THE LAST GAMBLER

DAN BLAKELY

For Kristi, Nate, Julia and Kate

May you always roll evens...

1

THE BLACK HOUSE

THE DARKNESS WRAPPED around Rye like a cloak, creating a sense of unease. She fixed her gaze on the narrow path winding through the woods ahead, leading her deeper into the forest. The creek, a ribbon of silver in the gloom, tracked alongside it. She'd thought herself clever, masking her tracks with care, but the sweat on her brow and the pounding of her heart told otherwise. Glancing over her shoulder, she quickened her pace, her footfalls hitting the ground with a soft thud, muffling any betrayal of her presence. As the trail curved closer to the creek, the gentle rush of water cascading over rocks whispered to her, but she ignored it. Her every nerve was stretched taut, every sense on alert for the slightest hint of pursuit. In the darkness, there were only two options: hide, or be hunted.

Her eyes darted about frantically, scouring the woods ahead for somewhere to hide, but the trees were thick, obscuring everything in shadows. Anger burned deep within as she pushed herself harder, faster along the twisting trail. *Why can't they just let me be?* Rye thought bitterly, her attention wandering. She returned her focus to the trail a moment too late, her foot catching on an exposed tree root. She stumbled, arms flailing to catch her fall, but her momentum sent her tumbling off the trail. Unable to regain her footing, she slid down the hillside and gracelessly crashed through the underbrush to the creek below. She gasped in surprise as the icy water splashed up her leg, flooding her shoes.

"Son of a bitch!" she cursed, momentarily surrendering her stealth, but she hated having wet feet. On top of that, she'd now left a trail that anyone could follow. Thankfully, a glance back up the hill revealed nothing, only the redwoods towering above her. She took a minute to collect her thoughts and rest. Her breath came in quick wisps, leaving ghosts drifting through the air before they faded away in the moonlight. Craning her neck, she sniffed the air, still learning to use her heightened senses. They were getting closer. Two against one—not good odds, even for her.

Pulling her grey stocking cap on tighter, she took a deep breath. *It'll be okay. Just keep moving*, she reassured herself. They'd played this game of cat and mouse over a dozen times in the past few years. She'd always been the mouse, always running, and they weren't far behind now. Turning back, she looked at the creek. The light of the moon reflected off the surface of the water, revealing its meandering path through the trees. She stepped out of the cool water onto a wide trail on the opposite bank and pressed onward, but her feet were now freezing, water squishing out with every step.

Around a bend in the trail, she suddenly caught the dull glint of metal in the moonlight. Whatever it was, she'd learned to keep a wary eye out when *they* were following her. She slowed her pace, inching forward until she could make out an ornate iron gate attached to two large redwoods flanking the trail. The gate stood taller than Rye, one side hanging off its hinges in obvious disrepair. Above the gate, an iron sign stretched between the trees, adorned with simple white block letters: BLACK CREEK CEMETERY, 1889.

Beyond the gate, a ghostly sheen of moonlight filtered through the trees, revealing a wide clearing pockmarked with a hodgepodge of gravestones of various sizes. The cemetery was overgrown with tall grasses and periwinkle, and a reluctant fog hugged the ground, casting awkward shadows all around. Stepping up to the gate, Rye shivered. This place looked gloomier the closer she came, and one never knew what might be lurking in the shadows.

Her hand froze as she tentatively reached out to open the gate. "Shit," she breathed. She took a small step backwards, tightening her jacket, then glanced behind herself. The thought of going into a creepy cemetery in the dead of night was almost too much. Her eyes searched for another passage, but the trail ended here. *Just keep moving.* That simple mantra pulled her forward. She reached out, pushing the gate open, going rigid as it let out a metallic shriek from years of neglect, echoing through the trees, shattering the silence. Her heart pounded, and again she turned, looking behind herself. Nothing. But it wouldn't be that way for long—not now. She had to keep moving.

Not wanting to risk any further noise, she squeezed her body through the narrow opening in the gate. Moving from gravestone to gravestone, she cautiously picked her way across the cemetery, trying to stay hidden. Suddenly, the tell-tale shriek of the gate sounded again, and she ducked behind a large tomb. Silence. Crouching down, she wiped the sweat from her brow, straining her ears for any sound.

"Hey, little magpie," a warm voice with a Southern drawl called out from the darkness.

Rye tensed. Liora was toying with her. Rye peered around the tomb, holding her breath. Liora wore an immaculate cream trench coat, and even in the dark, she sported her signature rhinestone-studded Dolce & Gabbana sunglasses. She had an uncanny way of sweet-talking people, spreading a bit of hope just before the hammer dropped. The hammer, of course, was her partner, Ciara, her opposite in all ways. Ciara dressed all in black leathers, blending with her jet-black eyes, and she was nothing short of dark and disturbing. Together, they made a frightful pair, even to Rye, and they knew she hated being called "magpie." She'd pleaded with the Lady to pick something different, but the Lady had held fast, calling the members of the Sorority her "flock."

Another screech of the gate, and it banged closed a moment later. Rye swore under her breath.

"I know you're out there," Liora called. "You can stop running if you just give us the necklace. I'm sure we could come to an arrangement—one that ensures your safety. Then you can go off with that sweaty boyfriend of yours, make some pups, live the good life." Liora's voice was gentle, almost pleasant, but it was much closer than Rye preferred.

Rye scoffed, almost giving away her position. She wanted nothing to do with Noah—not after what he'd done to her. She'd made that clear to him before she left him. Still, she'd grown weary of running. *Maybe there really is a workable arrangement*, she thought, the possibilities swirling in her head. That is, until Ciara chimed in.

"You can't leave the Sorority, and you certainly can't steal from it," Ciara said. "That's not how it works. You know that." Unlike Liora's somewhat melodic voice, Ciara's was like gravel in a wooden bucket, raspy and harsh. And unlike with Liora, kind words were not a gift Ciara possessed nor enjoyed. Instead, she opted to be direct, often employing threats to make her point.

Rye's face flushed, and she clenched her fists. It took everything she could muster to not yell out in protest. *The Sorority.* She sneered. She hadn't asked to be part of it, but

Ciara was right: once you were marked, you could never leave it. So, she'd run, leaving that world behind. And stealing? She resented the accusation. She hadn't stolen a damn thing. The necklace they hunted--she'd earned it for her years of service. Why else would the Lady have left it out the night Rye fled with Noah? Little happened by chance when it came to the Lady. Rye remained convinced it was a gift, and she didn't like being called a thief, especially by Ciara, of all people. They were goading her, and she couldn't believe that she'd almost considered an *arrangement* with them.

She leaned her back against the cool stone, taking a settling breath. Listening for footsteps, she heard nothing. Even the crickets were now silent as an unnatural stillness descended on the cemetery. Wispy tendrils of fog worked their way through the treetops, and the stars were disappearing one by one, as if a blanket were being pulled across the sky. Within moments, the fog had obscured everything in the sky, swallowing up even the moon. Only darkness remained. That was what Ciara preferred. Rye had seen Ciara call the darkness before, but never this fast. She was getting stronger.

Rye slowed her breath, sharpening her focus. In the past, she would've felt vulnerable in the dark, but Noah had changed that. He claimed he'd given her a gift, but it wasn't; it was a curse that she'd never wanted. In fact, he'd agreed to never visit it upon her. His failure to keep that promise was the final blow, driving a wedge deep between them. At the moment, however, his "gift" was proving useful. The shadows and shapes in the distance were unnaturally distinct, and Rye could even see Liora and Ciara at the gate, watching. The forest beyond the cemetery was visible as well, and she spied what looked like a faded game trail. That would have to do.

Just keep moving, she repeated, but then a sudden chill

breeze kissed her cheek. She grasped her jacket, pulling it around herself even tighter. The air around her had turned frigid, her breath prominent even in the gloom as a sheen of frost suddenly formed on the surrounding ground. A cool gust passed through her hair from behind, and goose bumps pricked her skin in warning. She spun around, seeing a shadow shift in the darkness before her. Whatever it was, it remained hidden in the mists. *This is precisely why I don't like cemeteries.* She'd heard stories about things that lived in graveyards, but it was unsettling to experience it in person. She searched the darkness for the shadow, glimpsing it again before something resolved in the distance. A smile touched her lips. Tucked into the woods, a small, dark house was hidden in the fog. This had to be her escape.

Bending over, Rye picked up a baseball-sized chunk of stone fallen from one of the crumbling gravestones. With all her strength, she wound up, lobbing the rock through the air toward the faded trail she'd seen on the edge of the woods. With a loud thud, the rock landed, crashing into a fallen branch and rolling through the underbrush before coming to a stop beside the trail. Rye crouched in silence, listening, hoping it was enough to bait them.

Ciara and Liora were arguing, but a moment later, the crunch of leaves confirmed that they were on the move. A final peek revealed their silhouettes moving through the gravestones toward the faded trail. Rye held her position, watching as they leaped the fence and continued down the trail before disappearing into the forest.

Still crouching, she picked her way across the cemetery, careful to stay hidden. Even though she could no longer see them, their scent hung heavy in the air, an unsettling mixture of flowers and rot. Luckily for Rye, their scent was fading. As she crept closer, the little house revealed itself. It was painted black, almost invisible in the darkness. It was smaller than she'd expected, but it would do. A chimney towered above the roof. The shutters were closed, but the front door stood ajar. The scent of mothballs and mildew wafted out, overwhelming her senses. That same strange stirring in the darkness pulled her forward, goose bumps once again peppering her skin. The open door revealed little. Inside, all was an inky black, with no beginning or end.

She knew they would expect her to run, just like last time at the music festival in Cologne, and the carnival in Lisbon before that. Cat and mouse, ad nauseam. But this time would be different. She took one last look behind her before squeezing through the doorway, careful to close the door quietly behind her.

Unlike outside, the inky blackness of the shuttered house was complete. She couldn't even see her own hand as she waved it in front of her face. She spread her arms, searching for the wall. Her fingers found the smooth wood, and she followed it, circling the room. A stone fireplace came first, followed by a few of the shuttered windows and another door. She settled into a corner, sitting with her back to the wall, careful not to get too comfortable, even though she was wet and cold. She'd slipped past them again. The darkness swam about her, and she thought of the shadow in the graveyard, wondering if she was alone.

"Thank you for your help," she whispered into the darkness, not wanting a good deed to go unrecognized. No response came. She let out a deep sigh, grateful for the silence.

Time moved like molasses dripping from a spoon, and she did her best to stay alert. She'd already recited the lyrics of her favorite songs a hundred times and had just started naming all the subway stations in London. Her attention waned as her head drooped, and her body slumped forward before she caught herself. She refocused, slapping her own face and starting on the subway stations again, still drifting in and out.

… until she startled to the sound of a door closing.

Shit! She wasn't sure if she'd dozed off and just imagined the sound. Dark places could mask the truth, and this room was awash in it, the pungent scent of mothballs suffocating her senses. Her heart raced as adrenaline surged through her veins. Closing her eyes, she took a calming breath, trying to convince herself that she'd imagined the noise, but it was too late. A bit of fear had seeped in, and she knew where that would lead.

A moment later, Liora's sweet voice washed in from outside the front door.

"No need to cower in a dingy old caretaker's house, little magpie," Liora called. "You're better than this. Just give us the necklace, and I'm sure we can work something out."

Rye stared into the darkness as a switch flipped inside her, taking hold of her blood. Only one word came to mind: *Run.* Before she knew it, she'd crashed into the back door, grabbing the handle and trying to open it, but it didn't budge. Blood pounded in her head as she moved to the window, throwing her body into it, but it held firm too. The mixture of fear and adrenaline had taken over, and the darkness seemed to deepen, closing its noose around her.

"You having some problems with the door?" Liora asked in that sweet voice. "Funny thing. The old caretaker was so afraid of the creatures of the night…" She rapped her knuckles on the front door. "Hear that? Rowan. He built this entire cabin out of rowan wood. You know, to keep certain things out—or *in*, in your case. Just so happens you stumbled upon the worst possible place to hide. Amazing, really, if you think of the possibilities. So, what do you say—ready to make that deal?"

Rye leaned her forehead against the wall. She couldn't

believe it. She'd trapped herself. Her thoughts flashed back to the shadow in the cemetery, hearing her mother's voice chiding her. *"Be wary of the things in the darkness. They often wish us harm."* So true, but unfortunately in hindsight. Out of habit, her hand moved to her chest, reaching for her necklace, but she already knew it wasn't there. Noah had stolen it. That's what had caused their breakup—that and his bite, which now left her trapped. There was no deal to be made with these ladies—not tonight or any other night. The only thing left was to fight.

"No? That's most unfortunate," Liora said.

A moment later, Ciara let out a shrill cackle from *inside* the house. A shiver coursed down Rye's spine, but she stood tall, ready for whatever would come next. She winced as her bones cracked and stretched, the hair on her skin filling out into a plush pelt. The change was still new to her. She found it unsettling, but she'd managed it before. She turned her body toward where Ciara's voice had been.

Too late. Ciara's face illuminated in the eerie glow of electricity arcing from a cattle prod she pressed into Rye's belly. In an instant, the adrenaline drained from Rye's body, and the burgeoning changes dissipated, along with any chance of her escaping this time. She fell to the floor, her body convulsing, as Ciara stood above her, releasing the button.

"You'd better hope you kill me," Rye said through gritted teeth, the scent of burnt flesh saturating the air.

"You only wish it'd be that quick," Ciara said from the darkness.

Rye recoiled as the metal rod pressed against her chest, followed by a subtle click. The blueish-white glow raged again, reflected on Ciara's sneering face. Something cold fastened around her neck, and then she blacked out.

2

THE ANVIL

Colm hurried down the sidewalk, glancing at his wristwatch. Late again. Lucky for him, mornings at the pawnshop were notoriously slow—something he frequently took advantage of. Turning the corner, he paused outside the coffee shop, where a line of customers spilled out the door onto the sidewalk. He glanced at his watch again, hesitating, as a friendly female voice from somewhere inside called out, "Hey, Colm! I've got your latte for ya."

He pressed his body through the people at the door, arriving at the counter.

"Here you go," she said, the tranquility of her voice matching the colorful floral tattoos that festooned her arm, holding out Colm's latte.

"Thanks, Zoie, I owe you one." He took the cup, laying some money on the counter. "See you tomorrow?"

"Yup, tomorrow. Now get out of here before your uncle gets himself in a tizzy," she said, smiling at him before turning to the next order.

Colm had been working his way through college at the Anvil, his uncle's pawnshop. Not a glorious job, but it paid the bills and his ever-increasing tuition. That is, until he'd dropped out last semester. He'd been going to school forever, never really understanding why; it was just something old people expected young people to do. They said it was where you learned how to be an adult, but he was learning far more about real life by working at the Anvil. He'd finally hit a point where he was done wasting his money. When people asked, he said he was just taking a break. That was the simple answer. People understood that, and it typically ended the conversation. He wasn't ready to have an honest conversation with anyone about it. He was barely having one with himself, and certainly not with his girlfriend, Tabitha. She would never understand.

Colm nudged his way out the door. A blanket of fog had settled in overnight, hiding the storefronts in a dirty haze. A fine mist saturated the air, its cool touch pricking his skin. This was typical for fall in Monterey, where the days often started a bit dreary. He pulled the hood of his jacket tight over his head, sipping his coffee as he passed under the cypress trees that lined the streets. Moments later, he stood before the pawnshop. His free hand was searching his jeans pockets for the key when the door swung wide.

"It's already open," a voice said from inside.

Colm raised his eyes. A wooden cane propped the door open, and his uncle stood waiting impatiently. He wore a pair of torn and faded black denim jeans, topped with a Metallica T-shirt that peeked out from underneath a black zip-up hoodie.

"Oh, you here already?" Colm said, and Andrew rolled his eyes. "What?" Colm took another sip of coffee.

"Thanks for getting *me* a coffee," Andrew quipped. "Now, hurry up. You're letting the cold air in." As he spoke, he swept Colm inside with his cane, closing the door. Colm remembered the days before the cane—before the night those guys thought they'd gotten a raw deal. But at least Andrew wasn't bitter about it. He just said it came with the territory. His cane tapped on the floor as he moved to the side, flicking the switch on the neon *OPEN* sign. It flickered to life, making a colored halo in the fog outside.

As they walked into the shop, Andrew stopped by the register, reaching under the counter to get Betsy—another new addition from that night a couple of years ago. The cane and Betsy went hand in hand now. He slid her into the holster hidden on the small of his back. Reaching under the counter again, he pulled out a second gun, holding it out to Colm. This had become a bit of a game with Andrew lately.

"You know," Andrew said, "you really should carry this. You just never—"

"We've already talked about this," Colm cut in testily. "I'm not interested in having anything to do with guns, and besides—"

"'There's too much killing in the world already,'" Andrew parroted him. "Right, I know what you think. But I'm telling you from experience," he said, tapping his cane with his free hand. "There's time for talking, and time for doing. When the talking's done, you're gonna want to have this." He again offered the gun.

Tired of the debate, Colm ran his fingers through his stringy black hair, going off script. "Look, I get it, I do. Let's just say I'll think about it and leave it at that today, okay? That's progress, at least."

Andrew's eyes softened, seizing on the sudden change. He sat on a stool, putting the gun on the counter between them. "Before your parents died, I promised I'd take care of you. That's all."

Colm hated it whenever Andrew brought up his parents. That wound had never healed, and rather than deal with it, Colm did everything in his power to avoid it, keeping those memories locked away. It was hard enough growing up without his parents; talking about them was too much. He let out a deep sigh, meeting Andrew's eyes. "You've done that."

Andrew pressed, "Dangerous people come into the shop every day, and this gun might help. I'm just trying to protect you."

"I know," Colm said, stepping forward to give his uncle a hug. "And I'm grateful for it."

"… So?" Andrew said after a brief pause.

"Okay," Colm said. "I'll think about it, but for now, it goes in the safe."

"Sounds good," Andrew said, slapping Colm on the back.

Colm headed to the back of the shop, the steel cold in his hand. The mere act of holding this gun was a betrayal of the memory of his parents, but Andrew couldn't understand. The final police report had called it a "fluke robbery." Bottom line, whoever had shot his parents, they'd never caught them. Powerless to do anything about it, Colm was forced to let it go. It was a bitter memory, best left in the past, forgotten.

"You know I get it," Andrew said from the doorway.

"Jesus!" Colm snapped, startled. "How can you be so sneaky with that cane?"

"I get it," Andrew repeated.

"Get what?"

"Get why you don't want the gun. You know, they took my sister away from me too," Andrew said, turning away, his cane clicking on the floor.

Colm had not once stopped to consider what Andrew had lost that night, but he didn't care. This was about him, not Andrew.

For the rest of the morning, Colm puttered around the shop as the fog outside gave way to golden sunshine. More sun always meant fewer customers. People flocked to the beach on sunny days, so Colm passed the hours watching an inane news show on the little television on the counter. The host spewed the latest celebrity gossip—Beyonce's baby, Elon Musk touting his latest venture, and other mindless tidbits.

As the afternoon wore on, Andrew stepped out from the back with his jacket on. "You handle the shop? I've got a dentist's appointment."

"Yep, got it. Just remember, I'm having dinner with Tabitha at six, so I'll close up a little early."

Andrew nodded, stepping out the door, leaving Colm alone with the afternoon talk shows. Colm thought back to the earlier discussion about his parents. He had no more tears to shed, but he thought of them every day. The world had taken so much from him, but he wasn't going to end up like his uncle, alone and working at a pawnshop forever. One way or another, he would take back what the world had stolen from him. It was just a matter of figuring out how— but once he did, nothing would stand in his way.

Outside, the lemony light of the streetlamps sprang to life, casting an amber glow on the sidewalks. Colm reached down, changing the channel as the door chimed. Raising his eyes, he saw a disheveled man holding a sizeable cardboard box. He wore a brightly colored jersey emblazoned with the oversized logo of some foreign sports team, looking look like he'd just come off the field. It draped down well past his waist, perhaps a size or two too big. Sooty ink wrapped his arms in a variety of striking but unpretentious designs, the work clearly done by the steady hand of an experienced artist. Arcane symbols and tribal knots stood out among them, but the most notable was a black heart on his right forearm that dripped blood down to the back of his hand, where it formed a delicate black rose. His hair was wild, poking out in all directions, and a pair of messy mutton chops followed his jawline, ending at his mouth, which was oversized for his head. The man gave a furtive look outside as the door closed behind him.

"Can I help you?" Colm asked, not doing a great job of suppressing his amusement.

"What's so funny?" the man demanded, his voice thick with an Australian accent.

This kind of brashness was a mainstay of the Anvil's clientele, and Colm had learned to brush it off. "So, you got some stuff to sell?"

The Aussie glanced at the television, then back at Colm, his right leg vibrating. "Yeah, lookin' to sell," he said, walking across the shop and setting his box on the counter. With his hands free, he feverishly scratched his scalp and all about his body.

Colm had a smooth way of talking to people looking to fence stolen goods, and this guy was clearly here to sell something stolen. The man telegraphed it in the way he kept looking out the door and twitching. Whatever he had to sell, he wanted to do it quickly.

"Let's see what you've got," Colm said, motioning to the box.

The man paused, glancing back to the door again before he started unloading. Some old vinyl records were the first to come out. Colm rolled his eyes. The shop already had too many records loitering in crates along the walls. He was about to pass when the Aussie lifted a few other things from the box that caught his attention. The first was a blade that could've been either a long knife or a short sword. It was a strange milky white he'd never seen before, and he couldn't tell if it was made of stone or some sort of glass. Next, the Aussie set down a wooden disc the size of a saucer, engraved with an intricate mandala pattern of a tree gilded with a dull gold leaf that had faded with age. The last thing pulled from the box was a simple carved wooden pendant on a leather choker.

"That's it. You a buyer?"

Colm picked up the blade, surprised at how light it felt in his hand. "What's this made of?"

"Glass, maybe crystal," the man said, shrugging. "Not sure. It's just somethin' me Gram had in her attic when she passed." The man scratched his head again, his eyes darting around the shop.

It didn't concern Colm that the man was lying. He'd learned long ago to just roll with whatever story was being told. He turned the blade over in his hands, studying it. The side was adorned with detailed scrollwork that flowed into the etching of an animal skull. Runes of some ancient language wrapped around the smooth grip, none of which he recognized. He set the blade down, picking up the wooden mandala. It too was exquisite, with a circular opening in the tree trunk of the gilded design. From the opening, the branches and roots extended to the edges of the mandala, joining a pattern that encircled the tree around the edge of the wooden disc.

"That was from me Gram's attic too. And them records, and that choker," the Aussie volunteered in hopes of speeding up Colm's assessment.

Colm ignored him, trying to tamp down his growing excitement. The blade and mandala were extraordinary, but he had no idea what they really were, let alone what they were worth. He wished Andrew were around to help, but if he asked this guy to come back later, he'd just head down the street to the next pawnshop. Colm wasn't going to let that happen.

His eagerness betrayed him. The Aussie leaned in, the stench of whiskey and rot heavy on his breath. "You like those? Nice, huh?"

Colm leaned back, not responding. He needed to play it cool, just as Andrew had taught him. The two pieces were clearly old and probably valuable, but that was about all he could say. In his mind, he added up all the money he had in the world, wanting to make this buy himself, not with Andrew's money. He didn't want to overpay, but greed was creeping into his thoughts. He paused as Andrew's voice echoed in the back of his mind: *"Never be the first to put out a number."*

"What do you want for the blade and the mandala?" Colm asked flatly, feigning disinterest.

"It's a package deal. All or nothing."

"I'm only interested in the two."

"Too bad. I need to sell all of them," the man said, starting to pack up the box.

Colm reached out, stopping him. "Fine. Package deal. What's your best number?"

"Ten grand," he said without hesitation, staring Colm in the eyes.

Colm laughed, leaning back in his chair. "That's crazy! You want ten grand for stuff from 'your Gram's attic'?" Sarcasm oozed from his words. He knew how to play this game. They'd always ask for the moon on the first offer. From there, the job was to help them come back down to reality. Colm shook his head, not saying anything more.

"Okay, eight grand. But that's it," the Aussie said, glancing back to the door again, his feet shifting in place.

The twenty percent discount was a good start, but Colm knew there was more. Andrew's voice urged him on. *"When they're on the ropes, go a bit lower than you think you should."* Initially, Colm had pegged seven grand as the number. It would stretch him pretty thin, but if he flipped these fast, he was certain he'd make some good bank.

"Five. That's all I've got in the shop," Colm said with authority. Another trick from Andrew.

Taking another quick look at the door, the Aussie moved closer, speaking in hushed tones. "Let's cut the shite. I heard from good sources that you can handle delicate matters here at the Anvil. I just need to get rid of these things—*tonight*. Just need to hear that you can fence these discreetly." The stench of whiskey again filled Colm's nostrils.

"Always. That's how we do business here."

The Aussie tapped his fingers lightly on the counter as if he were counting. "Six grand. That's as low as I go. If not, I walk down the street and take my chances with the wankers at the Gold Emporium."

"Deal," Colm said without any hesitation. He'd seen enough things come into the Anvil to feel confident that he'd just made a steal of a buy. "I'll get the cash."

Colm went into the back room, quickly scribbling an IOU for six thousand dollars to his uncle. He took the money from the safe—six bands of one thousand each—and put the IOU in their place next to his gun. He paused, looking at the gun. There was something unsettling about this guy and how quickly he'd caved on a steep discount. Maybe Andrew was right—but he still wasn't going to take that gun.

He returned to the counter, where the Aussie stood fidgeting. "You want me to count it?"

"No need," the Aussie said, taking the stack, reaching out to shake hands. As their hands met, the Aussie pulled him in close, baring sharp fangs and squeezing so hard that Colm's knuckles cracked. "Remember, don't tell a soul where you got this stuff."

Colm silently nodded, uncertain of how to respond or whether his eyes were deceiving him. The Aussie released his hand, no fangs in evidence, and then he turned, heading toward the door.

Halfway across the shop, he paused, turning back. His eyes met Colm's with a grave sincerity. Colm was getting nervous, grimly aware that the goods still sat on the counter, the Aussie had his money now, and no one else was in the shop. They both stood quietly, looking at each other.

"You seem like a decent fella, everything considered," he said, pointing back to Colm. "There's people—dangerous people—lookin' for that stuff. My advice, if ya don't wanna get killed, would be to sell it outta town, quick and quiet."

Colm nodded, still at a loss for words as the man turned, disappearing out the door into the darkness. The Aussie's last words echoed in his mind. *Did he say "killed"...?* Not an auspicious start to his plans to sell these things for a big profit.

The grandfather clock in the store chimed six times, bringing Colm back to the present. "Shit," he swore, tapping the counter. He was supposed to meet Tabitha down the street for dinner at six. Late again. Tabitha would not be happy—but then, she rarely was lately. He picked up the box, placing the records in it, and stashed the other items in his backpack. Throwing it over his shoulder, he turned off the lights, locking the door behind him.

THE WHISKERED STRANGER

Colm soon arrived at Dos Suenos, checking his watch. Fifteen minutes late. Could be worse. The smell of citrus and roasted chili peppers filled the restaurant as the hostess guided him to a secluded corner booth, where Tabitha sat glaring at him.

"You could've texted me," she snapped. "We've talked about this before."

"Yeah, sorry. I had a last-minute customer." He leaned over for a kiss, but she nudged him away. She'd been more vocal about his shortcomings lately, so he wasn't surprised that she was angry. Colm slid in across from her as the server came to the table, giving him a brief reprieve.

"Hey, guys! You want the usual?"

Colm looked at Tabitha, and she nodded. "Yeah, the usual. Thanks, Sam," he said with a smile, and the server whisked away.

Tabitha picked up right where she'd left off. "I'm just sick of trying to help you figure your shit out. I don't know what your plan is with college, and instead you work at a dead-end job where you literally buy and sell stolen things. *Stolen,*

Colm. Then, on top of all that, you're not considerate enough to even text me when you're running late."

"Well, not *everything's* stolen," he said with a smirk, trying to lighten the mood.

She just scowled back, not appreciating his attempt at humor. "That's not the point. I just don't feel like I know who you are anymore. Like, what do you want to do with your life?"

Colm wasn't sure she really wanted a response. They'd had conversations like this before, where she just needed to vent. He'd learned that if he withstood the initial assault and held his tongue, it would blow over.

Her eyes briefly turned away from his as she took a deep breath. When she turned back, Colm saw a misty sheen reflected there. When she spoke again, her tone had changed dramatically, all the anger gone. Her voice was steady, but cracking. "I've been accepted to grad school in San Diego."

"Wait," Colm said, confused, "I thought you decided to go to school here?"

"I changed my mind. The offer was too good to pass up. Full tuition, room and board, and I get paid to help on research projects."

Colm sat back, wondering where this was going, but her next three words made it crystal clear.

"I need space."

"Wait… Are you breaking up with me?"

Unable to speak, Tabitha simply nodded, looking away as tears streaked down her face.

Colm stared at her, stunned. His eyes teared up, but he didn't know if it was because he was losing her, or because she was rejecting him. Either way, it hurt, reminding him of when he'd lost his parents. He quickly regained his composure, tamping down the tears, hiding the pain.

Tabitha wiped the tears from her own face and turned

back, placing her hands over his in the middle of the table, speaking in a gentle voice. "It hasn't been good between us for a while now. We both know it, and I can't do it anymore. You need to let me go. I need to let *you* go." Tabitha pulled her hands back.

She had delivered her message with brutal compassion, and it had been received. The silence between them was deafening, and looking back, Colm realized their relationship had always been one-sided, driven by *her* needs and desires, never what he wanted. A flame ignited within him as it dawned on him that she'd planned all this out—probably even practiced it. Just the act of sitting in this booth with her bordered on torture. He didn't want to be here, and neither did she.

But she had one more checkbox on her list. Her eyes lowered as her hand slid to the center of the table, depositing a ring. "You should have this back, since it was your mother's."

He reached out slowly, taking the ring. She moved her hand, covering his once again, raising her eyes to meet his.

"I don't regret anything with you. I'd always hoped…" She stopped mid-sentence, seeing the look on his face, the anger swirling just below the surface. "Right," she said, pulling her hand back, "I understand. But you'll be okay. You always are."

"What about you?"

"I'll be fine."

The simplicity of her statement was almost more painful than anything else she'd said. Not *"It'll be hard,"* or *"I'll miss you"*—just *"I'll be fine."*

She slid out of the booth, suddenly in a hurry to leave. There were no heartfelt goodbyes. She just waved as she walked away from the table, wiping the tears from her eyes. The entire conversation had lasted maybe a couple of minutes.

Colm opened his hand, turning the ring in his fingers. The silver band was worked into two hands, reaching for a ruby in the shape of a heart that wore a silver crown, symbolizing love, loyalty, and friendship. It was his mother's Claddagh ring that she'd gotten from his father years ago. Now, the ring was just a painful reminder that other than his uncle, the people who'd loved him were all gone.

"Never again," he hissed. He slipped the ring onto the pinkie of his right hand, heart tip facing toward his wrist, telling the world he was in a relationship. From now on, he'd be watching out for himself.

A moment later, the server arrived back at the table with a carryout bag. Seeing the confusion on Colm's face, he set the bag on the table. "When she got here, she told me to pack up the food to go. She paid on the way out."

"Isn't that just perfect?" Colm muttered as the next table over summoned the server. Walking toward the booth was the mariachi band that played here nightly, all dressed in black, sleeves adorned in white frills, tassels shaking on the brims of their black sombreros. He and Tabitha had always liked the band; it made dinner feel more like a party. This had been one of his favorite places to eat, but like so many other things, she'd ruined this place for him now. Slinging his backpack over his shoulders, he slid from the booth, picking his way past the band and out the door.

Outside the restaurant, the darkness was periodically interrupted by the soft amber glow of the streetlamps that lined Alvarado Street, the main road through town. Monterey was a quaint coastal town full of shops and restaurants, its sandy white beach a short walk down the way. People, mostly tourists, littered the sidewalks, moving about haphazardly, congregating in small groups. The fog had once again started its creep in from the ocean, carrying a familiar dampness with it, but a few stars still managed to peek through. Colm fastened his jacket, pulling his hood tight over his head as a cool ocean breeze whipped up the street.

He started the short walk home, pausing briefly in front of Abalone's, the seafood restaurant where he and Tabitha had gone to celebrate things—mostly her things. He shook his head, the anger returning. She'd clearly been thinking about this breakup for some time, planning it out meticulously, like one of her science experiments. He had to admit, it was a bit cold, even for her. His feet mindlessly followed the path home as he toyed with the idea of calling her, then quickly dismissed it. If she ever wanted to talk, she could call him.

As he passed an alley, something hidden in its darkness caught his eye. Pausing, he saw an old man digging through a dumpster. Colm leaned in for a closer look, confirming what he thought he'd seen. The man was wearing a robe—not a bathrobe, but Benedictine-style robes, complete with a braided rope at the waist. Colm turned to leave, but not before the man noticed his presence.

"Help an old man out?" he asked, his soft eyes trained on Colm.

"Sorry, I don't have any money," Colm lied.

"Don't need money. How about those leftovers?" he pleaded.

Colm turned to leave, intending to ignore him, as he always did with street people. But this time, he stopped. He hadn't paid for the food, after all, and he didn't even like the vegan garbage Tabitha always ordered. "Sure, why not?" he said, turning back and holding the bag out to the man.

The old man wavered, stumbling against the dumpster and falling to the ground. Colm rushed over, helping him up. "You okay?" he asked, guiding the man out of the alley and sitting him down on a bench.

"All good. Thank you." He reached down, rubbing his ribs and wincing.

"You sure you're okay?"

"Yeah, it's nothing," the old man said, catching his breath.

Colm leaned against a light pole and reached into his jacket, pulling out a pack of cigarettes and placing one in his mouth. His hands went to his pockets, rummaging around for a lighter.

"You know those things will kill you," the old man said.

Colm nodded. "I've heard that," he said, his hands still searching. "You want one?"

"Thought you'd never ask." The man's wrinkled face lit up as his hand disappeared into a pocket of his robe, pulling out a matchbook.

Colm nodded, taking the matches. The deep purple cover of the matchbook was a funky retro design, speckled with pastel stars in different sizes, boldly advertising a casino called The Lair. He flipped it open. The inside read, *Where Fortune Lives*, like a promise of a better life. He'd always found old advertising interesting, snatching it up any time it came into the Anvil. It was a shame to use these, but it had been a long day, and the desire for a smoke won out. He pulled a match free, striking it. With a deep inhale, the end of his cigarette burned a dirty orange, the smoke fading invisibly into the darkness. Colm handed the old man a cigarette, striking another match, blocking the wind with his other hand, until the old man's cigarette flared, highlighting the rough whiskers on his face. They both took a drag in silence, blowing out the smoke as the man coughed, reaching for his ribs.

"No one smokes anymore," the man said, as if he were in a moment of deep reverie. "I miss the old days, when sharing a smoke meant something. A time to slow down and enjoy someone's company. Nowadays, people are always rushing around, staring at their phones," he said with an odd mixture of sentiment and resentment, taking another deep drag from his cigarette.

Colm was taken aback at how well spoken he was, especially since a moment ago, he'd been rummaging through a dumpster. Colm held out the pack of cigarettes. "Here, take a few more, then, for old time's sake."

"Thanks." The man smiled, taking a couple of cigarettes and placing one behind each ear.

"Your matches," Colm said, holding the matchbook out to the old man.

"No, you keep 'em. You never know when you might need a light to find your way. It's the least I can do."

Colm nodded, about to leave, but something had been gnawing at him. "So, what's with the robes?" he asked. "You some sort of preacher?" He'd seen these types of robes before in a book about medieval times, but he couldn't figure out why this old man would be wearing them.

The man either ignored the question or hadn't heard it, instead taking the conversation elsewhere. "You ever wonder how different the world would be if everyone made good choices? Always paying it forward," he said, looking at Colm, pulling another drag from the cigarette.

"Well, I guess I'd have to stop the smokes," Colm said, laughing, trying to add some levity.

The old man ignored Colm's attempt to lighten the mood and continued in a solemn voice, "We all choose our path. Right or wrong, light or dark. We each make the world we live in. Do you believe that?" He took a long drag, finishing his cigarette and using it to light another.

"Not really. But maybe someday, the world will be like that." Colm dropped the butt of his cigarette to the cement and stepped on it to extinguish the embers.

"'Someday'--that's just code for 'never.' Sometimes you

need to swallow hard and roll the dice instead of waiting for *someday*. Take a chance before you're too old, like me," he said, his eyes intent on Colm as he finished.

Colm nodded, growing tired of the conversation. It was sounding a bit preachy, confirming that he was in fact a man of the cloth, albeit a washed-up one. "Look, it's been nice talking with you, but I gotta get going." As he turned to leave, he heard the old man chuckle.

"Thanks for the food. It's hard to keep the darkness out, but it warms an old man's heart to know decent people are still around. You're a good man, Colm," he said, his voice trailing off into a fit of coughs.

Colm paused, a bit flustered as he retraced the conversation. He was certain he hadn't given the man his name. Could he be a customer of the Anvil, or a friend of his uncle's? Nothing solid came to mind as an unsettling feeling overtook him. He turned back to the old man, looking at him with renewed interest. "Who are you?"

The man spoke in the same gentle voice. "Just here to pay it forward myself. A favor for a favor." He lifted the bag of food from the bench.

Colm remained speechless, waiting with bated breath for whatever came next.

Rising to his feet, the old man stretched his legs and took a final drag from his cigarette. The fog had thickened, veiling the stores across the street and withering the streetlamps to fairy lights. The old man continued, "Let me do you one tonight. The only thing I ask in return is that when the lady in red comes to you, you promise to help her. She's lost, and she needs help finding her way home. You have to get her home. Fair enough?"

Colm nodded, answering dismissively, "Yeah, sure." The song "Lady in Red" was already churning away in his head, thanks to his uncle's love for sappy 1980s love songs. He wasn't certain if this old man was a loon or not, but either way, he'd have another good story for Andrew.

"Great. Then we have a deal," the man said, reaching his hand out, and they shook.

Colm felt as if he were watching a movie on the big screen, still not certain how the old street gypsy knew his name. Not to mention, he'd never gotten a straight answer on the silly robes that were now just a big question mark on the overall experience.

The old man leaned in, pointing across the street through the deepening fog, drawing Colm's attention to a storefront with its lights on and its door open. "Take a look in that shop," he said. "I understand they have some … *unique* offerings."

Colm stepped to the curb to get a closer look. He knew this street and its shops, but he didn't recall seeing this one before. New shops came in occasionally, of course, so it wasn't that surprising to him. He could barely make out the sign above it—something like THE DASERII. Through the open door, he saw someone moving around inside.

When he turned back, the old man had vanished. A prickle ran up Colm's spine, and it took a few seconds before he convinced himself that the old man had simply walked back down the dark alley to wherever he called home. Still, he had to admit, this brief encounter had been beyond strange.

Colm turned, looking across the street to the new shop that beckoned him with its warm glow.

4

THE DASERII

COLM STOOD OUTSIDE THE SHOP, the murky fog settling around him, slightly obscuring the simple wooden sign. Below the shop's name, in small type, was written, *Proprietor, Mr. Wynn Liddl.* Colm wasn't sure what *daserii* meant, but it piqued his curiosity. The shop wasn't large, perhaps just a quarter of the size of the Anvil. He peeked through the open door and saw several elegant mahogany display cases, and the walls were exquisitely paneled to match. A warm light reminiscent of a flickering fire filled the shop and spilled out onto the sidewalk in a welcoming sort of way. He glanced back up at the sign, straightening his backpack as a noise from inside the mysterious shop captured his attention. Looking deeper within, he saw a dwarfish man standing with his back to the door, cleaning the glass on the display cases. Curious, Colm stepped through the door.

A subtle chime echoed through the shop, announcing his presence. The man in the back of the shop spun around, his head on a swivel. A pair of eyes the color of a restless ocean peered out from a rotund face with a closely clipped beard and mustache greying with age. He puffed on a finely carved pipe that dangled from his mouth as thin wisps of smoke escaped from it, dispersing a pleasant aroma of sweet thyme. He was dressed rather formally in slacks and a matching tweed jacket, with patches on the elbows, like Colm's poetry professor had worn. His tanned skin was wrinkled with age, and his face lit up with a big smile as he took the pipe from his mouth.

"Welcome, friend! I'm thrilled to announce that you're my very first customer! Tonight's the grand opening. Now, please, come in," he said with a heavy accent, never dropping his smile as he ushered Colm into the shop. Colm wasn't good at placing accents, but he guessed that the man was from somewhere in England or nearby.

"Uh, thanks. I work down the street at the pawnshop," Colm said, pointing toward the Anvil. He carefully removed his backpack, not wanting to bump anything. "I hadn't noticed a new shop coming in."

The man's eyes twinkled as he took a small step toward Colm, his tiny feet shuffling on the wide-planked floor. It was made of the same wood that lined the walls, giving the elegant yet cozy impression of being inside a tree—a deeply polished, nicely appointed tree. "Just signed the lease last week, and with a little luck, I found an artisan to get the shop all shipshape for opening. The crew just finished these last display cases this afternoon," he said, pointing to the mahogany display cases.

Through the glass, Colm saw a variety of dice in all different shapes, sizes, and designs, some with the traditional six sides, some with more. He wasn't sure what he'd been expecting, but it was definitely not this.

"The Daserii... That's a strange name for a shop," Colm ventured.

"Not so much," the man said with a chuckle. "Daserii just means 'dice-maker.' That's me." He patted himself proudly on the chest, reaching his hand out. "Name's Wynn."

Colm smiled as they shook hands. "Nice to meet you. I'm Colm. Welcome to the neighborhood. You've got yourself a nice place here."

"Thanks. It's taken many years for me to pull the coin together to open this place, but here I am." Wynn took a short drag on his pipe, noticing the sour look on Colm's face. "Something got you down, my friend?"

Was it that obvious? It hadn't even been half an hour since Tabitha dumped him. Clearly, it was bothering him. Ordinarily, he kept things to himself, but there was something warm and inviting about this place and this funny little man in the tweed jacket. What could it hurt? Maybe he just needed to say a few things out loud to let go of them. With that thought, Colm opened up, recapping the derailed dinner with her. Wynn nodded, a look of compassion on his face.

"I just wish things could have gone differently," Colm finished lamely.

"Don't we all, don't we all…" Wynn puffed on his pipe, his eyes distant, as if his thoughts were somewhere far away. The next instant, he reached behind the counter, grabbing two glasses and a crystal decanter full of a ruby liquid. He slowly poured two stout glasses of it, handing one to Colm. "That's a real bit of bad luck, my friend. Calls for a drink, in my book." Without another word, he tossed the contents of his glass into the back of his throat, placing it on the display case with a satisfying thud, and Colm followed suit. The only difference was that Wynn remained unaffected, but Colm was now bent over coughing, the burn of the liquor leaving a trail of tears streaming from his eyes.

"Always hits you that way the first time." Wynn snickered and slapped his knee as he poured them both another glass. His eyes locked with Colm's as his laughter subsided. "I propose a toast to new beginnings! Plus, the second one's always a bit smoother." He winked at Colm, holding the glass out to him.

The toast strangely resonated with Colm, and he took the glass, clinking it against Wynn's. As promised, it went down smoothly, leaving a warmth within him. He thought of leaving, but something was nagging at him about this shop.

"So, you just sell dice here?" Colm said, confused.

"Yep, just dice."

"Like, for what? Yahtzee? Craps? Dungeons and Dragons?" Colm asked, his voice thick with mockery.

Brushing the jibe aside, Wynn's response came smoothly —melodically almost, as if he'd responded to this question a thousand times. "Yes, those, and others—gambling games and such. You know, all the things people use them for."

"And you can sell enough to support a place like *this*?" Colm asked, gesturing to their surroundings. But he held his tongue a breath short of telling Wynn he was doing something stupid and inadvisable.

To Wynn's credit, he again shrugged off the implication. "You'd be amazed at what some people would spend for a reliable, balanced set of dice. It's a craft, an art, and I have a bit of a reputation for it." He leaned in closer to Colm, whispering quietly as if telling a secret. "Some people even think my dice are lucky."

After a pause that was just a bit longer than was comfortable, he chuckled, and Colm nervously joined in.

Colm normally wouldn't have pressed, but the drinks had emboldened him, and he couldn't leave without knowing more. "What do you mean, 'lucky'?"

"Well, not so much lucky as *custom*. That's where the real money is," he said in a thoughtful voice.

"Custom? Like, loaded dice?"

"Sure, that—and more," Wynn said, pouring them each

another glass from the decanter while puffing away on his pipe. The smell of sweet thyme filled the air with an intoxicating aroma.

"Like what?" Colm asked, his hands sweating.

Wynn set his pipe down, picking up his glass and spinning the ruby-colored drink in circles, watching until it settled. Taking a sip, he raised his eyes to meet Colm's. "Some say my dice have powers … *magical* powers."

Colm tapped the rim of his glass with a wry smile on his face, waiting for Wynn to laugh. But Wynn didn't laugh. Instead, he held Colm's gaze, sipping from his glass again.

"Yeah, some people are pretty superstitious, huh?" Colm said nervously, uncertain if Wynn really thought his dice had magical powers, but he didn't want to offend him. What the hell was going on tonight?

"Well, not to brag, but there's a bit more to it than that. In some circles, they're known as Tyche Dice, and they can grant wishes—for a price, that is." Wynn spoke in a solemn voice, clearly believing every word he was saying.

Colm eyed him apprehensively, eyes wide, stifling his laughter. Surely, he'd misheard him. But Wynn had spoken clearly; there was no mistaking what he said. Colm glanced around, looking for hidden cameras, convinced that he was the butt of some prank on a TV show. Any second, a television producer would pop into the store, revealing the joke. But as each second passed, it became clear that wasn't going to happen.

He took a sip from his glass before speaking. "Did you just say your dice grant *wishes*?"

"Yes, wishes," he said matter-of-factly, like it was completely outside the realm of questioning. "But for a price," he emphasized, his brows furling. "All magic comes at a cost, Colm, always. Don't you ever let anyone tell you different. If they do, it's a straight-out lie."

"You mean *magic*—like, spells and fairies and that sort of shit?" Colm tipped the empty glass, his words spilling out with laughter as he sat it on the counter.

"Well, not exactly," Wynn said, smiling and joining in with the laughter. "But let's just go with it, if that's how you best relate to the idea."

"So, it's like a genie's lamp?" Colm asked, still laughing. "A guy pops out, and *bam*, three wishes!"

Wynn stopped laughing, seemingly offended. He sat with a stern look on his face as Colm stood quiet now too. "No. Genies are egotistical bores. Their magic is crude and unrefined," Wynn said, spitting the words out as if eating something rotten. There was not an ounce of humor or sarcasm in his voice. "My dice, on the other hand, are sophisticated and uniquely attuned to the user. And—this is a big *and*—the wishes with my dice can be *unlimited*, with the right lucky roll. The people who work with my custom-made dice are called Gamblers, but not the losers you find at some gaudy casino. The genuine kind," he said, his eyes fixed on Colm.

"I'm sorry," Colm said, backpedaling, concerned that he'd offended Wynn, and he matched his tone, the laughter gone. "So, the dice gives you unlimited wishes? As many as you want, for whatever you want?"

A tiny sparkle returned to Wynn's eyes as he chuckled at the question. "Heavens no, lad. Didn't ya hear me earlier? Magic is not free; it never is. Magic always has a cost, eventually."

Colm struggled to understand him through the growing haze in his brain. "So, these Gamblers, they use the dice to get wishes granted?"

"Well, they try—some better than others. Whether a wish is granted is based purely on the roll of the dice. Evens, the wish is granted. Odds, well, it's not, and that's when the magic takes its toll," he said, taking another sip from his glass and packing more tobacco into his pipe. "The problem with wishes is you only get out what you put in, and generally nothing good. But the Gamblers, they keep trying."

"Who are these *Gamblers*?" Colm asked, getting more interested in Wynn's story.

"Many Gamblers walk the earth, both now and throughout history. Just read the headlines. All those people with god-awful amounts of money, just hoarding it for themselves… Nero, Hearst, Zuckerberg, Musk—all Gamblers," Wynn said, pausing. "But in the end, they all flame out. Some spectacularly so." He lifted his pipe to his mouth, pulling in a breath, holding his finger to the bowl of the pipe. Colm could have sworn that a tiny burst of flame sprouted from Wynn's index finger, but the man deftly closed his hand, putting it into his pocket when he spied Colm watching him. Their eyes locked, neither of them saying a word.

Colm reached for his glass, and the light glinted off his mother's ring, reminding him of the promise he'd made to himself after Tabitha's harsh words at dinner. The world may have abandoned him, but he wanted to believe there was something better out there waiting for him. Maybe this was it. Maybe this was his chance to do things differently. He just had to believe this little man's story. What the hell did he have to lose? Nothing added up, which was why it all strangely made sense to him. Lifting his glass, he drained it one more time.

"So, how much for one of those dice?" Colm asked casually.

Wynn lifted his glass to his mouth, taking a measured sip, looking upon Colm with calculating eyes. A moment passed before he spoke again, but this time with a fatherly tone. "Those dice are not for sale. Not in the traditional sort of way, that is." He paused, holding Colm's complete attention.

"I can only make them for those who *make the offering to be bound.* And for my services, since you've found me on my grand opening, I only ask for some good word of mouth around town. You know, to get the shop off on the right foot."

"How do I make the offering?" Colm asked without hesitation.

Reaching into the display case, Wynn retrieved a single alabaster-white dice with six sides, placing it on the counter between them. Its corners were rounded, and each of the sides appeared to be etched with X's, not the typical dots. Wynn spoke, drawing Colm's attention from the dice. "Bone. In ancient times, it was valued for its intrinsic powers—some say magical. Through my craft, this single dice will bind itself to its Gambler. But remember, all magic comes at a cost. This dice is no different. It will take its sacrifice as luck demands. There is no avoiding that—ever." Wynn took a puff from his pipe before continuing. "Being a Gambler isn't for everyone. In fact, most would be best advised to avoid it. So, you can still turn around and walk out of this store. That path is still open to you—but once the binding begins, it's a done deal."

Colm took in Wynn's words. For a moment, he thought of leaving; why risk it? But glimpsing his mother's ring again, he reached out, picking up the lone dice from the counter. "No. I'm all in."

Wynn chuckled at the alacrity of the response. "Okay, good enough for me!" He walked over and pulled the door closed, turning the dead bolt. As the door closed off the sounds from the street, the room filled with an unnatural and expectant stillness. Wynn turned from the door with a gleam in his eyes and shuffled back over, rejoining Colm at the counter.

"Blood. We need your blood," Wynn said matter-of-factly

as he pulled a vicious-looking penknife from under the counter. "Your binding to this dice requires a blood oath."

Colm's heart skipped a beat. "What? You're not cutting me with that thing!" He leaned away, wondering if he'd made a terrible mistake.

"Right, I'm not. *You* are," he said, holding the penknife out to Colm. "You have to make the offering yourself."

"Okay, sorry, this just got weird," Colm said, tossing the dice back on the counter and crossing his arms with a recalcitrant look on his face. "I'm not into making oaths to anyone, especially one that requires blood."

"Let's try this a different way," Wynn said with a fatherly tone. "Your blood creates the connection between you and your new power, forging the bond with your dice."

As Wynn spoke, the word "power" resonated with Colm. Part of him still thought all this was crazy, and the idea of furthering the charade by drawing his own blood was almost too much. But the drinks coursing through his veins hid that part of him, clouding his thoughts. Still, he had enough sense to know that his life needed to change.

Colm stepped back up to the counter, looking at Wynn. "You know this is insane, right?"

"All you need to do is prick your finger and place it on the dice. From there, my craft will take over. Simple, really," Wynn said, failing to acknowledge whether he agreed. He proffered the penknife again.

Colm hesitated, but he knew he had to do it quickly before his mind intervened. Grabbing the penknife, he pricked his finger with the tip, wincing as he placed it on the dice. His blood beaded up on the polished surface. The crimson hue was striking against the bleached white, and he watched in shock as his blood slowly soaked into the bone, filling each of the etched X's.

Almost immediately, the surface of the dice became luminous, followed by a pulsing scarlet glow from deep inside, as if the dice itself had a heart. Colm's mouth dropped open. The dice throbbed in and out ever so slightly, as if brought to life by the offering. There was a subtle scarlet flare, and the pulsing stopped. The etched X's dried to the color of burnt henna, offset nicely against the alabaster-white bone.

"That, my friend, is how it's done," Wynn said with a smile, barely marking Colm's dumbfounded expression. "Over time, the more you use it, the darker its color will become, showing that your connection with it is growing. Don't be alarmed if that happens." He reached over, pouring them another glass from the decanter. "Let's have one last toast. To you and your new dice," he said, raising his glass, and Colm reluctantly joined him, wondering what the hell he had just gotten himself into.

Wynn sat his glass on the counter, placing his pipe back in his mouth, and pulled a leather-bound journal and a pen from behind the counter, flipping to a marked page. He studied the page, mumbling to himself. "Yes, now, just a few housekeeping items…" He wrote Colm's name at the top of the page and looked up. "Where on your person will you keep your dice?"

"In my pocket, I guess," Colm said, patting the front pocket of his jeans.

"Check," Wynn said, looking down, scratching some notes in the journal. "Okay, now, let's just try it out." Wynn picked up the dice, placing a small blue sticker on it, and he walked over to the door, unlocking and opening it. The chilly night air spilled into the shop, cooling the sweat that had formed on Colm's brow. Wynn held out the dice so Colm could see the blue sticker on it, and in the next instant, he tossed the dice out onto the sidewalk, pulling the door shut behind him.

"Wait!" Colm objected, moving toward the door.

"Just calm down. Check your pocket," Wynn said, motioning to Colm's jeans as he locked the door and circled back around the counter.

Colm hesitated, but he finally fumbled his hand into his pocket. To his utter disbelief, he pulled the white dice out. It was heavier than before and warm to the touch. The corners were smoothly beveled, and the only imperfections were the etched X's on each face. He spun it around, seeing the blue sticker. "How the hell did you do that?!" Colm asked with a thick tongue.

Wynn laughed. "That's what they all say, but it wasn't me. It's the dice. It can't be lost, or destroyed, or anything." He busied himself again with the page in the journal, tapping the pen on the counter while puffing away on his pipe. "Yes, and now the rules."

Between the liquor and his shock over the dice reappearing in his pocket, Colm was only half listening. He rolled the dice between his fingers, gazing at the sticker in wonder, still wondering how Wynn had done it.

Behind the counter, Wynn remained focused on his job. "Rule one: you can tell people about the dice and its magic, but it's strongly advised that you don't. People will just think you're lucky or unlucky, like every other sod in the world, but you'll know differently." As he finished, Colm nodded, and Wynn scribbled something in his journal.

"Okay, rule two: speak your wish out loud, then roll. It's that simple. Evens are good, and your wish will be granted. But if you roll an odd number, you lose one year of your life. That's where the magic takes it due."

"Wait—what do you mean, I *lose* it?" Colm asked in horror, fighting the cloudy fatigue of the liquor.

"I mean it's gone, just like it sounds. Because of that, Gamblers need to have a healthy respect—or fear—for the odds. Whatever motivates you. You'll pick your own path, weigh your own choices. Only you can decide what might be worth trading your life for. So, that's number two," Wynn said, as if he were discussing the weather, looking down and writing in his journal. Colm swallowed, trying to keep his cool.

"Okay, on to rules three and four. You can't make the same wish twice, even if it's not granted. And you can't wish for lost time back, or more time, or time travel, or anything to do with time at all—that's beyond the power of the dice." Wynn checked two more boxes before moving on. "Now, rule five…"

"I can't do this anymore," Colm cut in. "I don't know what's in that drink, but I need to get myself home." His attention was fading, his eyelids growing heavy.

"Humph," Wynn intoned as he moved his hand to the bottom of the page, marking something before he continued. "Well, there are some more rules. I'd suggest—"

Before he could finish, Colm interrupted again. This was about the point where the liquor would finally overwhelm him, the last glass working its way through his system, pushing him over the edge. "I can't focus. I'll pop in tomorrow, and we can finish this then," Colm assured him, the sweat beading on his forehead, his skin turning a pale white.

Wynn's eyes turned again to the checklist, his hand moving to the bottom, making another mark. "I suggest you let me finish. This is very important. I can only share these things while the dice is being crafted. The magic prevents—"

"I understand how it works," Colm interrupted yet again, slightly slurring his words. The room was spinning, and he could sense the nausea welling up within him. "Make a wish and roll. Evens, it's granted; odds, it's not. I think I need to get going."

Wynn's eyes lowered to his notebook, and his hand moved to the bottom, making a third mark. "Three times asked, three times denied," he muttered. With those words, he set his pen down, and the journal vanished, but Colm was well beyond the point of noticing.

"Is that it?" he asked, throwing his backpack over his shoulder, leaning heavily on the counter.

"Just one more thing," Wynn said, and the unnatural silence seemed to deepen. "The Lady rules over other people's fates, but not yours. Not anymore. You are left to the winds of chance. Use that freedom wisely."

Colm nodded perfunctorily, tucking that wisdom away somewhere it would probably never be found as his eyelids sagged.

"Now, I'd appreciate some good word around town," Wynn said, winking at Colm and ushering him to the door, closing it tightly behind him before locking it.

5

THE ROOST

The room was cavernous and reeked of something long forgotten. Filtered light from the fading sunset streaked downward through a broken window, revealing rubble and trash littering the floor. In the spots where the cement peeked through, rainwater and milky bird droppings collected into puddles, leaving a greasy sheen reflecting the dimming light. An eerie silence enveloped the room, only broken by the periodic dripping of water from high above, which echoed into the shadowy corners as it splashed to the floor. This place was abandoned, except for a single chair that stood squarely in the middle of the sunlight, where a lone figure sat, slumped over, wearing a simple grey cable knit stocking cap.

Rye was conscious, but she remained motionless, keeping her head hung down, feigning otherwise. Her stocking cap had been pulled down, covering her eyes, making her other senses do the work. Wherever they'd taken her, it reeked something awful of feces and death. She inhaled, desperately wanting to breathe through her mouth to avoid the smell, but they'd gagged her. The knot dug into the back of her head, just as the ropes binding her arms and legs ripped into her flesh—merciless, just like them. She cautiously moved her fingers, probing the bindings, but stopped when she heard the echo of footsteps behind her.

"Finally awake, little magpie?" Liora said, her cream-colored gloves reaching out, moving Rye's stocking cap above her eyes. "You got yourself all worked up in that house. Still learning, huh?"

"Glad I was there to help you," Ciara said, her raspy voice joining in from across the room, feet splashing through the puddles as she moved closer.

Rye cursed herself for being so stupid. Why would she think a ghost would help her? They never did. And now look at her. She'd walked right into a trap, thanks to Noah.

She pushed her anger down. Noah wasn't the actual cause of her frustration. It was more that she'd done it to herself. She'd been reckless, first with him, and now with Liora and Ciara—and it was definitely going to cost her. But cost her what? She didn't have the necklace or even know where it was. That would put them in an even fouler mood, which came quicker than she thought.

From behind, Ciara knocked off her stocking cap, grabbing her hair and pulling her head back. Rye gritted her teeth, not wanting to show them any sign of weakness. Her eyes met the seedy black stones of Ciara's, which looked as if they were made from the darkness itself. Cropped black hair framed Ciara's face, her lips dressed in a matching black. She wore black leathers that fit her athletic physique like a glove, and she held one of her blades in her free hand, the other remaining sheathed on her back. Her signature blades were of the darkest obsidian, the guard of each wrought into an eerie raven's head with the same hollow, beady black eyes and stilted, pointy beak as Ciara. The rumors told that her blades had been a gift from Death herself—something Rye knew to be all too true.

"Welcome to our roost. Do you like it?" Ciara said with a sneer, spraying spittle on Rye's face. She held fast to a handful of Rye's hair as she cast the tip of her blade around the room. Now that Rye could see, the room was even bleaker than she'd imagined, and she crinkled her nose at the stench. "Oh, what's wrong? You don't like it?" Ciara said, feigning tears, moving her face closer, holding the obsidian blade against Rye's throat as the pointy beak of the raven skull dug into Rye's shoulder.

"Oh, stop it, Ciara," Liora said. "Let's just get this done. There's no need to play around with her. There are other ways to get what we need." A cream-gloved hand swept in, gently pushing the obsidian blade away from Rye's throat as Ciara finally let go of her hair. Rye turned her venomous look toward Liora. As always, Liora wore a sleek cream trench coat that fashionably buttoned up the front and cascaded downward just past her knees, enveloping her entire wiry frame with a subtle purity. A pair of matching lace-up boots peeked out, completing the outfit that somehow—even in this dingy, disgusting place—was still sparkling clean. As she stepped closer, she brushed her bleach-blonde hair over her shoulder, revealing her pale white face. Rye looked up to meet her eyes, but they were hidden behind sunglasses. Liora wore her sunglasses every-where, day and night. The cream outfit and the sunglasses—that was quintessential Liora.

"You're wrong about that," Ciara said, but stowed her blade.

Rye tried to speak through the gag, but it came out in mumbles. Liora reached in, pulling the gag down.

"It's good to see that you kept your nice white coat clean.

I'd hate to see you off brand," Rye said, voice thick with sarcasm.

"Cream," Liora retorted.

"What?"

"It's *cream*, not white. And some of us have an image to uphold."

"Whatever. You're both demented," Rye spat, struggling against her bindings in defiance as she snuck a peek around her. An unbroken mound of ash formed a line on the floor encircling her chair, and her sleeve was rolled up, revealing a small wound on her inner arm. Things were worse than she'd thought.

"Yes, you're a bit stuck," Liora said, following Rye's glance. "Ciara thought the rope would be enough to hold you, but the ash… Well, that's just an extra safety precaution of mine." Her creamy gloved hands reached down to the bindings, tugging on them to confirm that they were still taut.

Ciara chuckled as she stood back, picking the dirt from under her fingernails. "You're wasting time. We should just beat it out of her. I'm sure she'd tell us where it is within seconds."

"Come, come, Ciara. Surely, even in your eternal gloominess, you can find some light for a fellow member of the Sorority," Liora crooned.

"*Ex*-member. She left the Sorority of her own volition, after she stole the necklace," chided Ciara, her cold, beady black eyes fixed on Rye.

"I didn't leave the Sorority, and I've stolen nothing," Rye protested. "I'm just on a little hiatus. Anyway, she pushed me out with her decision. But you know that."

"Oh, right—the *boyfriend*." Liora drew her words out and threw her arms up in the air dramatically. "That's right: *you* wanted Noah to join. Not to pick at old wounds, but I was always a little confused about a *man* joining a sorority. Still, that boyfriend of yours, he's a cutie! How is the old chap, anyway?"

Rye cringed at the mention. She wasn't certain if it was out of embarrassment over trusting him or lingering anger at what he'd done, but neither sat well with her. "I couldn't care less. Now, let me go before things get out of hand," she said, her words clipped as she teetered on the edge, about to lose control. To focus her mind away from their barbs, she bit down hard on her tongue, and her mouth filled with the metallic tang of blood. She couldn't afford to do anything stupid right now.

"Trouble in paradise? That's too bad, little magpie," Liora said.

"Stop calling me that," Rye said through gritted teeth.

Ignoring the plea, Liora continued, "But back to the Sorority. I do admit that we have a little confession to make. We also left the Sorority, shortly after you did. When the Lady went into hiding, we got a better offer from someone else—a new employer. Different places and different faces, but with a renewed sense of purpose. The Lady had gotten so pedantic about the Stone of Fates, lording over everyone's fate and dispensing good and bad fortune with a light touch. We felt it was high time to transition the control of people's fates to someone new—someone with a fresh vision and growing ambitions. We're helping our new employer realize this vision, and we just need what you stole from the Lady to lure her out."

"Enough!" yelled Ciara. "You're sharing too much. She just needs to give us the damn necklace. That's it." She stormed over to Rye, baring her obsidian blades. A flicker in Rye's eyes grew, and adrenaline filled her veins once again as her bones cracked.

Just then, she felt a prick in her bicep and turned to see Liora injecting a murky violet liquid. Almost immediately, the surge subsided, and Rye's shoulders drooped against the ropes.

"What the hell is that?" Rye asked, eyes wild in protest.

"See?" Ciara cried, erupting with an unsettling mixture of glee and laughter. "I told you the lichen would work!"

Liora stepped away, setting an empty syringe on the table. *"Lethoria vulpina,"* she said, turning back to Rye. "Small doses won't kill you, but too much can be fatal—*for your kind.*"

Ciara kneeled, gloating in Rye's face. "You'd best stay calm, little magpie. Things can only get worse from here."

Rye was furious, and doing a poor job of hiding it. These were people she used to think of as friends—more than friends. How could they do this to her?

Liora pulled Ciara away, glaring at her before turning back with a soft look as Ciara's laughter continued, only more subdued. "Rye, please. It doesn't have to be like this."

Rye's brows crinkled with concern as her eyes moved from Liora to Ciara. She knew their tactics were vastly different. Liora was the more civil of the two, always pulling on people's hopes and dreams. Ciara was the opposite, preying on people's fears, always dealing in pain and confusion. When left unchecked, hope led people to do foolish things, while fear made them unable to act. Only the balance between the two kept people in line, and that was where Liora and Ciara thrived. They were a balanced pair, and they were notorious for getting jobs done. Even the Lady had praised them for it. However, something wasn't sitting right with Rye. Why were they hell-bent on getting the necklace? And if it was so important, why would they risk killing her without getting it? Better yet, why did they want to kill her at all? It made no sense. Still not ready to test them further this early in the interrogation, Rye settled, wondering what more she could learn.

"There, now, that's better. We're all calm now," Liora said, gently laying her hand on Rye's shoulder. Rye sat still as a stone, staring coldly at Liora. "You know, we could stop all this if you just told us where it is," Liora suggested.

Rye continued to glare, not saying a word.

Ciara scoffed, "I can't believe you're dumb enough to not wear it all the time."

Rye agreed: it was insane. She *always* wore it—at least, before Noah had stolen it and refused to give it back to her. He'd hoped that if he got rid of it, maybe Liora and Ciara would stop hunting her. Clearly, that was wrong, as were so many other things about him, many of which had only now become clear to Rye. Still, she didn't take well to being lectured by Ciara. "I didn't steal it," Rye insisted. "I earned it for my service to the Lady. You're just mad that she didn't give it to you."

"Whatever. We all know you stole it, but I love that you're convinced she *gave* it to you. Either way, she won't be happy that you lost it. Just think if it fell into the wrong hands... She might be driven out of hiding. That'd be a shame," Ciara said, her words thick with sarcasm.

But as long as they were talking, Rye could think. "I didn't steal it," she repeated, "she left it for me to take." She wished no harm to the Lady, even though she was done with her and her Sorority. She'd simply moved on with her life—something that Liora and Ciara clearly hadn't done.

"Right. Whatever makes you feel right in your world," Ciara snapped.

Rye spat back as convincingly as she knew how, "Well, it doesn't matter anyway, because I don't have it anymore. I was sick of you hunting me for it, so I sold it just to be done with all of this. I don't need its magic, I don't need you hunting me, and I don't need the Lady or the Sorority ever again, so screw off!"

Almost in unison, Ciara and Liora howled with laughter.

"You always were the worst liar," Ciara managed as tears rolled from her eyes.

Liora joined in, "Your nose—it *twitched*!" She could barely get the words out as she laughed along with Ciara.

Rye just sat there, glaring. They knew her too well to fall for her lie. "You two are the worst," she said. "There's no way—"

"You know, there was one little thing we omitted earlier," Liora said, speaking over Rye. "I didn't mention it, but we were able to find that boyfriend of yours, and I'm guessing he might know where the necklace is. What do you think?"

Rye hesitated before speaking, her face betraying her again. "I told you, I couldn't give two shits about him. He's not my boyfriend. Anyway, you're lying."

"Unlike you, we opt to trade in truths," Liora said, holding up a cell phone that Rye immediately recognized as her own. "Amazing what these things can do—and *track*. Did you know Noah is sharing his location with you?"

Rye looked back at Liora with a blank expression.

"Didn't think so, but lucky for us, he is," she said, tossing the phone onto the table. "We'd prefer to just deal with you, but if you push us, we could pay him a little visit and see what he knows."

Rye's eyes glistened with moisture as she turned to Liora. She was mad at Noah for what he'd done, of course, but she'd never wish a visit from Liora and Ciara upon him. That would not end well. She looked around the bleak room one more time. She'd had enough. All the running had finally worn her down, and she was trapped. She knew Noah had sold her necklace—at least, that's what he'd said—but she didn't know exactly where.

Playing the only card she had left, she said, "I can get it for you. Just promise me that you'll leave him alone and let me go if I do."

Ciara leaned in close, her steamy breath washing over Rye's face. "We don't make deals," she said—just before landing a series of heavy blows on Rye's face, leaving her streaked with blood.

Rye's tongue lapped up the blood as she raised her head defiantly at Ciara. The games were over. She knew there would be no deals. She held her head up, smiling, blood trickling down her face. Meeting Ciara's eyes, she spit a loogie into her face that sprayed wide, casting bloody spittle across Liora's immaculate cream coat.

Liora jumped. "God dammit!" she cried, looking at her soiled coat in disgust. Rye laughed, further enraging them.

"You know you can die without your necklace, right? You can remember your own mortality, right?" rasped Ciara.

Rye rose to meet the threat one last time. "And you would be wise to remember that the Lady will not take kindly to it if something were to happen to a member of her Sorority. You can remember that, right? You can recall her wrath, right?" Rye said, mocking Ciara. "She still holds the Stone of Fates, last I heard. I don't know what's come over you two, but you'd better check yourselves before it's too late."

The retort appeared to have struck a chord, as they both took a small step back. Apparently, even they could recall what it meant to be a member of the Sorority. It was a membership for life in the eyes of the Lady.

"You cannot avoid the consequences of membership as long as she holds the Stone of Fates. Those are her words, not mine," Rye reminded them.

"Right—*as long as she holds the Stone of Fates,*" Ciara repeated. "You always were the teacher's pet, weren't you? In fact, that's what we're counting on. She'll either come to rescue you, or to get that necklace." Ciara glanced at Liora as she spoke.

Brushing her coat off, Liora chimed in, "You're not

leaving here until we have it, or you tell us where to find it. I suggest we take a break from this lovely little reunion and pick it up later."

"Yes, I'm certain I can find ways to better *motivate* our little magpie to share her secrets," Ciara said, wiping the blood from her hands on Rye's jacket. Leaning in, she pulled Rye's stocking cap back on her head and slid the gag into place. "You be a good little girl and wait here for us," she whispered, laughing and softly patting Rye on the cheek. Then she stepped over the circle of ash, making sure not to disturb it.

Rye sat resolute in the chair, trying her best to stay upright. Once they disappeared out the door, she slouched over against the ropes, her face throbbing as the blood trickled down. The revving of their car echoed loudly through the room, only to be replaced by silence once again.

6

SOMEDAY

Morning light flooded the room as Colm pulled the covers up, blocking it out. His head throbbed, and all he wanted to do was sleep. He rolled over, expecting to be in his bed, but instead he fell to the floor with a crash, banging his head on a table. Rubbing the sleep from his eyes, he saw a tacky green couch, like the cheap velour of an outdated jogging suit. He was still wearing the same clothes from the day before, and his mouth was dry, like a spider had woven a web in it. He rolled over, swishing his tongue around his mouth, trying to get some moisture back into it.

"You finally awake?" his uncle asked, sitting at the dining room table behind the couch.

Colm yawned, pulling himself up and holding his head in his hands. "How did I get here?" he asked, confused.

"Roget called me." Andrew lifted the newspaper, turning the page.

"Detective Lemmek?" Colm covered his face with his hands.

"That's the one," Andrew answered casually, finishing the eggs on his plate.

"Where was I?" Colm asked, trying to piece together the woolly images floating around in his head.

"Just outside Dos Suenos, sitting against a tree."

"That makes sense," Colm said, the memories of his dinner with Tabitha breaking through the fog. "Tab dumped me last night."

"Ah." Andrew lowered his newspaper. "I'm sorry to hear that, but it explains a lot. There are some pancakes and bacon over here, if you can drag yourself off the couch. But I've got to go; I have a meeting at eight a.m. sharp. So, let's catch up when I get back to the shop." He folded the newspaper as he got up from the table, heading toward the door.

"Thanks, that sounds great." The smell of the bacon wafted over, and Colm got up from the couch, taking his uncle's place at the table.

Andrew turned back. "I'm headed out to see Oliver. You got anything for him?"

That explained Andrew's urgency. Oliver was an antiques guy Andrew worked with to help him price things at the shop, and he loathed when people were late. His advice came at a high price, but he'd saved Andrew from underpricing things on numerous occasions, more than making up for his fees and fussiness.

"No, not—" Colm stopped mid-sentence, snapping his fingers. "Wait… Where's my backpack?"

Andrew motioned to the bench by the door, and Colm brought it over to the table. He laughed, remembering the Aussie as he pulled out the mandala and necklace, placing them on the table. "Have him take a look at these."

Andrew stopped, walking back to the table. "Nice. Where'd you get these?"

Colm told the story of the Aussie showing up just before closing, pausing as he reached into his backpack, pulling out the milky blade. "I got this too." He laid it on the table, where it made a crystalline sound as it settled. "But I'm gonna hold onto the blade for now. It'd be a cool mantelpiece at my place."

"Nice haul, but what'd you pay?" Andrew asked.

"Six grand," Colm said flatly, and seeing the irritation enter Andrew's face, he quickly added, "I bought them with my money, not yours."

Andrew's eyebrows raised. "You got the money to cover that?"

"Yeah, I've got it," Colm said, reaching for another piece of bacon.

Andrew relaxed, picking the pieces up one at a time, studying them with a disapproving look on his face. "Well, it'll be interesting to hear what Oliver has to say. Might've been a good idea to have him look at them first."

"There wasn't time," Colm said, sitting back down at the table. "This guy was hot to sell. He would've just gone to one of the other shops in town, so I jumped in."

"Well, we'll see if your little gamble pays off. You sure you don't want me to take the blade too?" Andrew asked as he picked up the mandala and necklace.

"No. Let's just start with those."

"Never took you for a knife guy," Andrew said, chuckling as he zipped up his bag. At the door, he turned back, just as the Aussie had done the night before. Colm had a bit of déjà vu remembering the Aussie's warnings.

"What is it?" Andrew asked.

"Well, before he left the shop, he told me other people—*dangerous* people—might be looking for this stuff, and to be discreet when I sell them. He even suggested selling them out of town."

Andrew paused, his eyes narrowed as he looked at the blade on the table. "Well, first step, let's get these to Oliver and see what we've got."

Colm nodded, putting the blade in his backpack and finishing the food on his plate.

"You've got the shop this morning, but please take a shower first," Andrew said as he whisked out the door, closing it behind him.

Colm reached for the bottle of Advil on the table, downing a couple with a swig of orange juice. Already, his stomach was feeling better, but his head was still swimming. Pressing his hands against his pants as he got up from the table, he felt an odd bulge in his pocket. Reaching in, he pulled out a single dice, holding it in his palm. The burnt henna color of the imprinted X's contrasted beautifully with the white of the dice, and his mind wandered back to the night before. The face of a funny dwarfish man and his opulently adorned shop flashed into his mind. He combed through the foggy memories, recalling the man's name, and with that came the memory of the pipe and its smell of sweet thyme, and that syrupy sweet drink. Colm flushed at the sudden memory of the liquor, his stomach churning once again as he ran to the bathroom, spewing up the breakfast he'd just eaten.

Wiping his mouth, he sat down on the bathroom floor as more memories came trickling back. His mind objected to the tedious work of piecing together the night before, and he couldn't help wondering if he'd been drugged. He opened his hand, looking at the dice, turning it in his fingers, then noticed a small wound on his forefinger. He looked back and forth from the pinprick to the dice, and in that moment, the memories of the night before fell into place.

Closing his hand tightly around the dice, he remembered Wynn telling him his dice were magical and granted wishes. Was that guy crazy? Magic and wishes were the stuff of fairy tales, not the real world. Yeah, he must've been drugged. That was the only thing that could explain his willingness to believe all of that garbage.

Still, he had to admit that he wanted it to be true—desperately. And how could he explain the strange things he had witnessed last night? Could this dice really be magical?

Recalling Wynn's trick, he rose, stepped over to the bathroom window, opened it, and tossed the dice into the alley below.

"Please be real, please be real," he whispered, crossing his fingers. He took a deep breath before reaching into his pocket. His heart skipped a beat as his hand closed around it, pulling out a white dice with burnt henna X's. Unable to believe just yet, he opened the window, tossing it out again and again, only to find it in his pocket each time.

"This shit is *real*?!" he whispered, a mixture of disbelief and wonder in his voice.

But now he had questions—so many questions he hadn't asked the night before. His view of the night was becoming more fluid, and he now wished he'd been present enough to really listen to Wynn's spiel about the rules.

He knew what he had to do. He splashed some water on his face and straightened his hair in the mirror before heading back to the kitchen, where he grabbed his backpack and clicked the lights off on his way out.

Colm walked briskly down the sidewalk, dodging the morning dawdlers as he went along. Andrew lived in town, so it didn't take him long to get to the dice shop.

But when he arrived, there was no shop. There wasn't even a door there. It was as if The Daserii had never existed. Thinking his memory might be off, he retraced his steps, walking up and down the street, but it was nowhere to be found.

He stood on the sidewalk, running his fingers through his

hair. He didn't understand. How could a shop literally be there one day, and simply gone the next, like it had vanished?

"What the hell?" he muttered, trying to convince himself he wasn't crazy. He shook his head, letting out a resigned laugh. Was he really starting to believe that a little man in a nonexistent shop had made him a dice that granted wishes? He pulled out the dice, looking at its burnt henna X's, puzzling over it. The dice was undeniably real, but how? The only answer was magic, but he didn't believe in magic—at least, not until this moment. It was the only thing that could explain it all, and he had to admit, he found the idea of magic and wishes alluring.

But why him? He paused, holding his gaze on the dice as if it would give him answers. He recalled the old homeless man's words: *"Sometimes you need to swallow hard and roll the dice instead of waiting for someday."* But the words now resonated with Colm differently. This was the old man who had pointed out the shop to him in the first place—a shop that wasn't there now—and had also told him to "roll the dice." The implication couldn't have been clearer to Colm in this moment, and he couldn't ignore its call any longer. He might not have heard all the rules for the dice, but he'd heard enough. Moving down the street toward the Anvil, all he could think of now was getting somewhere private to try it out.

"Sorry, we're opening late today," Colm said, dismissing a few customers who were waiting for the shop to open. "Come back in an hour." With that, he closed the door.

His mind was spinning with all the possibilities, both good and bad, as an uneasiness settled over him. Turning the bolt to lock the door, he saw his mother's Claddagh ring on his finger, reminding him instantly of Tabitha. He hadn't had much time to think about her in the morning's excitement, but the pain of the breakup sat raw in his stomach.

Out of nowhere, a voice in his mind told him he could solve the whole Tabitha thing with one lucky roll. Could he use the dice to *make* Tabitha come back to him? He wasn't entirely sure, but it was a thought that he knew he should've quickly dismissed. Still, it ended up lingering a bit too long, and against his better judgment, he formulated the words of the wish in his mind. Was the chance of getting back together with her worth one year off his life? He paused, mulling it over. Could he, in good conscience, *make* her live that lie?

He was dangerously close to uttering the wish and letting the dice decide when the shop's phone rang. It if hadn't rung at just that moment, he wasn't sure what he would have done. He liked to think he wouldn't have made the wish, but he was grateful for the interruption, just in case.

Colm ignored the phone, rolling the dice in his fingers as he took a seat behind the counter, cycling through other wishes. With a sudden inspiration, he snapped his fingers and leaned in, blowing on the dice as it jiggled in his hand. He might not be willing to force her to come back to him, but a good bankroll could go a long way towards smoothing a lot of things out in his life—maybe even things with Tabitha. "I wish for five million dollars."

As soon as the words were spoken, he sent the dice skittering across the counter, where it bumped into an old clock radio, coming to a stop. Overwhelmed with excitement, he pulled it back, only to see three X's glaring back at him. He hesitated, waiting for the magic to descend, half expecting an ethereal whirlwind to spin around him, leaving him with a beard down to his knees. But he couldn't discern any change at all, which left him wondering if it had worked. Picking up the dice again, he gave it another go, this time not being shy about wishing for even more cash.

"I wish for *ten* million dollars," he said, rolling and failing again, before making two more wishes for progressively more insane amounts of money, rolling odds both times. "What the hell?" he whispered, picking up the dice and wondering if he was doing something wrong. Still, he couldn't discern any changes, so he steadied himself for another go when a noise at the front door startled him. Looking up, he saw Andrew shuffling in, welcoming in the customers Colm had shunned earlier. Andrew turned, giving Colm a curt look as he walked across the store.

"Why's the door locked?" he asked in a pithy voice.

Colm stood, nervously tapping the dice on the counter, debating how to tell his uncle about it. "Sorry. I just..." He hesitated, glancing at the customers milling about the shop before he continued, "There's something I need to—"

"Jesus, you look terrible. You alright?" Andrew interrupted, coming to a stop on the other side of the counter.

Colm shrugged. "Yeah, my stomach's off. That's all." But then he caught a glimpse of his reflection in the mirror on the wall over his uncle's shoulder. It was still him, only slightly different. He bore a few more defined wrinkles, a scruffy beard, and a darkness under his eyes. The changes were minute, but as clear to him as they were to Andrew. He peered vacantly at his reflection, not hearing anything his uncle was saying. The words *all magic comes at a cost* echoed in his mind. Fear coiled in his stomach. The magic *had* taken its due, just as Wynn warned him it would. Colm tried to recall how many wishes he'd just frivolously made, but found he couldn't remember; he'd been too caught up in the thrill of it all, which he now found disturbing. For a moment, he wondered how many wishes he might've made if Andrew hadn't come in, and he didn't like the answer. The reality of this magic was sinking in.

"I thought I told you to clean up before you came in?" Andrew said, irritation growing with each word as he leaned in, taking a sniff. "Jesus, you smell like a mix of puke, cigarettes, and liquor. Get out of here. Go home and shower, get yourself cleaned up. I've got a delivery you need to make this evening, so you can rest until then," he said, making a shooing motion with his hands.

"Yeah, okay, but I really need to tell you something first," Colm said, setting the dice on the counter between them.

Andrew's eyes narrowed, and creases lined his forehead. "I'm already upset that the shop wasn't open on time. We can talk later," he said, pointing to the door, handing Colm a small manila envelope about the size of an index card.

Colm started to object, then noticed the address scribbled on the envelope. "Wait... You're shitting me with this address, right? The docks have been abandoned for years."

"If you're worried, you could take your gun with you," Andrew suggested, sensing Colm's apprehension.

"I'm not taking a gun! It's just... That place gives me the creeps, especially at night," Colm said, his body quivering.

"You'll be fine. Now, go." Andrew turned, and his cane clicked across the floor on his way to visit one of the customers browsing the shop.

Colm quickly left the Anvil and made his way to the alley behind the shop, where his motorcycle was still parked from the day before. Taking a seat on the bike, he dumped the contents of the envelope into his hand. A dingy gold coin roughly the size of a silver dollar landed in his palm. He flicked it with his finger, hearing a soft but resonant thud. Solid gold. Both faces of the coin were identical, displaying an elegant Celtic knot in the shape of a pentagram. An embossed triskelion sat in the center, enclosed in a circle, and weaving its way through the lower half of the pentagram was a crescent moon arching upwards.

"Well, that's not creepy or anything," he said out loud as he returned the coin to the envelope, stashing it away in the pocket of his jacket.

7

COWARD IN THE CLOSET

Colm opened the throttle on his motorcycle, adjusting the position of his feet on the foot pegs. As he sped down the road, his feet were almost numb in the biting wind whipping at him. The autumn sun had ducked behind the horizon, and the light from his headlights flooded out ahead before being swallowed up into the fog and darkness. The shadowy silhouette of the docks loomed in the distance, catching the last hints of the day's light.

Moments later, he turned off the road, slowing to a crawl as he maneuvered around the scattered boxes and debris littering the docks. His eyes moved from building to building, searching for the address that Andrew had written on the envelope. Not surprisingly, most of the buildings' numbers were absent and had never been replaced, because no one came here anymore. The fishing industry had collapsed years ago, and these abandoned buildings were the remnants. There had been talk of revitalizing the area, turning it into a swanky community of art studios and galleries, but like most things that required funding, it had never moved beyond talk. So, the buildings had sat derelict for years now, only frequented by vagabonds or the periodic curious developer. Otherwise, the only rumors about what went on here were bad ones, and Colm wanted nothing to do with any of it. He just wanted to make the delivery, get in and out, wholly intending for it to be a quick affair.

Ahead at the end of the dock, two large buildings stood, dimly lit. He picked his way down the dock, pulling up to the door of the nearest one. Coming to a stop, he killed the headlight and the engine. Reaching into his pocket, he pulled out the little manila envelope that read, *23 Wharfside B*. He dismounted the bike, walking closer to get a better look at the address above the door. Some of the letters had fallen, but their shadows remained. The address was a match, but looking closer, he saw that there was grunge over where the letter *A* had previously hung. Wrong building. He stowed the envelope, looking down the dock to the other building, guessing that was 23 Wharfside B.

Pulling his hood up, he turned, moving forward almost at a slow jog. The quicker he made the delivery, the quicker he'd be out of here. With each step, he heard the waves splashing in the darkness, but otherwise, it was eerily quiet. No moon and no stars decorated the sky. Tonight, the fog hid them. Only the soft lights from the two ramshackle buildings stood out. He wiped the mist from his face, drying his hands on his jeans as he stopped at the doorway. A faint light from inside trickled out into the night, and he let out a sigh of relief at seeing the letter *B* in place. The door was mostly closed, just a sliver of light escaping. He paused for a moment, looking around, wondering what his uncle had gotten him into this time. Who the hell would want a delivery to this place? *This is crazy.* He momentarily thought of turning around and just telling his uncle he couldn't find it, but a muffled noise from inside grabbed his attention.

Leaning into the window by the door, he craned his neck

to peek inside. The room was open and expansive, the only light coming from a single sodium lamp dangling from somewhere high above. A lone chair sat directly under the lamp, and as Colm leaned in for a better look, he made out the figure of someone sitting in it with their back to the door. "This must be it," he whispered out loud, almost as if trying to convince himself. He took a step toward the door, uncertain whether he should just go in or knock, but he ultimately decided that they had left the door ajar, expecting the delivery. His hand reached out, pushing on the cold metal of the door handle. The door opened with a loud creak, and he cringed.

As he was about to call out to the person in the chair, a pack of rats scurried out the door, frantically rushing over Colm's shoes before skittering away into the darkness. "Son of a bitch!" he yelled, jumping back. This wasn't exactly how he'd intended to make introductions with his uncle's latest customer. "Sorry, just some … rats," he called out apologetically.

There was no response, and he paused in the doorway, looking at the chair, wondering if his eyes were just playing a trick on him in the low lighting. He spoke in a slightly louder voice. "I'm here for the delivery. Andrew sent me." He tentatively took a few steps forward into the building, confirming that there was in fact a person in the chair. They looked to be struggling, and he heard mumbling he couldn't quite make out.

"Dammit," he muttered to himself. What the hell was going on? The floor was littered with debris and dark puddles, and the place reeked of dead things. Putting his nose into the crook of his elbow to mask the smell, he cautiously stepped forward, doing his best to dodge the puddles. "Hello?" he called, his voice shaking.

He scanned the room, and his eyes landed on a table covered with various things—shiny things, rusty things, sharp things, and some things that were just strange, adding to the overall creep factor. The closer he got, the louder the incoherent mumbling, but he'd still gotten no real response. With each step, the idea of quickly making this delivery and getting out of here was evaporating.

As he approached the chair from behind, he circled it widely, seeing the smooth curves of her body and the long, silky red hair sprouting out of the grey stocking cap. His eyes drifted down, finally seeing why she hadn't responded to him: she'd been tied to the chair and gagged.

Colm almost turned and ran, but morbid curiosity and perhaps compassion propelled him forward. He continued his arc, circling around her, keeping his distance, until she turned her head to look at him. She was young, like him, adorned with a simple tattoo of a small black star under the corner of her left eye. His eyes connected with hers immediately. They were a beautiful emerald color—but they were not happy. They were rife with concern, pleading with him to help her. Blood streaked her face and had soaked into her stocking cap, making small blurry polka dots. She'd been beaten badly—and recently, judging from the color of the blood.

"What the fuck?!" he muttered without realizing it. He stood frozen, looking at her, trying to convince himself of what he was seeing, but his mind was struggling to pull the pieces together. She mumbled again, wriggling her body in the chair as her eyes widened, trying to get him to snap out of his stupor. Seeing her struggle, his senses finally reengaged, and he rushed forward, pulling the gag down from her mouth.

"Quick, untie the ropes," she said, eerily calm and matter-of-fact. "We need to get the hell out of here. They'll kill you if they find you here."

He saw the truth of it in her eyes, sending shivers down his spine. Colm didn't know who *they* were, or whether *they* were Andrew's customers, or whether this girl was the customer, or something else altogether. It didn't matter; all he heard was *"They'll kill you."*

"Right." Colm's eyes moved to the ropes binding her, his hands probing for the knots. He glanced back into her eyes. There was something about her that was comfortable, disarming, and wild at the same time. As he worked to loosen the knots, his hands brushed against her skin. It was soft, but well defined with muscle. She was clearly an athlete, not just some college girl. Out of the corner of his eye, he saw the blood on her face. The strangeness of it all sent questions echoing through his mind.

"I'm just here for a delivery. Are you Andrew's customer?" he asked, his eyes meeting hers momentarily before he turned his attention back to the knots.

"Does it *look* like I'm a customer to you?" she snapped, clearly trying to hold back her temper.

"No, I guess not." He struggled with the knots as her first words echoed in his mind. "When you said, 'they'll kill you,' did you mean—"

"Yes, kill you. Like, dead," she cut in. "Just hurry, they'll be back soon. We've got to get out of here. They've gone completely nuts this time." She urged him to focus on the knots, but they were tight, double- and triple-knotted in places, and his hands were shaking in his panic. Whoever had tied her up didn't want her to break free, that much was certain, and he was getting a better understanding of what the scary things on the table were for. Looking at the blood on her face, he shuddered.

Just as the knots were loosening, he heard the unmistakable throaty sound of a vintage muscle car off in the distance, working its way up to the docks.

"Shit!" she breathed. "That's them. Hurry!" She struggled against the ropes.

He'd made some progress, but it was clear he couldn't get the knots untied before they arrived. Lowering his head in defeat, he stopped his work moments before the car pulled up outside the door of 23 Wharfside B.

"I can't—they're too tight," he said apologetically as his face flushed with guilt.

Their eyes met in a silent acknowledgment as she spoke in a harried voice. "On the floor behind you, break the circle of ash, but subtly. Then hide." Her eyes motioned behind him, and he turned to see a door hidden in the darkness.

"But I can't just leave you—"

"There's no time. Go!" she spat.

They exchanged a nod, and he turned, asking no questions as he dragged his toe through the circle of ash, making an almost imperceptible break in it. The words *"They'll kill you"* echoed loudly in his mind, sending his heart racing as he looked to the door in the shadows. In his panic, he was beyond the point of questioning anything; he was simply following her orders.

A moment later, he opened the door, expecting to see the dock outside, but instead it was a small broom closet. He glanced back, hearing voices outside the front door. Stepping inside, he pressed his body into the closet, pulling the door shut quietly behind him, but not before he glimpsed the girl, her amber hair framing those emerald eyes. Their gazes locked one last time before she lowered her head, closing her eyes.

As the door closed behind him, the shame of what he'd

just done flooded over him. Andrew would never have done this; he would've stood his ground. But not Colm. He'd only saved himself, and now he was hiding in a freaking broom closet. It reminded him of the night his parents were murdered—a night he rarely talked about, but thought of almost every day. That night, he had hidden in his room with the door locked, and now he was hiding again, even though he knew the right thing to do was to help her. But he couldn't. In this moment, he was still that cowardly little boy who hadn't saved his parents. Why put his life on the line to save a complete stranger? He struggled with his thoughts, but the voices entering the room interrupted him.

Inching closer to the door, he found a small crack in the wood, allowing him to see bits and pieces of the room, but not enough to make out faces. To his surprise, he overheard the voices of two ladies, and as he pressed his face to the door, he saw someone dressed in black carrying a box with what looked like wires hanging over the edges. He tried to adjust his angle to get a better view, and as he did, a raspy voice sounded from across the room.

"Still here, magpie? Course you are," she said, chuckling. "We talked about a lot of different options that might get our favorite little loup-garou talking, and we landed on an oldie, but a goodie." She dropped the box to the floor with a loud thud as Colm caught a flash of another lady, this one wearing a cream outfit.

"Do what you want. I'm not scared of you," the voice of the emerald-eyed girl rang out, boasting the very courage he lacked.

"'Do what you want, do what you want,'" the raspy voice mocked her mercilessly. "I told you we should have just started with the boyfriend."

"We owe her a chance. Perhaps she'll see the benefits of cooperation," said the one in cream. Her voice was sweet, almost syrupy, and strangely, it made Colm feel a bit more relaxed.

He leaned back from the door, gathering his wits. There must be something he could do to help this girl…

His dice! He reached into his pocket, feeling the smooth contour of it as he mulled over the idea. His uncle would say this was "a time for doin'," but thinking back to earlier at the Anvil, he recalled his reflection in the mirror. The magic of the dice had taken years from him already. How many, he didn't know, but he felt certain it was real. Why should he risk years of his life for someone he didn't know? And what if … what if she *deserved* this? After all, who knew what she'd done to get caught up with these two ladies? He paused for a moment, then released the dice, pulling his hand out of his pocket.

He looked through the crack again, seeing the two ladies circling their captive, talking to her in low voices. Maybe he wouldn't use the dice, but surely he could handle two women.

Still, she'd warned that they'd kill him. The girl had been clear about that. What if they had guns? The idea of charging out to her rescue quickly cooled in his mind as he shifted his body, trying to hear what was being said. As he adjusted, his arm hit an old forgotten broom leaned up against the wall of the closet. It clattered to the floor, and Colm swore under his breath.

The voices immediately stopped. Even though he couldn't see them, he felt all their eyes glaring at the door.

"What the hell was that?" asked the raspy voice.

"Not sure, but it came from the closet," said the other one.

The flash of a pale coat moved toward to the closet as the raspy voice called out, "Maybe we've got us a rat."

Colm froze, heart hammering against his ribs, barely breathing as he caught the blurry images of the two ladies approaching the closet. As their feet shuffled closer to the door, a deep grunt sounded from behind them. Looking through the crack in the door, Colm saw the grey stocking cap rise from the chair. In a blur, the girl bolted for the front door, slamming it shut behind her.

"Get her!" the two ladies yelled, turning away from the closet to chase the girl. They swore loudly as they fought through the debris, finally making their way out the door. A second later, there was a familiar loud rumble outside. Colm reached into his pockets, searching frantically for his keys. The dice was there, but his keys were not.

"Shit!" he cursed. The rumble grew louder as his unattended bike throttled and sped off down the dock, quickly followed by the throaty engine of the ladies' car coming to life. The squeal of their tires echoed through the warehouse, rattling the windows as the car grumbled away in hot pursuit.

Colm leaned back against the wall of the closet, running his fingers through his hair. Andrew would never let him hear the end of this one. He wasn't sure what he'd just walked into, but he hoped the girl with the emerald eyes had gotten away—even though she had just stolen his motorcycle. He craned his neck, listening to see if he was alone, and his mind wandered back to her red hair. There was something about it…

Then it hit him. Was she "the lady in red"—the one that the old man from the night before was talking about? She couldn't be. How would that make any sense? But he had to admit, not much of the last twenty-four hours made any sense to him, and the coincidence of it all was too great to ignore. It had to be her.

The warehouse had fallen silent, and his muscles were sore from being cramped in the small space. Cautiously pushing the door open, he emerged and walked across the room to the chair, looking at the ropes dangling from it. Some knots had come loose, while others were still tightly in place. He kneeled by the chair, inspecting the ropes more closely. Something sharp had sliced clean through them. He stood, turning to look at the grey circle surrounding the chair, now broken and jagged in many places. The girl had said it was ash. But why? And why had she asked him to break it? Each question seemed to create three more. He stood looking about the large room. There was definitely something different about her, but he couldn't grasp it. But at the moment, he got the distinct feeling that he'd overstayed his welcome. It was time to go.

He stepped outside, pulling his phone from his pocket, the glow of its screen piercing the darkness. No service, naturally. As he'd told Andrew, no one ever went to the docks. He recalled passing a dingy little bar not too far away on the ride up, but he did not relish the idea of the walk. But at least he had made it out alive.

Pulling his coat tightly around him, he heaved a sigh and started to walk down the dock to the road beyond. As he dragged himself through the darkness, a few cars passed, and he momentarily thought of hitchhiking, but quickly dismissed it; he'd already had enough weirdness for one day. He pressed on. His mind was preoccupied, working methodically to cook up a story about why he hadn't managed to deliver the coin and what had happened to his motorcycle. The story needed to be seamless to fool Andrew. Different scenarios flashed through his mind, but most were too crazy to work on his uncle, and he finally decided to just tell him the truth—the whole embarrassing truth, including how he'd abandoned the poor girl and hidden in a closet.

After what seemed like an hour, he finally saw the lights of the bar shimmering through the fog like a washed-out mirage. Coming closer, he breathed a sigh of relief at seeing a couple of cars parked out front. He had signal now, and he'd thought of calling Andrew, but when he glanced at his phone, it was ten o'clock. Andrew wouldn't appreciate a call to come pick him up this late. He'd have to call a taxi and catch up with his uncle tomorrow.

8

CATCHING UP WITH THE AUSSIE

Liora pointed to a driveway tucked discretely amidst a dense cluster of ceanothus, and Ciara turned in, slowing the car to a stop behind a row of hedges. Liora stepped out of the car, her cream coat flashing up the short earthen drive, heading toward a quaint little cottage nestled in the woods by the river. Ciara lagged behind, retrieving a box from the trunk. They knew he wasn't home; Rye's phone had told them that much. But she'd otherwise shared little helpful information, aside from the fact that she and Noah were on the outs. Liora couldn't put her finger on it, but she suspected there was more to Rye's story than she let on.

Now that Rye had escaped them again, the only way to get answers was from Noah—a visit Liora wasn't particularly thrilled about. He had been a respected member of his Garou before they'd exiled him because of his tryst with Rye. The details of his exile weren't clear, but even without his Garou, he was strong, meriting a healthy dose of respect. Before coming, she and Ciara had agreed it would be best to avoid escalating things with him, but just in case, they had a backup plan. That was the purpose of Ciara's box.

Liora approached the cottage quietly, peeking through the windows to ensure no one was home. There were no lights on, and she saw no one moving around. When she turned the doorknob, it was unlocked.

Once inside, Ciara set her box down, turning to Liora. "Look around for it. I'll get to work."

Liora nodded. She would've preferred to find the necklace on the counter or stuffed away is a sock drawer, so they could leave before he got home, but she knew it wouldn't be that easy. Honestly, they didn't even know if he had it or if he knew where it was, and Liora had a gut feeling the answers wouldn't come easy. Rye had clearly been holding something back, and she'd had no qualms about her feelings toward Noah. It wasn't an enormous leap to think he might know something. Maybe the rift between Rye and him would bear fruit under the right circumstances. That's where Ciara's plan would come into play if needed.

The night wore on, and Liora found no trace of the necklace. She returned to the living room, where Ciara was finishing up. There were only two doors in and out of the cottage, and Ciara had arranged her little surprise perfectly. Unlike most days, when Noah came home to a respite from the world, today would be a little … *different*. Ciara handed Liora a small box with several buttons, similar to a garage door opener. She explained the plan to Liora, who nodded.

They didn't know when he might return, so they settled in. Ciara sat brooding as she relentlessly sharpened her dark blades. Liora stood across the room, taking off her coat and hanging it on a hook by the door. Lifting her hands, she removed her cream gloves, exposing hands and fingers singed black from use. She sprayed some peroxide she'd found in Noah's bathroom on the bloody spittle, watching it disappear before slowly brushing it to clean off the day's grime.

"Why do you do that?" Ciara scoffed from her perch at the top of the staircase leading to the upper floor, her blades flashing melodically against her sharpening stone.

"I like to look nice, and you like your blades sharp. We both like to have our things in order when we meet people," Liora said as the morning's first light glowed through the windows.

"Well, one of us needs to be sharp," Ciara said coarsely, still fuming over Rye's escape.

"Agreed. That's why I'm blessed—"

She stopped in mid-sentence as Ciara hushed her. "Someone's coming!" Ciara took up a position where both doors were in sight. "You ready?"

Liora removed her coat from the hanger, putting it back on in one smooth motion as she quietly glimpsed herself in the mirror by the door. Nodding to her reflection, she smoothed down her coat and took a deep breath, sliding her gloves back into place, covering her darkened fingers. "Ready," she said, stepping away from the door and placing the contraption Ciara had given her in her pocket as she settled into a chair in the living room.

A moment later, the front door opened, and Noah stepped inside, holding a bundle of clothes over his privates, otherwise naked. Dried blood splattered his chest, and his hair was all askew, littered with twigs and leaves. He looked directly at Liora, then at Ciara on the stairs. "I could smell you two a mile away."

Liora's face reddened at his nakedness as Ciara chimed in, "And you still came in?"

"I've got nothin' to hide."

"Yes, apparently," Ciara said with a wry smile.

Noah pointed to a pair of sweatpants on the couch by Liora. "You mind throwin' me those, doll, or would ya prefer I get 'em myself so you can take a gander?"

If it was even possible, Liora's face turned a deeper red as she leaned over, taking the sweatpants and throwing them to him. She quickly recovered her usual poise. "You're disgusting, as always."

He chuckled as he turned away, pulling on his sweatpants. "Why are you here, anyway? I'm not with her anymore."

"That's what she said, but I needed to hear it for myself," Liora answered.

"So, you finally caught up with her after all these years? You two are tenacious, I'll give ya that," he said, turning back to face them.

"We've come for the necklace," Liora said, following the plan.

Noah laughed. "Well, too bad. I don't have it. She never let that thing outta her sight. But you two know that already. So, again, why are you here?" He fixed his gaze on Liora, baring his fangs at her.

Liora stood, holding his gaze, about to speak, when Ciara interrupted her, going off script. The plan they'd agreed on promptly went out the window. They were apparently doing Ciara's plan now, and she'd been adamant that she wanted to face him down, especially after the fiasco with Rye.

"Cut the shit. She told us you have it," Ciara snapped.

It was a lie, but Liora was now interested to see where this ruse would take them.

Ciara crept down the stairs, blades in hand. "We've had a long night, and we're not leaving until we have it."

Noah turned his attention to Ciara, holding his position. "Is that right? Are you sure you want to do this? Rye's not here to protect you anymore." He flexed his hands as razor-sharp claws appeared from nowhere. "I've had a long night too, but I can extend it," he said, letting out a rumbling growl.

Liora moved aside as Ciara entered the living room, blades at her side. "This doesn't need to get all messy. You said it yourself: you're not with her anymore. So, why not just tell us what you know?"

Noah stepped forward. Liora could see him physically changing as the breaks in his flesh revealed fur, and there was a noticeable cracking sound as his bones elongated to meet the larger size of his transforming self. This was getting out of hand quickly. Liora reached into her pocket, at the ready.

"I told you, I don't know anything. Now, I suggest you ladies leave while ya still can," he said, glaring at Ciara, still inching forward, his transformation almost complete as his claws clicked on the hardwood floor.

"You always thought you were so tough, but you don't have your pack here to protect you. Rye got you banished, but you still protect her. Why?" Ciara asked as she spun the blades in her hands.

"Get outta my house!" He dashed forward, taking a wild swipe at Ciara, but she'd anticipated it and pushed off the wall with her leg, doing a backflip over his head and landing in a crouch behind him. With one smooth stroke, her blade flashed through the air, cutting clean through his Achilles tendon. His leg buckled as he let out a loud roar, but he recovered quickly, turning to land a blow with the flat of his palm, throwing Ciara into a curio cabinet that tumbled over, crashing to the floor.

"Now!" Ciara yelled, blood trickling from the side of her mouth.

Liora clicked the first button. A muffled sound of compressed air popped from the side of the room, propelling a barbed bolt attached to a wire squarely into Noah's back. He let out a high-pitched yelp and advanced on Ciara, snapping his jaws, but the injuries slowed him down just enough. Ciara smacked his face with the flat of her blade before rolling to the left, dodging his advance. "Now, now, Noah. No biting," she said in a mocking tone.

"You're a dead woman!" He lunged forward, grasping onto her ankle as she scrambled to escape, falling to the floor.

"All of them, now, Liora!" Ciara yelled as she frantically kicked at Noah with her free foot.

Three more pops sounded from around the room, and three more wired bolts found their target. Noah released his grip on Ciara, reaching for the bolts and pulling one out of his flesh, leaving a raw wound gushing blood.

"Turn it on!" Ciara commanded, keeping her eyes fixed on Noah as she crawled out of reach.

Liora mashed the red button of a small generator positioned on top of several car batteries hidden behind the couch, and the hairs on her arms raised from the static electricity now flooding the room. The wires attached to the bolts embedded in Noah's flesh crackled to life. His back arched as he scrambled, straining to pull the bolts from his body, but the surge of electricity was too much, too fast, and he fell to the floor. His body shrunk back to its human size, fangs and claws retracting, and he immediately fell unconscious. Liora pressed the button again, stopping the flow of electricity.

"Geez, that was a rush!" Ciara lay on her back, licking the blood from her lips.

"That wasn't the plan," Liora snapped.

"You just can't let a girl have a little fun, can you?" Ciara sat up, patting Noah on the chest. "Two werewolves in two days. We're doing pretty good."

Liora pointed a finger at Ciara. "It could've gone wrong, fast. Now help me get him in the chair."

They lifted him into a wingback chair, binding him with ropes. Reaching into her jacket, Ciara pulled out a tarnished silver collar that was studded with spikes on the interior, removing a small silver lock from the collar. She snapped it into place around Noah's neck. Blood dripped down onto his bare chest as the spikes dug into his skin.

"That'll keep him in check," Ciara said, fastening the lock in place. "Now, let's get some answers."

Liora took a bottle from her pocket, removing the cap and placing it under his nose. Noah's eyes snapped open, and his muscles bunched as he struggled against the bindings, trying to free himself. He furled his brows, growling as he looked at Liora.

"What've ya done to me?" he asked, wincing in pain as the collar dug deeper into his neck with his words. His eyes darted downward, trying to see what it was, but he could only see trails of blood streaking down his chest.

Ciara's raspy voice filled the room. "You just had to make things difficult, didn't you? Now look at where we are. We had to put this nasty collar on you. You might want to start talking, before something *unfortunate* happens."

Noah regained his composure, turning his glare to Ciara. "I'm still a part of my Garou, and when my exile's over, you're both dead."

"Enough with the threats! You can give it a rest, already." Ciara placed her hand over her mouth, feigning a yawn.

Liora took over, using her sweetest voice. "Let's start over, shall we? It's good to see you again, Noah."

Noah turned to her, speaking in a resigned voice. "I wish I could say the same, Liora—or do ya like to be called the Dove nowadays?"

"Either one," she said amicably, reaching out and picking a few leaves from his hair. "We were hoping you'd be more reasonable."

Noah glared at her. "I already told ya. I don't know where it is."

"Right. There's just one little problem: I don't believe you."

"Screw you! I've lived too long to answer to the likesa you bitches," he snarled.

Ciara leaned in, spitting in his face.

"My, my, a little testy today? Was the hunting not good last night?" Liora still used her sweetest voice as the spit dripped down his face. "Perhaps if you knew a bit more, you'd be inclined to help us, as I assume you have no love lost for the Sorority or the Lady."

"You're just her cronies, doin' her bidding," he said. "I've no mind to help you or the Lady—ever. Not after what she did to me."

"Your Garou would've learned of your lies sooner or later. She simply expedited the truth," Liora said with a smile.

"She got me exiled."

"A temporary penance for your lies."

"Twenty years isn't 'temporary,'" he corrected her while struggling against the bindings, which showed no signs of loosening.

"It's unfortunate, but that should make it easier for you to decide which side you want to be on," Liora said.

"Side? Why would I want to be on *your* side?" he demanded. "You two are nothin' more than the brutal hands of the Lady."

Liora held his eyes. "That may have been true once upon a time, but things have changed. The Sorority has fallen silent. The Lady has gone into hiding. No one's seen nor heard from her in years."

"I don't see no evidence that the Lady's absent at all," Noah replied.

"That may be," Liora said, "but I assure you that her prolonged absence has weakened her control over the Stone of Fates. At first, her seclusion was distressing, but as time passed, we came to see it as an opportunity, as did others. To that point, we've been engaged by a new employer—one who's committed to carrying the power of the Stone of Fates into the future, without the Lady and her secretive Sorority."

"Good luck with that," Noah said, letting out a thunderous laugh. "Fortune won't be on your side—"

Ciara's fist slammed into his face with surprising force for her lithe frame, and the chair rocked back, almost falling over. Liora grabbed her arm, and they stepped aside, exchanging hushed words. Ciara glanced at Noah before turning away, cracking her knuckles in frustration.

Liora ran her hands over her immaculately clean coat as if pressing out some wrinkles, turning back to Noah with a settling breath. "Now, as I was saying, we've been engaged to flush the Lady out of hiding—something that can best be done with Rye's necklace. We're quite certain the Lady will come for it if our new employer were to get it." She met his eyes. "We've been authorized to make you a one-time offer. If you help us, our new employer has committed to making a place for you in the new order that comes about—you *and* your Garou."

"It never ends up good for people who cross the Lady," he reminded them.

"After all she's done to you, we were hoping you'd be interested. The offer's a legitimate one, but it's now or never," Liora said optimistically.

Noah tipped his head back, his eyes far away.

"If you don't tell us, I'm sure we can get it from Rye, *eventually*," Ciara threatened.

"How do I know this offer's even real?" he asked.

"You have to trust us," Liora said, grinning.

"See, that's the problem," he said, looking Liora dead in the eyes, his face reflected in her sunglasses. "I don't trust you."

"So, you still choose to protect Rye?" Liora asked in a resigned voice.

He gave no response as Ciara's voice swept in from behind. "See? I told you."

Liora nodded to her, stepping away. "Do what you must."

A crazy screech erupted as Ciara swooped in, landing a furious round of blows on Noah's face. Blood was streaming down his cheeks, but he lifted his head in defiance once again.

"That wasn't funny, you crazy little bitch." He spit blood on the floor, keeping his gaze on her.

Ciara reached into her jacket, pulling out a capped vial and dangling it before his eyes. "Know what this is?" she asked, swirling the vial's contents. Inside, a clear liquid spun, catching the morning light, revealing what looked to be a subtly shimmering silver thread that danced in and out of sight.

Noah glanced at it, not responding.

Ciara spoke as she circled behind the chair. "I was told it's called Afterglow. A deeply held secret amongst your type. Lucky that some of you are willing to spill ancient secrets for the right price. The recipe cost me a fortune, and then I had to wait until the next full moon. Amazingly simple to make. But you know that, don't you?" She stood quietly in front of him, a grin spreading across her face as she came around the chair. "So, when Liora told me we were coming to see you," she said, leaning in and gently wiping the blood from his face, "well, I got pretty excited." She twisted the cap from the vial, taking a sip. "See? No effect on me. But for you, well… I understand that's not quite the case."

Noah looked at the vial, his body stiffening as she moved it closer to his lips before capping it.

"So, I'll let you pick. This can go one of two ways. After-glow," she said, holding the vial out, "which we both know could be messy, but kind of cool. Or, you just tell us where the necklace is, and we untie you and let you scurry away."

Liora moved back to Ciara's side, joining in. "We need that necklace. Give it to us, and we'll be on our way. Simple as that."

Noah turned his head to her. "What about the deal? Is it still good?"

"The deal stands," Liora said as Ciara stepped back.

"Fine. I'm sicka all this and the games you Sorority girls play with each other, so I'll tell you," he spat. "I needed money to buy a plane ticket, so I sold it to one of them pawnshops down in Monterey."

Liora held her fingers up, as if measuring something small. "I need a bit more. Which pawnshop?"

He lowered his head, taking a deep breath. "I'm bein' honest with ya. I don't remember its name, but it's the one right down from the coffee shop on Main Street."

"Does Rye know this?" Liora asked.

"What'd be the point of that? Sure, I did it for the money, but also to set her free from you both chasin' her for it," he answered.

"Why not just give it to us, then?"

"It felt like less of a betrayal to pawn it."

"Well, you just told us where it you pawned it, so you pretty much just gave it to us," Ciara said with a chuckle.

"Right, well, I guess I'd rather live another day at this point, and I don't really care who has the necklace anymore," he said, shrugging his shoulders.

"That's the first honest answer I've heard from you," Liora said. "But I'm concerned about your commitment to the cause."

"I'm not committed to any cause. You can do whatever you want with it," he said as sweat beaded on his forehead.

"That's the problem," Ciara said as she handed the capped

vial to Liora and leaned down, picking up a large funnel. "We can't have any loose ends. Not when we're this close."

"Liora, come on," he said, his eyes pleading with her. "You're better than this."

Liora avoided eye contact as she took the cap off the vial.

"I promise I'll leave town straightaway. Hell, you can drive me to the damn airport," he said, looking at Ciara as she approached, circling behind him and firmly grabbing hold of his chin. "You don't understand what'll happen—"

His voice cut off as he struggled against Ciara's grip, but eventually she subdued him enough to slide the funnel down his throat. Her beady black eyes peered down at him from above as she struggled to hold the funnel in place. "You're right about one thing. I don't know what's gonna happen— but I have a pretty good idea."

Liora stepped forward, looking into Noah's eyes as she poured the Afterglow into the funnel. "You're too much of a risk. But if it's any consolation, Rye will never know the full depths of your betrayal. Goodbye, Noah." She dropped the empty vial and turned to leave.

"What goes 'round comes 'round, and you'll get yours. The Lady will make sure of that!" Noah spat, bloody spittle spraying from his mouth. "I don't know what's come over you two, but it's no good, and—"

His words cut off as Ciara gagged him.

"You sure this will work?" Liora asked, glancing back at Noah. The black heart-and-rose tattoo on his arm writhed, as if something wanted to get out of his skin, and his muscles rippled as he railed against the bindings, fighting desperately to get loose. The chair rocked wildly as his skin bubbled and flattened, his bones elongating and then retreating.

"I'm certain." Ciara took up her roost at the top of the stairs. "What I'm not certain of is how long it takes, but we have all day to make sure it works."

9

THE MORNING AFTER

THE ALARM BLARED, startling Colm awake. He shielded his eyes from the morning light flooding in through the window. It had been a long night. His dreams vacillated between the girl saying, *"They'll kill you,"* and Tabitha saying, *"I'll be fine."* Each haunted him, but in different ways. Not surprisingly, it had taken him a while to fall asleep, and the sleep he got was fitful.

He rolled over, feeling like he hadn't slept at all. Swinging his legs over the edge of the bed, he sat up, rubbing the sleep from his eyes. His thoughts continued to race between Tabitha and the girl, but finally settled on the dimly lit warehouse. Over the course of the night, Colm had replayed his conversation with the old man from the alley more than a hundred times, and he'd become convinced that the emerald-eyed redhead was the lady in red. The deal with the old man seemed to be an unspoken quid pro quo: the dice for his promise to help her. As he played it back in his mind, it didn't just sound insane; it *was* insane. But all the same, on some base level, he knew it was true.

Beyond that, there was something else bothering him.

The circle of ash reminded him of something, but he couldn't quite place it. Everything about last night made him uneasy, and a shiver ran down his spine. His thoughts returned to the emerald-eyed girl, and his face flushed, thinking about how he'd left her alone, bound and bloodied. Did he really do that?

He rose, trudging to the bathroom, looking in the mirror before turning away in disgust. What the hell was his uncle doing getting mixed up with people like that, anyway? He had known going to the docks was a bad idea, but for now, he needed to get to the Anvil and tell his uncle about it—all of it.

He grabbed his backpack as he hurried out the door, double-timing it to the pawnshop. But when he arrived, he was surprised to see that the shop was still dark inside. Unlocking the door, he stepped inside, calling out for his uncle, but there was no response. He flicked on the lights, taking the dice from his pocket as he walked to the counter.

A moment later, he heard the door chime and turned to see Andrew struggling to hold two coffees in a beverage caddy atop his cane, along with a pink box in his other hand.

"You're late," Colm said in a mocking tone, turning the tables on Andrew for once.

"Ha. Nice try. I've already been here and left, sonny boy. Figured you could use some coffee and donuts this morning."

"Why's that?" Colm asked hesitantly.

Andrew paused, holding the door open with his hip, looking up. "Tabitha stopped by with a box of your things. It's in the back. Now, can an old man get some help?"

"Yeah, sorry." Colm rushed over and carried the coffee and box to the counter. Andrew was right behind him, and he reached down behind the counter, grabbing Betsy.

"You got the coin?" Andrew asked, catching Colm off guard.

"What?"

"The delivery. They called yesterday afternoon and said they needed to reschedule. I tried calling you, but kept getting your voicemail, so I left a message." He took a swig of his coffee and a bite from a maple bar.

"Well, that would've been nice to know. I went, and you will not *believe* what happened…" Colm shivered, vividly recounting the events of the night before. The words *"They'll kill you"* still haunted him, and he cringed, embarrassed when he shared that he'd hidden in the closet, leaving the girl alone.

Andrew leaned on his cane, deep in thought. "And you're sure there were two of them?"

"Yeah. I'm sure." Colm set the little manila envelope on the counter.

Andrew stashed it in his pocket. "They called this morning. They're coming here today to get it."

"What?! They're coming *here*?" Colm's mouth went dry.

"Just relax. They never saw you, so you're good," Andrew said, sipping his coffee like they were talking about the weather.

"So, you're not at all freaked out?"

He shrugged. "We deal with lots of unsavory types here. What they do on their own time is no business of mine. Now, as for your motorcycle, I'd suggest you call Detective Lemmek and just tell him it was stolen from the alley. No need to go gossiping about our customers' extracurricular activities," he said with a knowing look.

Colm laughed sarcastically, taking a swig of coffee. "That's one way of putting it."

Andrew retreated to the back room, returning with a business card. "Here's his number. Good guy. He owes me a few favors," he said with a wink.

"Thanks, I'll call him. But there's more," Colm said as he took the card.

"Okay. What's more?"

"This dice," Colm said, setting it on the counter. "You won't believe it, so I'll just show you." He picked up the dice, shaking it in his hands and blowing on it as Andrew watched. "I wish this box was full of donuts," he said, knowing it was a patently stupid wish, but he had to make an impact on his uncle. He dropped the dice on the counter, and both of their eyes watched it roll to a stop, two X's facing upwards.

"How the hell'd you do that?" Andrew asked, dumbfounded.

As Colm raised his eyes from the dice, he saw Andrew looking at a pink box that was now overflowing with donuts. *Yes!* Colm thought to himself. He hadn't rolled an even number yet, and this was finally proof positive that this freakin' dice was real––its magic was real!

"What do you think?" Colm said, barely containing his excitement. "It's magic!"

His uncle turned slowly, meeting his gaze. "What?!"

"I had to show you. I knew you'd never believe me otherwise. Hell, I barely even believe it myself!"

Andrew sat down on the stool by the counter, looking from Colm to the donuts to the dice. "How?" he asked in disbelief.

"I can't explain it, but it's real." Colm quickly relayed to Andrew everything about meeting the old homeless man in the alley, and how he'd sent him across the street to a now nonexistent shop called The Daserii, and how Wynn had given him this dice. "I wanted to tell you about it yesterday, but you made me leave before I could."

"Well, next time, tell me to shut the hell up!" Andrew

picked up one of the new donuts and tasted it, as if to confirm its authenticity.

"Imagine what we can do with this thing, if we play it right!" Colm said.

Andrew nodded, gathering himself. "Right. Well, never make a stupid wish like that one ever again. You need to be more careful. May I?" He motioned to the dice.

Colm nodded. "It's like when we talk about winning the lottery," he said excitedly, watching Andrew study the dice. "We need to come up with our list of wishes."

"Makes sense, but only you can decide what's worth years of your life. And we should sit on it for a bit, get our thoughts about us. For now, just put it away. Go in the back and call Lemmek about your motorcycle, but no word about the ladies. Got it?" Andrew said sternly. "Business as usual for now."

Colm nodded, taking the dice from Andrew and grabbing a donut. Once in the back, he parked himself at the desk, moving the box Tabitha had dropped off earlier. Taking his phone from his pocket, he dialed the number on the card. The man answered straightaway in a friendly voice—not at all what Colm expected. Most police officers he ran into had sharp, snarky attitudes oozing with skepticism, but not Detective Lemmek.

"You feeling better today?" the detective asked.

"Yeah. Much better. Thanks, Detective," Colm answered, remembering that according to his uncle, Lemmek was the one who had found him in front of Dos Suenos the night Tabitha had broken up with him.

"Please, just call me Roget," he said. After a brief pause, Roget asked how he could help, and Colm shared the concocted story about his motorcycle being stolen from the alley. Roget reeled off all the standard questions, and Colm made up answers as best he could.

"Great, that's all I need," he said. "I'll let you know if we find anything."

The phone went silent, and Colm sat at the desk, the glint of his mother's ring catching his eye. Not a day went by that he didn't think of his parents, their murder. Deep down, he'd always wanted to punish their killers, but they'd never been caught. Almost absentmindedly, his hand found the dice hiding in his pocket, and he pulled it out. The dice changed things for him. Now he could do it—he could make them pay. A tear formed in his eye as he shaped the words to make it real, but just before he spoke, he closed his hand around the dice. No matter how much he wanted revenge, he wasn't a killer. He leaned back in the chair, taking a deep breath, but the dice was still pulling at him.

Next thing he knew, he'd made three successive wishes to get his motorcycle back, each slightly different, and three successive failed rolls. So much for putting it away; it was easier said than done. He tapped the dice on the desk, making one last wish. "I wish the girl would bring my bike back," he said, rolling the dice. But this time, four X's faced up.

Just then, he heard the door chime, followed by the sound of his uncle's cane clicking across the floor in greeting. After a few moments, Andrew appeared in the office with a grin on his face.

"There's a good-lookin' young lady here for you," he said with a wink. "She's looking for a *necklace* that her ex may have sold here. Told her I haven't bought any necklaces lately, but you might've. She's hoping she can talk to you?"

Andrew was good at playing dumb with angry spouses and partners, exes or otherwise. Often they'd come in wanting to reclaim whatever was sold, sometimes for free. Colm nodded, standing up. He didn't like these encounters, and Andrew knew that, but it was the unwritten rule of the shop. He'd bought the necklace off the Aussie, so he had to deal with it.

He turned to head out front, peeking at the monitors showing the shop's security camera feeds. The video was grainy, but what he saw was clear. She stood at the counter, and her stocking cap titled back as she looked up, revealing her eyes. The video was black and white, but he knew they were emerald, and he could just make out the small star tattoo under her left eye. He flashed back to the night before as his heart rate increased palpably, wondering if this was a coincidence, or if the dice had actually delivered. Either way, how could he face her? He'd left her there to get beaten, or worse, while he hid in a closet. The shame of it flushed over him as he struggled to find the words to make it okay.

Casting further doubt on the situation, he thought of the Aussie's warnings about "dangerous people." Was she dangerous? Maybe he'd made some wrong assumptions about her, and there was a reason they'd tied her up. He looked at the dice, and then at the camera. It was exactly what he'd wished for, but now he was second-guessing himself.

Andrew noticed his sudden change in demeanor and leaned in closer. "What is it?"

"She's the girl from last night," Colm whispered.

Andrew rapped his knuckles on the counter. "Well, how about that? Why don't I stay back here and give you two some privacy?" He sat down in the chair at the desk. "But don't forget, those ladies are coming for the coin soon, and I'm guessing it'd be best if she was gone before they get here."

Colm nodded in agreement before taking a deep breath and stepping out behind the counter. Their eyes met, and they stood frozen a few feet apart. It was as if he were seeing her for the first time, and Andrew was right: she was undeniably attractive. Her long red hair spilled from her cap, and she wore a dark outfit with a dusty old leather bomber jacket that fit her so well, it looked like it had been tailored just for her. Colm guessed that her mind was racing through their meeting at the warehouse, assessing him, and making judgments. Her eyes flashed to either side, hunting for something as she took a tentative step backwards, creating more space between them before her eyes settled on him once again.

He opened his mouth to speak, but hesitated, looking away. He didn't know what to say to make up for what he'd done, but frankly, he'd never thought he would see her again. It struck him that she must be wondering how he was associated with the two ladies. He wanted to tell her he had nothing to do with them, but that wasn't entirely true. So instead, he opted for honesty, looking her in the eyes.

"I'm so glad you're okay," he said, a wave of relief flushing over him at hearing the words out loud.

"You look tired," she said, her voice sweet and comforting, but her emerald eyes continued scanning the room.

"It was a long night. When I left you out there..." His voice cracked. The guilt registered not only in Colm's face, but in the tone of his voice as he lowered his eyes for a moment before meeting hers again, this time with renewed purpose. "I shouldn't have left you there, alone. I should've stayed and helped you."

She shrugged, nervously looking at the cameras watching them. Her demeanor hadn't changed, and she held her distance as she spoke. "Why were you there?"

"I was just making a delivery," he said as she took another tentative step backwards, the hesitancy again rising in her face. Colm raised his hands, trying to settle her. "It's not like that. Those ladies purchased something from the shop. I was just a delivery boy, that's all," he said, pleading with her with words unspoken.

He must have appeared sincere. She relaxed, taking a step forward with a bit of urgency, the hesitant look gone from her face. "A necklace? With a wooden charm? Was that what you were delivering?" she asked, her voice suddenly filled with hope.

"No, not a necklace," Colm answered. "Just an old coin."

Her shoulders slumped as she murmured, "So, you must be Colm Stokely."

His eyebrows raised, wondering how she knew his name.

Seeing his confusion, she clarified, "I got it from the registration card for your bike." He nodded in acknowledgment. "Thanks for leaving the keys in it. That was a literal lifesaver."

"Glad I could help in some way," he muttered. The Colm of a week ago would've been pissed that she'd stolen his bike, but after his display—or lack thereof—the night before, he was simply glad he'd helped her out somehow. "What should I call you?" he asked politely.

"Rye. But let's just leave it at that for now," she said with a tone of finality.

"Okay. It's nice to meet you, Rye. I'm glad you got away," he said, leaning back.

"Me too," she agreed, "and thanks for what you did."

"For what? Abandoning you?" he said, the embarrassment returning. "I don't really think that deserves any thanks."

"No, you loosened the bindings just enough for me to work my way out. And if you hadn't broken the circle, I'd still be there, and they certainly would've found you. It was risky, but the noise you made from the closet was brilliant. I'm guessing leaving the keys in your Harley was a mistake, but it was a stroke of good luck for me. So, thanks to you, I'm here," she said, smiling now for the first time.

It was as if the sun had come out after a string of rainy days. Colm returned the smile, electing not to dispel her version of reality. It painted him as more heroic than what he knew to be true, but he could live with that. "You're welcome. But I should've done more."

"Well, I'm okay," she said, smiling as she turned to grab something from her purse, "and I've got your keys right here. So, you have your Harley back, and I'm not dead, so things are looking up for both of us." She laughed sweetly as she turned back to him, setting the keys on the counter.

"Well, I guess that's the positive spin." Magic or not, things were falling into place for him. But something was still gnawing at him. Why had she been tied up and beaten in the first place? He recalled the cuts and bruises marring her face the night before. Looking at her now, he saw zero bruises, and the cuts that remained were faint, as if she'd gotten them long ago. How was that possible? There had to be something more to it.

Picking up the keys, he mustered the courage to ask, "You know, you don't have to answer this, but why were you tied up? And your face, the cuts—how did they heal so quickly?"

She looked at the cameras before turning her eyes back to Colm, hesitating before she spoke. "It's a long story, for another day, perhaps." She again flashed a smile, but this time as if to say he'd asked enough.

Not taking the hint, he pressed on. "It's just that, well ... nice girls don't get themselves tied up and beaten."

"Oh, that's sweet. You think I'm a nice girl? But how did you get to that? You just met me." But her smile was no longer shining, and they both stood looking at each other awkwardly.

After a moment, her eyes dropped, breaking the stalemate. "Those ladies, they're looking for my necklace—the one that my stupid ex-boyfriend stole and sold, but he wouldn't tell me where. I've been going from pawnshop to pawnshop looking for it. It'd be a strange coincidence if you have it, but if you do, I'll pay good money for it. And then I'll be gone, out of your life."

"That seems to be going around lately," Colm said with a chuckle, but the humor was lost on Rye, and she just looked at him, confused. "Sorry, poor timing," he muttered. "It's just that my girlfriend just broke up with me, saying something similar." He cleared his throat uncomfortably. "So, your necklace—can you describe it?"

She leaned in. "The charm is made of wood, about the size of a quarter, and has carvings like a Celtic knot."

Before she'd even said a word, he already knew he had it. "Coincidence" was the word she'd used, but to him, she was the lady in red. He knew all of this was well beyond mere coincidence, and it was strange how the events of the past few days all blended together, leading to this moment.

"So, this Aussie came in a couple of nights ago," Colm said. "I assume that's your ex?"

"Noah, yes. That's him," she said, spitting the words out.

"Well, he was hot to sell, and fast. So, yeah, I've got it," Colm said, but he opted not to say anything about the other items Noah had sold, since she was only asking about the necklace.

"So, I've really found it?" she asked in disbelief, her eyes lighting up.

Colm nodded as she stepped forward. It made him feel good to finally do something to help her that didn't involve him hiding in a closet or losing his Harley. They stood in silence, then her eyes darted away with a misty sheen.

"I just can't believe he actually sold it! I was hoping he was lying about that, but..." She sniffed, wiping her eyes. "He knew how important it was to me."

Colm understood her feelings of betrayal. He'd been dealing with his own demons. "I know how you're feeling.

Sometimes you think you know someone, only to find out they've been plotting to betray you."

"Your girlfriend?" she asked, raising her eyes.

Colm nodded, pushing down his anger. "Ex, but let's just say I know what you're going through." Then he recalled Noah's parting words. "You know," he said, scratching his head, "Noah warned me that 'dangerous people' would be looking for your necklace."

"Right, those two ladies," she said, regaining her composure. "And they'll stop at nothing to get it."

"Who are they?" he asked against his better judgment, his curiosity piqued.

Rye hesitated, casting a nervous glance behind her before returning her gaze to him, speaking in a hushed tone. "Liora and Ciara, but on the streets, they're known as the Dove and the Raven. Trust me, they *are* dangerous people—the deadly kind."

"What about you? Are you dangerous?" Colm asked. He'd intended it jokingly, but quickly realized he'd struck a chord.

Rye let out a snicker, as if it were a silly question, which left Colm feeling unsettled. He wasn't certain from her laugh whether she was or wasn't dangerous. Either way, he'd delved into something he wished he hadn't.

Rye reached out, gently touching Colm's hand, catching him by surprise as she whispered to him in a soft voice, "A little bird told me you're going to give me my necklace back. Once you do, I promise I'll be out of your life, and I'll make certain Liora and Ciara will never bother you."

Her touch resonated warmly inside him, and his heartbeat settled. Any tension vanished, allowing him to think clearly. It was obvious that Rye posed no threat to him. But those ladies… They were dangerous, and he preferred to steer clear of them. In fact, he had an acute desire to get the necklace out of his life as quickly and quietly as possible, just as Noah had recommended. He recalled not even wanting to buy the necklace, so giving it back to Rye was the easiest way out. He'd already intended to give it to her, but now he was more certain of it than anything in his life. And perhaps with the power of the dice, he could even help her find her way home, just as he'd promised the old man in the Benedictine robes.

She held his gaze, but sheepishly pulled her hand back, her face flushing. "I'm sorry, it's just important to me. I didn't mean to…" She cut her explanation short, diverting her eyes from his.

But he wasn't sorry. Her touch felt good. He wanted to reach out to her, to take her hand and reassure her that everything was okay. But before he could work up the courage, she turned back to the business at hand. "I've got money. Do you have the necklace?"

"So, about that. I actually don't have it here at the shop…" Seeing a worried expression cross her face, he quickly added, "But I know exactly where it is. I have an antiques dealer looking at it to tell me what it is."

"Okay. So, let's go get it."

It wasn't a question, and it was stated so emphatically that Colm knew better than to suggest otherwise. Plus, he wasn't put off by the idea of spending more time with this girl. Maybe he'd even get to know her a little better, which was probably important if he was going to help her find her way home.

"Yeah, sure. His place is just across town, by the fairgrounds," he said, picking up his keys and calling out to tell Andrew he'd be stepping out. Andrew's head popped through the door, followed by the clicking of his cane. He was about to say something, but was interrupted by the throaty rumbling of a car pulling up to the curb outside the shop.

"Shit," Rye cursed, "it's them!" She had a renewed look of concern on her face as she looked back at Colm and Andrew.

Andrew leapt into action, clearly understanding her concern. Looking at Rye, he spoke quickly and calmly. "You're safe here, I promise. They're just customers coming to pick up a coin. That's all." He held her eyes for a moment before turning to Colm. "Get her in the back, and stay quiet. I'll get them out of here as fast as I can. Now go!" He shooed them both into the back of the shop.

As the door closed behind them, Colm looked at the security monitor, seeing his uncle settle onto the stool behind the counter. Rye joined him, looking at the screens, hearing the door chime, and seeing the two ladies come into the shop.

"How do we get out of here?" Rye asked.

"We can't. We just need to wait. He'll get them in and out. Trust me," Colm said, his attention still focused on the monitors.

Rye continued looking around and paused, seeing a large vintage Coca-Cola sign leaning against the back wall. Moving closer, she looked behind it to find a small window, high up on the wall. She turned back to Colm with a frenzied look. "Does this window open?"

Colm didn't respond, his attention focused on the monitor. He turned the volume up, leaning closer to listen. After some small talk, Andrew handed the coin to Liora, and she stowed it in the pocket of her cream coat as Ciara perused the cabinets.

Rye returned to Colm's side, and the images on the screen caught her attention.

"You have any necklaces with wooden charms?" they heard Ciara ask.

"Yes, a nice Australian man told us he'd sold a necklace here. It's quite the collectible, and we'd pay top dollar for it," Liora said, stepping to Ciara's side.

"That little bastard," Rye said, watching them. "Colm..." She grabbed his arm, turning him from the monitors. "We need to get out of here. Does that window open?"

The fear in her eyes caught hold of him, and he followed her to the window. Together, they lifted the sign, moving it aside. A moment later, she jumped up, grabbing the windowsill with one hand and unlocking the window with the other. In one swift movement, she pushed the window open and was gone, leaving Colm alone in the back room. He tried to grab the windowsill as she had, but it was too high, and he turned to grab the chair.

"Pssst, Colm!"

He turned back to see Rye hanging through the window, her arms outstretched, reaching for him. "Give me your hands!"

Colm let out an audible sigh, not even trying to hide his doubts. There was no way this little girl could hoist him up to the window.

"Stop it. Just give me your hands," she repeated, this time a bit more forcefully.

"Wait," he said, turning back to the desk and grabbing his backpack. He tossed it up to her, and she dropped it out the window. He reached up, and she grabbed his wrists, pulling him up to the window with ease as if he were a baby. When he grabbed onto the windowsill, she dropped back outside. Struggling, he pulled himself up and pushed his way through the small window, awkwardly falling into the alley behind the shop, landing in a heap of arms and legs.

"How'd you do that?" Colm asked, wondering how her little frame could manage his weight so easily.

Rye leaned over, helping him up and ignoring his question. "You said the antiques guy is by the fairgrounds, right?"

"Yeah," Colm said, grabbing his backpack.

"Good. Noah's place is on the way, and I've got a bone to pick with him."

Her eyes went dark, but he didn't know her well enough yet to gauge whether her look was one of revenge or disappointment. Regardless, he never wanted to be on the receiving end of that look, because neither seemed good.

"Are you sure that's a smart thing to do right now?" he asked. "Maybe we should get your necklace first."

That plan made sense to Colm, but apparently not to Rye. In her current state, she was hell-bent on confronting the Aussie.

"Yeah, I'm sure," she said, moving down the alley. "I parked your motorcycle by the coffee shop."

Colm was stunned by her athleticism. There was something different about her, that much was certain. But before he'd taken a step, she turned to see him still standing by the window. "Come on!" she yelled. "I can't do this without you."

Colm ran up the alley, pulling his phone from his pocket, hitting redial. "Hi, Detective Lemmek, this is Colm again."

"Yes, did you forget something?" he asked.

"No, it's just that I had to leave the shop in a hurry, and there were a couple of customers in there looking to cause some trouble. I'm concerned my uncle might need some help, and I'd rather not call 911. I'm sorry to ask this, but could you stop by?"

"Sure, anything for Andrew. I'm just down the street and have one thing I need to see to, then I'll stop in. Anything I need to know?" he asked.

"No. Nothing specific. I've just come across these customers before, and they're nothing but trouble."

"Got it. I'll stop by."

Colm hung up, finally catching up with Rye, and soon they were motoring off down the street, her arms clenched tightly around his waist.

10

BETSY'S LAMENT

"Necklace?" Andrew said. "We get lots of necklaces. Let's take a look. Can you describe it?" he asked, moving over to the display case, which held various pieces of jewelry he'd bought, mostly from jilted lovers and thieves. It didn't matter to Andrew how they came into his possession; they paid the bills. The two ladies followed him to the case as he jingled his keys, trying to find the one to unlock it.

"We understand it would've been sold here in the past couple of days," Liora said pleasantly.

"Hmm," Andrew said, "it's not ringing a bell with me, and I'm good with faces. Not that many people come in here this time of the year looking to pawn jewelry. That's more around the holidays, when people need money to buy gifts."

"Cut the shit!" Ciara yelled, her nostrils flaring. "We know the Aussie was in here! We *know* he sold it here."

Andrew reeled back, looking at her wide-eyed, uncertain of how to respond.

"Yes, yes," Liora's sweet voice cut in as she brushed her bleach-blonde hair from her face, giving a curt nod to her companion to be quiet. "My apologies. She can get excited at times. Perhaps a description would help. It's a carved wooden charm on a black leather cord. Simple little thing, really, but a perfect complement to our collection. Have you seen such a necklace?"

"Well, I don't recall seeing it, but perhaps Colm—" He paused, cursing himself for mentioning his nephew, but it was second nature. In a flash, he turned his attention back to the case, looking furtively for a necklace that might match her description. But the search was pointless. Nothing in the case looked remotely like it, and he knew the necklace they wanted was across town at Oliver's. Playing out the ruse, he pointed out a few necklaces in the case. At each one, Liora politely shook her head.

"He's playing us," Ciara said, looking at her companion and taking a step forward. "Let's just cut to the chase—"

Just then, the door chimed, surprising them.

"I thought you locked the door," Liora snapped at Ciara.

"Just an oversight, but hey, the more, the merrier!" Ciara turned, looking at the new visitor.

"Tabitha," Andrew said, realizing she must be looking for Colm. "Colm's not here. He left earlier, might be grabbing a bite to eat or something," he said dismissively, hoping she would take the hint and just leave, which she did after a quick thanks.

"The door," Liora said to Ciara with a slightly annoyed tone.

Ciara glared at her as she walked over and deliberately spun the lock on the front door before bending down and unplugging the *OPEN* sign.

Andrew heard a muffled noise from the back of the shop and did his best to ignore it, but Ciara's senses were too keen to miss it.

"What was that?" She moved toward the closed door to the back room.

"Hey, you can't go back there!" Andrew objected.

Ciara turned to him with a cross look. "I go where I want, old man." She continued to move toward the door until Andrew moved in front of it, blocking her.

Ciara laughed, brushing him aside. He stumbled, catching himself on the wall, his cane falling to the floor. Andrew moved his hand to his lower back, searching for Betsy. The cold steel of the gun provided him some reassurance, but just before he was about to pull it out, Liora stepped in, picking up his cane and handing it to him. His hand released Betsy, as he preferred not to get into a real dispute, hoping they'd leave once he convinced them he didn't have the necklace.

"Now, now, Ciara," Liora said with a smile. "No need to rough up an old man who's already been quite helpful to us. He did find us the coin."

Andrew turned to her, noticing a simple black star tattoo under her left eye, just like that girl with Colm had. Glancing at Ciara, he saw that she wore the same mark.

"I'm not in the mood for any surprises," Ciara said, opening the door to the office. Her eyes searched the room, and seeing nothing, her attention turned back to Andrew. He was relieved to see that Colm and Rye had escaped somehow, and he stood leaning on his cane. Now, to get these two ladies out of here too...

"Are you good?" Liora asked her, and seeing Ciara nod, she turned back to Andrew. "So, the necklace. We know for a fact that it was pawned here, and I don't see it in the case. Perhaps it's in the back? You know where you keep the good stuff," Liora said, motioning to the back room.

Over the years, Andrew had learned how to sell a rather convincing lie. Even if the necklace had been here, he wouldn't sell it to them—not after hearing the story of what they'd done to that girl. And if things got too out of hand, he always had Betsy.

"I only have what's in the case. Perhaps your *source* is not as reliable as advertised?" he said calmly.

Ciara stepped toward him menacingly, but Liora restrained her before continuing her conversation with Andrew. "Perhaps. Those sorts of things can happen when dealing with scum, but I don't have to tell you that. However, if you know where it can be found, I'm sure we can come to a satisfactory arrangement. You found some nice additions to our collection, and we'd hate to see that blossoming relationship come to an end," Liora said as Ciara settled.

"As would I," Andrew agreed, but he was now nervous about where this was going.

Liora leaned in closer. "Yes. We would like to—"

"Enough of this!" Ciara said, impatient with the banter. "Don't make us hurt you," she threatened as her eyes settled on a family photo hanging on the wall. "Or your family," she added, stabbing one of her obsidian blades into the picture, shattering the glass. As she pulled her blade back, the photo crashed to the floor.

"That's not my family, that's my sister's family. But they're all dead, except for the boy," Andrew said in a rush, shying away from her blade.

"What?" Liora bent over, picking up the photo. She rose, holding the picture of the family in her hands with a look of growing concern on her face. The family was smiling in front of a quaint little cottage.

"It's not my family," Andrew repeated. He had a habit of rambling when he was nervous. "I'm a bachelor. The photo's for appearances, you know, to make customers think I have a family with mouths to feed. But I don't have a family. Well, I mean, I did, but Karelyn and her husband are dead. Now it's just me and the boy, but he's in college now."

Ciara joined her partner, looking at the photo. Liora

tapped her finger on it, showing it to Ciara, who now wore a similar look on her face.

"No! Is that…?"

"Yes, it seems so," Liora said. "Perhaps fate is in our favor, and we can finally finish an old job." Andrew looked on, uncertain as to what they were talking about as Liora turned to him once again. "Did you say your nephew's name is Colm?"

"Yeah, but that man, that's not me. Kind of looks like me, especially from a distance, but—"

"Doherty?" Liora interrupted. "Karelyn Doherty?"

"Yeah, Doherty, but he's got my name now. I adopted him. But how…?" The rest of his inquiry went unspoken, but was understood. How could they know his dead sister's name? It made no sense.

"Well, that makes things a little more interesting, now, doesn't it?" Ciara muttered, laughing as she looked from the photo to her partner.

Liora gave Ciara a smug look of confirmation as she set the photo on the counter, lowering her head and taking a deep breath. After a moment, she looked up at Andrew. "You're a strange little man. Perhaps in another time or place, things would be different. But right now, we need that necklace."

Nervously, Andrew waded back in, sensing that perhaps there was a way out of this yet, but not entirely certain of what that was. "Look, I'm your guy. I got you the coin, and maybe I can find you this necklace, but trust me when I tell you I didn't see any Aussie come in here. So, you don't have to threaten me, or my fake family. I promise I'll keep my eyes peeled for that necklace, and if I see it again, I'll call you straightaway. Okay?"

Ciara's ears perked up. "What do you mean, 'again'?"

Before Andrew could call on old Betsy, a cold, dark

obsidian blade was pressed against his throat. It had been a simple but unfortunate slip.

"Did I say 'again'?" Andrew questioned aloud, slowly backpedaling, both verbally and physically, until his back was against the wall.

Ciara pressed on him with two blades drawn, crossing each other at his throat. "I say we just end this liar now."

"No, he's still useful. I'm certain he has information. Maybe with the appropriate … *motivation*, he'll open up to us," Liora suggested as Ciara stepped to her side. "So, you have a choice. Share everything you know, or Ciara will get it out of you piece by piece. Eventually, I'm quite certain you will tell us what we want to know."

"Okay, calm down. I can find it for you," Andrew said with a sudden change of strategy, spurred by the razor-sharp blades against his throat. "But it's been sold, and I don't talk about who I sell things to. I'm sure you can appreciate that, since you buy from me as well. However, given the present situation, I can make an exception."

"Yes, well, that makes some sense. Still, we do not enjoy being jerked around. We *need* that necklace. Am I clear?" Liora said, her nostrils flaring with an anger that didn't suit her, but made it even more disturbing to him.

"Crystal," Andrew said. "I just need to make a call to see if I can find out who bought it." He tried to move, but the blades were still at his throat. "I can't do it here. The numbers are in the back, and the phone is too."

Liora waved her hand lazily. Ciara pressed harder with the blades, drawing a little blood before she finally pulled back, allowing him to head to the back room. They followed closely behind. Andrew thought of reaching inside his jacket for Betsy, but he let it go as one of the black blades poked into his back, urging him forward. The situation was growing more dire by the moment, so he opted to tell them what he knew, hoping they would leave.

"Look," Andrew said, "you're valuable customers, so I'll cut the shit. My nephew was working at the shop when the Aussie came in, looking to sell the necklace. Colm bought it, and I took it over to this antiques dealer we use to help me value things, and sometimes he sells them for me to interested buyers who know how to be discrete. Anyway, I told him to sell it, and before I left, he already had a buyer lined up."

"Perfect, then all you need to do is call him and get the name of the buyer," Liora purred.

"I can try," he said as he flipped through his Rolodex, looking for Oliver's number. "It's unlikely that he'll tell me, just like I wouldn't tell anyone about the stuff you buy from me."

"Enough," Ciara snapped. "Just figure out who he sold it to. Got it?"

Andrew nodded, picking up the phone and dialing. After a brief conversation, he hung up and hesitantly turned back to them, not sure how to deliver the news, so he kept it short. "He wouldn't tell me."

Andrew winced as a fist slammed into his face, and he felt blood trickling from his nose, the pain wrapping around his head like a winter scarf.

Liora stepped between him and Ciara. "That's most unfortunate for Oliver. Now we'll have to pay *him* a visit," she said, snatching the card from the Rolodex.

Andrew was still reeling in pain, but had enough sense left to know that Colm was likely headed to Oliver's too. "Wait, just wait," he said, wiping the blood from his face. "I know other people. Just give me a chance to call around. I might be able to find out who bought it. There're only so many people who buy that kind of stuff around town. Since he sold it that fast, it's got to be someone local, and Oliver's local buyers are mostly the same as mine." He lowered his eyes, feverishly thumbing through the Rolodex cards.

"You get us this necklace," Liora said, "and we'll take care of you, so you'll never need to worry about buying or selling this crap ever again. Friends take care of friends, right?"

As she spoke, her phone rang, and she glanced at the screen. "One moment," she said, turning to Ciara with a pained look before stepping away.

"Yes," she answered curtly. "No, no, we don't have it yet, but we'll have it by the end of the day… Yes, of course. You'll be my first call when we get it." Clearly, whoever was on the other end of the line was not happy, as her responses were short and subservient. "Yes, understood… No, you needn't do that. We're the right people for the job… Yes, at all costs." She hung up and motioned to Ciara as she slid her phone back into a pocket inside her coat.

Ciara lunged forward, pinning Andrew's hand to the desk. "You've got ten chances to get us the necklace," she said, spreading his fingers, resting her blade on his pinkie, her beady black eyes looking squarely at him. "Do we understand each other?"

"Yes, just relax," he pleaded as she released his hand and turned to Liora, nodding. Things had gotten out of hand. It was time for Betsy to come out and play.

"It's good that you've decided to cooperate," Liora said from across the room.

"Cooperate this!" he yelled, pulling Betsy from his belt, pointing the gun at Liora.

A deafening boom echoed through the small room just as the hilt of a black blade slammed into his temple. He dropped the gun, hearing it clatter to the floor as he looked up to see that the bullet had gone astray, but still hit its mark. Blood flowed freely out of Liora's shoulder, soiling her cream coat. With a sudden burst of energy, Andrew caught Ciara off guard and shouldered her to the floor, sprinting for the door. But Ciara recovered just enough to stick her foot out, sending him tumbling headlong into the counter, knocking him out cold.

He awoke to their voices, groggy with pain. Looking down, he saw that he was sitting in the office chair, the phone in front of him on the desk.

"Time to make those calls," Ciara said, tapping him on the back of the head.

Andrew was still trying to grasp the situation. His whole body hurt, and he was spinning in and out of consciousness.

"Yes, you find the necklace for us, and perhaps we can forget about your little *outburst*," Liora said, holding a towel to the bullet wound, but the blood had already left its mark.

11

THE VOICE FROM BEYOND

COLM'S MOTORCYCLE rolled to a stop by a little cottage nestled in the trees, with Rye still holding tight around his waist. It reminded him of when he'd taken Tabitha places, but she'd never liked the motorcycle, and rides together had become increasingly rare. She'd tell him that grocery shopping was impossible on the bike, or that the helmet messed up her hair. But to him, it was a way of life—something he appeared to share with Rye.

She removed her hands from Colm's waist, sliding off the motorcycle. As her feet hit the ground, she moved with purpose toward an old, rusted-out BMW parked in the driveway. Colm dismounted, placing his helmet on the handlebar of the motorcycle as Rye turned back.

"It'd probably be best if you waited here," she said.

Colm nodded, leaning against his bike as he watched her walk to the door of the cottage. Pausing, she peeked through the window before turning the knob and slowly opening the door without knocking. She took a step forward, disappearing into the cottage.

Colm relaxed, peeling off his backpack as he heard her

voice inside. A moment later, the lights flicked on, and Rye screamed, startling him.

Before he knew it, he was at Rye's side. He half expected to come face to face with the ladies from the warehouse, but the dim lighting revealed something far more disturbing. It was as if a human and a wild animal had collided, leaving the room littered with blood, guts, teeth, and matted fur. No surface was spared. Hunched over and bound to a chair in the middle of the room were a man's skeletal remains, a studded silver collar dangling around his neck. Noah.

Bile rose in Colm's throat. "What the hell happened here?!" He glanced around the blood-splattered room, searching for some kind of explanation.

"I'm not sure, but I'll give you one guess who did it," Rye said grimly, turning to him.

He didn't have to guess; he knew. The truth was written in her eyes.

She spoke quietly, taking a step backwards. "You're right: we shouldn't have come here. It was stupid. There's nothing for us here but death." Rye turned, racing out of the cottage, leaving Colm alone with the scattered remains of Noah.

For a moment, he felt lucky that he'd hidden from the ladies in that closet, but that sentiment subsided as he stood looking at what remained of the Aussie covering the floor. Every fiber of his being told him to leave, but he couldn't. She'd come here to get some closure with Noah, and he was supposed to help her. Turning to leave, he slid his hands into his pockets, feeling something unexpected.

He pulled the dice out, looking at it. Maybe he could still help her. He nodded to himself, and with no more thought, he scrambled to the table, saying his wish out loud and rolling the dice. As it hit the table, a tremor rumbled through the house, shaking it violently. Colm grabbed the table to steady himself as the dice settled on two X's. Picking it up, he was shaken by how readily he'd rolled the dice with little thought for the consequences. He felt warm, and beads of sweat formed on his forehead as he buried his nose in his elbow to block out the stench of the room. He needed some fresh air. But as he turned to join Rye, he witnessed the first telltale signs that something had gone freakishly wrong with his wish.

The scattered pieces of Noah were slinking their way back to his skeletal remains, although not necessarily going where they belonged. Colm looked on in horror, shuddering as the flesh, bone, and gore smushed themselves back together into a mismatched, fleshy blob. A moment later, Noah had taken on the semblance of a humanoid form with the texture of cottage cheese, the heart of his tattoo now married with the rose below it in a strange mishmash of black ink.

Rye came rushing back into the house. "Did you feel the quake?" she asked, then stopped short, her eyes landing on Noah just as he made a wet gurgling sound. "What the hell is that?!" she asked in shock.

"I think it's Noah," Colm answered in grim disbelief. This wasn't what he'd intended with his wish. He'd expected something different, like a friendly ghost, or maybe a written note.

"Holy shit, that's disgusting," she said, calming down as she circled the chair. "It's like—"

"He's been turned inside out," Colm said, finishing her thought.

"Yeah." She'd completed her circle and came to stand next to Colm.

Noah appeared to be gathering more control as his flesh pulsated and oozed. He raised his head and cleared his throat, looking at Rye.

"Hello, Rye," Noah said, his words sloshing out with great

effort as he coughed, struggling to maintain his composure. "It's me, back from the dead. *Ohhhh-weeee!*" he wailed, trying to mimic a ghost, while Rye stared at him in shock.

"Jesus, is that really you, Noah?" She stepped closer, seemingly unfazed by the situation.

Noah did his best to nod, but was still trying to master his newly cobbled-together form. "I'll admit, this is strange, even for—"

"Why'd you steal it?" Rye interrupted, her voice cracking. "You knew how important it was to me! You never gave me a good answer." She lowered her head, looking away to hide the tears.

"We'd been runnin' for so long," Noah said. "No matter where we went, they found you. I thought it was the only way."

"Don't be fooled by my tears. I'm still pissed at you for everything you took from me. But what they did to you isn't right. I never meant for you to get mixed up in this…" Her voice trailed off in a strange mixture of anger and sorrow.

"That was my choice," he said, looking away momentarily, clearing phlegm from his throat before turning back. "What I did—I was only tryin' to protect you. It wasn't you they wanted. It was the necklace, and I knew you'd never give it up, so I did it for ya. I thought it was your best chance to be free of them. But now I see I was wrong."

Rye looked away, not saying a word.

Noah let out a resigned sigh. "They did this to me. Imagine what they'd do to *you*. You should forget the necklace and run like hell while you still can."

Rye turned back, her eyes blazing. "You had no right to sell *my* necklace! I'm not gonna let them have it! You don't understand. You never did."

There was an awkward silence as the skin oozed from his face, and he struggled against it in obvious pain. "Yes, well, probably not the apology you were expecting," he said, "but it's the honest truth. If I'd wanted to save myself, I woulda just left."

"That clearly would've been better for both of us," Rye said, holding his gaze.

Noah let out a wet chuckle. "You still don't see it, the gift I gave you. Most people would—"

"Don't even!" she yelled. "You violated me! You gave me your curse, even though you knew my feelings about it. My mother was right: your kind can't be trusted. Maybe you didn't deserve this, but you deserved *something*," she spat, her words clean and crisp, full of venom.

Noah looked away, deep in thought before he turned, meeting Rye's eyes. He said in a cordial voice, "Please tell my Garou of my passin'." Redirecting his attention to Colm, he continued, "I know ya had good intentions, and I thank you for the opportunity, but there's too much water under the bridge."

Without a word, Rye turned, streaking out the front door. Colm and Noah exchanged an awkward look before Colm followed, finding her pacing on the front patio.

"I don't understand how he's even here," she said, "but I can't leave him like that. He needs to go back. You got a gun —anything?"

Colm lowered his backpack to the ground, pulling out the milky white blade. "I have this."

"What the hell?!" She took a step backwards, her eyes tinged with fear. "What else did he sell you?" she asked, the disappointment obvious in her tone as she lowered her eyes, turning away.

Colm had seen her do the same to Noah inside, but this time it was directed at him, and he didn't like the feelings it stirred in him. He was struck by how attached he'd grown to her in their short time together as he stepped in front of her, catching her eyes once again. "No more secrets," he said in a quiet voice. "When he came into the shop, he sold me your necklace, this blade, and a wooden mandala. Nothing else."

"That's it?" she asked, her eyes narrowing.

"That's it, I swear," he answered, thinking back before correcting himself. "Okay, he sold me a bunch of old records too, but that's it."

"God dammit, he sold you *my* records!" she said crossly.

"Yes," Colm replied, the answer barely squeaking out.

Rye chuckled and punched him in the arm, wiping the tears from her face. "I'm just shittin' you. Those were his." Colm laughed with her as she pointed to the blade. "Did he tell you what that is?"

Colm shook his head. "No, he just wanted to sell, and it looked old, so I was a buyer."

"It's a Moonblade, and you're right. But it's not just old; it's ancient. It's the weapon of choice for Hunters. They're rare these days, but they still exist."

"What do they hunt?" Colm asked curiously, excited to learn that he was holding something *ancient*.

"Lycanthropes," she said without hesitation.

"Lycan— What?" Colm asked, confused.

"Werewolves. You know, loups-garous. Also known as lycanthropes."

Colm waited for her to punch him in the shoulder again and tell him she was joking, but that moment never came. "You're serious?" he asked, wondering if she was under the influence. Rye just held his gaze, nodding her head. "You're telling me that this blade is used to kill *werewolves*?" he asked, as if he even believed in werewolves, which he most definitely did not. Werewolves were in the domain of scary stories and fairy tales, not the real world—the world he lived in.

Rye held his eyes, nodding again, letting her truth creep

its way deeper into him. She was dead serious, and he was smack dab in the middle of it—whatever *it* was.

"Noah kept this as a memento," she said, "a reminder that Hunters are still out there. He took it from the last Hunter who showed up on his doorstep."

"Are you telling me *Noah* was a werewolf?" he asked, incredulous.

She nodded. "I know this must sound insane, but trust me, it's true—all of it and more. If that blade you're holding pierces the heart of a lycanthrope, it will turn it to stone— forever, period, end of story. It's even said that just a cut from a Moonblade will cause incredible pain and blistering, slowing the werewolf down just enough to allow the Hunter to land the final blow."

She closed her eyes briefly, then opened them, catching his eyes again. "There's something I need to share with you," she said, stepping closer to him and reaching out with both hands. She slowly placed one hand around his, guiding the razor-sharp blade across the soft flesh of her other forearm. Blood welled along the cut as it sliced smoothly into her skin. Her eyes firmly held his as she flinched, wincing at the burn.

He reeled back, yanking the blade away from her arm. "Are you crazy?!" he cried, shocked at what she'd done. But as he looked at the cut, he saw that the surrounding skin had blistered, and Rye bent over, the pain overtaking her.

Understanding spread across his face. It was true—everything she'd said was true. "You're a werewolf too," he murmured, the implication of his words washing over him.

Well, if magical dice exist, why not werewolves? his mind pointed out. After all, was this any crazier than what he'd just witnessed in there with Noah? He had known there was something *different* about Rye, and this would certainly explain it, but the reality that the stuff of fairy tales might all be true left him uneasy about the promise he'd made to the old man in the robes.

"Well, technically, a she-wolf. Getting involved with Noah is what caused a rift with my mother," she said, grimacing as she grabbed a bandana from her purse.

"Your mother *knows* about werewolves?"

"Yes, my mother's well versed in the occult. She can be stubborn, and she didn't approve of my relationship with Noah, but I now understand that was for good reasons." The blistering from the cut was spreading up her arm, and she reached out, handing the bandana to Colm. "Quick, tie it off."

He quickly wrapped it around her arm, tying a double knot. "Too tight?"

"It can't be tight enough."

The moment of silence allowed Colm's mind to catch up with the deluge of information. "Wait… Those two ladies—are they Hunters? Are they after you because you're a she-wolf?"

"That I could understand, but I'm afraid not," she said, her eyes flicking back into the cottage. "Give me the blade. I need to finish this."

Colm reluctantly handed her the ancient weapon. She turned, heading back inside, but her steps were hesitant and uncertain. Then she stopped, turning back to Colm. Her face was streaked with tears, her voice was barely audible. "I can't do it."

Colm's stomach flipped at the implication, but he couldn't blame her—that was her ex in there, after all. And at the end of the day, this was all his own doing. He'd said, *"No more secrets,"* but he'd held onto the secret of his dice, and he wasn't certain he wanted to tell her about it. Now he had to man up and take care of the mess he'd made. He stepped forward, giving her a tender hug and taking the blade from her hand. "I'll do it."

She nodded with relief. "I'll meet you at the motorcycle," she said, turning and walking down the driveway.

Colm stood in the doorway, trying to rouse his courage. Even though Noah was a self-proclaimed revenant, Colm would still have to kill *something,* and that did not sit well with him. He spun the hilt of the blade nervously in his hand, testing its weight. He resolved to do it quickly, but as he stepped into the cottage, Noah's wet voice broke his trance.

"You must do as you promised and help her," Noah said.

"Who are you?" Colm asked, his mind flashing back to the homeless old man once again.

"You wished me here, so you know who I am," he answered. "The real question is, who are you, and what will you do with your gift?"

"How do you know about that?" Colm whispered as he stepped closer to Noah.

"Death brings a certain ... *clarity* to the world of the living. The ability to see things otherwise not seen in life. And speaking of death, didn't anyone tell you the rules?"

The mention of the word "rules" brought Colm squarely back to The Daserii and its gregarious proprietor. "Wynn didn't mention any rules about death."

"Yeah, well, that's obvious," Noah said, laughing as his face contorted into an awkward smile. "Let me help you out. You can't bring people back from the dead. There's an absoluteness to it."

"If that's true, then how are you here?"

"Do I really look like I'm here?" Noah asked. Colm shrugged as he continued, "You felt the tremor when you rolled. There are boundaries that must be respected. I don't belong here. I belong to the other side now, so you need to finish what your bloody dice started."

He motioned to the creamy white blade. Colm nodded once and took a deep breath, raising it up to the level of

Noah's heart. When he hesitated, Noah's fleshy hand snapped out, pulling Colm's arm forward, driving the blade deep into his chest. His hand tightened its grip on Colm's arm as their eyes met one last time. "There's a plane ticket on the kitchen table. Take it, and help her. Just as you promised."

Noah's hand fell limp at his side, and Colm withdrew the blade, watching as Noah turned to greyish stone. With a shuddering breath, Colm walked over to the table, picking up the plane ticket. It was to Dublin, a world away from here. He stowed it in his jacket and turned, looking at the statue of Noah, wondering what the hell he'd gotten himself into.

Walking down the driveway, he saw Rye sitting at an old picnic table. He gave her a confirmatory nod. Nothing more needed to be said.

"That was weird," Rye said, rubbing the back of her neck.

"This is all beyond weird to me—him, and *you*," Colm said, feeling like he was living a lucid dream, not knowing where reality began or ended.

The look on her face softened, matching the tone in her voice. "I'm assuming your uncle knows who has my necklace...?"

"He wouldn't tell them anything," Colm said, understanding her implication. "That's not how it works. Anyway, his detective friend is probably at the Anvil now. There's no way they'll do anything crazy with the police there."

"Are you certain of that?"

Her tone said it all. If she wasn't certain of it, how could he be?

Feeling panic creep in, Colm reached for his phone, dialing the shop, but he got a busy signal. "Shit!" he cursed loudly. He slid the phone back into his pocket, bumping his dice. He hadn't told Rye about it, so it would be easy to use its magic without her knowing. Taking the dice from his pocket, he nonchalantly tapped it on the picnic table.

"Dammit, I wish Andrew would just answer the phone," he said, carefully enunciating the words, then rolled the dice.

Rye's eyes narrowed and her head tilted as she watched the dice skitter to a stop just in front of her, four X's facing up.

"What are you doing? Just keep trying to call him," she said, her eyes alternating between him and the dice. As she glanced back to the cottage, a flash of clarity spread across her face, and her tone changed. "Wait… Did you say, 'I wish'?"

"… Maybe?" he answered, a sheepish look on his face.

"Where did you get that?"

"Get what?"

"The dice. I told you, my mother's into the occult, so I've heard about lots of different things, and you just made a wish and rolled. That can only mean one thing," she said, pointing to the dice sitting on the table in front of them.

"What's that?"

"You're a Gambler."

It seemed that everyone knew about his magic dice—Noah, and now Rye. He'd said no more secrets, but he viewed this as more of an omission rather than a lie, and now that she was bringing it up directly, he didn't want to keep it from her. In fact, she might even be able to help him with it. "Okay, but how—"

"I don't know a great deal about these dice, but I know enough," she interrupted. "They most certainly are not good luck. Whoever gave it to you did not have your best interests in mind, and I'd suggest you stop using that thing before it takes over your soul."

"Takes over my *soul*? What are you talking about?" Colm scoffed at the suggestion.

Her eyes held an edge that could cut diamonds. "The stories of Gamblers are well known, and they never end well,

Colm—*never*. Your greed, or even your desire to do good with it will *always* pull you to use it. It will become irresistible, preying on your deepest desires. That's what it does. It pulls you in, and it takes your life from you along the way. Mark my words, it's a curse, not a gift. You're destined to become a slave to it," she said, waiting for some response, but her ominous warnings left him speechless. Slowly, a darkness clouded her eyes. "Wait... Did you wish for Noah to come back? Was that what he meant when he thanked you?" she asked, the pain clear on her face. She already knew the answer.

Colm quietly nodded in confirmation, not wanting to speak the words aloud even to himself.

Tears once again streaked down her face. "See, you had good intentions, but wishes *never* turn out the way you think. They're always perverted somehow. You may think you're in control, but you're not. Trust me, you need to get rid of that thing."

"I can't. If I do, it just shows up in my pocket again," he said, picking it up from the table and throwing it across the driveway. Reaching into his pocket, he pulled it out again. "See?"

"It's bound to you," she whispered, a quiet recognition spreading across her face. "You've got to find a way to get rid of it."

"I literally have no idea how to do that, so I guess I'll just have to figure out how to control myself."

"It doesn't work that way. You may think you can, but it will win in the end," she said, taking a deep breath before continuing. "I *never* want you to use that dice to make wishes for me again. I can handle my own fate. Got it?"

Colm nodded, acknowledging her request, when his phone rang loudly. He glanced down to see it was Detective Lemmek. He picked up immediately.

"Hi, Detective. Is everything okay?"

"Hi, Colm," he said quietly.

It was only two words, but ice stabbed at Colm's insides. He had heard that tone before, and he knew what the detective was going to say before he uttered another word.

"I'm sorry, but your uncle's dead." There was a long pause before he continued. "It looks like there were two of them, but other than that, we don't know a lot yet. I just..." The detective hesitated, blowing his nose, the sorrow heavy in his voice. "Sorry, I've just known Andrew for a long time, and this is a hard one... Colm, are you there?"

Colm hadn't said a word since answering the phone, but a few now faintly escaped. "Yes, still here." He thought of his parents' murder, and now his uncle. All the family he had left in the world were gone, taken from him. It wasn't fair. He might have a magic dice, but it did little for him in this instance.

"You said you saw them or knew them from around town. Is there somewhere we can meet, so I can ask you some questions?"

Colm cleared his throat, wiping the tears from his eyes. "Sure. We're over by Parada Cantina."

"Perfect. I'll head over in a few minutes." With that, Detective Lemmek hung up, and Colm's hand dropped to his side.

Rye had heard the whole thing. "Colm, I'm so sorry," she said softly. "This is all my fault."

Colm just looked at her with glassy eyes. "It's not your fault. It's *their* fault. Someone has to pay..." Maybe he could use the dice to settle the score, but if Rye was right, it would likely be at the cost of his own life—something he wasn't presently certain he was interested in wagering.

She reached out, touching his hand, her eyes pleading with him. "No, it's the dice weaving its demented magic, pulling on you. You're in over your head with that thing. If you keep it, it will destroy you eventually. They *always* do. But you can choose to change your story, Colm," she said, taking a small step closer. "I'll probably regret this, but if you promise to help me get my necklace back, then I promise to help you get rid of that dice and save what's left of your life. I owe you that much."

There was a prolonged pause as Colm choked back his grief and thought about her proposal. He couldn't help but wonder if Rye might be wrong about the dice. He hadn't told her how he'd gotten it, but then, she hadn't asked either. There had to be a reason the strange old man had asked him to help her and then sent him off to The Daserii. Why else would the dice have been given it to him if not to help her? Doubts swirled in his head, but he'd felt its compulsion, and he'd already surrendered years of his life for little in return.

She was right: he was in over his head. And for some reason, he trusted her. But with or without the dice, there was still the business of his promise to the old man, which he intended to keep, and the only way to do that was to keep her close. So, blindly, he jumped at the deal. Either way, he'd keep the dice for the time being and suss it out a bit more. Meeting her eyes, he let out a sigh, responding in a soft voice, "I'll probably regret it too, but I'm in. I can already feel it's pull."

1 2

PARADA CANTINA

RYE SWUNG OFF THE MOTORCYCLE, the wind whipping her hair as she spoke. "Let's make this quick. I'll breathe easier once that necklace is in my hands."

Colm trailed behind her, his expression uneasy. "I'm not exactly thrilled about this either," he admitted.

Rye pulled him in close, speaking in hushed tones. "Nothing about me. Okay?"

Colm nodded. He had no intention of telling Detective Lemmek about how he'd hidden in a broom closet from the very women who had just murdered his uncle.

The Parada Cantina was a treasure trove of petroliana collectibles, its walls covered in memorabilia from a bygone era. Sunlight poured in through the towering windows, casting the bar in a golden glow. Colm pulled out a stool for Rye and took the one next to her. The bartender gave her a second glance, but said nothing as he strolled over. "The usual, Colm?"

"Yeah, a burger and a beer. Thanks, Dennis."

"And for your lady?" he asked.

Colm gave him a cross look as he noticed a grin touching the corners of Dennis's mouth. He turned to ask her, but Rye answered for him. "Just bring me whatever he's having, and make it snappy."

Dennis's eyes widened as he nodded and stepped away from the bar to put their order into the kitchen.

"Colm?" a familiar voice said from behind. Colm turned, standing up. "I wish we were meeting under better circumstances. Your uncle was a good man—better than most."

Colm reached out, shaking his hand, doing his best to stifle his emotions. "Thanks, Detective. He spoke highly of you too."

"Please, call me Roget," the man said. "This must be especially hard for you, after what happened to your parents."

Colm wished he hadn't brought it up. He preferred to keep that firmly in the past, so he gave a simple nod before moving on. "Would you like to join us?" he asked as they sat down at the bar. "We just ordered a quick bite to eat."

"No, no time. I just have a few questions."

It was a quick conversation. Colm shared descriptions of the two ladies. Notably, he omitted any mention of the delivery gone wrong, the warehouse, or Rye. "There's security footage too. That should help," he said.

Roget rose to leave, placing a hand softly on Colm's shoulder. "I'm really sorry, Colm. Please, if there's anything that I can do, just call." He turned to leave, then paused, speaking in a hushed tone. "Oh, one more thing. This is a small town, lots of tourists. Let's keep this quiet for now, until we know more. No need to go getting people all worked up."

They both nodded, and a moment later, he was gone.

"You lost your *parents* too?" Rye asked in a soft voice.

"Yeah, when I was fifteen," he said. Her face was a mixture

of sorrow and grief, but he wasn't looking for her pity. People had told him it would "get better," but it never did. He'd just learned to live with it and avoid obsessing over it. Not talking about it was the key.

"I'm so sorry, Colm."

"It's okay. It happened years ago. They never caught the people who did it. I just woke up to the police swarming the house, and somehow I was lucky enough to survive."

"Looks like someone has a guardian angel."

"Is that a real thing too?" he asked with a sad smile.

"It is," she said, nodding.

He looked away, uncertain of how to respond.

She stood, looking around. "I need to hit the restroom." Colm pointed to the end of the bar, watching her walk away.

Dennis returned from the kitchen, a smug grin on his face. "I heard about you and Tabitha. Didn't expect to see you in here with another lady so soon." He slid two beers in front of Colm, spilling a bit on the bar.

"News travels fast, but I'm not *with* her," Colm said. "She's just a customer."

"Right," Dennis said with a wink as Colm took a sip of his beer, glancing down the bar toward the restroom. "She's a sassy one. Sure you can handle her?"

Colm let out an exasperated sigh. "I'm not trying to *handle* her! I'm just trying to drink this beer," he said as someone in the kitchen yelled to Dennis, and he disappeared again.

It had been a hell of a day, and Colm was relieved to have a minute to himself. His thoughts should've gone to his uncle, but instead they went immediately to the dice nestled in his pocket. Visions of hoards of money, sports cars, and paparazzi flashed through his mind. But it didn't feel the same to think about it without Andrew. They should've been talking about how they'd use it. But not now. Now he was alone—more alone than ever. He set the dice on the bar, spinning it with his fingers. *Why did Wynn give it to me?* There had to be a reason. The old man with the robes had talked of paying it forward, and how one's choices shaped the world.

He leaned back, taking another sip of his beer as his eye caught the television above the bar. A news anchor was telling a story about the eviction of a local homeless encampment. He reached for the dice, but paused. Why should he help them? No one ever helped him. If he had to keep the dice, any wishes had to be worth it to him. He'd already sacrificed too many years for nothing, and now his uncle was dead. From now on, one thing was certain: he wouldn't pay anything forward, and any choices would be his own. He picked up his pint glass, taking a big gulp.

"Hey, slow down there, puppy," a voice from behind said as a hand gently touched his shoulder.

His eyes narrowed as he turned. "Tabitha. What are you doing here?" he asked in a cool tone, glancing nervously at the second glass of beer sitting on the bar.

"I just… I…" she stammered, and he was in no mood to help her out. She'd made her desires crystal clear, and the cuts were still raw. "Maybe I should…" She turned to leave, but paused, taking a deep breath. "No, I came here to apologize. I said some mean things the other night."

Colm scoffed, rolling his eyes. "Ya think?"

"I didn't mean it—not all of it. Sure, we have some things to work on. All couples do. Anyway, I've done a lot of thinking, and, well…" She sat down on Rye's stool and leaned in, taking his hands in hers.

He pulled away. "What do you want me to say, Tab? That I forgive you? That it's okay? You've always wanted things your way, on your terms. This breakup—that was typical *you*," he said, spite heavy in his tone—likely spurred by the death of his uncle, but he wasn't going to tell her about that. He didn't want her pity.

"No, that's not why I'm here. I'm here because I'm sorry," she said, taking a deep breath before pressing on. "I'd like you to come with me, to grad school. You can take some time, see what you want to do, whatever. But we'd be doing it together."

Colm glanced down the bar, still seeing no sign of Rye. Strangely, he found himself getting worried about her. She'd been gone for an abnormally long time, and things had been strange the last couple days, to say the least.

"Are you going to say anything?" Tabitha asked, waiting for a response.

"I don't know. You said a lot of things the other night."

"Okay, well, that's not a no. So, think about it," she said, a measured smile meeting the corners of her lips as she wiped her eyes.

"Yeah, I just need some time."

"Time for what?" Rye asked, looking to join in on the conversation.

Tabitha turned to see who'd interrupted them, and Colm jumped in, introducing them.

"Tab, this is Rye. We're on our way to get a necklace back from Oliver that she sold at the shop," Colm said nervously.

Rye immediately understood. She reached out her hand to Tabitha, smiling warmly. "First, it's nice to meet you, but second, to be clear, I didn't sell my necklace at the pawnshop; my dimwit ex-boyfriend did. Colm here is just helping me get it back."

"Yeah, he's good like that," Tabitha said as Dennis returned with the two burgers.

"Do you want to join us?" Rye asked.

"No, that's nice of you, but I've got some errands to run. I'll let you two get back to your business." With that,

Tabitha turned, heading out of the bar as Rye settled onto the stool.

"She seems sweet, but not what I expected," Rye said. "I mean, she doesn't have horns or a forked tail or anything." She laughed as she took a bite from her burger.

"Is that a thing?" Colm asked.

Her lips turned up. "It is, sorry. But it looks like she came crawling back to you?"

"I wouldn't call that 'crawling.' I'd call it someone trying to clear their conscience."

"What'd you tell her?" she asked, wiping her mouth with a napkin.

"I told her I needed some time, and that's when you saved me."

"You're welcome." She glanced down, noticing his dice out on the bar. He reached out, putting it away, but she called him on it. "See what I mean? It's relentless."

Colm shrugged, changing the subject. "What took you so long? I was getting worried ... you know, with everything that's happened."

"Just a long line for the bathroom. But funny thing," she said, pausing to chew her burger before continuing. "As I was waiting, I caught this overwhelming smell of thyme, and I look over, and there's this trippy little dude in the corner booth, puffing away on a pipe. Like, who smokes pipes anymore?" she said, laughing, expecting Colm to join in.

He didn't. "Wait... Did you say thyme—like, the herb?" he asked, his voice a mixture of excitement and disbelief.

"Yeah, definitely thyme," she said, finishing her beer and setting it on the bar.

Colm leaned in. "And his pipe was made of carved black wood, and he's wearing a tweed jacket, right?"

She raised a brow. "How'd you—"

"Holy shit, it's him!" Colm stumbled as he got off the

stool, and Rye caught him, their faces mere inches apart. There was an awkward silence until he gathered himself.

"Who's *him*?" asked Rye, glancing at the corner booth.

"The Daserii—the guy who gave me the dice!"

"Oh, *that* guy."

"Right, and I've got some questions." He walked toward the corner booth, and Rye quickly followed.

Sure enough, there he was. Without a word, they slid into the booth across from the little man, causing his goblet to rock back and forth. Just before it toppled, the man caught it, but much of its contents spilled on the table.

"What the hell?" cursed the little man as he used his napkin to soak up the spilled drink.

"Hi, Wynn," Colm said with a cool smile.

The man looked up, irritated. "I'm afraid you must have me confused with someone else. And really, where are your manners?"

"Bullshit!" Colm said, not buying it.

"Yes, well, you Americans always seem to think that all Irish people look alike, but I assure you, I am not this 'Wynn.' My name is Liam Paxton, and I'm just here to enjoy a drink and some food. So, if you wouldn't mind … bugger off!"

At that moment, Dennis shuffled over to the table, placing a cheesesteak in front of the man. "Everything okay here?" he asked as he wiped up the spilled drink.

"Just catching up with an old friend," Colm said, his eyes locked on the man who now called himself Liam. Dennis nodded, taking his leave, and "Liam" reached for his goblet, which was curiously full again.

Colm pinned the little man's forearm to the table.

Liam—or whoever he was—sputtered on his drink. "I would strongly suggest you remove your hand from me before things get out of control," he said, his words of warning crisp and clear.

"Things are already out of control," Colm said, glaring back as he pulled the dice from his pocket with his free hand, setting it on the table.

Liam glanced at the dice and let out a nervous laugh, his eyes flashing around the room.

"Don't make me do it," Colm threatened. "I've had a couple of crazy days, and I've got some questions."

Liam released his hand from the goblet, pulling it back, and Colm followed suit. "What are you gonna do with that? Shove it up me arse?" Liam said, chuckling softly, but no one else joined in. "I've got better things to do than deal with rabble like you." He huffed, grabbing his cane and sliding out of the booth, intending to leave.

Colm picked up his dice, letting out a sigh. "Remember, you asked for this… *I wish you could only tell the truth for the rest of your life.*"

Before the dice even hit the table, Liam's hand shot out, snatching it in midair. His voice was bitter as their eyes met. "Is this your new path in life, Mr. Stokely? Teenage antics and frivolity to impress your lady friend?" he mocked, begrudgingly setting his cane against the edge of the table and settling back into the booth. He took a bite of his cheesesteak, followed by a long drink from his goblet.

Colm smiled, reaching into his pocket and magically pulling out his dice again. "I've got questions about this."

Liam laughed into his napkin as he wiped the grease from his face. "Sorry, but the time for that has passed. *Three times asked, three times denied,*" he reminded him, stowing his now empty goblet in his jacket as he slid out of the booth, looking at Colm with a sneer. "Enjoy your short life, *Gambler.*"

Colm rose, pushing Liam back down on the bench. "Sit down. I'm not done," he said with a wild look in his eyes as he placed the dice on the table between them.

"Check yourself, Mr. Stokely. You're on a dangerous

path," Liam said, flashing a stern look as he straightened his jacket.

"I can do this all day," Colm said nonchalantly as he settled back into the booth.

"There are other ways to deal with this," Rye interjected, trying to calm Colm down.

Liam cast a curious eye toward Rye, sensing that he'd found an ally. "Perhaps you should listen to the little lady."

"Who the hell are you calling 'little lady,' you greenie jack-hole?" Rye said through gritted teeth, trying to keep her voice down.

Colm turned to Rye, speaking in a subdued voice. "It's okay. I'm willing to give up a year if I roll an odd number. I just need answers."

"Wait—*what* happens if you roll an odd number?" Rye asked, eyebrows raised.

"That's right, dearie, it's all trophies and cupcakes until your boy here rolls an odd number. Then he loses a year of his life—just like that," Liam said, snapping his fingers for emphasis. "He may rule over his own fate, but the magic doesn't work without an occasional sacrifice."

Rye clasped her hands over Colm's, holding the dice in place. "I knew these dice were bad luck … but time? Time is your only real currency. It's more precious than anything that dice could ever give you. You need to stop," she pleaded with him.

Her hands were warm, and he made no move to pull back. He was touched that she actually cared what he did. Looking at her, he felt conflicted. He knew she was right, but there was a good chance he'd never be able to get rid of it, and in that case, he needed to know more about it. Liam had crafted it; he had to know its secrets.

Almost as if she were reading his mind, she shook her head. "You've been tricked by him, Colm. It's their way."

"Not tricked, dearie, but *gifted* something of immense power, if harnessed and used properly. It holds great potential, but admittedly, Gamblers often fail in their original intentions, letting greed and selfishness seep in. I suspect he is no different."

With his frustration growing, Colm slammed his free hand on the table. "You're wrong. I'm *helping* her—" He cut himself off, not wanting to delve into the promise he'd made to the old man. He preferred to think he was helping her out of the goodness of his heart, rather than a sense of obligation. "I know my path. Now choose yours, Liam—or whatever your name is. I can roll all day," he said as he gently peeled Rye's hand away from his, giving her a confident nod. She relented, but held his gaze. He wasn't sure where this would go, but he was prepared to see it through, and he returned his focus to Liam, dice in hand.

Liam leaned back, pulling his goblet from his jacket, which was once again magically full somehow, taking an absurdly long drink. Setting it on the table, he wiped the foam from his upper lip and spoke in a subdued, conversational tone. "You know, it's *highly* unusual for a Gambler to meet his Daserii after the bonding. In fact, I'm not aware that it's ever happened, but such are the days we live in, I guess," he said, shrugging his shoulders before leaning forward with a smirk. "You took a few more drinks than most. Guessing they hit you pretty hard the next day?"

"You *drank* something he gave you?" Rye asked incredulously as Colm nodded, unconcerned. "Fairy drink is way too strong for normies!"

"Whoa, lassie! I'm no fairy, you take that back," Liam snapped, clearly offended.

"Or what?" she said, leaning forward and glaring back.

"I'm afraid I haven't been formally introduced to your little vixen here. Got a little fight in her, she does. I like that in my ladies," Liam said, his eyes twinkling, highlighting the depraved grin that had formed on his face.

"You. Are. Gross," she said, enunciating each word slowly as she settled back into her seat.

"This is Rye," Colm said.

"Just Rye?"

"Yes, just Rye," she said with cool conviction before turning to Colm. "Don't trust this guy. Leprechauns are liars and cheats."

"*Leprechaun?*" Colm repeated, not certain he'd heard her correctly.

Rye nodded as Liam sat smugly across the table, not saying a word.

Well, hell, why not leprechauns too? Colm thought. It intuitively made sense, given what he knew of them from fairy tales. They were mischievous, magical creatures who loved a good drink, and Liam seemed to fit the bill.

Colm glanced down at the dice in his hand, feeling it pulling at him. Between the two, his trust lay with Rye, and she was right: he was in way over his head. "I don't know what game you're playing, but I want out," he declared, sliding the dice across the table to Liam. "Here's your dice. Just take it and give me back all the years it's stolen."

Liam pushed the dice back to him. "Can't do it. It doesn't work that way. Only the Lady herself could take it back, but she's a hard one to find."

Rye leaned forward, suddenly acutely interested in the conversation. "Wait—who?"

"The Lady," Liam repeated. "She goes by many names—Lady Luck, Lady Fortune, Tyche. But give you back your lost years? I doubt even she could do that. The past is the past; it's already written. But the future... Now, that's malleable. You can still shape it."

Rye leaned in, whispering to Colm. "The Lady controls

the fates of all those in the Land Between, and she can be..."
Rye searched for the right word. "... *difficult.*"

"She speaks the truth," Liam added with a chuckle.

"What's the Land Between?"

"This is," Rye answered.

"Okay, so, what's it between?" Colm asked, more confused than ever.

"Good and evil. Light and darkness. Heaven and hell. Whatever you believe," Liam said calmly. "An ancient war for souls once raged between the two, until the Triumvirate Treaty finally resolved it in the Last Skirmish. In that treaty, they created the Stone of Fates to control the fortunes of all living souls on Earth, or the Land Between, bestowing it upon an ancestor of the Lady, and the stone has now passed down to her. The Land Between is her exclusive domain, free from their meddling, provided she maintains a somewhat balanced flow of souls to each side—no winners, no losers."

"Even if you can't find her to give it back, you need to stop wasting your life with it," Rye pleaded with Colm.

"Some wishes are not wasted, lassie. Would saving a life be worth the risk of giving up a year of your own life? Seems to me it could."

"Then why don't *you* have a dice?" Rye asked.

"It's the Lady's magic. I can only make them for people at her request."

"Since you work for her, you must know where I can find her?" Colm asked.

"*Worked* for her, past tense. I'm no longer in her employ. Your dice was my last commission from the Lady," Liam said, leaning back.

Rye had a concerned expression on her face. "Maybe it'd be better to just stop using it. Meetings with her rarely turn out as expected."

"No, I need to give it back. You said it yourself: I'm in

over my head," Colm said, and Rye gave a half-hearted nod. He turned back to Liam. "How do I find her?"

"It's not easy. She's become more fearful of her own fate and gone into hiding. Since then, my jobs have come to me in missives from woodland creatures, and in your case, from the Whiskered Stranger himself."

"Wait… Is he an old man who wears priest's robes?" Colm asked.

"That'd be him," Liam answered. "But—"

"That's who sent me to your shop!" Colm interrupted. "Do you know where I can find him? Maybe *he* can help me find her."

Liam laughed, taking a sip before answering, "I'm afraid you can't find him. No one can. He only appears on a whim, which is random and quite infrequent."

"He's telling you the truth," Rye said.

"And there's no way to call him. People have tried, and they've always failed," Liam added.

Rye tapped her fingers on the table with a puzzled look at Colm. "So, the Whiskered Stranger visited you?"

Colm nodded. He didn't know the import of it, or who this Whiskered Stranger really was, but it seemed that Rye was quite interested.

"Did he say anything that might help us out here?" Rye asked.

Colm looked at her, hesitating, "He asked me for a favor, and we kinda shook on it."

"Kinda, or did?" Rye was now laser-focused on Colm.

"We did. I mean, I thought he was just a crazy old home-less guy," Colm answered sheepishly, lowering his eyes as Rye and Liam stared at him, waiting.

"What did you shake on?" Rye asked gently.

"He said the only thing he wanted in return was that when the lady in red came to me, I would help her," Colm said, raising his gaze from the table to Rye, looking into her emerald eyes as they widened in disbelief, framed by her amber hair.

"Am *I* the lady in red?" she murmured.

"Ya think?" Liam chuckled, thick with sarcasm.

"He asked you to help me?" Rye asked, ignoring Liam.

"It seems so," Colm answered.

They all sat in silence for a moment. Liam pulled his pipe from his pocket, packing it with tobacco. As he did, Rye reached out, grabbing Liam's goblet, and took a drink of whatever he was fancying. She sat back, turning the goblet in her hand. Her eyes glazed over, her expression distant. "The stories of the Whiskered Stranger are ancient," she said, "centuries old, maybe more. No one really knows where they originated, but one thing is certain: a visit from him is always an omen, and not always a good one."

"She's definitely right on this one," Liam said, casting her a probing look before continuing. "It's been said that he only shows himself in the direst of situations."

"Right, the situations that..." Rye paused mid-sentence, looking from Liam to Colm. "Did he say *how* you're supposed to help me?"

"Well, I guess..." Colm said, his breath coming in brief pulses as it dawned on him that he'd made a promise to an ancient mystic.

"And?"

"He said that you're lost, and I need to help you find your way home."

"Well, you can stop helping me, because I don't want to go home. That chapter of my life is closed," she said definitively, turning away.

"But it's the Whiskered Stranger. How can you ignore that?" Liam pleaded.

"Because I can, and it's none of your business," Rye said, the tension returning as the two stared at each other.

"Look, I'm not gonna tell you what to do, but at least you have a home," Colm said, turning to her. Rye opened her mouth, but Colm spoke over her. "I promised I'd help you, and that's what I'm doing. We're going to start by getting your necklace back. As for me, I need to get rid of this dice. Are you still willing to help me with that?"

Rye let out a small breath, pursing her lips. "But I'm not going home, no matter what that crazy old man said to you."

"Whatever you want," Colm said in agreement.

She paused, taking another drink from the goblet, looking from Colm to Liam. "Yeah, I'm still on board. We'll help you try to get rid of your dice once I have my necklace back."

"'We'?" Liam echoed.

"Yeah. If we have to find her to give it back, we're gonna need your help," Rye answered, setting down the goblet.

"Sorry, lassie, not gonna happen." Liam waved his hands in front of him. "She and I have a sordid history, and I've no desire to go stirring things up with her—not over you two, anyway."

"Are we really going to do this again?" Colm asked, reaching into his pocket.

Rye placed her hand gently on Colm's leg and spoke softly. "I said there are other ways." She turned to Liam, sliding her hand across the table, touching his arm and whispering to him in a soft, syrupy voice. "A little bird told me you're going to help us find the Lady and give Colm's dice back. Once you do, I promise I'll be out of your life, and I'll make certain you're never bothered by us again."

Liam flushed with embarrassment as she pulled her hand back. "You're no bother, lassie. Still, I don't know if we'll find her. But let's give it a go."

"Good to see you've had a change of heart. Any ideas on where to start?" Rye asked Liam. Colm just looked at her, perplexed as to what had just happened.

"Well, there is…" Liam hesitated, reaching for his goblet.

"There is what?" Colm asked impatiently, turning his attention back to Liam.

"Someone called the Tin Maiden," answered Liam.

"Never heard of her," Rye said, toeing the line of calling him a liar.

"Rumor has it that if you find this Tin Maiden, you can find the Lady," Liam continued, ignoring her tone.

"How do we find her?" Colm asked.

"That, I'm afraid, is where my knowledge ends. The stories range from unclear to downright unreliable, and I don't know where one would even start."

"Are we done with story time?" Rye sneered. "I'd like to get my necklace."

"Yeah, let's go," Colm said, getting up from the table.

"We can take my car," Liam said, grinning widely. "It'll fit all of us and then some." He rose from the table, leaning heavily on his cane.

The trio headed out to the parking lot, and Liam pressed a button on his keychain. The lights on a vintage golden Cadillac flashed brightly, and it lowered to the ground.

Rye sighed, turning away. "You've got to be kidding me. I'm not getting in that pimpmobile."

"Whoa, now, she's a lady too. You've got to treat her nice and speak to her respectfully," Liam said, settling into the driver's seat.

After some cajoling, Rye reluctantly joined Colm in the back seat. Liam lovingly rubbed the dashboard and tapped his little Hawaiian girl bobblehead softly, starting her dance. "Leilani, she's my protector, always keeps me on the straight and narrow."

Rye scoffed and turned to Colm, whose attention was currently fixed on the oversized fuzzy dice hanging from the rearview mirror.

Liam turned, looking at them both as a broad smile covered his face. "I know, right? She's awesome." He slapped his hand on the seat in excitement. Then he fired up the engine, speeding away as he yelled over the car's obnoxiously loud grumble, "Where're we going, anyway?"

13

LE PETIT CHATEAU

LIAM'S CADDY crawled down the street as Colm pointed ahead to a cottage resembling a miniature storybook castle. On a post by the gate, a small wooden sign read, *le petit chateau*, written in a scripted lowercase. The houses in the area had all been given names, some fanciful and some descriptive, but always quaint. The Caddy pulled to a stop in front of the chateau, and Liam cut the engine, silencing the beast.

"Jesus, that's loud!" Colm said, his ears practically ringing.

"Right, I know. It's awesome!" Liam cackled with an enormous grin as he tapped Leilani on the head to stop her from dancing.

"This is it?" asked Rye.

"Yeah, this is it," Colm answered, closing the door behind him.

The yard about the chateau was well maintained, an homage to a garden one might find in a countryside villa in France. Lavender, thyme, savory, and an abundance of flowers painted a vibrant and fragrant scene. Colm reached out to open the gate when the front door popped open, revealing a tall, gaunt man who was so thin, it was like he'd disappear if he turned sideways. His clothes were tidy, and a close-cut goatee adorned his face, as manicured as the gardens.

"Colm, so good to see you!" the man said, waving them in.

"It's good to see you too, Oliver. How are things?" Colm asked as he opened the gate, dodging the errant honeybees on his way into the chateau.

"No complaints, but couldn't miss hearing you pull up," he said with distaste, casting a scornful eye toward the Caddy.

"Yeah, sorry about that…" Colm shot Liam a crusty look.

"No worries." Oliver cast a suspicious glance at Rye and Liam. "Who are your friends?"

"Right. Where are my manners?" Colm took a moment to introduce them all, and after some pleasantries, Oliver invited them inside.

"I've just been puzzling over one of your finds," Oliver said as he closed the door and directed them into his workroom at the end of the hall.

Oliver's workroom was outfitted with bookshelves and worktables sporting various sizes of magnification devices, from eyepieces to handheld glasses to a sturdy table-mounted magnification glass that looked so heavy, Colm wondered how the table did not simply tip over under its weight. An assortment of chairs and cushions finished off the room, and everything had a place. White outlines reminiscent of those used for a dead body at a crime scene were clearly marked for every tool, with tiny labels under each. Colm had known organized people before, but this took it to a whole new level. Even the bookshelf appeared to have an index of all the books it contained, with their location noted.

Oliver noticed Colm's interest as he popped in behind him. "Kaizen."

"What?" Colm turned to him, confused.

"Well, Kaizen 5S, technically: sort, straighten, scrub, standardize, and sustain. It's a Japanese management and organization system. Everything has its designated place when not being used. See, this magnification glass goes here," he said, lifting it from its outline, and the words MAGNIFICATION GLASS 1:50 were written below it. He set it back down in its place, squarely inside the white outline. "That way, you always know where things are when you need them."

"Wow, that's ... really organized," Colm muttered, still absorbing the immaculate detail of the room, now wondering if Oliver had done it throughout the entire house.

Rye sidled up to Colm, reminding him of why they were here. Colm snapped out of it and turned back to Oliver. "So, I'm here to pick up the stuff that my uncle dropped off for me."

"Right, that's what I wanted to talk to you about." He pointed to the large magnification glass on the workbench as he flicked a switch, powering it on. The glass magnified the detail of the gilded tree on the flat wooden mandala to the size of a basketball, showing the engravings in astonishing detail. "This piece is fabulous—extraordinary, really—and quite old," he said as he walked to the bookcase.

"The Tree of Life," Liam whispered, the dark wood of his cane clicking on the floor as he stepped forward, looking at the mandala.

"You know what it is?" Colm asked, stepping next to Liam.

Oliver ignored them, taking a book from the bookcase and flipping to a bookmarked page. He laid it on the workbench, but before he said anything, Liam answered Colm with a deep sigh. "It's kinda like a lock and key, or a puzzle."

Looking at Liam in surprise, Oliver pointed to a diagram in the book. "Yes, that's a wonderful description. A *key* would have been made to uniquely fit into the round opening in the middle," Oliver said, pointing to the center of the mandala that split the tree into the upper half, where the branches spread out, and the lower half, dominated by roots. "The design of the Tree of Life was unique to—"

"The Great Seer, Haesel." Liam's brow furrowed. "But it's more than just a design. It was her calling card, and she hewed her mandalas from the Tree of Life itself." He lifted his cane, pointing it at Oliver. "You're right to call this piece extraordinary. It's known as a Haesel's Mandala, and each was handmade by her to protect her most delicate prophecies."

Oliver's mouth was agape as he pointed to the tiny words below the diagram that confirmed it was indeed a Haesel's Mandala. "How did you know? Are you a professor, a collector...?"

"Neither. I'm just very old, and I've seen this mandala before. I'm wondering how it got here?" Liam asked, rubbing his chin.

"No big mystery," Colm answered. "Rye's ex pawned it to me, along with her necklace."

Liam glanced at Rye with raised brows as Oliver brought them all back to the mandala, pointing to some additional text from the book.

"It says these mandalas were believed to carry prophecies concerning the gods themselves … but wait, there's more." Oliver picked up the book and flipped a few pages, running his fingers along the text. "Yes, here it is: 'It was believed that only with the revelation of the full prophecy through the insertion of the given mandala's key would the prophecy come true.'"

Liam frowned. "Well, that's not quite right. See, the prophecy of a given mandala was always true, but it was unknown to all except Haesel herself. The fitting of the 'key,' as you call it, into the mandala revealed the prophecy to the world and gave the god to whom the prophecy was directed an opportunity to change the course of future events, to avoid the realization of the prophecy."

They had all now turned their full attention to Liam, realizing they didn't need a book to tell them anything.

"Who are you?" Oliver asked, transfixed by Liam's sheer depth of knowledge.

Liam ignored the question and pressed on. "In the early days, some nefarious gods would obtain Haesel's prophecies to use as weapons against the others, often resulting in unspeakable atrocities. Now, understand, her prophecies are always in play, regardless of whether or not they are known. But once they become known, they have a weird knack for coming to fruition in an expedited fashion. So, long ago, the gods determined it was best for Haesel to keep those prophecies concerning them secret, and let the fortunes unfold in their own time and manner. From that point on, Haesel inscribed these mandalas and their keys at the time of seeing, and then each key was kept separate from its mandala, ensuring that the prophecy was known only to her. Even though it's nearly impossible to escape the realization of her prophecies, legend tells us that in the direst of circumstances, the fates will reveal a mandala and its key, thereby offering the potential to avoid what she foresaw."

They all stood mesmerized by Liam's words. Rye glanced from Liam to Colm. "Where the hell did Noah get this?" she asked rhetorically.

"He stole it from the Lady. That's the last time I saw it," Liam said matter-of-factly, flipping to the next page, which portrayed the marks of the various gods. He pointed to a black pentagram. "That star is the sign of the Lady."

"The Lady? Who is that?" Oliver asked as he closed the book, returning it to its designated spot on the bookshelf.

Ignoring the crosstalk, Rye stepped closer to Oliver. "What about my necklace?"

"The necklace, right… Splendid item in its own right," Oliver said. "Old, precise carvings, and did you know it's made from sprush? An ancient wood—extinct now, so it's quite rare."

Colm stepped beside Rye. "That's why we stopped by. Can we have it?"

"Afraid not, as I'm proud to tell you it's been sold—and for a rather handsome price too. But don't go expecting this kind of result all the time," Oliver said, beaming with pride.

"What?! You didn't say you had it up for sale!" Rye glared at Colm as the blood rose in her face, matching the color of her hair.

"That's because I didn't," Colm muttered, Rye's anger catching hold of him as he looked upon Oliver. "I didn't tell you that you could sell it!"

With a mixed expression on his face, Oliver took a step back, raising his hands defensively. "When Andrew dropped it off, he told me to get rid of it quickly and quietly, which I did. I thought you'd be thrilled. It's a lot of money for an old piece of wood."

"Dammit," Colm swore, running his hands through his hair. He knew it was true; "quickly and quietly" had been his uncle's mantra with items like these. Plus, he had told him that the Aussie suggested he get rid of it quickly and quietly, so he didn't blame Andrew.

"Yes, well, I'll go get your cut," Oliver said, now keen on bringing the visit to a close. He stepped out of the room and skittered down the hall, entering another room and closing the door behind him.

"He *sold* my goddamned necklace! Now what?" Rye asked, trying to contain her frustration.

"We're still okay. We'll find it before those ladies do. We

just need him to tell us who he sold it to," Colm said in a calm voice.

Liam lifted his head, stepping closer to Colm with renewed pep. "Ladies? Did I hear you talking about some ladies?"

Rye rolled her eyes, turning away.

"Rye's got these two crazy ladies chasing her, looking for her necklace," Colm answered, going on to describe Liora and Ciara to Liam.

Without missing a beat, Liam looked to Rye once again. "You've got the Raven and the Dove on your tail? Those are two very dangerous ladies, and you're just telling me this *now*?" Liam flapped his hands in the air.

Rye turned, responding in a fiery tone, but careful to keep her voice down. "I told you, it's none of your business! I just want to get my necklace back, and then you'll never see me again—and neither will they."

Liam chuckled. "How's that been working out for you so far?" She gave him a crusty look, flaring her lips before turning away. "That's what I figured," he said. "You can't escape those two. They're relentless. You know they're part of that secret society of fanatics who work for the Lady, protecting her and the Stone of Fates?"

"You mean the Sorority," Rye interjected.

"Yeah. Those two ladies do her dirty work, and they're exceptionally good at it," he said, pacing the room, his cane clicking across the floor. "But there've been rumors swirling that they may be working freelance for someone looking to shake things up and take the Stone of Fates from her."

"I've heard similar things," Rye said.

"Hmm… Without the Lady keeping them in check, that makes them unquestionably more dangerous." He paused, looking from Rye to Colm. "I just wanted a simple life, but it looks like that's not in the cards for us right now. Seems like the fates have driven us together."

The creak of a door sounded from down the hall, and Colm shushed them. Rye moved over to look out the window as Oliver nervously stepped into the room with a small paper bag.

Rye turned to Colm, her eyes pleading.

Colm nodded, stepping closer to Oliver. "Please, just tell me who you sold it to?"

Oliver's eyes flashed from Colm to Rye and back before he spoke tentatively. "You know that's not how it works. My customers, they're confidential."

Colm pressed him. "Come on, Oliver. Her ex stole it from her, and I promised her I'd get it back. What if you just kept the money in that bag?"

Oliver squirmed as he considered Colm's offer. "Look, I'd really like to help, but you're talking about my livelihood. If word got out—"

"Word will not get out," Colm cut in with a confident tone. "You have my promise on that. You keep it all," he said, motioning to the bag. "Just tell me who bought it."

Oliver hesitated, clutching the bag tighter, but finally shook his head, handing it to Colm. "I'm sorry. I can't risk it."

Before he realized it, Colm had his dice in hand, vaguely hearing Rye's muted objections. "I wish you'd tell me who you sold the necklace to," he said, and as soon as the words were spoken, the dice skittered across the table, careening into the mandala under the lighted glass. Three magnified X's faced up, mocking him. "Shit!" Colm cursed, rubbing the back of his neck.

Oliver laughed, looking at the dice. "What are you doing?"

With the laughter ringing in his ears, Colm remained singularly focused on getting the necklace back and immediately landed on another wish as he retrieved the dice from the table, shaking it in his hand.

"Colm, stop!" Rye begged him as she surged forward, trying to grab for his hand, but she was a moment too late. The wish was made, and the dice clattered across the table. They all watched as it spun to a stop, revealing a single X. Oliver's laughter stopped as Rye finally took hold of Colm's hands.

Liam joined Rye, grabbing Colm's shoulder. "You need to think before you roll, boy," he said. "You only have so many in you, and you've just lost two years in a matter of seconds. You'll be dead by the end of the week, at this rate."

Colm looked at Liam as if he'd woken him from a dream. *Two years, just like that,* he thought. If he'd had any illusions that he could control himself with the dice, they'd just fluttered away. There was no way that he could keep it, and he nodded at Liam, acknowledging as much.

Oliver stared at them, utterly confused. "Dead? What are you talking about?" he asked, but they all ignored him as if he weren't there.

Rye flashed a reassuring smile to Colm as she let go of his hands. "There are *other ways* to get the information. Trust me, I've got this," she said, turning to Oliver with an impish smile.

"What are you smiling about?" Oliver asked as he slowly stepped backwards.

She continued her approach, and Oliver retreated until he found his back against the bookshelf. Her smile widened as she leaned in closer, but he was trapped with nowhere to go.

"It's okay, you're going to like this," she said in her soft, syrupy voice.

"I'm a married man," Oliver objected, but relented as she leaned closer.

Rye took his hand in hers and spoke to him in that same

voice. "A little bird told me you're going to tell us who bought my necklace," she said, releasing his hand and taking a step back.

Oliver shook his head and wiped his brow before clearing this throat. "Right. So, one of my regulars, Adam Merkel, purchased your necklace. I delivered it to his house earlier today."

Colm laughed, slapping his hand on the table, startling Oliver. "I should've known. He's the curator at the local museum, and he's been all over town letting people know he's buying."

"So, where do we find him?" Rye asked.

"I've got his address," Colm said, pulling out his phone. "There we are... 535 Oakvale Lane."

Rye turned back to Oliver, but this time he gave no signs of hesitation. "A little bird told me you're going to go to sleep and forget everything about this little visit."

With that, he crumpled, and she caught him, laying him softly on a bench by the window.

"What the hell?!" Colm said, standing above them, confusion reigning again.

"That was a fancy little trick, lassie," Liam said to Rye. "Do you want to tell him, or me?"

"Trick? What's he talking about?" Colm asked, looking at Liam and back to Rye.

She stood up, turning to Colm, but unable to meet his eyes. "You're not the only one with magic."

Liam was now smiling widely at Rye as he nudged Colm. "She has the gift of charm. I should've guessed it."

Colm wasn't certain what Liam was telling him, but then it hit him. "Wait... You did *that* to me at the pawnshop?" he asked, recalling her gently touching his hand and using those same unique words just before he agreed to help her.

Her face flushed, and she turned her eyes away.

"So, you can make people *do* things?" Colm asked, stunned at the possibility of it.

Rye turned back, her eyes answering him before she spoke. "I didn't know if you'd help me. Now I know better."

Colm silently absorbed her words. At first, the manipulation left him feeling violated. But at the same time, he'd enjoyed his time with her. She'd opened his eyes to a world he'd never imagined existed, and he felt more alive than ever because of it. On top of that, she'd committed to helping him. She didn't have to do that. Still, it hurt that she'd tried to use him. "You know, I'd already decided to help you before you did it."

"I'm sorry. I'm not proud of myself for doing it. Sometimes I just lose myself to the power," she admitted, her eyes glistening.

Colm immediately understood what she meant. It always sat just below the surface, waiting for its opportunity. He'd experienced it several times already with his dice and presumed it must be similar for her. He held no illusions about what she'd done, but just like she needed him to help her get her necklace back, he needed her to help him get rid of his dice. But he had to admit, there was more to it than that. Deep down, he wanted this little adventure with her to last as long as it could.

"I want you to know I'm helping you because I want to," he told her sincerely. "Not because you charmed me, or whatever it was you did."

"I know that now, and I'll never do it to you again," she assured him, pulling Colm into an unexpected hug. He returned it gladly.

"Perfect. It's settled, then. You don't charm me, and I won't make wishes for you," Colm said, and they both nodded in agreement.

"You can *charm* me anytime you want to, lassie," Liam

quipped, giving Rye a lusty wink. "I haven't felt this frisky in years."

"That's disgusting." Rye scrunched her nose as she looked away.

"It's good to know you're not just some silly girl looking for a necklace," Liam said, moving over to the worktable and picking up the mandala. "I have a hunch that we're gonna need this."

"So, you're still going to help us?" Colm asked, wondering if Liam would bail now that he knew Rye had charmed him.

"Sure, I'm interested to see where all this goes," Liam replied. "The Whiskered Stranger, the Lady, and now the Raven and the Dove… It's too much to pass up on, and seeing as I'm recently retired, I've got the time."

Colm stepped closer, taking the mandala from him. "I'm glad you're coming, but if it's all the same to you, I've got a lot of money in this, and I'd rather hold onto it myself." Picking up his dice from the table, he noticed it now had a subtle grey tone to it.

"You're growing more attached to it," Liam said matter-of-factly.

"What do you mean?"

"The more you use it, the darker it'll get. I've seen too many Gamblers succumb to the call. Avarice, power, revenge—those are all powerful motives, even without the dice. But with it, for most, they're irresistible. Once it turns black, then it's game over," Liam said emphatically.

"I can't keep it," Colm said softly, the realization firmly entrenched now.

"Well, then there's only one thing to do," Liam said, patting Colm on the back. "Let's go find us the Lady."

"*After* we get my necklace," Rye added, and with a final glance at a now sleeping Oliver, they all filed out of the chateau, closing the door behind them.

14

535 OAKVALE LANE

THEY TURNED the corner onto Oakvale Lane, the car crawling along as Colm got his bearings.

"That's it," Colm said a moment later, pointing to a house down the lane with a tall Victorian lamppost by the curb.

"Stop the car here," Rye said in a calm but disconcerted voice as she leaned forward from the back seat.

"What is it?" Colm asked, turning to her.

"The black Rambler—that's their car," she said, pointing to a classic car parked by the lamppost.

The vintage vehicle immediately reminded Colm of his dad. He recalled going to car meets with him, seeing all the vintage corvettes, but the AMCs were the ones his dad always stopped to look at a bit longer than anything else. The Rambler was always a favorite, and even from this distance, Colm could see it was a mint-condition 1959 Nash-AMC Rambler coupe. Given their rarity, he hadn't ever actually seen one in person. The chrome bumpers glistened in the sunlight, highlighting a vanity license plate: RAVEN. The car was painted a custom matte black, shaded to look like it was flocked with feathers. "Whoa, that's nice!" he said in awe, his mind still aflutter with thoughts of the dingy car meets, not yet appreciating the danger it represented.

"We're not here for the car," Rye snapped. "We're here for my necklace."

"Right, sorry," Colm said. "What are they doing here? How could they have known?" But then the answer hit him even before Rye chimed in.

"Andrew," she said. "They must've gotten it out of him before…" Her words trailed off, but Colm understood, and like with his parents, he didn't want to talk about it. "This is not a good thing."

Liam turned to Rye. "I've suddenly got a bad feeling about joining you two."

"We have to get that necklace," Rye said matter-of-factly, as if there were no other option.

It surprised Colm to find himself nodding his head in agreement, even though the memory of Rye's bloodied face at the warehouse still haunted him. But these two women had murdered his uncle, and knowing that the police were likely to prove useless once again, the desire for some blood in payment was taking root in him.

"They'll most likely be in his office, or the living room. Both are on the far side of the house," Colm said, having been to Adam's house once before.

"Alright, let's go, but follow my lead." Rye turned to Liam and looked him in the eyes. "Got it?"

"Wouldn't it be better for me to keep the car ready?" Liam asked.

"He's got a point," Colm answered. "If we actually get it, we're gonna need to get away fast."

They had a brief conversation and decided Liam would wait in the car, but it needed to be closer. Rather than risking the ruckus of starting the beast up again, they put the car in neutral and pushed it up the street. A moment later, it coasted into place in front of 535 Oakvale Lane, behind the Rambler. Rye turned from the car, and Colm hesitated, looking back to Liam.

"Come on," Rye said, pulling on his arm as she crouched behind the camellia bushes in the front yard. Colm settled in next to her, surveying the house. "So, the far side?" she asked, motioning in that direction.

"Yeah," Colm answered. With that, Rye started to slip out from behind the camellias just as Colm caught the flash of a cream coat through the front window. Reflexively, he reached out, jerking Rye back. Not a second later, the woman turned, glancing out the window as they safely ducked behind the bushes once again. Rye turned to him, annoyed, but Colm spoke first, his heart racing.

"They're in the front room," he said. "Liora was at the window. She would've seen you for sure."

Rye nodded, leaning her head against his shoulder. He could see that the near misstep had shaken her. That would have been the end of the element of surprise, the end of getting the necklace back, and the end of God knew what else. They both took a deep breath. They'd never make it through the front yard without the distinct possibility of being seen, so Colm suggested they work their way around back and come at the room from the other direction.

"You lead," she said, nodding in agreement.

Crouching, they skirted their way behind the bushes as Colm glanced to the window to see that it was now empty. They carefully picked their way along the fence line, finally sprinting the last few yards to the side of the house, pressing themselves up against it. They paused, catching their breath and listening. Hearing nothing, they worked their way around the back of the house, staying hidden until they were crouching next to the living room window. It was cracked open, allowing some fresh air into the house, but more importantly, allowing the mumbled voices inside to drift out. The conversation was heated, as Colm had expected. He mostly heard Liora's warm, syrupy voice, but Ciara's raspy voice cut in here and there, as she was so fond of doing. Then a man's voice joined the fray, furious.

"That's Adam," Colm whispered back. But then he heard something more, and he risked a quick peek through the window. Rye grabbed him, pulling him back, but not before he got a chilling glimpse of the scene inside. It wasn't just Adam whom they'd caught. His wife and daughter were in the room too, gagged and tied to kitchen chairs. Their eyes were red with tears, their faces wrapped in fear, unlike Adam, who sat defiantly tied up to another chair.

Liora's voice sang out through the open window, "We were hoping to come to an agreeable arrangement for the purchase of the necklace."

"I already told you, I don't know what you're talking about. I haven't got your goddamned necklace!" Adam roared.

"Well, as we politely tried to tell you, we have information to the contrary. We understand you bought it from…" She removed a Rolodex card from her pocket, wincing in pain as the cream-colored sling holding her left arm in place pinched her shoulder, pressing into the fresh gunshot wound. The bullet hole and blood were gone, her coat somehow restored to its pristine state. But the wound still sat painfully beneath, a reminder of their close call at the Anvil. She finally righted the card in her hand and read the name aloud. "… from a certain Oliver Zane. You do know Oliver, correct?"

Something almost imperceptible flashed across Adam's face, but left as quickly as it arrived. Stiffening, he held the line. "I don't know what you're talking about." He glanced at his wife as tears ran down her face.

"Is it really worth putting your family at risk?" Liora asked. "I mean, look at them. Surely, they're worth more to you than a silly old necklace, and as we offered at the door, we would pay you handsomely for it. We're not trying to steal it from you."

Adam said nothing, sitting firm in the chair, not making eye contact.

True to form, Ciara stepped forward, growing tired of the banter, and sent the little rendezvous in an entirely different direction. With a smooth sweep of her hand, she slapped Adam's wife across the face, snapping her head back. A red handprint marked her face, and blood glistened at the edge of her mouth.

"Stop it! Just stop it!" Adam yelled. "You should know I tripped a silent alarm when you came in. The police will be here any moment. You still have time, so I suggest you leave!" he threatened.

Liora turned, stepping over to the window below which Colm and Rye were hiding, and they pressed firmly against the side of the house as they heard her footsteps approaching. She looked out into the distance before speaking. "Funny, I don't see the police. I certainly hope you're not trying to play games with us. But if you did call them, then perhaps we need to move things along a bit more quickly…" Turning to Ciara, she nodded, and in an instant, Ciara had an obsidian blade pressed to the young girl's throat.

"We have no time for this! Give us the necklace," Ciara demanded, pressing the blade harder. The girl leaned her head back, trying to distance herself from the blade, but it still drew a trickle of blood.

"God dammit! Stop, just stop! It's not here!" Adam insisted.

Before he even finished, Ciara was upon him, the hilt of her blade crashing into his skull as he reeled back, blood flowing freely from the wound. "That's for lying to us," she growled, her black hair sticking to the sweat on her face.

Adam turned his head to the front window. In the distance, the faint sound of sirens echoed down the valley. "Screw you! The police are coming," he announced, a snarky smile creasing his face.

"Hmmm, that is distressing for certain. But for you, right now, your time is running out," Liora said calmly.

"No, *your* time is running out," he spat, sitting up in his chair, emboldened by the sound of the sirens that were creeping closer by the moment.

"That is distinctly not how I see it," Liora said, motioning to Ciara before continuing. "You know, it would be terrible if the gas main to the house were to break. Fires can be most disruptive to human flesh, wouldn't you agree?" As she spoke, Ciara was already in the fireplace, fully opening the gas valve. Within seconds, the smell of rotten eggs filled the room, and Ciara was already down the hall, heading to the kitchen. They heard the range being pulled out and pipes being broken as the smell permeated everything.

Ciara returned, looking at Adam. "Are we still doing this?"

The sirens grew louder, but were still a good distance away.

"Fine. Untie us, and once we're outside, I'll tell you," Andrew muttered, fear finally creeping into his voice.

"Hmmm, yeah, given that you called the police and all, I don't like that offer. Sorry," Ciara said smoothly, pulling a lighter and pack of cigarettes from her pocket. She placed one in Adam's mouth, the rotten egg smell now soaking into their bones. She raised the lighter to the cigarette, about to strike the flint.

He turned his head, spitting the cigarette onto the floor.

"Are you fucking crazy?! You'll kill all of us—yourselves included!"

Colm leaned over to Rye, whispering, "We need to get the hell out of here! They're going to blow this whole place up!" He moved to leave, but Rye caught his arm, holding him close.

"No, they won't," she whispered back. "They're just working him to get the necklace."

Colm was growing nervous. Without thinking, he pulled the dice from his pocket.

Rye shook her head and closed her hand around his. "No, just let it play out. Be patient."

Begrudgingly, he slipped the dice back into his pocket and craned his head over the windowsill to see Ciara engaged with Adam.

"I'm willing to take that risk," Ciara said, pushing another cigarette into Adam's lips, once again raising the lighter.

He spit the cigarette out again. "I told you, it's not here! It's at the museum, in my office," he finally confessed, sweat beading on his forehead.

Colm pulled his head back, relaying the information to Rye.

Rye rose, taking Colm's arm. "Let's go. We can beat them there."

They moved cautiously to the corner of the house. Liam was still waiting in the car, bobbing his head obliviously as he tapped out a rhythm on the dashboard. Colm waved his hands, trying to get Liam's attention as Rye touched his shoulder, pointing to the Rambler.

"Let's get us a new ride. No car, no chase," she said with a diabolical smile.

Colm had to admit, it was genius. But he glanced back to the house, the ladies mere yards away.

"Don't worry," she added, "I know how to hot-wire a car. And if I can't, no problem, you can just slash the tires."

He nodded in agreement. Either way, the Rambler would be out of commission for Liora and Ciara.

Rye looked into Colm's eyes. "You ready?"

He nodded, flinging his backpack over his shoulders.

"Go!"

They dashed across the front yard. Colm headed to the Caddy, filling Liam in on the plan. Then he turned, looking nervously at Rye, expecting to see her pulling wires out from beneath the dashboard, like in the old movies. But instead, she had inserted a small device into the keyhole. She motioned to him, calling out, "I need your phone!"

He reached into his pocket and rushed over, handing it to her. She connected it to the device with a cord and pressed a button. The phone went blank momentarily, and then a barrage of numbers, letters, and symbols started flashing across the screen. The light on the device was blinking red, and then with a sharp beep, it blinked green. Something clicked inside, and she disconnected the phone, handing it back to him.

"Get in," she said, then turned to yell to Liam to meet them at the museum, and he gave a thumbs-up. The Caddy roared to life, closely followed by the deep, throaty growl of the Rambler. Rye slammed on the gas, spraying dirt and rocks across the hood of Liam's Caddy. As they all sped off down the street, Colm turned back to see a flash of cream bolt out of the front door before they turned the corner and went out of sight, happy to leave the two ladies behind.

15

HOT PURSUIT

LIORA'S CREAM trench coat spun in a wide circle as she turned from the front window, crying out in alarm, "It's Rye!"

Ciara turned to face her, confused, still holding the pack of cigarettes and the lighter.

"She's outside with some young guy, running toward the street!" Liora said, turning back to the window. She watched, mesmerized, as Rye made a beeline for the Rambler, glancing back to the window. Their eyes met briefly as Rye turned, jumping into the front seat. Liora watched the young man with her approach a Caddy parked behind the Rambler and exchange words with its quirky driver, who was wearing a bowler hat. She'd seen the driver before, but was having a hard time placing where. But the younger man with Rye she instantly recognized from the family photo at the pawnshop.

"It's Colm! He's with her," Liora announced, sounding surprised, but there was no doubt. It was definitely him—the one from the job they'd failed to finish years ago, something their employer was unaware of, because the two ladies always finished their jobs. All except for that one. They'd kept quiet about it ever since, not wanting to tarnish their flawless reputations, and they were never directly asked about it. She smiled. Fortune was shining upon them today; she'd always hoped this moment would present itself. It was a perfect opportunity to quietly remedy their previous oversight and maintain their reputation, but more importantly, to stop him from helping Rye.

"Perfect! A chance to kill two birds with one stone," Ciara said delightedly. "Get the necklace, and correct that little oversight." She stowed the cigarettes and lighter, reaching for her obsidian blades. Rising effortlessly, she pushed past Liora toward the front door.

However, what should have been a simple escape was anything but in the house of a museum curator. The room was cluttered beyond hope with every type of collectible, some entombed in oddly shaped curio cabinets stacked deep with trinkets and oddities, while others were lovingly placed on oversized tables protruding into the room in annoying ways. Moving through the house quickly would've been a challenge for a seasoned gymnast, and even though the ladies were extraordinary in their own right, exiting was proving a challenge even for them, especially with Liora's injury slowing her down.

Finally, at her wits' end, Ciara crashed through the curio cabinets, toppling them over. Leaping over tables, she smoothly scattered all the previously pristine collectible objects to the floor in a hodgepodge of pieces and parts. From behind, Adam objected loudly to the destruction and utter disregard for all the things he'd tediously curated over the years, but it did nothing to slow Ciara down.

By the time Ciara and Liora made it out the front door, both cars were speeding off down the street, the tacky gold Caddy following the Rambler.

"God dammit!" Ciara yelled in anger, slashing her blades

through the air as the rumble of the cars became distant, only to be replaced by police sirens pulling ever closer.

Liora finally arrived at Ciara's side, nudging her and pointing to the garage, where Merkel's Land Cruiser sat gleaming in the midday sun.

"I saw the keys on a hook by the door. I'll grab them." Ciara instantly spun on her heels, rushing back through the front door. She briefly glanced across the room at Adam and his family, the stench of rotten eggs so pervasive that it flowed out into the front yard through the door. The wife and her daughter had tipped their chairs over and were struggling against their bindings as they gasped for air.

Adam's eyes went to Ciara as she lifted the keys from the peg on the wall, and he yelled out, pleading with her to untie them. "You can take the damn car, just let us go!"

"No loose ends," Ciara said in a barely audible voice and turned, walking out the front door. She had no plans to leave any trail behind. Reaching into her pocket, she placed a cigarette in her mouth, lighting it. Then she turned, flicking the lit cigarette into the entryway, pausing for a moment to make sure the ember survived the fall. The red glow held steady, and she turned, sprinting toward Liora. Once upon her, she grabbed her arm, pulling her to the detached garage and stuffing them both into the Land Cruiser before the place blew.

There was a deafening *boom* as the house exploded, lifting the car off the ground and shattering all its windows. The house was engulfed in a raging inferno, while the Land Cruiser remained steadfastly parked in the garage.

Ciara brushed the glass off herself and flipped through the keys. "Shit!" She tossed the keys on the dashboard.

Liora turned to her, covered in glass while rubbing her ears, trying to get the ringing to stop. "What?"

"Wrong keys," Ciara said, shrugging her shoulders.

They both jumped out of the car, stepping through the glass that covered the garage floor. The sirens were virtually upon them now.

"Perfect, just perfect! You know, you didn't have to blow up the house," Liora admonished, wincing again as she readjusted the sling on her arm.

"No witnesses, no loose ends, per the boss's orders. Plus, they knew too much, and he was being a petulant little prick," Ciara grumbled.

"Well, that's for sure, but now you've now gotten the attention of the entire neighborhood. A little discretion would—" Liora stopped mid-sentence, looking at the street, where the neighbors were congregating, gaping at the blazing house. "You're a genius!" Liora squealed.

"I am?" Ciara asked, confused by Liora's sudden change of heart.

"Yes, pure genius! With all these people, we can just blend in. Let's go."

They nonchalantly stood in the driveway, gazing upon the inferno with the others, seemingly distraught. The first fire truck rolled up, along with two police cruisers that had finally made their way here. With the smell of rotten eggs still heavy in the air, a burly firefighter jumped out of the passenger side, ushering all the lookie-loos further away from the blaze. A second firefighter jumped out, grabbing a large wrench from the truck, and sprinted to the corner of the house, turning the gas off. As he headed back to the truck, a second and third fire truck rolled up, and now firefighters were streaming into the property.

Liora and Ciara pranced down the short driveway to the sidewalk, joining the others looking on from the street. Once at a safe distance, Liora turned to Ciara, speaking loudly over the din of the three fire trucks parked at the curb. "Rye must've overheard our conversation. We need to get to the museum, and fast, or we're back to square one with this whole thing, and he will *not* be happy."

Ciara nodded, and without a word, she climbed into one of the fire trucks left idling at the curb. Moments later, the passenger door opened, and her head emerged. "Get in!"

"Hey, get the hell out of that truck!" yelled one of the firefighters from the front yard, lumbering towards them.

"Hurry up, already!" Ciara snapped, her head disappearing back into the truck as she put it in gear, and it lurched forward. Liora took another look at the firefighter heading her way, and letting out a sigh, she scaled up the truck into the passenger seat, pulling the door closed behind her.

"So much for discretion," she muttered, giving Ciara a cross look as the truck crawled forward, picking up some speed.

Before they'd even made it down the street, the firefighter leaped onto the step outside the passenger door, grabbing hold of the handle. Ciara glanced over, pressing the gas pedal to the floor as she swerved wildly to the right, smashing the side of the truck into a large cypress tree, crushing him. Liora shrunk back from the door as Ciara righted the truck onto Oakvale Lane.

Looking out the window, Liora saw the firefighter's hand still clutching the door handle. She opened the door, giving it a firm shake, but he didn't let go, so she placed the toe of her boot on the man's body, pushing him into the street. "Nice," she said, her voice thick with sarcasm as she imagined this little episode on the front cover of the local newspaper. "He will not be happy with all this attention."

"Oh well, sometimes you have to get a little dirty to get the job done," Ciara said with a grin.

"Unless, of course, none of it had to happen—which was

distinctly the case here," Liora snapped, growing more uncomfortable with her partner's impulsive tactics.

"He'll understand—especially when he has the necklace in his hands," Ciara assured her.

"I can only hope you're right."

As if on cue, Liora's phone rang. She fished for it with her good hand while her body twisted side to side as Ciara weaved and dodged her way through traffic, ever so slowly making their way to the museum. Finally, phone in hand, Liora shot Ciara a concerned look. Reaching forward, she turned off the radio, leaving only the noise of the truck rumbling down the street.

"It's him," Liora said curtly, clearing her throat and taking the call. The conversation was a series of stops and starts, with Liora mostly listening. "Hello. ... Oh, yes, hello... I'm sorry. ... Yes. ... No. ... No, we haven't given up. We've just gotten back on the trail and are heading out to get the necklace now." Liora paused, turning to Ciara, her brows raised. "Yes, it's at the museum, in the curator's-- ... No, we won't let you down." There was another long pause as Liora held her gaze on Ciara, growing tired of the tongue-lashing she was receiving from their employer. "Understood. ... No, we've got this. It'll be in our hands before the sun goes down, and we'll eliminate anyone who gets in the way."

Ciara nodded, slapping her hand on the steering wheel as a grim smile spread across her face.

16

LOUVRE DE MONTEREY

THE RAMBLER PULLED to a stop at the curb next to an understated wooden sign reading LOUVRE DE MONTEREY in a simple block typeface. The museum behind it, however, was noticeably different and towered above the surrounding park. It was easily the largest building in town, one of the few with three floors, designed with a curious mixture of Gothic and mid-century modern architecture. The museum itself would not have been here if not for the ostentatiousness of its original benefactor, Harvey John Dingleberry, a wealthy socialite of Monterey's distant past, desperate for an enduring monument to his life. During his final years, he had committed to building this behemoth and attaching his name to it.

For the first couple of decades, the museum proudly bore his name, but over time, locals came to simply call it "the Dingleberry," which did not sit well with the museum's board. Years later, when the museum needed renovations, the city council seized on the opportunity and introduced a ballot measure to rename it. Ready to cut the Dingleberry loose, people voted overwhelmingly in favor of the measure.

But interestingly, there had been a resurgence of nostalgia running through town, and some folks were now calling to restore its original name, which had resulted in a wave of T-shirts and bumper stickers declaring, RESTORE MONTEREY'S DINGLEBERRY. Colm himself had one of the T-shirts, which he'd picked up at a meeting he attended with Tabitha. But at the end of the day, he couldn't have cared less about what it was called——especially now. He still thought the T-shirt was funny though.

Colm and Rye stood on the sidewalk as Liam pulled into the space in front of them, bringing the Caddy to a stop. A moment later, he stepped from the car, reaching for his cane in the back seat.

Rye looked at Liam. "Wait here. It'll be easier for two of us to get in and out."

"You'll get no argument from me," Liam said, leaning back and taking his pipe from his pocket.

"We need to keep moving," Rye said to Colm as she turned and briskly walked away, following the winding path to the museum through the park.

Catching up, Colm recalled something from the warehouse. "Why did those ladies call you 'magpie'?"

She turned to him with a sour face. "It's just a silly nickname, because I have a knack for finding things that are lost. What about you? What's the story with that ring?" she said, motioning to Colm's hand.

"It was my mother's. I just keep it as a reminder," Colm said, looking away, closing his fist to hide it.

"Right. Well, may I borrow it? I have an idea," Rye said as they climbed the stairs to the museum.

Colm glanced at her curiously before taking the ring off and handing it to her.

They pushed on the pretentiously oversized glass-and-bronze filigreed doors marking the entrance to Mr. Dingleberry's creation. Surrounding the arched doors, the glass-and-bronze work continued outward, creating a sun motif that covered the entirety of the building's facade. The doors floated inward, and as Colm stepped inside, he was awestruck by the cavernous room, leaving him feeling rather insignificant. Of course, that was the intent of Mr. Dingleberry's design, and Colm had to admit that it might have succeeded, if not for the hastily added security barriers, metal detectors, and related personnel milling about.

"Let's do this," Rye said, sliding the ring onto her left hand, the tip of the heart facing out. She stepped forward, bantering with the two security guards by the metal detector. Colm paused, watching her as the reality of what they were about to do hit him. They weren't just going to *ask* for her necklace back; they were going to steal it. This could have dire real-world consequences for him—consequences he hadn't anticipated when she'd shown up at the pawnshop earlier. He lowered his head, seeing the hilt of the Moonblade peeking out of his backpack. *Great—armed robbery,* he thought, then looked up to see her motioning for him to join her. With a resigned sigh, he zipped up his backpack and joined Rye at the security gate as the guard motioned for her to go through.

Rye turned as the guard gestured for him to proceed too. Colm hesitated as beads of sweat gathered on his forehead. He could feel the weight of the blade in his backpack and wondered if the Moonblade would trip the metal detector.

"Come on, sweetie, it's just a metal detector," Rye said, turning to the guard and speaking in a motherly tone. "He always gets nervous about these things. You should see him at the airport." She again motioned for him to come through, her eyes betraying the calmness in her voice.

Taking a step forward, he partially closed his eyes, waiting for the blare of an alarm that never came.

The guard smiled at Rye, pointing across the atrium. "Elevator's that way. The curator's office is on the third floor. Best of luck, you two. This is a great venue."

"Venue?" Colm asked, confused.

She furrowed her brow, looking at him sternly as she strained to maintain the sweet tone. "Come on, honey, the curator's waiting to discuss our wedding plans with us."

Colm stood in shock at the intimate nature of her ruse, snapping out of it as he felt Rye's arm interlock with his, guiding him across the atrium.

"That was unexpected," Colm said, stating the obvious.

"Right, I know. Sorry, it just popped into my head when I saw your mother's ring. Anyway, doesn't matter now," she said, dropping his arm as they walked to the elevator bank and she pressed the button.

"So, how the hell are we getting into his office?" Colm asked.

"I don't know. It's a work in progress."

The elevator door opened, and they both stepped in, surprised to see it was a glass elevator. Colm watched as they slowly ascended, revealing the true grandeur of the atrium's design and how it was integrated with the bronzed image of the sun on the outside of the building, allowing the day's light to flood in. The bell dinged, and the elevator shook to a stop at the second floor. Colm turned to see a janitor standing at the door, a mess of keys jangling about his belt, and the man paused, seeing that the elevator was occupied.

"You folks go on, I'll catch it on the way down," he said, smiling and stepping back as Colm nudged Rye, directing her attention to the keys.

"No, that's silly," Rye said, returning the smile.

Colm motioned for him to join them, holding the door to keep it from closing. With a warm smile, the man thanked them and stepped into the elevator, rolling a trash can behind him.

"Appreciate it, folks. No service elevators here, so I have to use this one. Sometimes I have to wait fifteen or twenty minutes, but I don't mind; I'm still getting paid."

Rye glanced at his name tag. "No problem, Samuel. There's more than enough room for all of us." She smiled and touched the man's arm, talking in that soft, syrupy voice. "A little bird told me you're going to let us into the curator's office," she said, removing her hand as Samuel smiled back.

"Sure, ma'am, I can do that for you. Been workin' here for over ten years now, so I got keys for everything," he said, jangling his keys as the door opened on the third floor and he pushed his trash can out, motioning to them. "This way, folks."

They skirted a railing overlooking the atrium, then turned and headed past a few exhibits. People were bustling about, and there was a group of school children on a tour. As they wormed their way through the group, Colm overheard the chaperone talking about the gods of the old world and the role of ancient prophecies. Rye and Samuel moved along, but Colm paused, taking a step closer, looking over the shoulder of one of the children's grandparents. The chaperone was pointing to various artifacts in a glass display case, but as the gaggle of children moved on, the old man remained. He turned, noticing Colm, and stepped aside, making room for him.

"Sorry, don't mean to dominate the exhibit," he said with a chuckle.

"Yeah, no problem. Thanks," Colm said, smiling back as he stepped forward for a better look.

A few paces away, Colm heard Samuel tell Rye that the office was just ahead, and he glanced over to see it nestled in a small alcove on the far side of the room. Rye turned to catch his eye, and Colm raised a finger, motioning that he'd be there in a minute. Rye shrugged her shoulders with an impatient look and rushed to follow the rolling trash can.

Colm turned back to the display, surprised to see several mandalas of different shapes and sizes, some etched with designs, others with a bizarre script. There were openings for the "keys" that Oliver had spoken of in various shapes, from squares to diamonds to stars. Alongside the mandalas, various keys were arranged, each cast in antique gold, bearing similar etchings. The information cards on the display referred to the artifacts as *ancient auguring tools used to predict the future; rumored to be the cause of many ancient wars and plagues.* But there was no mention of the Seer Haesel or her prophecies.

Glancing to his left, he saw that the old man was holding a tarnished brass handbell, intently looking back and forth from it to the items on display. Intrigued, Colm risked a closer peek, seeing that the bell was adorned with strange engravings and what looked to be some sort of script. The old man turned to look at Colm, but before their eyes met, Colm's eyes flashed across the room to Rye. She was hovering over Samuel as he methodically moved along the large key ring, trying to fit each key in before moving to the next. Rye turned, catching Colm's eye, the impatience clear on her face as she briskly called out to him, motioning for him to come over.

He rushed across the room to join Rye as Samuel continued his struggle with the keys. What they'd thought was a good idea was quickly fading, even as Rye continued to shower him with encouragement. Colm turned, furtively scanning the area for the ladies, knowing it wouldn't be long before they arrived. They needed to get the necklace and get the hell out of here. Colm reached into his pocket, thinking of the dice just as Samuel dropped his key ring to the floor, totally losing his place.

Stifling a curse, Colm pulled his dice out, pausing. "Think," he whispered to himself. Why was he so keen on helping Rye, anyway? He couldn't help but wonder if the charm she'd used on him was warping his thoughts, or maybe it was just the dice taking hold of him. He shook his head, not convinced that either was the case. It felt *right* to help her, and that was enough for him. It was settled: he'd roll once, but put it away if it was an odd. He looked at Samuel one last time, but the key was no closer to being found.

"I wish Samuel would find the right key," he whispered, shaking the dice. But just as he was about to roll, a wrinkled hand closed over his, stopping him. Colm turned to see the old grandpa from the exhibit looking at him with soft brown eyes.

"Hold, brother," the man said in a gentle voice, opening his other hand to reveal a dice as black as the moonless midnight sky, marked with burnt henna numbers. "Sometimes, rather than rolling the dice, you just need to let things work themselves out."

Laughter rang out in the background. "Ah, this is it," Samuel announced, and Colm heard the door unlock.

"See? Things can work out, even when you don't roll," the grandpa said, chuckling as he answered the question written all over Colm's face. "Yes, I'm a Gambler, like you. But I've learned many things since getting this dice—mostly the hard way. Believe me, I know it's difficult to ignore its call, but you must learn, or you'll end up like me—old and wrinkled, or maybe even dead." The man released Colm's hand with an understanding look, but Colm was too shaken to respond, since he'd essentially confirmed what Rye had been telling him.

Looking over the man's shoulder, Colm saw Samuel with a boyish grin on his face, fast asleep in a chair.

Rye turned, her eyes trained on the newcomer, clearly unhappy. "Who's the old guy?" she asked, moving toward the open door to the curator's office.

"He's a Gambler, like me," Colm answered. "He was over by the exhibit. They have some mandalas like the one Noah sold me!" he said excitedly, pointing across the room.

The man turned to Colm with a curious look, a wry smile cracking his lips. "Interesting. Perhaps we seek the same things, and fate has brought us together."

Rye laughed, mocking his sentiment. "I doubt that." Her voice was sharp, leaving no room for ambiguity. She had no trust for this newcomer, which was abundantly clear as she glared daggers at Colm. "Whatever! I don't have time for this. Just stay out of my way." With that, she disappeared into the curator's office, and Colm held his position outside the door, watching for the ladies.

"What are we watching for?" the man asked as he crouched next to Colm.

"Two ladies. One dresses in all black, with beady black eyes, and she looks scary. The other dresses in cream, like Mary Poppins, only she's anything but," Colm answered. The hair on his arms prickled just at the thought of them. He stole a glance back at Rye to see her rifling through cabinets, spilling their contents haphazardly.

Suddenly, from the direction of the atrium came an explosive sound of shattering glass and metal scraping metal. The whole museum trembled, and Colm braced himself against the wall. He looked back at Rye, who stood frozen in a wide stance, looking wildly toward the source of the noise. There could be no mistaking what it was.

"Just find it! I'll keep watch," Colm called to Rye, then turned to the old man. "Go help her. She's looking for a necklace." He quickly described it, and the man nodded, heading in to join Rye in the search.

Turning back, Colm saw a security guard ushering patrons down the back staircase. A moment later, something blared across the walkie-talkie at his shoulder, and he headed down the hallway across the room that led to the elevator. He paused at the end of the hall, raising his hands and shuffling backwards. Colm couldn't hear what was being said, but judging from the guard's posture, it was obviously serious. Seconds later, a cream trench coat flashed around the corner, followed by her dark companion.

"Shit!" Colm cursed under his breath.

The next thing he knew, Liam was at his side, leaning on his blackened cane, slightly out of breath.

"What the…? How did you get here?" Colm asked.

"No time for questions. Get in the office and find that necklace! I'll hold them off as long as I can." Liam spun the cane in his hand, stretching his neck from side to side. Colm objected, but Liam cut him off with a wink. "Don't worry, lad. I've got a few tricks of my own."

Colm retreated, heading into the office as Liam took a few steps forward. The lone guard continued his posturing, but was retreating step by step, periodically looking over his shoulder for backup. Finally, the guard stopped, holding his position, but before he could react, Ciara flashed forward, sweeping her leg behind him, grabbing him by the collar of his shirt, and pulling him backwards. He let out a yelp as he tumbled over her leg. She drove the back of his head squarely into the floor, the thud echoing through the room. The few patrons that remained were now screaming and fleeing for the stairs, adding to the mayhem as the guard lay motionless in a growing pool of blood. Ciara smirked, looking across the room to see Liam standing in front of the curator's office. A moment later, Liora joined her. The two ladies strolled leisurely across the room, like they were window shopping on Main Street, stopping a few yards short of Liam.

"This is not your battle, leprechaun," Liora said with quiet confidence.

"That's right, it's not. But friends take care of friends," he said, leaning heavily on his cane, positioning it in front of him.

"I'm up for a little appetizer," Ciara said, letting out a cackle, her blades drawn as she flashed toward Liam. He disappeared and reappeared just feet away to send his cane crashing down on her back, dropping her to the floor. As she tumbled to a stop, Liam once again flashed away, only to reappear by Liora, delivering a jab to her injured shoulder, reopening the wound. She doubled over in pain, kneeling above Ciara.

In an instant, Ciara rose, now more cautious, but brimming with venom. "You can't do that forever, greenie, so make it good while you can!"

"Maybe I can't, but maybe I can," he said with a sneer. "You want to push your luck with me, little lady?"

She leapt toward him, blades slashing furiously. Liam's cane was up for the onslaught, meeting her movements stroke by stoke, his deftness belying his age. The exhibit hall rang with the sound of her blades striking the unbending strength of his cane. She channeled her frustration into a flurry of strikes as Liam flashed away again, appearing behind her with a snicker.

"Over here, lassie!" he called mockingly, and she turned with a ruthless glare.

In the office, Colm looked over the chaos. Chests of drawers were overturned, their contents strewn across the floor. Rye and the old Gambler were in the process of ransacking the cabinets lining the walls. Colm glanced back to see the ladies in a furious battle with Liam, but two against one was not good odds. They needed to find the necklace, now—and he was the only one who could make that happen.

He turned his back to Rye, reaching into his pocket once again. At this point, using the dice seemed like a means of self-preservation, and the loss of years meant nothing if he was about to end up dead at the hands of Ciara. Caressing the dice with his fingers, he quietly made a wish, rolling it on the curator's desk. It settled on two X's.

Almost instantaneously, the old Gambler pulled a book from the shelf, opening it to reveal a necklace.

"Is this it?" he asked, holding it toward Rye as Colm turned to them.

A smile of relief spread across her face as she caught sight of it. "That's it!"

The old Gambler walked over, placing it around her neck. The charm hung high on her chest, resting against her worn T-shirt, and Colm had to admit that it was just her style. It had the look of petrified wood, casting an aura about her that he'd not noticed before. They rushed to join Colm at the door, and Rye stepped forward to give him a hug. As she rested her head on his shoulder, she glanced down to see the dice on the desk. She breathed a deep sigh, and her voice quivered as she spoke.

"You rolled?"

"I know, I know, you told me not to use it for you. But we need to get out of here. It was the only way—"

"Stop," she interrupted him as she leaned back, looking into his eyes. "Thank you, Colm. I can't tell you what this means to me," she said, pressing her hand against her charm.

"You're welcome." He wanted to say more, but he bit his tongue. For now, he didn't want to let her go.

"But you're right, we need to get out of here," she said, stepping away.

Colm nodded in agreement, realizing that this was her

life: running, hiding, being found, and running, over and over again.

They joined the old Gambler at the door, looking out to see Liam still facing off with Ciara, brandishing his cane like a sword. Liam glanced at Rye, losing his concentration just long enough for Liora to surprise him from behind, knocking the cane from his hand. She locked her arm around his neck, wincing in pain as she held him tightly against her injured shoulder.

"Not so fast," he said, blinking away, causing her to lurch forward into empty air. He reappeared a few yards short of Colm, falling to his knee and breathing heavily as he raised his eyes to meet Colm's.

"I can't hold them off much longer. You need to run," he said in a labored voice, then rose with a resigned look and turned back to them, flexing his hand slightly. His cane slid across the floor, snapping back into his hand with a satisfying thud. "Let's do this!" he cried, his eyes fixed on Liora and Ciara, positioning himself between them and the stairs.

"Step aside, greenie, and we'll let you go. It's *them* we want," Liora said in a steady voice.

"Not gonna happen." Liam tapped his cane on the floor in front of him, leaning on it heavily.

Ciara took a step forward, looking past Liam. "Hello, *Colm*, long time no see." Her beady black eyes settled on him, sending shivers up his spine.

Colm hesitated as Rye took his hand, trying to lead him toward the stairs, but he didn't budge. *How does she know my name?*

Seeing his confusion, Ciara continued, "Yes, I know you—and now we have our chance to kill two little birdies with one stone." Reaching into her pocket, she took out the gold coin they'd purchased from Andrew. "I've got a deal for you.

How about heads, you die, or tails, you die?" She cackled, the coin flipping through the air.

Rye frantically turned back to Colm, squeezing his hand so hard it hurt, her pupils dilating as she pleaded with him. "Colm, we need to go, *now!*"

Colm stepped closer, speaking quietly. "We can't leave Liam—"

"What is he doing?" Rye asked.

Colm turned, following her gaze to see the old Gambler standing beside Liam, holding up a set of charcoal-colored stones in the palm of his hand. Ciara's coin flipped upward as the old Gambler whispered something indiscernible, almost as if he were speaking to the stones, and softly blew on them.

The result was immediate. Across the room, the ladies crumpled to the floor as if all their bones had suddenly left their bodies, and a moment later, the gold coin clattered to the floor next to Ciara, momentarily spinning on its side until settling.

Colm looked to Rye and gave her hand a reassuring squeeze, seeing her eyes relax. She nodded, letting go of his hand as they turned and raced over to Liam. Colm arrived first, bracing Liam as he teetered, exhausted from the fight. Leaning heavily on Colm, Liam turned to look at the old Gambler as he closed his hand over the stones, looking back to see that they were all staring at him.

"What the hell was that?" Liam asked, his eyes narrowing.

"Just a little something I was given," he said, his eyes turning downward and his shoulders slumped as he stowed the stones in his pocket. "It only works once, and I don't know for how long, so we'd better go."

Colm couldn't help but notice Rye and Liam exchanging a worried glance before her eyes fixed upon the old Gambler once again. Liam was about to speak, but Colm stopped him.

"He's right," he said. "We need to get the hell out of here. There's no time for this now."

They all turned to Colm, nodding. The questions would come later. They moved in lockstep toward the back stairs, but just as they were about to descend, Colm pulled up short, the sound of the coin hitting the floor echoing in his mind. He recalled the earlier discussion about the mandalas and the keys, and he couldn't help but think that there must have been a reason the ladies were looking for *that* coin.

"I'm going back for the coin," Colm said, spinning back. Rye reached out, trying to grab his arm, but he was already out of reach.

Ciara lay crumpled on the floor, the coin beside her. Colm slid in like he was stealing third base and reached out, snatching up the coin as Ciara's eyes popped open. She was still mostly catatonic, but alert enough that her hand shot out, concealing a small blade that cut deeply into the back of Colm's hand. He yelled out, covering the open wound with his free hand as Ciara dropped the blade, grasping Colm's ankle, holding him in place with the deadweight of her body.

"You miss your parents, Colm?" she asked with a sneer, her beady eyes locked on him. "We should've finished you when we finished them. We never like to leave jobs undone, so we're back for you."

Colm froze, anger surging through him. What she was saying made no sense. But there was no time for this now, and he wriggled, trying to get free. She held a tight grip on his ankle, but the rest of her body remained useless. Whatever the old Gambler had done to them, it was still affecting her.

"You can't run forever. We'll find you, just like we did your sniveling parents."

Their eyes locked. In the background, Colm noticed Liora's motionless cream trench coat—and then it hit him.

There had been two of them that night when his parents were murdered. He didn't understand it at all. Glancing back at the others, he saw that Rye was making her way back to him. That wasn't how it was supposed to work; he was supposed to help her, not the other way around.

His brow furrowed, rage welling up from deep inside, and he pulled the knee of his free leg up to his chest. "Screw you, you crazy bitch!" he cried, thrusting the heel of his boot squarely into Ciara's face with a satisfying crunch.

Blood trickled from her nose, and her eyes flicked shut. Her hand went limp, and he rose, sprinting to meet Rye halfway across the room. She tore his sleeve from his shirt, quickly wrapping it around the wound, and they ran back to the others, who were already heading down the stairs.

Reaching the atrium, they saw the cause of the earlier commotion. A fire engine had crashed through the front doors and now sat in the atrium, its lights still garishly flashing. Police cars were rolling up outside, adding to the pandemonium. They slowed their pace, and Colm concealed his bloody hand in the pocket of his jacket, not wanting to draw any attention.

The officers in the atrium were ushering people out of the fire exits, and the group was quickly out of the museum. Liam's cane clicked heavily along the sidewalk through the park as he jingled his keys, unlocking the car doors. He sat heavily in the driver's seat, his little Hawaiian girl furiously dancing away on the dashboard.

Colm grabbed Rye's arm, holding her back, speaking in a subdued tone. "It was them. I don't know why, but Liora and Ciara killed my parents."

17

TIME TO FLY

LIORA AWOKE TO THE COLD, smooth floor of the museum pressing against her cheek. The last thing she remembered was an old man stepping up next to the leprechaun, holding something in his hand. Ciara muttered something behind her, and Liora rolled over to see her holding a blood-soaked handkerchief to her nose. A moment later, she made a swift movement that was followed by a wet crunching sound.

"That little bastard is gonna pay for this," Ciara vowed, pressing the handkerchief to her nose as she rose to her knees, looking at Liora.

Liora stood, adjusting her sunglasses and smoothing out the creases that had formed in her coat when she'd fallen unexpectedly. She rubbed the bump swelling up under her bleach-blonde hair, checking for blood, but her hand came away clean. "What the hell was that?" Liora asked as Ciara finally rose to her feet. "And what happened to your face?"

"Colm's foot happened to my face—and he took the coin," she muttered, picking up her blades from the floor. "My body was frozen or something, but I was still able to grab him for a moment. That is, until he booted me in the face."

She pressed the handkerchief to her nose to stop the bleeding.

"Who was the old guy? Did he do that to us?" Liora asked, bewildered.

"Whatever it was, it was some pretty powerful stuff to do that to *us*," Ciara answered.

Liora nodded. She could still feel the old man's magic ensconced in her bones, and although it was left unspoken, they both knew he was a dead man if they ever caught up with him again.

The sound of sirens and bustling people echoed from the hallway, catching their attention. They turned, moving past the pool of blood surrounding the fallen guard, stopping at the railing overlooking the atrium. The fire truck had proven to be a perfect distraction and allowed them easy entry to the curator's office, but just a minute too late. The lights of the fire truck spiraled around the atrium, joined by the flashing lights of half a dozen police cars outside. Pulling in front of the police cars, a big black van with the letters SWAT stenciled on the side took up its position. The back door of the van opened wide, and a stream of officers in tactical black gear scurried out. They dashed into the museum, spreading out, weapons in hand. A moment later, Ciara caught sight of an officer in plain clothes pointing up to them, and the surrounding officers turned their attention upwards, quickly speaking into radios pinned to their shoulders.

The ladies stepped back from the balcony, disappearing from sight.

"I'll see you out front," Liora said.

Ciara nodded as Liora shed the sling from her arm. They simultaneously raised their arms, sweeping upwards into the air and back down, but Liora was having a difficult time with the movement.

Ciara glanced at her nervously before speaking in a firm voice. "You just have to suck it up. You can do it."

Liora nodded, wincing as she pressed on, sweeping her arm up and down, joining Ciara. Their bodies became enveloped in a misty haze as they ran forward. The sounds of flapping wings rippled through the air and echoed off the walls of the hallway. Wings outstretched, they flew over the railing and through the open air of the atrium. They glided toward the opening made by the fire truck, but the pain was overwhelming, and the dove squawked, losing too much altitude too quickly. Just as she was about to crash into the fire truck, the black raven swooped in, grasping the dove in its talons and flying them both out of the museum. A few officers pointed to the two birds, momentarily watching in amazement, but just as quickly, they turned their attention back to the matter at hand on the third floor of the museum. The raven flew past the police cars before the mist returned and they morphed back into human form, standing on the stairs of the museum as if what they'd just done were perfectly ordinary.

"Thanks," Liora said to Ciara. "But damn, I hate that feeling. I always come back with an appetite for worms." She shook her arms, putting her injured one back into its sling.

"I don't know," Ciara said, "I kind of enjoy it. Plus, it certainly made that much easier, and less deadly for them."

Liora shrugged, conceding the last point as they descended the stairs.

"Still, that didn't go as expected," Ciara said flatly.

"No, most certainly not."

"He's not gonna be happy."

"Nope, that's for sure," Liora agreed. "And did you say they took the coin too?"

"Yep," Ciara said with a scowl.

"Yeah, he's really not going to be happy."

"Seems like we're back at square one on this whole thing," Ciara said, her eyes already turning a light tinge of black from the kick Colm had delivered to her face.

"Right. No coin, no necklace, no Rye, and now it looks like she's got some legit help too," Liora said, rubbing the back of her head again.

"Dammit!" Ciara motioned off to the right, and Liora turned to look.

All they could do was watch as the golden Caddy from the Merkels' house sped away down the street, turning a corner and heading out of sight.

In the grass nearby, a little girl was walking a cute little black lab puppy. "Good girl, Blackie." "Slow down, Blackie," the little girl said repeatedly.

Ciara turned from the Caddy, pounding her foot into Blackie's side as the dog yelped. The little girl started crying and ran across the park, Blackie limping behind her.

"Jesus, Ciara, really?" Liora snapped, rolling her eyes.

Ciara turned to Liora, but her eyes were focused on something in the distance. "Well, at least that's some good news, finally."

Liora turned to see the black Rambler sitting at the curb. It was too late to chase the Caddy, but at least they had a ride out of here, because within a few minutes, word would be out that they were no longer in the museum. The search would then spread outward, and with Ciara's latest outburst, they would likely find a little girl crying about a lady in black who had just kicked her dog.

The ladies casually walked to the Rambler. "I'm hungry," Ciara said. "Let's get a bite to eat before we call him and break the news."

"Sounds good. Tikka Masala?"

"Yeah, Tikka Masala."

They both climbed into the Rambler, and Ciara fired up

the engine. As the car moved away from the excitement of the museum, Ciara turned to Liora. "What was the name of that tight little package who came looking for Colm at the Anvil?"

"Tabitha."

"Maybe we can salvage something yet."

"Maybe," Liora agreed.

18

FATEFUL FRIENDS

"WHAT?" Rye said, her eyes puzzling over what he'd told her.

"She said it was them who killed my parents," Colm said, agitated.

"She's just messing with you. That's what she does," Rye said dismissively.

Colm pressed on. "She said something about a job, and that they should've killed me too."

"Job? Why..." Rye hesitated. "It doesn't make sense. How would they even know who you are? You're a nobody."

"Ouch," Colm said, leaning back.

"Stop it, I didn't mean it like that. It's just, why you?" she asked, eying him curiously.

Colm shrugged his shoulders. "I have no clue, but we need to get out of here. My uncle has an Airbnb down on the beach. It isn't far away. We can head there and regroup," Colm said, turning to get in the car, but Rye tugged his arm.

"So, you don't think it's weird that another Gambler showed up out of the blue to help us, right when we needed it?" she whispered.

"I don't know. Maybe it's fate," Colm offered.

She rolled her eyes. "I don't like this. It's just too damn convenient. He could be dangerous."

"You might be right, but let's just see where it goes. First sign of trouble, we'll dump him," Colm whispered back.

She let out a sigh, nodding as her voice lowered. "Okay, but you need to keep my secret." Her eyes went to the wound on her arm.

Colm nodded, and they turned, joining the others in the car, Colm settling in the back seat with the old Gambler. Leaning forward, he gave Liam directions to the beach house, and they sped away.

Sitting back, the old Gambler introduced himself as Jake Morar. Their conversation quickly turned to their experiences with their dice, and to his horror, Colm learned that despite his weathered appearance, Jake had been born only five years before him.

"You either become a sinner or a saint. That's what my mom would say," Jake said, peering off as he reached into his coat, pulling out a tarnished silver flask adorned with a skull-and-rose motif. Through the embedded crystal eyes of the skull, an electric-green liquid peeked out. Twisting the stopper, he took a small swig, wincing as it went down. "I searched for ways to quiet its call to me. I even tried Gamblers Anonymous. Why not? You know," he said, laughing, "it worked for a while, but the pull of the dice was too much. I did learn one important thing from that though, which is that all things eventually break. So, I know I'm on borrowed time. But for now, this works for me," he said, lifting the flask and taking another swig. "It gives me the fortitude to hold it back."

Colm looked upon Jake. *Will this be me? Is this what I have to look forward to? What have I done? Is there a way out of this, or did I sell my soul the moment I picked up that dice?* He recalled his conversations with Liam and Rye. There was a way out, but he had to find this Lady they spoke of. On the positive side, Rye was committed to helping him find this Lady, and Liam had worked for her until recently. Still, Colm was wary of Liam, and it wasn't lost on him that despite knowing what would happen, Liam had still crafted the dice for him. *Why did Liam make the dice for me in the first place if he's now so ready to help me get rid of it?* Colm had many questions, but for now it seemed everyone was intent on helping him get rid of his dice, and that calmed him. He just needed to listen to Rye and control himself, at least until he could give the dice to the Lady. As for Jake, he'd turned to drinking the green liquid to stymie the call of the dice, and perhaps Colm would get there too, but for now he was emboldened by the idea of finding the Lady before things got to that point.

The Caddy pulled to a stop outside the beach house underneath a grove of wind-blown cypress trees. Colm hopped out of the car, keys in hand, unlocking the front door. The others followed at a slower pace, marveling at the stunning meeting of sea and stone as the ocean disappeared over the horizon. The house itself was reminiscent of the English countryside, sporting walls made of sturdy cobblestones and tall, pitched roofs that stood proudly in the afternoon sun.

They moved inside, and Liam settled into a chair, resting his feet on the coffee table. Following his lead, Jake sat on the couch and pulled out his flask, taking another swig before offering it to Liam.

"The Green Fairy," Liam said knowingly, his brows wrinkling as the scent of licorice filled the air. "That's some nasty stuff. Messes with your mind."

"You leprechauns are all the same," Jake said, lowering his hand with a sigh.

"What do you know about my kind?" Liam asked, taking offense.

Jake leaned forward, wagging his finger in Liam's face. "I know that—"

"Everyone, just calm down," Colm cut in. "We don't need this right now."

"Amen," Rye chimed in from across the room, peering out the front window.

"Jake's a Gambler," Colm explained to Liam, in hopes of easing the tension.

"Yeah, I heard all about it on the ride over," Liam said, his voice thick with sarcasm as he reached his hand out to Jake. "Let me see your dice."

Jake handed it over without hesitation, the deep black contrasting with Liam's pale skin.

"It's gotten ahold of you," Liam said, speaking in a fatherly tone.

"Not right now," Jake said, tapping his flask. "I've traded one demon for another."

The creases in Liam's forehead deepened. "The Green Fairy's a quick ticket to the madhouse, and even if you keep your wits, it won't work forever."

"It's my choice," Jake said, shrugging his shoulders.

Liam nodded, concern still marking his face as he turned his attention to the dice. "Not one of mine, but it's not really yours either. You're a Drifter," Liam said with disdain, tossing the dice back to Jake.

Colm didn't know what a Drifter was, but obviously Liam didn't like it.

Jake, however, remained amazingly calm and noticed the concern on Colm's face. "It's okay," he said. "It's typical from his *kind*. They don't like to share their magic. They're kind of greedy that way."

"You'd be nothin' without that dice," Liam said, glaring back at Jake.

"See, that's where you're wrong," Jake said, leaning

forward. "Without it, I'd be fine and still have a full life ahead of me. But it's easy for you to forget that I never asked for it. It was given to me by my father, who was so corrupted by it that he couldn't see the truth."

"You got yours from your *father*?" Colm asked in surprise, again trying to ease the tension.

"Yes. Shortly after he took his own life, I was given a box and a handwritten note," Jake said, setting the dice, the hand-bell, and two white stones on the coffee table. "That's what was in his precious box to me."

"And it wasn't until you got his letter that it was bound to you," Liam said, his mood softening as he pulled his pipe from his pocket, packing it with tobacco.

"That's my understanding," Jake said, nodding to Liam. "He was convinced that things would turn out differently for me, and he went to extraordinary lengths in that letter to share everything he'd learned. But he was wrong. We all eventually succumb to its call."

Did Jake just admit that trying to control the call of the dice is pointless? That he tried and failed, even knowing his father's experiences, and now he has to rely on some strange elixir to quiet its call? If that was the case, then things were even more dire than Colm had been led to believe. The idea of *controlling* the dice seemed like a pipe dream, absent the use of "the Green Fairy," and apparently even that couldn't hold back the call of the dice forever. Both Jake and Liam had admitted as much. Colm leaned against the wall heavily, lowering his head and running his fingers through his hair. It was like they'd just levied a death sentence on him. Things seemed to be spinning out of control, and he had the distinct feeling that time was not on his side.

"What's a Drifter?" Rye asked, looking away from the window and joining the conversation.

"A Drifter inherits a dice through blood lineage," Liam

said, taking a puff from his pipe before continuing. "Let's call it a loophole of sorts, but it's not widely known."

"I don't care what he calls me," Jake said, leaning back. "All I know is I have this thing I never asked for, and it's killing me. It'd almost be funny if it weren't," Jake said, laughing to himself. "But *I wish* I could get rid of it, only they don't make it that easy."

Colm winced at the words "killing me," knowing that the words applied to himself now too. The dice had taken years from Colm already—he could feel it in his bones—and it was poised to take more at the next opportunity. The only hope Colm had left was to give it back, something which Jake clearly understood.

"Best I can tell," Jake continued, "the only way is to convince—"

"—the Lady to take it back," Colm jumped in.

Jake turned to Colm, nodding. "That's right. That's why I was at the museum," he said, tapping the handbell. "My father was convinced this has something to do with her."

"I'm trying to get rid of my dice too," Colm said as he moved across the room, taking a seat beside Jake, his excitement growing.

"In that case, I've got a proposal," Jake said with an intent gaze. "Let's team up and help each other find her."

"No way," Rye said, stepping forward, at the same time that Liam joined in with a scowl, reiterating her objection.

"Please," Jake pleaded, leaning forward on the couch. "My time is running out, all because of a derelict father. This may be my only chance, and you all seem like you know where to look. I don't even know where to start," he said, his tone changing, as did his demeanor, but Rye and Liam remained silent. Jake stood, his hands at his sides. "Look, I didn't ask for this dice," he said, clearing his throat. "It never should've been given to me, and I only ask that you help me return it to the Lady. That's all I want—just the chance to live a normal life again."

Colm stood up, joining Jake in his plight, his eyes flashing from Rye to Liam and back. "He never even asked for it. It was pressed upon him," he said, turning his attention to Liam. "Seems like you should be happy that he wants to give it back."

"I don't know," Liam said. "Everything about him is concerning, from his dice to his drinking."

Colm's eyes intensified, the tone of his voice firm as he looked from Liam to Rye. "He's just like me. Would you give up on me?"

Rye stood in silence, her eyes meeting Colm's until finally she turned away. "Fine," she said, keeping her back to Colm, "but he's your responsibility."

"And you?" Colm ask, turning to Liam.

Liam nodded in agreement, picking up the pearly stones from the table. "So, these stones—they were black before. What happened?"

"Beats me," Jake said, shrugging his shoulders. "Maybe they turned when the magic was used. My father called them Siren Stones. Said they're used to make someone do something, but they only work once. I'd been saving them for the Lady, but I guess we were lucky to have them."

Liam grumbled, returning the pearly stones to the table.

"What about this?" Colm said, tossing out Ciara's gold coin. "Could this be one of those mandala keys Oliver was talking about?" He took the mandala from his backpack, setting it on the table.

"Perhaps," Liam said, picking up the coin. His fingers traced along the embossed design of the pentagram, pausing at the crescent moon woven through it. "A crescent moon," he said, his eyes closing.

Rye turned from the window, joining them. "The pentagram is the Lady's sign, but I've never seen it married with a crescent moon."

"It's not a good thing," Liam responded, opening his eyes as he flipped the coin over to see the design repeated. "The crescent moon with the points arching upwards portends dark omens."

"But why is it married to her pentagram?" Rye asked, watching Liam.

Liam hesitated, setting the coin down. "If this is in fact the key to that mandala, then Haesel's prophecy about the Lady has ill tidings."

"What do you mean, *ill* tidings?" Colm asked.

"Usually the grave kind," Liam said, puffing on his pipe, all pretenses gone from his voice. "But there's something more we need to discuss."

"What?" Rye asked, sitting on the arm of the couch by Colm.

Liam took his pipe from his mouth, looking squarely at Rye. "It's time you came clean with us."

"About what?" she asked.

"Your star tattoo," Liam said, tapping his finger below his eye. "Liora and Ciara wear the same tattoo."

Rye turned away, lowering her head.

"What is it?" Colm asked.

Liam started to speak, but Rye cut him off, turning back. "It's the mark of the Sorority of the Lady," she said, looking to Colm, her eyes glistening in the light.

"What?" Colm asked, more confused than ever.

"She's a member of the Lady's secret service," Liam answered.

"It's complicated," Rye said, looking only at Colm. "I left the Sorority years ago."

"Does that mean you know where she is?" Colm asked, a mixture of hope and confusion swirling inside him.

"No, I don't. I'm sorry," Rye answered.

"So, Liora and Ciara, they're, like, co-workers of yours or something?" Colm asked, trying to understand.

"In the distant past, yes, in a way," Rye answered. "But not anymore. Like I said, I left years ago, due to some personal differences with the Lady."

"Why didn't you just tell me?" Colm asked. "Now it's just a little weird to have it coming out this way."

Rye paused, briefly turning away before answering. "I didn't want to overwhelm you, and I didn't really want to get into it. That's all."

"Is that supposed to be an apology?" Colm asked, though keenly aware that he'd also deliberately hidden his dice from her earlier in the day, but somehow that seemed different to him.

There was an awkward silence as Rye looked out the window. "I've been running for so long that it's second nature to keep things about myself hidden," she answered, pausing briefly to find her words. "And after Noah betrayed me, I lost faith in everything and everyone. Not that that's any excuse," she said, turning back to Colm. "But I am sorry for not telling you about the Sorority. That was my mistake. I wasn't expecting a guy like you when I walked into your pawnshop, so you can take it or leave it as an apology. I wish I could trust people easier, but I can't. It's just who I am. Still, I was being truthful when I said I'd help you get rid of that dice."

The room was silent as Colm took in her words, her emerald eyes imploring him to believe her. Deep down, it still stung, but he appreciated her honesty, and for some reason, he did believe she wanted to help him, even though she was still keeping much of her past hidden from him. It was enough for now.

"I get it," Colm said. He didn't like to talk about his past either—especially his parents, and now Andrew. He wanted to bury that deep too. So, yes, he did understand, and he hadn't been expecting someone like her either.

"Are we good, then?" she asked, looking into Colm's eyes.

"We're good."

"Phew! Now that that's in the open," Liam interrupted, "we can get back to the matter at hand, which is, how did Noah get the mandala? Like I said, the last time I saw it, the Lady had it."

"I don't know," Rye said, regaining her composure. "We were together when I left the Sorority, so he must've taken it then. Do you really think that coin is the key?"

Liam sighed, tapping the coin with his finger. "Unfortunately, I do. It's too much of a coincidence for the coin and the mandala to come to us days after the Whiskered Stranger visited Colm. Seems to me that fate wants us to know this prophecy, but revealed or not, we need to get this mandala and its key back to the Lady. It's the only way that she can protect herself. That must be why they were given to us."

"I don't know," Rye said as she traced her finger along the edge of her necklace. "There's no guarantee that the prophecy would help you find her, even if you did reveal it."

"True," Liam said, nodding, "but I cannot just sit back doing nothing while she's in danger. Some bonds run deep, and I owe it to her to try and help."

"This isn't just your decision," Rye pointed out.

"You're right. We should all have a say." Leaning forward, Liam picked up the coin and mandala, looking around the room at each of them. "I've spoken my mind. This is a time of action, not idleness."

"Let's get on with it," Colm said impatiently. "You already know I want to find her, and if this might help us do that, then I say reveal it."

Jake reached over, grasping Colm's shoulder. "My

remaining time in this world slips away with each day. I no longer have the luxury to wait for other options. If there's a chance that revealing this prophecy will aid us in finding her, then I implore you to do it. If not for my sake, then for Colm's. He's still young, and finding the Lady could allow him to avoid my fate. The sooner we find her, the better for us and for her."

They all turned to Rye. She had a brooding look about her as her finger continued to trace the edge of her necklace. "Fine," she said in exasperation. "But let's all be clear here. There's no promise that revealing it will help you find her, and even if it does, she may not want to help you. Remember, I already told you that she can be difficult, and on top of that, she may not want to be found," she said, looking squarely at Colm.

"So, this is the decision?" Liam asked, and they all nodded. He slowly lifted the coin to the mandala, and as if by magnetic attraction, the coin slipped from his fingers, locking into place in the opening with a muffled click. Almost immediately, the branches and roots of the tree on the mandala pulsed with a burst of light that flowed outward. Liam turned the mandala to see a glowing script reveal itself on the edge, as if being written with ink of pure sunlight.

"The language of the gods," Liam said in awe.

"What does it say?" Rye asked, leaning in closer as Liam turned it in his hands, examining the script, which morphed into English before their eyes.

A moment later, he looked up with a grim frown. "The closest translation is, 'At odds with her feats, the Lady retreats. In hiding, the fratricide completes. Upon her death, her bondage torn, the world's fate is reborn.'"

"What's fratricide?" asked Colm in confusion.

Jake turned to Colm. "It's an old word, but today it's mostly used during wars. It means killing your own soldiers."

"Or family members," added Liam with a snarky tone, setting the mandala down. "But more importantly, she's already in hiding. The prophecy is already in motion."

"No, more importantly," Rye joined in, "the prophecy reveals nothing to us about her location. So, now we've revealed the prophecy, and we still have no idea where to find her."

The vibe in the room was awkward as Rye turned away.

"What about the bell?" Colm asked, looking to Jake. "You mentioned that your dad was convinced it has something to do with her. Do you know why?"

"I don't," Jake answered. "His letter was short on details."

"Let me see it," Liam said, picking it up. He shook it by its wooden handle, but it made no sound. "Curious. Is it broken?"

"It's always been like that," Jake said, shrugging his shoulders.

Confused, Liam turned the bell upside down, inspecting it, but it appeared that all the necessary parts were there. He turned it over, shaking the handle again in disbelief. No sound.

"It looks like there are some etchings on it," Rye said, scooting closer.

Liam spun it in his hands, his fingers tracing the etchings encircling the bell's rim. "It's rubbed off in places, but what I can make out says something like 'to summon or call,'" he said, his finger continuing to trace over the etchings. "No, 'to reveal'—that's a better translation," he corrected himself.

"To reveal what?" asked Colm, watching Liam study the etchings.

"The Tin Maiden. 'To reveal the Tin Maiden,'" Liam said. "That's all I can make out from what's left."

"The Tin Maiden? Who's that?" Jake asked, leaning back.

"You mentioned her back at the bar," Rye said, looking at Liam.

Colm joined in. "That's right. You said if we can find the Tin Maiden, we can find the Lady."

"So, this Tin Maiden—she's real?" Jake asked eagerly.

"Well, I can only suspect she's real. I've only heard her name once in passing," Liam said, looking off into the distance.

"And?" Colm prodded.

"It was long ago, when the Lady selected me as her new Daserii. Those early days were the best of my life," Liam said, smiling as he retreated into the memory.

"Liam," Rye said, snapping her fingers. "We need you to focus."

His eyes came back to center. "Right, sorry. She was going over my responsibilities when we were interrupted by someone in the hall wearing a dark cloak. The Lady stepped aside to have a brief conversation, and just before she turned back to me, I overheard her reference this Tin Maiden. She waved her hand in an irritated manner, telling the cloaked person to stay in the Divide. Then she turned back to me."

"That's it?" Colm asked, hoping that there would be more.

"Afraid so," Liam said, setting the handbell down on the table as he finished.

Rye craned her neck, squinting at Liam. "You're holding something back. There's got to be more."

"I'm done with the games, lassie. That's all that I know of this Tin Maiden."

"How does that even help?" Colm asked, kicking the table in frustration, and the bell silently toppled over. "What good is knowing the prophecy if we can't even find her?"

Rye ignored Colm, instead focusing on what Liam had said. "So, it seems like the bell is supposed to *call* or *reveal* the

Tin Maiden. Maybe it's just broken and needs to be fixed, so it rings again."

Colm turned back, looking at Rye. "That's actually not a bad idea."

"Hmmm," Liam said, puffing on his pipe. "I might know someone who could help, but he's a bit testy. Sorta feels like the world has left his little people behind."

"What do you mean, 'little people'?" Colm asked curiously.

"They're a group of travelers—gypsies of sorts—but they're the best artisans you'll ever find," Liam answered.

"You don't mean the Picts?" Rye asked reverently.

"Yep, the tiny people. But don't go callin' 'em that, or it'll be a short road to somewhere you'd rather not go. Just believe me on that one. Their leader calls himself the Pict, and if anyone can fix that bell, it'd be him."

"You know where to find him?" Colm asked.

Liam nodded. "Their Dun's just outside of town, in the hills."

"Let's go," Colm said, and they all stood up.

"Wait," Rye said, looking at Colm's bandaged hand. "We need to clean that cut on your hand before it gets infected. You got a first aid kit?"

"Yeah, I'll grab it and meet you on the patio," Colm said as the others stepped outside, but Jake paused, catching Colm's arm.

"Hey, you got any guns here?" he asked. "We might need something to defend ourselves."

"Yeah, under the floorboards in the back bedroom," Colm said, pointing down the hall, and Jake disappeared. Colm grabbed the first aid kit, joining Rye and Liam on the patio, the waves rhythmically crashing and receding on the rocky beach.

Liam glanced toward the house before speaking in a

hushed tone. "The stones that your new friend used on the ladies—see how they're pure white?" He pulled the white rocks from his pocket, handing them to Colm. "I'm not convinced we're getting the whole story with these. Something's not right. And drinkin' the Green Fairy like that— that's never good. They say it rots your brain from the inside out," Liam said, glancing to Rye as she opened the first aid kit.

"This is deep," she said. "It'll need a few stitches. You ready?"

"Have you ever done this before?" Colm asked, his eyes widening.

"I've sewn up lots of things," she said, smiling as she deftly ran the blue nylon thread through the needle. She prodded at the cut, and Colm winced as she started the first stitch.

"Did you tell Liam?" she asked.

Colm raised his eyes, a darkness swirling behind them.

"Tell me what?" Liam asked, doing his best not to look at Colm's wound.

Colm quickly relayed to Liam what Ciara had said to him in the museum, and Liam leaned back, scratching his chin. "Why would they be interested in normies?"

"Right. It makes no sense," Rye said in agreement.

Colm tensed up, turning away as Rye finished a stitch. He had never liked blood or pain, and this was both. She leaned in, snipping the thread above the knot as Colm's thoughts turned dark. "All that matters is that they're going to pay," he muttered.

"Is that you or the dice talking?" Liam asked.

"It doesn't matter," Colm said, turning back, trading out the stones for the dice in his pocket.

Liam reached out, placing his hand on Colm's arm. "I'm sorry for making it for you. I can see the pain it brings you, and it gives me no happiness to see it. Perhaps this is why the Lady forbade her Daserii from meeting their Gamblers."

"Who cares?" Colm said, his anger growing. "She doesn't control me anymore. Isn't that what you said?"

"Yes," Liam answered, "but I also said to use that freedom wisely. You have the power to choose your fate, if you're brave enough to fight for what you desire."

"They don't deserve to live. Not what after they've done," Colm growled, gripping his dice, the hunger for revenge growing. What had his parents or Andrew done to them? Those two ladies didn't deserve anything better than what they'd brutally dished out. Why should he care about them? He wasn't even part of their world, knowing nothing of them other than the pain they'd brought upon him.

"There's no turning back from a wish like that. Trust me," Liam said quietly.

"Trust?!" Colm lashed out, his patience worn thin. "What have *you* done to earn my trust?"

Liam lowered his head as Colm glared at him. Raising his eyes to meet Colm's, he spoke calmly. "I understand your scorn for me, but I don't have to be here, risking my life. I choose to be here, to help you, to right the wrong that I've done to you and others. Maybe trust is too tall a hurdle, but my intent is sincere."

Rye set the needle down, placing her hands softly over Colm's. "Think, Colm. The dice is goading you on, but its magic won't even work on members of her Sorority, myself included. And even if it did, you're not the killing type."

Colm's eyes finally softened as they moved between Rye and Liam, tears streaking down his face. "I hate what this thing has done to me! It's not fair. Nothing about my life is fair." Pulling his hand away from Rye, he hurled the dice onto the rocks. Turning back to her, he wiped away the tears, sniffling. "Let's just get this done," he said, pressing his hand against the table, motioning for her to continue.

Rye picked up the needle, continuing where she'd left off.

Liam stood, leaning heavily on his cane. "I'm in this to the end. I know we didn't start off on the best of terms, but I'll fight to the death for my friends, and you're both squarely on that list now."

Colm turned to Liam, his anger relenting. "I know. They could've killed you in the museum. So, I know. It's just... I've had so much stolen from me, and sometimes it's hard to see past that. I'm trying to hold it together, but it's getting harder. They killed my parents, and now Andrew..."

Liam patted Colm on the shoulder, nodding. "I'll get the car ready. We've got some little people to visit."

As the patio door creaked shut, Rye tied off the last knot. "Good as new," she said, placing a bandage to cover it.

"I know you guys have my best interests at heart, but the dice doesn't. It brings out my dark side," Colm said, standing up, the salty air filling his lungs.

"That dice doesn't define you—not yet, at least. We'll find her and get rid of it. You have my word," Rye said, joining him.

Colm turned to Rye, taking her hands in his. "I need you to promise me something."

"What?" Rye asked, her eyes widening with concern.

"You can't let me use it to do stuff like that—evil stuff," he said with a steady voice. "I need you to promise that you'll kill me if you see me doing shit like that with it."

Her voice wavered. "Colm, I can't—"

"Please, you're the only one I can ask. You have to promise me."

She let out a deep breath, lowering her head in thought.

"Please," he repeated, his voice cracking.

Her eyes met his, her voice barely audible. "Yeah, okay. I promise."

At least he had her. He squeezed her hands, leaning his head against hers in silence until she stepped back, her eyes distant. "Go find Jake. We need to keep moving," she said, then turned, gazing out at the ocean in silence.

Colm headed back into the house. As he walked into the bedroom, Jake was sitting on the bed with his back to the door, muttering in a low voice as Colm rapped his knuckle on the doorframe. Jake turned, holding his flask and a snubbed shotgun. He rose, whispering to Colm as he leaned in. "Thanks for sticking by me earlier."

"It's the least I can do," Colm said, patting him on the shoulder. "We're a lot alike."

"Agreed, and to that point, let me give you a piece of advice. All this may not pan out, so you need to learn how to live with your dice. Figure out how to keep your wits about you, and make it as hard to use as you can, or at least a very conscious decision when you do. Create some space—anything that adds a little time for reflection. And just remember, time is a one-way street. Once it's gone, it's gone."

The room went quiet, filled with an awkward silence until Jake straightened up, taking a swig from his flask and holding it out to Colm. "Or you can use this."

"What is it?" Colm asked, the licorice scent heavy on Jake's breath.

"The Green Fairy—absinthe. She numbs the call of the dice."

Colm's stomach objected, recalling Liam's syrupy drink. "I'll pass."

"Let me know if you change your mind," Jake said as they walked to the living room.

Colm opened his backpack, putting away the mandala, and with Jake's approval, the handbell. As he adjusted the contents of his pack, the Moonblade slid out, clattering to the floor.

"That's a beauty! Can I see it?" Jake asked, pointing to the Moonblade.

"Sure." Colm handed the blade to Jake as Liam came through the door. He froze, eyes fixed on the Moonblade.

"Where the hell'd you get that?" Liam asked, clearly agitated by the sight of it.

"Rye's ex pawned it to me," Colm answered.

"You don't just *pawn* something like that. Do you even know what it is?" Liam asked, inching backwards.

"Yeah. Rye called it a Moonblade. Said it's used to hunt werewolves."

Liam stopped him. "It's not just for werewolves. It can kill *anything* magical or immortal. Just a nick from that blade would leave me in a world of hurt."

Jake let out a low whistle through his teeth. "Well, that certainly makes things more interesting."

"Just put it away," Liam said, turning to leave. "We need to go."

As they walked to the car, Colm's phone rang. It was Detective Lemmek. Colm didn't really want to answer, to hear any gruesome details about Andrew's death, and he almost sent it to voicemail, but his curiosity got the better of him. He picked up with a heavy sigh, his gut twisting with grief.

After some pleasantries, Roget dove in. "I'm down here at the museum," he said, "and you're not going to believe it."

"What?" Colm asked nervously, his mind flashing to the ransacked curator's office and the stolen necklace.

"It sounds like two ladies matching your description blew up the curator's house, stole a firetruck, and rammed it through the front doors of the museum, then killed a security guard outside the curator's office before ransacking it."

"What?!" Colm said, feigning surprise.

"We're still piecing it together. Can you think of anything that might help us find them?" he asked.

"Hang on," Colm said, hitting mute and turning to Rye. "I need to tell him about the warehouse, but I'll leave you out of it. Maybe he can help, or at least slow them down."

She pursed her lips, reluctantly nodding.

Colm unmuted the phone, launching into the story about the delivery to the warehouse, even sharing how he'd hidden in the closet.

"Thanks," Roget said. "That helps a lot. We'll check out the docks."

A moment later, Colm hung up and immediately dialed Tabitha's number. After a few rings, it went to voicemail, and he left a strange and garbled message, telling her about Andrew's murder, and asking her to lay low and call Detective Lemmek if anything weird happened.

19

A NEW ANGLE

Tabitha's phone lay on a table just out of reach as she watched Ciara move across the warehouse, each step carefully placed to avoid the rubbish littering the floor.

"I wonder when lovey-bird will call again?" Ciara laughed as she picked up the phone, flashing a picture of Colm on the lock screen. Tabitha turned away, her face caked with the crusty trails of dried tears.

Liora joined Ciara, adjusting the sling holding her arm, speaking in a girlish voice. "Oh, play back the message! I wish I had a boyfriend like him, so sweet and concerned."

Ciara flicked the phone around, pressing Tabitha's finger on the home button. A few taps later, Colm was speaking as if he were in the room with them. Concern weighted his voice as he warned Tabitha about the strange things that were happening, and of Andrew's murder at the shop. His message ended with an impassioned plea for her to lay low for a bit until things blew over.

"Whoops! Seems like you didn't get the message in time, huh, sweetheart?" Ciara rubbed her thumbs softly across Tabitha's cheeks, wiping the dried tears away. Tabitha defiantly turned her head away as she stood bound to a wooden column. Unfortunately for her, they'd found her before she heard his message, but they had been kind enough to repeatedly play it for her ever since.

"I bet you're wishing you would've listened to that message earlier, huh, sweetie?" Liora said as she paced the room, carefully avoiding the milky puddles. "Seems like you just got yourself hitched up with the wrong guy at the wrong time."

"He's not my boyfriend. Not anymore. I broke up with him the other night. I'm leaving for grad school, and he's just having a hard time coming to terms with that reality," Tabitha said in a firm voice.

"Right. Is that why you came into the pawnshop earlier, looking for him, and he's leaving you lovey-bird messages?" Liora asked, pausing for a moment. "You see, it just doesn't add up to me. It stinks of lies." She moved her face closer to Tabitha's, taking a sniff of her skin. "See? Stinky. Perhaps if you're helpful, I could find it in my heart to let you head off to grad school. You seem like a sensible young lady. What do you say?"

"I already told you, I had a few things of his to return. That's why I stopped by the shop. Honestly, that's it." Tabitha winced as the ropes tore deeper into her skin with each little movement.

Liora stood, turning away. She'd been through this with Tabitha several times already, and she was getting nowhere. She believed the girl was being mostly truthful, but she was having a hard time teasing out where the truth ended and the lies began. Still, she was convinced Tabitha had to know something helpful. She mulled over what to do next, but was interrupted by the phone ringing.

"Maybe it's your lovey-bird again?" Ciara said, lifting the

phone, but she frowned as she saw that it wasn't Tabitha's phone ringing.

Liora scrambled, pulling her own phone from her pocket. It was their new employer calling again. She motioned to Ciara, and they hurried to a corner of the room, away from Tabitha, as she put the call on the speaker. The last time they had spoken was after their fiasco at the museum, but to their surprise, their employer didn't see it that way; he was elated by how things had gone down. Given that, it was no surprise that he was in a good mood, and they both let out a sigh of relief. Still, their brows raised at the latest instructions.

"Do not harm the girl; she may yet come in handy. Just hold tight and wait to hear from me again," he said.

Ciara, never really knowing when to keep quiet, didn't like this new plan and spoke out. "That's not why you hired us," she said as Liora silently waved her hand, frantically trying to get her to calm down, but it was futile. This was Ciara's way, and she bulldozed forward. "We don't *wait* for things to happen; we *make* them happen. That's why you brought us on board."

The voice snapped, "Don't be insolent. Do I need to remind you that I caught you lying to me about the boy? It was something I graciously overlooked, but I can change that if you push me." There was a pause before he continued. "Perhaps you need a little reminder of who I am and what I've done for you? She abandoned you, the Sorority, and the world when she decided to save herself by hiding away. Cowardly, even for her, but I offered you a way out, a new hope," the voice echoed into the room as Liora gasped for air. It felt as if her chest were being crushed, and her life was ever so slowly being drained, breath by breath. She turned to see Ciara in the same predicament.

"Let that be a warning to you," the voice echoed out from the phone as the pressure subsided and Liora could breathe freely once again, the color returning to her face. "The terms of your employment were made clear to you. You are bound to me, and you will not be released or rewarded until I get what was promised to me. She's just a thief using the Stone of Fates for her own gain, and none of us will rest until that stone is mine. Do you understand?"

"Yes, understood," they both said, still recovering from the stern rebuke.

"Now, back to the matter at hand," he said. "Things are in motion since your little run-in at the museum, so we've got a new plan. It's possible that Rye and her ragtag group of vagabonds will lead us to where the Lady's hiding, so we no longer need her necklace to coax her out. Once I learn more, I'll be in touch."

Liora was still recovering, but Ciara, who never seemed to know her place, plunged back in with a scowl on her face. "You promised us the necklace. If you let Rye keep it, she's untouchable, even by you. She's essentially a god."

"She's no god!" the voice thundered. "She's just a silly little girl who stole something the Lady foolishly made, weakening her greatly." The line went silent before the voice returned, calmly chiding them, "Just do as I say. No harm to the girl, and wait to hear from me. Do you understand?"

They both agreed, but the scowl never left Ciara's face. She wasn't happy with their new orders. They were no fun, and now they had to babysit Tabitha. Before the screen even went black, Ciara's face flushed, and she raced across the room toward Tabitha, blades drawn, screeching as she went. "No one tells me what to do!"

"Calm down!" Liora said, still catching her breath. "You felt that. We cannot risk our lives for her."

Ciara's blades landed in the post just above Tabitha's head, splintering deep into the wood. Her face hovered close to Tabitha's as she whispered, "Your time will come." Then she slowly licked the girl from her cheek to her forehead, tasting the saltiness of her dried tears.

"Looks like you've got yourself some black eyes," Tabitha said defiantly, having overheard the entire conversation. "Must hurt."

"Just leave her. I'm not risking anything over this girl," Liora said, as if they had a choice. But deep down, she knew they didn't, and so did Ciara. The girl was to be left unharmed … for now.

"That's right," Tabitha said. "I heard it too. You can't touch me."

"Well, what's a little cut or a bruise, or heck, even losing a pinkie? That doesn't really *harm* her in any meaningful way, right?" Ciara mused.

"I suppose you have a point," Liora said, clearly not thrilled that Tabitha was playing them against their new employer. "It's just a job. We don't really have to follow those orders, sweetie." She stroked her fingers gently across Tabitha's cheeks.

"There are probably loads of things we could do without causing real *harm*," Ciara said with a menacing smile.

"So true," agreed Liora, her smile widening. "No reason two girls can't have a little fun."

THE PICT'S DUN

THE CADDY ROLLED down a country road, passing under a tunnel of ancient oak trees periodically interrupted by fields of tall golden grass. Colm had always loved the rolling hills outside of town. It was easy to get lost in them. Craning his neck, he looked for the old fire tower that lorded over the town, but it was nowhere in sight.

"Where are we?" he asked, leaning forward.

Liam glanced at him in the rearview mirror. "To find the Dun, you have to make at least half a dozen wrong turns, and then there's still a chance you'll never come across it."

"That makes no sense," Rye chimed in from the back seat, having just awoken from a catnap.

Liam turned to Rye, cracking a smile. "Glad to see you're awake, lassie."

"The road—watch the road! And stop calling me 'lassie.' I'm not some cheap date you're trying to pick up at a bar," Rye said crossly. "Just answer his question and spare us the BS."

"Spoken like a true lady. Talk like that just gets me britches goin'." Liam winked at her in the mirror as the car crested a ridge, entering an open meadow. Looming above them in the distance, a stark white fire tower reflected the late afternoon sun.

"No need," Colm said, spotting it. "I see where we are now."

Liam pointed ahead. "The Dun sits south of the tower. It's a bit tricky to get there, but that's the way the Pict likes it."

The fire tower sat on a rocky outcrop above what appeared to be a small commune on a flattened section of land. Liam pulled the car to stop a few paces from the entrance to what that looked like a ranch from an old Western movie. Rock fence posts spaced six feet apart were connected by sturdy cuts of redwood, and atop each was a single round white stone the size of a grapefruit. The fence tracked away from the entrance in both directions until it disappeared into the oaks and chaparral. The entrance itself was as wide enough for two good-sized trucks to pass through, flanked by girthy redwood posts four feet wide and fifteen feet tall. At the top of each, a deep notch was cut, holding a flat piece of redwood that stretched between them. The words THE PICT'S DUN were inlaid into the wood in a grungy black metal that matched the open gate below.

Looking beyond the gate, Colm saw that the Dun was a welcoming amalgamation of smallish redwood cabins, with one larger house made from a clever mix of river rocks and sandstone. The Dun was sprinkled with dozens of old oak trees, and at the center of it all was a communal firepit surrounded by chairs and tables of various shapes and sizes. There were a number of pint-sized people milling about, and a large wooden barn sat in the back, where much of the activity of the Dun was focused. Peering out the car window, Colm saw a few people look their way before disappearing into the large stone building.

Liam turned to face everyone. "So, this Pict guy... He

doesn't like having a lot of visitors to the Dun, especially uninvited ones, and…" He rubbed his neck. "He sorta doesn't like me either."

"Shocker," Rye deadpanned. Colm broke out in laughter.

Liam shot them all a dirty look. "Ha, ha. Glad I could be the butt of your joke, but it's not what you think. We just have *history*, that's all. I suggest that only one of us go in, and I think——"

"It's *my* bell," Jake interrupted, leaning in. "I should go."

Liam looked at Jake and spoke quickly before anyone else could respond. "I hear you, but coming uninvited and knowing him like I do, it's best to send in the most naïve of the lot. So, no offense, but that's you, Colm."

"None taken," Colm said, looking at Liam and Jake. Jake's eyes remained on Liam, measuring his words, clearly questioning the plan as he pulled his flask from his pocket, taking a swig.

Liam glanced at the flask, pursing his lips in disapproval. "Look, I know you don't know me, but you have to trust me on this one. If we want his help, this is the way to do it."

Jake eyed Liam a moment longer, sliding the flask back into its hiding place. He nodded, and they all got out of the car.

"How do I find him?" Colm asked, looking to Liam.

"Don't worry, he'll find you. Show him this when he does." Liam handed Colm a business card adorned with shamrocks and a variety of dice that read, *Liam Paxton – Daserii, retired.* "Like I said, the Pict may not like me, but he knows I always send him good referrals. Just show him that, and he'll fix that bell for sure."

Moments later, Colm walked through the gate, a cool autumn breeze washing over him. As he glanced around the Dun, his eyes settled on the pint-sized gypsies dressed in hippie clothes swarming about the barn. Liam wasn't kidding: they were small. Even the tallest among them was barely half his size, and he couldn't help but feel like he'd just stepped ashore in Lilliput. He thought about turning back, but before he could, a stout older fellow emerged from the stone house wearing a T-shirt with the sleeves torn off.

"You here for the flamingo?" he asked in a brisk but somewhat friendly voice.

"Flamingo?" Colm echoed, confused.

"Yeah, the flamingo," he said, pointing to the barn.

Colm turned to see a giant metal flamingo that must have been fifteen feet tall. Somehow he hadn't noticed it towering above the workers. "No, I'm not here for that," he said, turning back to the crusty man, laughing as he caught sight of his vintage Popeye T-shirt that read, *I yam what I yam.*

"Something funny?" the man asked curtly, crossing his arms.

"No." Colm stiffened up, taking another look at the gigantic bird.

The little man leaned to the side, looking around Colm, eyeing the golden Cadillac parked outside the gate. "If you're not here for the bird, then what're you doing here? This is private property," he said, his expression turning from crusty to downright inhospitable.

"I'm sorry for intruding," Colm said nervously. "But I'm looking for the Pict."

"The Pict? Is that some sorta joke?"

"No, I don't think so," Colm said nervously, taking a step back.

"That makes no sense, boy. You're wasting my time. Now get off my property before I really get irritated." He shooed Colm away and turned, heading for the barn.

"Liam sent me," Colm called out as he kneeled, holding out the business card.

The man paused, turning back in disgust, making no move to take the card. "I don't know any Liam."

Colm froze, uncertain of what to say, but the thought crossed his mind that perhaps Liam hadn't been completely forthright about unannounced visits.

The man glared at him, pulling a small wooden case from his back pocket, clicking it open. Inching back, Colm was convinced that the case held some contraption that would cause his immediate death. But instead, the man pulled out a pair of old spectacles, placing them gingerly on his face.

"Eyes aren't what they used to be," he said, reaching for the card. "What do you have there?"

"Liam told me to give this to you," Colm answered tentatively.

The man took the card, pulling it close to his face. Flipping it over, he ran his finger slowly across it to reveal a glittering golden seal that disappeared as quickly as it came. Flicking the card between his fingers, the man chuckled. "Liam? So, that's the name he goes by now?"

Colm nodded as the man took his glasses off.

"Watch out for him. He's a trickster," the man said, exhaling deeply. "But you can't blame him too much. It's the way they're raised. Like they say, you can take the leprechaun out of Sidhe, but you can't take Sidhe out of the leprechaun."

"I take it *you* are the Pict, then?" Colm asked as he stood up, towering over the little man.

"'The Pict'? That's like saying you're here to meet the human," the man said tersely, snapping his glasses case closed. "You know, we have names, just like you do."

Colm blushed, realizing his mistake. Picts were a race of people, not a person. "This is all new to me. I meant no offense."

The man nodded with a gruff expression. "Liam wouldn't dare send you into my Dun without good reason." He paused, sizing up Colm with a critical eye. "So, should I call you Human, or do you have a name?"

"I have a name," Colm said sheepishly before he introduced himself, apologizing.

"Apology accepted. My *name* is Grigs, and yes, I'm *a* Pict, but by no means *the* Pict." He stepped forward, placing his hand on Colm's shoulder with a warm smile. "What do you say we head inside, talk about why you're here? It's not every day that a Gambler visits my Dun."

The blood drained from Colm's face. *How the hell does he know that?* Things continued to get stranger by the moment as he silently followed Grigs into the stone house.

"How did you know I'm a Gambler?" Colm asked once they were inside.

Grigs ignored the question and walked across the room, throwing a few pieces of wood into a large stone fireplace, spinning a metal arm from which a tea kettle dangled. The house was rustic but cozy, the shelves and surfaces littered with trinkets.

"Tea?" Grigs asked.

Colm nodded, thinking that Grigs hadn't heard his question. "Yeah, sure, but how—"

"Patience," Grigs spoke over him in a calm voice. "We'll get to that, but first, some tea."

Colm nodded, engulfed by the silence of the room, his questions swimming through his mind with no mooring.

After a few minutes, Grigs placed a piping-hot cup of tea in front of him and settled into a chair across the table. "Now, on to your question. No magic can come into my Dun without me knowing. When you passed through my gate, I could feel the heavy load you carry."

"I didn't ask for it," Colm said, placing his dice on the table. "Not really, anyway. I mean, who would believe it could actually grant wishes? I just thought he was joking, but now I know this is dead serious."

Grigs nodded, periodically blowing on his tea and taking careful sips. "May I see it?" he asked, motioning to the dice. Colm nodded, pushing it across the table, and Grigs set his teacup down, taking the dice in his petite fingers. "Excellent craftsmanship. The magic in it is tight, purposeful. I've gotta hand it to him, he certainly does fine work." He looked up from the dice, his gentle eyes meeting Colm's. "This dice brings with it the possibility to do truly good things, but the lure of power and greed is often overwhelming for your kind. It casts a net, corrupting your thoughts, drawing you in like a hummingbird to sugar water. Your dice already shows signs of your growing addiction," he said, holding it out, his finger tracing its grey veins. "We all choose our own path, come to our own end. Until then, you must be forever vigilant against the lure of its magic. It's intoxicating to your kind."

It was hard for Colm not to notice the repeated references to "his kind," which in another scenario he might have found offensive. But presently, it seemed Grigs was saying the cards were stacked against him, and Colm agreed. "That's partially why I'm here. It's too hard to resist. I've already surrendered too much time to it, and I want to give it back to the Lady."

"That would be wise. But unfortunately, I've never heard of it happening, and I've been around for quite a while," he said, laughing softly, blowing on his tea again.

"I just want my normal, boring life back. I want out," Colm said, trying to convince himself it was true by saying the words out loud.

"Well, I hope you get what you're after, but I'm not certain your life will ever be normal again—not after what you've seen. Perhaps it's best to just accept your lot, maybe be the anomaly, strive for light and goodness with it," Grigs suggested.

They both sat quietly for a moment, sipping the tea, looking into the depths of the fire until Grigs cleared his throat. "But you've also brought something else here—something old and dangerous."

"What do you—" Colm paused, recalling the milky-white blade. "Wait… Do you mean this blade?" he asked, pulling it from his backpack and laying it on the table.

Grigs stood, gingerly picking it up and addressing it with a wide grin. "Hello, old friend."

"You've seen it before? Are you a Hunter?" Colm asked.

Grigs let out a raucous laugh, but Colm didn't understand what was so funny.

"My friends said Hunters use blades like these to kill werewolves," Colm said, "and Liam even told me it could kill anyone magical, himself included. Is that true?"

Grigs smiled, turning his attention back to Colm. "Well, your friends didn't lie, but Hunters hunt more than just werewolves. The ore used to forge this blade fell from the very moon itself, and it is deadly to anything magical or immortal, which is why they became the favored weapons of the Hunters. But me, a Hunter? Gods, no." He chuckled as he shifted the blade, stoically pointing to a small bumble bee design on the blade. "That there is my mark—the mark of the Pict."

"So, you *are* the Pict?"

"Well, I guess, in a way. Everything that comes out of the Dun has that mark, whether I make it myself or just oversee that it's made right. But this piece here—these hands made this one."

"It is nicely made, but Liam looked at it like it's pure evil."

"Can't say I blame him. It's a dangerous thing to our type, but there's nothing inherently good or evil about it, only how it's used. Just like your dice." He placed the blade back on the table. "Do you mind me asking how it came to you?"

"I bought it from a guy at the pawnshop where I work. Why?" Colm asked.

"Well, I don't think it's quite that simple. You must have it for a reason, because these blades always find their way to where they're needed. That's part of its innate magic."

Colm nodded, not saying a word as he placed the blade back in his backpack.

"But your dice, the blade—that's not why you're here," Grigs said, sitting down.

"You're right." Colm reached into his backpack, removing the handbell and placing it on the table. "I need to get this fixed. For some reason, it's stopped ringing, and Liam thought you could fix it."

Grigs reached out, picking up the bell, turning it over in his hands and shaking it silently. "No, I can't do that," he said, setting it back on the table and sipping his tea.

"But Liam said you can fix anything," Colm pleaded.

"Liam's right. But your bell's not broken."

"What do you mean?"

Grigs set his teacup down. "Make sure you tell Liam he's not as smart as me," he said with a smirk. "This is an Abbot's Bell, but not just any Abbot's Bell."

"What's that?" Colm asked, confused.

"Back in the day, the abbot of an abbey had a bell he used to call people to service, prayer, meals, or anything, really. He'd ring it, and the monks would do things. All very orderly. Do you want to venture a guess as to why this bell doesn't ring?"

Colm drummed his fingers on the table in thought until he finally made what he thought was an outlandish guess. "Because it's dead?"

Grigs's eyebrows raised, and a smile touched his eyes.

"Well, kind of, but it's not dead; it's *dumb*. You see, sometimes abbots were special people who did miraculous things, for which they were graced with sainthood, but sometimes that didn't happen until after their death. Either way, upon their death, or once they were sainted after death, their bell would go 'dumb,' or silent, as you say. So, I assure you that this *dumb bell* is in perfect working order and needs no repairs."

Colm's eyes turned downward, settling on the bell. He should've known finding the Lady wouldn't be easy, but maybe Grigs knew something about the Tin Maiden. Picking up the bell, he pointed to the faint etchings that encircled the rim. "What about the Tin Maiden? Liam said the etchings that haven't rubbed off refer to her."

Grigs took the bell from Colm, running his fingers along them. "Hmm, I do not know this Tin Maiden, but I can assure you that the etchings say much more than that. You just have to know how to coax them out—which I do."

Colm's head rose with renewed optimism as Grigs turned, reaching for a pair of fireplace tongs, gently gripping the bell. He stood by the fireplace, carefully dipping the bell in and out of the flames until all the etchings encircling the bell's lower rim were aflame with a radiant brilliance. Returning to the table, he sat down, taking his spectacles out once again before spinning the bell by its wooden handle, studying what was newly revealed. "Well, it does mention this Tin Maiden, but it also references the Lady."

"What?!" Colm said in disbelief. "What does it say?"

Grigs ran his finger around the rim of his teacup, staring deeply into it as if he were searching for something. "It's written in the ancient script of the gods. It's difficult to express in your tongue, but I believe it reads, 'Resonating from the chapel of the Lady's patron, only he can unlock the secret way to the Forest of Blood and Bone, revealing the path to the Tin Maiden, who hides in the shadows of the Lost City.'"

"What does it mean?" Colm asked.

"I can only tell you what was written, but if I were you, I'd seek the owner of this bell in the chapel at the abbey of the Lady's patron."

Colm nodded, stowing the handbell in his backpack and standing up. "Thank you for the information."

Grigs motioned to the chair. "Sit. I never let guests leave my Dun empty-handed. That is not the way of the Pict. Perhaps there's something else I can craft for you?"

Colm wracked his brain for ideas until his hands settled on his lap, feeling the stones Jake had used at the museum. He placed the two pearly white stones on the table between them, uncertain of what to ask for.

"Okay, so you've got a couple of stone shards. What are you thinking?" Grigs asked, sipping on his tea.

Colm shared how they'd been used by Jake to immobilize Liora and Ciara. "They were pure black, but once he used them, the power left them, leaving them like this. He called them Siren Stones. Can you recharge them?"

"I haven't heard of Siren Stones in centuries, and I wasn't really convinced they actually existed," Grigs mused as he picked up the stones, inspecting them. "If that's what these are, then their magic is very old and beyond even my skills, so I wouldn't know how to begin to remake them." With that, Grigs set them back on the table.

"I guess I'm striking out today," Colm said, reaching for the stones.

"Slow down. I said that I can't *remake* them, but I think I can use them to make you something else—something quite helpful to you. We just need to settle on payment. Nothing's free, ya know," he said with a smile.

Colm hesitated, not certain if he was joking, but as the

moment stretched on, it became clear that he wasn't. As he glanced around the room, it was as if he were seeing it for the first time. Every shelf was full of kitschy knickknacks, things that other people threw away, like Trollkins, Beanie Babies, Precious Moments figurines, and Chia Pets. It was a museum of all things tacky and nostalgic.

Colm snapped his fingers. "Give me a minute. I'll be right back."

Grigs nodded, refilling his teacup as Colm bolted out the door, heading to the Caddy.

"Did ya get it?" Liam asked as he laid back on the hood of the car, soaking in the sunlight.

"Not yet. I need to pay him," Colm said, sliding into the driver's seat and reaching for the Hawaiian girl, struggling to pull her free.

Liam scrambled to his feet. "You can't take her!"

"We need this to pay him," Colm grunted. With one last tug, the little lady squirmed loose from the dash, and he got out of the car, now face to face with the leprechaun. Liam's face was flushed as he glared at Colm.

"Stop it," Rye said, pressing her body between them, facing Liam. "It's just a stupid bobblehead. Go," she said, turning her head to Colm. "We're wasting time."

Colm nodded and sprinted away, hearing Jake and Rye working to calm down Liam. Arriving back at the house, Colm slowed to a walk, wiping his brow. Cracking the door open, he saw Grigs patiently waiting at the table, and he walked over, setting the Hawaiian girl down as an enormous smile broke out on Grigs's face.

"I've never seen anything so beautiful! May I?" Grigs asked, and Colm nodded, smiling. He spun it in his hands, running his finger along her face. "This is Liam's. He agreed to surrender this to me in payment?"

"Yeah, sort of," Colm said, shocked that the bobblehead

would be sufficient payment for anything, let alone something from the Pict.

Grigs turned, placing the Hawaiian girl front and center on the mantel over the fireplace. "She's a fine addition. Thank you for the generous payment, and express my gratitude to Liam as well for his sacrifice."

Sacrifice? Colm stifled a laugh, feeling like he'd just pulled a fast one on Grigs. "I'll be sure to tell him."

"I think that you'll find this to be a fair trade, indeed," he said, sitting down and picking up the two stones. "I can join these two shards to craft a Catholicon, which can be used to erase the effects of magic. So, for you, it can restore the years of your life taken by your dice."

"That's incredible! Thank you, Grigs," Colm said in shock.

Grigs nodded as he took the two stones, pressing them together tightly between his hands and whispering a few words Colm didn't understand. His eyes closed and his muscles strained as he pressed the stones together with all his strength. An ethereal green light spilled out, filling the room. A moment later, the light faded, and Grigs opened his hands. A moss-colored stone spilled onto the table. Opening a drawer, he retrieved a little velvet bag and a small card embossed with the Pict's mark, placing it in the bag along with the mossy stone. "For your payment," he said with a thick tongue, his body resting heavily on the table.

"Are you okay?" Colm asked, stepping to Grigs's side.

"There was no magic in those shards," he said, slurring as if sleep was about to overtake him. "I had to expend a great deal of my magic to fulfill our agreement. The Catholicon is yours. It will do as I promised, but I must rest now."

Colm helped him to his bed, and Grigs looked up at him, grasping his arm with fatherly concern. "The Catholicon— use it wisely. It only works once."

"But how do I use it?" Colm asked, kneeling beside his bed.

"When the need arises, you will know," Grigs whispered before falling fast asleep.

Colm pulled a blanket over Grigs and turned to leave. Pausing at the fireplace, he saw the Hawaiian girl bobbling away, though there was no breeze in the room. He stepped closer, placing his hand on her head to stop the motion, but as soon as he removed it, she resumed her dance. He chuckled, then remembered that Liam wasn't going to make this easy.

He could see Liam as he approached, and as soon as he walked through the gate, the leprechaun was on him. "Did you get the handbell repaired?"

"No, but I got the etchings on the handbell deciphered," Colm said, deciding it was best to keep the Catholicon to himself.

"God dammit!" Liam yelled, his anger reignited.

"Just hear me out. He could read *all* the etchings on the handbell, even the ones that were rubbed out," Colm said, looking to Rye for support.

"No, you hear *me* out!" blurted Liam, pressing forward into Colm's face as spittle rained from his mouth. "You traded my Leilani for information? That's what I get for sending a boy to do a man's job!"

Rye eyed Colm suspiciously and let out a deep sigh as she reached out, grabbing Liam's shoulders. "Shut it, Liam! You can get a new trashy Hawaiian bobblehead."

"Not like that one. It was a totem, Rye—*my* totem! He gave up my totem for words—words that we have no way of confirming! The Pict can be just as devious as anyone."

Rye took a step back, letting go of Liam, her eyes lowering. "Oh, that makes a lot more sense," she said quietly.

"What's a totem?" Colm asked, seemingly in a perpetual state of confusion.

"A totem rejuvenates someone and protects them from harm," Jake said. "Stuff like that."

Rye slowly raised her head, looking at Liam and speaking in a calmer tone. "Just stop. He didn't know. None of us did, so just let him explain."

Liam's anger melted just enough as he turned back to Colm. "Why didn't you just get the bell fixed?"

"He said it isn't broken. But he told me more about it. And the etchings—they mention the Lady." Colm recounted his conversation with Grigs about the handbell and its etchings.

"So, we're looking for a dead abbot and his abbey?" asked Rye.

"It seems so," Liam said quietly, looking away.

"What is it?" Colm asked.

"Do you recall what I told you about the cloaked fellow who visited the Lady?" Liam asked.

"Vaguely," answered Rye. "But honestly, it's hard to know what you're making up and what's real sometimes. Remind us."

"Yes, she told him to stay in the *Divide*."

"So?"

"Well, I'm thinking the chapel might be at that old monastery out past China Camp in Church Creek—the Church Creek *Divide*, as some call it. It's the only abbey I can think of around these parts, but it's been abandoned for ages."

"Yeah, I've heard of the place," Jake joined in, "but that's way out in the sticks. Who would go out there?"

"Exactly," Rye said, looking at the others. "No one would. What a perfect place to hide, right?"

"This is no coincidence," Liam said, grinning. "It's got to be the place. If it isn't, then we're plumb out of luck."

"Do you know how to get there?" Rye asked.

"I do," Liam said, nodding, "but I'm more than a bit worried about the other part of the etchings."

Colm glanced at Rye to see that she wore the same concern as Liam. "The Forest of Blood and Bones?" he asked.

"That and the Lost City," Rye said, glancing at Liam.

Liam cleared his throat, speaking in a hushed tone. "I've never set foot in the forest, and I've only met a handful who've claimed to, but I have my doubts about those stories as well."

"Same here," Rye agreed without elaboration.

"It's rumored that the trees grow from the remains of fallen heroes, and it's lorded over by the Black Nameless Thing and its horde of Unspeakables. They're always watching and waiting," Liam said quietly.

"Waiting for what?" asked Colm, sweat collecting in his armpits.

"Dinner, souls, slaves? I don't exactly know. The stories are shrouded in darkness, and I'm not terribly excited about the idea of wandering around that forest searching for this Tin Maiden," Liam said.

"What choice do we really have?" asked Jake. "It seems that a path to the Lady is laid out before us. Are we going to back away now?"

Rye turned to Liam, speaking in a gentle voice. "What of the Lost City? Are you welcome there?"

"I was not banished, if that's what you mean," Liam said gruffly, "but they may not exactly hold a ticker tape parade upon my return."

"What do you mean, your *return*?" Jake asked, stepping closer to Liam.

Rye turned to Jake. "All fae, including leprechauns,

retreated to Sidhe and the perpetual darkness of the under-world after the Fifth War. Ever since, the people of the invisible kingdom watch from the shadows, and all paths to the Lost City are no more unless you're a being of magic."

"My concern lies with the forest, not Sidhe," Liam snapped.

"But I'm not a being of magic. So, how can I go there?" Colm asked.

"It seems there is still a way—a *secret* way. The handbell's etchings say as much. The path to the Lost City and the Tin Maiden is through the Forest of Blood and Bones," Liam said. "That's how *you* get there. Now, we're wasting time. It's a long drive to the abbey."

With that, Liam jumped into the car, gunning the engine, waiting for the others to pile in. Colm gently took Rye's hand as they moved toward the car, and he looked at her, trying to tell her with his eyes that there was more that he needed to share with her. He wasn't sure she understood, but she didn't let go of his hand either.

FLAT TIRED

As the Cadillac sped down the dirt road, Colm glanced at the dashboard, seeing the sticky residue where Liam's totem had once stood. He felt guilty about taking it, especially since he'd omitted that he used it to get the mossy green Catholicon now tucked safely in his pocket.

Outside, the day finally submitted to night while Jake and Liam debated Saturday morning cartoons from the eighties. *He-Man* was currently the topic of heated discussion, and just as Colm was about to join in, the car bounced up like they'd run over something, then it swerved sideways, fishtailing. Liam fought to get the car under control, cursing as his arms worked the wheel. The road they were on was narrow, and the shoulder was studded with old trees and rugged boulders that flashed in and out of the car's headlights until the tail of the car finally won the battle, sending them spinning wildly down the road. Dust and dirt filled the light of the headlights, blinding them as Rye grasped Colm's arm tightly. With a last burst of cursing from Liam, the car jerked to a stop mere inches short of a large oak tree that loomed threateningly in front of the car.

"What happened?!" Colm asked, stretching his neck out.

"Not sure. Felt like a tire blew or something," Liam said, popping his seatbelt off.

"If you didn't drive like such a maniac, this stuff wouldn't happen," Rye said, scowling at Liam, clearly irritated, but Liam ignored her while Jake tried to soften the mood.

"It's my fault. I should've just let him drive instead of all the *He-Man* stuff. Even though we all know Skeletor is the stronger one," Jake said with a smirk.

"Is not," Liam snapped back, snagging his cane from the dashboard and jumping out of the car to start his inspection. Colm followed Rye, scooting across the rear seat to get out of the car. It was dark out, but the headlights still shone brightly as they watched Liam trudge around the car with a scowl on his face, periodically bending over to look at something, then moving on with a grunt.

Liam rounded the back of the car, calling out, "Yep, blown tire."

They all circled around to join him as he opened the trunk, pushing a set of golf clubs aside and grabbing a small electric lantern. Turning it on, he held it close to the blown tire. The slice in the tire's sidewall was clean, almost as if it had been slashed.

"Hmm… Strange," Liam said as he ran his fingers over it.

Colm thought the same thing, but guessed Liam had accidentally hit a rock in the road with an unusually sharp edge. It was impossible to know for certain, and for now, they just needed to change the tire and keep moving.

"I'll get the spare," Colm said, turning back to the trunk. Moving the golf clubs aside, he lifted the floorboard, assuming the spare would be stored beneath. Instead, he found a horde of used golf balls filling the cavity. "Please tell me you have a spare?" Colm said, worried.

"Well, here's the thing…" Liam hesitated.

Rye let out an audible sigh. "You've gotta be kidding me! I mean, really, how have you lived this long?" There was not a stitch of sarcasm in her voice. "What do we do now?" she asked irritably as she scratched her neck.

Colm stepped closer to Rye. "Are you okay?"

"Yes, it's just dark, and we're stuck in the middle of nowhere," she said, her voice cracking, sounding like she was about to cry as she stepped away into the shadows.

Colm froze. He had never been good with this type of thing.

"Go," Liam said, motioning toward where Rye had disappeared into the darkness. "Take care of her. I'll call for a tow truck to bring us a spare, but we're gonna be here for a spell." He turned to Jake, dialing on his phone as they got back into the car.

LIORA LEANED FORWARD, blowing on the reddened embers, infusing them with life and sending dark smoke billowing upward from the fire, masking the foul smell permeating the room. Ciara barked at her to move as she dragged over more of the fallen rafters, feeding them to the growing blaze. Liora rose, stepping to Ciara's side, holding a jar of shiny grey powder.

"Step back," Liora said, placing her arm softly against Ciara's chest. Turning to the fire, she took a pinch of the powder, casting it into the flames before shuffling back to join Ciara. Almost immediately, the fire flared with a blinding white light that danced in the lenses of Liora's sunglasses, the blast of heat reddening her pasty skin. Ciara let out a shrill cackle, watching the fire rage momentarily before settling.

"That was just a pinch. With the whole bottle, it will burn

hot enough and long enough for certain." Liora turned to the table, sliding a small cast iron smelting pot toward Ciara and reaching for a hook attached to a long wooden handle. "Pour her blood in."

Ciara stepped forward, taking the vial from her pocket and pouring it into the pot as directed. "Things are about to get exciting for her new little friends."

Liora winced as she attempted to lift the pot with the long-handled hook.

"Here, let me do it," Ciara said, reaching for the hook and taking over. Even though she could be rough, she did always look out for Liora, as Liora did for her.

Liora walked beside her to the fire, giving her instructions. "Just set it on something flat so it doesn't spill, and flip the lid closed."

Ciara obliged and stepped back from the fire. "Can I do it this time?" she asked Liora, rubbing her hands together, her eyes wide with excitement.

"You really are a pyro, aren't you? I thought that after the curator's house, you might dial it down a bit, but I guess that's just a dream too far."

"Yeah, so?" Ciara said, craning her neck forward, opening her eyes even wider.

Liora laughed, handing her the jar. "You are ridiculous."

"That I am," Ciara said, turning to the fire.

"You need to be care—"

Before Liora could finish, Ciara opened the jar, emptying it into the fire with a flourish as it went supernova with a brilliant white flash. A wave of heat swept through the room, and they both retreated to where Tabitha stood, turning her head to shield her eyes from the intense light.

"That's some crazy shit," Ciara said with an oversized grin.

"It's just chemistry," Liora said. "A little magnesium. So, at least we know it'll be hot enough to spark the Blood Bane."

COLM TURNED, trudging into the darkness toward Rye. The clouds blocked out the moonlight, but it momentarily peeked through, revealing her ghostly silhouette. Her head was down, but she raised it as he walked over. The clouds slid across the moon, and darkness reigned once again as he stepped to her side, his heart racing.

"I need to go. I can't stay here," Rye said with urgency.

"Yeah, okay. I understand," Colm said. It was the same story all over again: everyone left him one way or another, and it was silly for him to expect anything different from her. She didn't have to be here, and it was clear that she'd finally come to the same conclusion. The funny thing was, he wasn't mad at her; he was just sad to see her go. Reaching into his pocket, he took out the plane ticket to Dublin, holding it out to her. "You should take this and get as far away from them as you can. You can hitch a ride to the airport from the tow truck when it gets here."

Even in the darkness, he could feel her eyes upon him. "Are you finished?" she asked gently.

"Umm, yeah," he said slowly.

She stepped in, taking his hand, speaking softly. "We have no time for this. I'm not leaving you, but something is happening. Something is making me *change*, and I can't stop it."

"You mean the werewolf thing?"

"She-wolf, but yes, that," she corrected him gently.

Colm was getting nervous as the darkness filled his mind with unknowns. "What do you mean, *something* is making you change?"

"Just that. I can feel it in my blood, like it's boiling, and I can't calm it down," she said, scratching at her arm. "Shit," she muttered to herself.

"What?" Colm asked, growing more nervous by the minute.

"Nothing," she answered dismissively. "You need to go."

This is crazy. Colm stood holding the hand of a girl who would soon change into a she-wolf, which was not a settling position to be in at night, in the darkness, alone. He felt his heart rate pick up, pounding in his ears.

She spoke almost as if she sensed it. "I've never killed a human," she volunteered.

"What, is that supposed to be comforting?" he said in a high-pitched voice.

"Sorry, you don't need to worry. I've got this, but I need you to cover for me, because I don't want them to know," she said, squeezing his hand. "It's private." She glanced toward the car, where music thumped from inside and Liam leaned over, sharing a drink from his magic goblet with Jake.

Colm nodded in agreement. "Your secret's safe with me."

She leaned in, kissing him on the cheek, and he blushed, relieved that he was hidden in the darkness. "Thanks. I knew I could count on you," she said, stepping back and releasing his hand.

Colm gripped it tighter, pulling her back. "This is the first time we've been alone since leaving the Dun," he said, and hearing her breathing slow, he stumbled on his words. "There's something more I need to tell you."

"You have to hurry. It's coming," she said, reaching for her neck, scratching irritably.

He plunged his hand into his pocket, pulling out the mossy stone, placing it in Rye's hand. "This is what I traded Liam's totem for."

"What is it?"

"He called it a Catholicon. He took the two white stones from Jake, and he melded them into this. When he gave it to me, he said I could use it to remove the effects of magic and even restore the years of my life I've lost. But he said it only works once."

"I can see why you kept that quiet. It's a rare piece of magic he made you. It's lucky you had those stones."

"Well, that's what I thought, and he must've too. But when he finished crafting them, he told me that those stones didn't have any magic in them, and he had to use a lot of his own magic to make this for me. Then he pretty much passed out."

"Well, it's good that you traded him Liam's totem. It probably saved the Pict's life. But I don't really trust either of our traveling companions, so let's keep my she-wolf thing and your magic rock just between us for now."

"Agreed," Colm said as the clouds blanketed the moon once again.

"Now, I really need to go, so put your arms out, and I'll make this quick," Rye said.

"What?" Colm said, confused.

He could see her silhouette moving as her arms raised above her head. "Put your arms out like you're carrying firewood," she said, reaching out, lifting his arms up and laying her jacket and shirt across them, soon followed by her pants, boots, stocking cap, and undergarments, all subtly infused with the powdery floral scent of her perfume.

Colm blushed, averting his eyes from her, knowing she was stark naked, but the darkness hid the secrets of her body from him.

"Don't lose my clothes. Do you hear me?" she said sternly.

"Right," Colm said, still averting his eyes.

"Just hide them behind the big tree by the car, and I'll get them once it's passed," she said, about to leave. But then she hesitated, turning back to him, pulling the ring from her finger and placing it softly in his palm. "Here's your mother's ring. Thanks for letting me borrow it."

He felt the warmth of her hands brush against his palm as she stepped away. "Wait," he pleaded as a wild thought entered his mind. "Maybe I can remove your curse with my dice, or maybe the Catholicon can remove it. Maybe that's why I have it: to help you."

She turned back to him, placing her palm on his face. "You are a sweet man, and I do appreciate the offer," she said, lowering her hand, "but I chose my fate when I left with Noah. I will not let you sacrifice anything for the choices I've made in my life. Anyway, I doubt it'd even work. The magic of the Werewolf Curse is too ancient, and it's already poisoned my blood." She shooed him away. "Now go, I really can't hold it back any longer."

With that, she turned, leaping down the hill into the darkness. He heard branches breaking, and then nothing. Colm stood there for a moment, holding his mother's ring as he got a better hold on Rye's clothes. He turned the ring in his fingers as he thought of the touch of Rye's hand when she gave it back, which was markedly different from how Tabitha had just set it on the table for him.

With his thoughts flashing back to Tabitha, he realized he hadn't heard back from her, which was strange. He closed his hand over the ring and turned, heading back to the car, stowing Rye's clothes behind the oak tree. Walking around the tree, he found Liam and Jake in the car, singing along with the tunes pumping from the radio. Grabbing his phone, he was about to dial Tabitha's number when the car door opened.

Jake got out, laughing. "Oh, I didn't know you'd come back. Whatcha doing?"

Colm stood, holding his phone. "I was just gonna try Tabitha again. See if she's okay."

The light from the phone cast a ghastly ruddiness on their faces as Jake stepped closer, the laughter gone. "Why worry about the ex? Seems like you and Rye are really hitting it off."

Colm shrugged. "My parents and uncle have already been killed. I don't need any more blood on my hands."

Jake turned, leaning against the car and looking off into the night sky, taking his flask from his pocket for a quick nip. A moment later, he spoke in a flat voice, devoid of empathy. "We always think that we can control how things go down, but maybe, for us, it's just better to let life unfold on its own terms. Sometimes it'll work out, and sometimes it won't."

What Jake was suggesting didn't feel right to Colm, especially since a simple phone call might put Tabitha out of harm's way. However, just as he was about to object, Jake snapped out of it, turning to Colm with a grim chuckle.

"But that's not who we are, right? I guess that's why we ended up with these dice. Someone knew we were the type that can't leave things be. So, just call her, and then you can move on with the opportunities that are right in front of you. As for me, I've gotta take a leak."

Jake stepped away to the edge of the darkness. Colm raised his phone, dialing Tabitha, but it went to voicemail again. Regardless of Jake's lack of concern for her, Colm was worried. Sure, she'd dumped him, but he didn't want her to get hurt.

Reluctantly, he reached into his pocket, taking hold of his dice. He replayed all their warnings, telling him to think before he rolled, or questioning *if* he should even roll at all. Still, he felt guilty and had to protect her from any crap he'd inadvertently pulled her into. He made his wish, sending the dice rattling across the trunk of the car. With the glowing light of his phone, he reached out to take a look, but he could feel the X's this time before he saw them, and he stiffened. Another year gone, just like that.

His head drooped as a hand gently touched him on the back.

"You need to let her go. You gonna squander your life away over a girl who dumped you? No woman is worth that. It's a cruel life, being a Gambler, not a simple one, but it's the only life you have now," Jake said quietly.

Colm shook his head and laughed softly. "Well, if that's not the pot calling the kettle black…"

"Yeah, but black dice or not, I'm still here, aren't I? Maybe you should listen to me."

Colm took the dice from the trunk of the car. Jake was right: he'd kill himself if he kept going down this path, but stopping was easier said than done. "I just don't get it. What's the point of having it if I don't use it?"

"See, that's how it works. It wants you to think you're somehow special or have a calling. But trust me, you're not, and you don't. Just stop a minute, and you can literally feel the years it's already taken," he said, holding the flask out to Colm. "You sure you don't want a swig of this?"

"Why doesn't Liam like that stuff?" Colm asked.

"The Green Fairy? Maybe because it counteracts his magic. That's why," he said with a laugh, taking another swig. "You sure? It might help with the urges."

Colm looked at the flask, considering it briefly, but he recalled Liam's reaction to it and felt that perhaps Jake wasn't being entirely honest about it. For some reason, he chose to trust Liam on this one and waved it away.

Jake shrugged. "Your call, Gambler, but let me know if you change your mind."

Just then, the radio went quiet, and Liam emerged from the car. He quickly caught sight of the flask in Jake's hand, and his eyes flicked from it to Colm.

Jake piped in, returning the flask to his pocket. "You can relax. You've sufficiently scared the boy away from it."

Liam nodded, turning to search the darkness. "Where's Rye?"

"She said she needed some time and wanted to be alone," Colm said.

"What? You left her out there *alone*?" Liam asked as he circled around the car.

Wanting to keep his promise, Colm jumped to the first thing that came to mind. "She said it's *that time of the month*, and she needed to walk a bit."

"Are you that dense?" Both he and Jake snickered, looking at each other.

"If you haven't noticed, she does a pretty good job of taking care of herself," Colm said.

"Can't you see it, boy?" Liam asked.

"See what?"

Liam and Jake still could not contain their laughter. Liam stepped closer. "Okay, let me connect the dots for you. Girl meets boy. Girl *likes* boy. Girl makes up a reason to be alone with boy outside, in the dark." He paused, looking at Colm, but Colm still said nothing. "Oh, come on! Don't you see it? She likes you!"

They were both laughing out loud now, tears streaming from their eyes, and finally Colm joined in.

"You don't think that maybe she made it up, hoping that you'd offer to keep her company—in the dark, all alone, just the two of you?"

Colm rolled his eyes, confident that now was not the time to share that she'd also stripped down and given him her clothes. He knew the truth, but he'd sworn not to tell, so he played along. Still, he had to admit that their viewpoint was intriguing, and he couldn't deny that his feelings for her had grown as well. "You think so?"

They both nodded, and Liam handed Colm the lantern

from the back of the car. "Now, go find that little vixen and make sure she's safe."

Colm was getting caught up in the moment, but he had no intent of finding her. He stumbled down the hill, the lantern casting a dim halo of light barely bright enough to reveal a few yards ahead. He stepped behind a large bush as the lantern light flickered and went out. The hillside was plunged into darkness, with only the faint light of the moon peeking periodically through the clouds. Colm smacked the lantern, and it lit again with a flickering light that was getting dimmer by the moment.

His plan was to walk a bit farther, then sit for a little while before returning to tell them he couldn't find her. It was a good plan, but being outside in the pitch black could unnerve even the bravest of men, and this was one of those moments.

Down the hill from Colm, the crunch of fallen leaves and the crack of a branch echoed through the crisp night air. A lightning chill shot up his spine, setting off a wave of goose bumps as he peered out to the edge of the light. He stood in a clearing, holding the lantern up in the direction of the noise, and as luck would have it, the lantern flickered one last time before going dark. He smacked it again, but this time nothing happened. Growing nervous, he shook it and smacked it again. No light came, and the dark clouds ominously snuffed out any remainder of the moon. Growing closer, the rustling continued, this time accentuated by a muffled growl. He frantically searched his pocket for his phone to illuminate the night, but realized he'd left it on the trunk of the car.

Hearing a rustling of leaves on the far side of the clearing, he squinted his eyes, trying to make anything out in the darkness. She'd warned him to stay away, and now he wished he hadn't strayed so far from the car. He stood staring across the clearing, flinching at the sound of something darting out of the underbrush. Colm's muscles tensed as the clouds momentarily parted, allowing the moon to illuminate the clearing, revealing the fur of a snow-white rabbit. It held its position twenty yards away, its nose nervously sniffing the air. The clouds shifted again, dimming the light of the moon, and before the rabbit could make its next move, something sprang out of the darkness behind, crushing it. The newcomer raised its head, looking at Colm with a throaty howl, then taking a step forward with a low, rumbling growl.

He swallowed. "Rye, it's me, Colm," he said, voice shaking, recalling reading somewhere that werewolves could some-times recognize people and hold back.

Rye paused, her ears pricking up.

"That's right, Rye, it's Colm. I'm not gonna hurt you."

As he spoke again, Rye tilted her head slightly. She stepped back, picking up the rabbit in her jaws, and started to turn away, when the sound of breaking branches from behind Colm pierced the clearing, drawing her attention. From the bushes, a single beam of light pierced the darkness, illuminating her face, showing her fully transformed. Her green eyes glinted back, and she dropped the rabbit, letting out a vicious growl.

Behind the beam of light, Liam and Jake scurried out of the bushes to Colm's side. Liam held the light steady on Rye's face, and Jake kneeled next to Colm, raising the sawed-off shotgun and leveling it at her.

"No!" Colm slammed the barrel of the gun down just as Jake pulled the trigger, and a deafening boom thundered through the clearing. Rye let out another howl before picking up the rabbit and disappearing through the brush.

Jake turned to Colm. "What the hell?!" he said, his frustra-tion boiling over into anger.

A calm voice from beside Colm chimed in. "Was that Rye?" Liam asked as he stood frozen, holding the flashlight steady on the far side of the clearing where she'd disappeared.

There was an awkward silence, but Colm's lack of a response answered the question as another howl echoed up the hillside.

"Well, now, that makes a bit more sense," Liam said as they looked out into the darkness on the far side of the clearing. They finally turned, working their way back up to the car slowly. No one was talking. Instead, Liam and Jake seemed to be processing this new reality.

Liam turned to Colm. "You know, you're lucky she didn't tear you apart. Why didn't you just tell us?" he asked. "We're all adults here."

"She just wanted to keep it a secret and asked me not to tell anyone, which I've clearly failed at. I'm sure you two have your secrets as well," Colm grumbled, climbing into the back seat of the car and pulling a blanket over himself so he could get some sleep. Liam and Jake settled into the front, and the rest of the night was a blur. Colm briefly woke as the tow truck arrived and he heard Liam get out to help.

Later, in the early morning hours, the back door opened, and Rye slipped in, nestling under the blanket next to Colm.

The morning sun peeked over the hills as Colm woke to whispered voices in the front seat. Rye was still fast asleep, but looked to be a wreck. She finally stirred as Liam started the engine to warm up the car.

Liam turned to Rye. "You know, lassie, you could've just told us. It was a bit of a surprise coming across you like that. Lucky for you that Colm was there. Anyway, I assume that we're safe from that thing for now."

She rubbed her eyes, yawning. "It's not a *thing*, it's me. And yes, you're safe—*for now*," she said with a snarky tone as she picked several small sticks from her hair before pulling her stocking cap back on.

"Let's get going," Colm said matter-of-factly, and Liam nodded, putting the car in gear.

"Sorry," Colm whispered, leaning close to Rye, but she didn't acknowledge him and sat staring out the window. After a few moments, she turned to him with tears streaking her face.

"That was my secret. It wasn't yours to share," she whispered, wiping the tears from her eyes. "Why did you come back out there, anyway? I warned you to stay away."

"It was stupid, I know, but it's done now. Anyway, Liam knew it was you, so there was no point in me lying about it. How do I fix this?" Colm asked.

Rye didn't respond, turning to look out the window as she readjusted her stocking cap. The pause was bordering on awkward as she turned back. "You know, Jake was lucky you were there to knock the shotgun down," she said, looking him in the eyes. "If he'd hit me, things could've gotten real ugly, real fast."

"I guess I'm not good at keeping secrets," Colm muttered, shrugging his shoulders.

"I guess not," she said, turning back to the window.

LITTLE LIES

SMOKE STILL LINGERED from the smoldering fire across the room, casting a shadowy haze in the early morning light. Liora had been awakened by her phone, having a hushed conversation before hanging up. She leaned over, tapping Ciara on the shoulder.

"Oh, it's just you," Ciara said as she rolled over, flashing her obsidian blades at the ready.

"We have new orders. We need to go," Liora said, rubbing the sleep from her eyes.

"What about her?" Ciara motioned to the bundle next to her. The soft inhale and exhale of Tabitha's breathing moved the surface of the bag they'd placed over her head.

"She comes. Seems that our employer thinks she might come in handy."

"She seems pretty useless to me," Ciara said, scowling. "We'd be better off if we just did away with her, already."

"I don't disagree, but the orders were quite clear. She's to come with us and not be harmed." Liora put her sunglasses on.

"Great," Ciara said sarcastically, standing and putting her

blades away. Tabitha had recently taken on the tactic of going boneless, which required them to drag or carry her everywhere. "Wake up," Ciara snapped, delivering a solid kick to Tabitha's side. A muffled sound of pain emerged as Ciara knelt, removing the bag from Tabitha's head. She was still gagged, but her mascara had run down her cheeks. "We've got to go, kiddo. You gonna make this easy or hard?"

Tabitha lay flat on the floor, again going boneless. Ciara rose, winding up to kick her again, but before she could, Liora grabbed her arm, pulling her away.

"She's never going to play nice if you keep treating her like that," Liora said, pushing past Ciara, kneeling by Tabitha to offer her some water. Tabitha looked at Ciara with a grin as Liora removed her gag and helped her sit up. Liora held the glass to Tabitha's lips, giving her drinks like a baby bird getting food from its mother. When she finished drinking, Liora said in a calm voice, "Look, Tabby... May I call you Tabby?"

"No one does, but—"

"I've got nothing against you, really. You just got mixed up with the wrong people, that's all. I want to help you, but you've got to start helping us."

"Why would I help you?" Tabitha spat.

"You're wasting your time," Ciara said from across the room, where she had settled at the table for a quick breakfast of yesterday's coffee and stale donuts.

Liora turned and shot her a cross look before turning her attention back to Tabitha. "So, we have two options here: self-preservation, where you cooperate and make things easier on yourself and Colm, or the opposite, where you make things less easier on yourself and Colm."

"'Less easy,'" Ciara said from across the room.

"What?" Liora turned, irritated at Ciara for interrupting her again.

"It's 'less easy,' not 'less easier,'" Ciara said nonchalantly, stuffing half of a donut in her mouth.

Liora turned back to Tabitha, ignoring Ciara. "So, your choice: you can make things easier on yourself and your friend, or *less easier*." Ciara muffled a sarcastic laugh from across the room as a donut hit Liora in the back of the head. She again ignored Ciara, keeping her eyes on Tabitha. "Well?"

"What do I get?" she asked in a restrained tone.

"Perhaps we can make a simple exchange. You give me some cooperation, and I give you something you want. How about that?"

"I'm listening," Tabitha said.

"Let's say you stop doing this boneless thing this morning and get into the car like a good little girl."

"And in exchange?"

"I'll let you call your lovey-bird," Liora said with a smile.

"What?" said Ciara from across the room. "Are you crazy?!"

Liora turned to Ciara with a stern look. "Please, I've got this." She turned back to Tabitha, talking over the continued objections from Ciara. "You'll tell him you're okay. That'll be a lie, of course, but what relationship doesn't involve a few little lies here and there? I doubt this will be the first time you've ever lied to him."

Tabitha's eyes darted away briefly.

"See, lies are normal," Liora said, "especially ones that give people hope, and he won't have to get all worried about you. But to be clear, it'll just be some white lies that you're okay and appreciate his concern. Do you think that's a fair exchange?"

"Why would I do that?" Tabitha asked, eyeing Liora suspiciously.

"Oh, Tabby, you're not doing it for yourself. You're doing it for *him*, so he can stop worrying about you. I've heard that people can literally worry themselves to death. You wouldn't want that to happen to your lovey-bird, would you? Plus, you'll get to hear his voice and know he's okay. We're willing to do that for you—"

"If you just stop being such a pain in the ass," Ciara finished as she crossed the room to stand at Liora's side.

Tabitha paused, looking at Ciara and then back to Liora, nodding her head. "Okay, agreed."

"Excellent," Liora said with a bright smile, helping Tabitha sit in a chair by the table. "Shall we call him?"

Tabitha nodded and cleared her throat as she lowered her eyes.

Liora pushed Tabitha's chin up, and their eyes met. "Nothing about us. You hear me? You're packing up for school, and everything is okay. Got it?"

Tabitha nodded, but Ciara moved in and briskly pushed her chair back against a wooden post. With one swift movement, she drew a blade, placing the point of it against Tabitha's forehead, pinning her head against the post. A small trickle of blood glistened where the blade rested, and Tabitha let out a gasp as she shuddered, looking into the hollow, beady eyes of the raven's head carved into the guard of Ciara's blade.

"Just a little insurance to make sure you stay on script, *Tabby*," Ciara said, tired of all the pleasantries.

"Dammit, this isn't necessary," Liora cursed, irritated at Ciara's outburst.

"I disagree. *This* situation makes me a bit more comfortable with the deal you made. You may proceed," she said, waving her free arm to Liora, who proceeded to get Tabitha's phone.

"Ready?" Liora asked, looking at Tabitha.

Tabitha was frozen, looking up at the blade resting on her skull. She closed her eyes, taking a deep breath and blowing it out slowly. Then she opened her eyes and nodded, wincing as the blade dug in a bit deeper.

Liora pressed the button to dial Colm's number. "Stick to the script," she reminded her one last time.

The phone rang a few times before the call connected.

"Hello?" said a soft female voice. Tabitha hesitated, not saying anything, and the voice repeated, "Hello?"

Ciara's knife dug in a bit more, and Tabitha winced in pain.

"Answer her," Liora said in an almost inaudible whisper.

"Umm, hi. I'm trying to reach Colm," Tabitha said, working to settle the tremor in her voice as she recalled the girl who had been with Colm the day before. "Rye? Is that you? It's me, Tabitha. We met at the Parada yesterday?"

A cheery voice on the other end responded with a clear acknowledgment. "Right. Hi, Tabitha. Colm's been trying to get a hold of you. Hang on, I'll get him."

Liora nudged Tabitha, motioning for her to hurry it up.

"I don't have a lot of time right now. I'm heading off to college. Maybe you can just let him know that I got his message, and I'm okay," Tabitha said with a steady voice.

"No need. I can see him heading back now, so you can tell him yourself. It'll take a load off his mind to know you're okay. Just hang on a sec."

"Perfect. Thanks, Rye," Tabitha said, looking to Liora, who nodded to her approvingly and mouthed the words, *"Stick to the script."*

"So, your necklace—was Colm able to get it back for you?" Tabitha asked. Ciara pressed the blade harder, and she winced, tears now streaming from her eyes. Liora reached up, grabbing Ciara's arm, shaking her head and pulling some pressure off the blade.

"He did, just as promised," Rye answered. "And here he is."

"Tabitha? Why didn't you call or text me back? I've been

really worried, especially after what happened to Andrew. Are you okay?" Colm asked.

"Yeah, I'm sorry. I've just been busy packing for school, and frankly, I didn't really know what to say about Andrew. You know I'm not good with that kind of thing. But I should be asking if *you're* okay. Are you?"

He sighed. "Yeah, I'm okay—or will be, I guess. I haven't had much time to think about it, but right now I'm worried about you. You haven't had two strange ladies visit you, have you?"

Liora glared at her, mouthing, *"the script"* once again as Ciara's blade dug in a bit deeper, causing Tabitha to let out a subtle gasp.

"What's wrong?" Colm asked immediately.

"Nothing, it's just..." She hesitated, settling herself. "Your message was a little weird, and then it was strange to call and have *her* answer your phone. Is there anything you need to tell me about her?" Tabitha asked.

"No. It just took a little longer than I thought to get her necklace back, that's all. But you—you're safe?"

"Yeah, I'm okay. Nothing to worry about here. Did you give any more thought to our talk at the bar?"

"No, I'm just in the middle of something that I need to take care of before I can answer you. Okay?" Colm said, his voice almost a whisper.

Tabitha took a deep breath, steadying herself as tears flowed from her eyes. "I'm sorry, that wasn't fair of me to ask right now. Just know that I'm here for you, but I can't wait forever," she said, lowering her head as Colm told her to let him know if anything changed. Just as she was about to respond, Liora pressed the button to hang up.

"Perfect, bravo!" Liora clapped as Ciara removed the blade from her head. "That was better than I'd hoped."

"You bitch!" Tabitha screamed, struggling against her

bindings. "You two are the worst! How can you *do* this to people?!"

"Well, it's kind of an art, really. But thank you, that's a huge compliment, and you played your part perfectly," Liora said, beaming with delight.

Ciara turned to Liora. "I have to hand it to you. I doubted that was the right thing to do, but with my modification, it seemed to work out well."

"How can you live with yourselves?!" Tabitha fumed.

"It's what we do, Tabby, it's what we do," Liora said matter-of-factly. "Now, for your part, I assume you never intended to live up to your end of the bargain."

"You got that right," Tabitha said, spitting in Liora's face. "How do you like that?"

Ciara's hand had reeled back to strike, but Liora caught her arm as she wiped the thick spit from her face. "No, it's okay. Perhaps I deserved that. But enough fun and games for today. Gag her and bag her. Our employer told me we need to get to some abbey out in the country—asap."

A moment later, Liora walked across the room, Ciara following as she toiled with Tabitha's limp body draped over her shoulder. Arriving at the door, Liora paused, hearing the din of diesel engines thrumming outside. She stepped to the side, peering out the window by the door. There was a line of police cars at the end of the dock, and just behind them was the black van from the museum with SWAT stenciled on the side. In front of the police cars, a number of officers dressed in black tactical gear had formed a line, carrying riot shields. The other officers congregated behind them, guns drawn, and they all inched forward with the speed of a garden slug.

"Looks like we've got company," Liora said, turning to Ciara.

Ciara dropped Tabitha with a thud, joining Liora at the window. "Oh, goodie, some fun! I've got this, but be ready."

She slipped out the door, lifting her arms wide above her head and clenching her fists. The morning sky darkened as clouds and fog flushed in from the ocean behind the warehouse. The line of officers stopped, and an officer in plain clothes stepped out with a bullhorn that crackled to life.

"We've got the dock blocked off. There is no escape." He stood tall, his eyes not leaving her.

Ciara cackled as she squeezed her hands tighter, and a thick fog suddenly descended on the dock, the clouds almost entirely blocking out the sun now. The officer with the bullhorn gaped upward at the looming darkness and took several steps backwards. When he looked back towards Ciara, she was gone. Behind him, the other officers retreated, slowly walking backwards, but as the darkness flooded the dock, they broke rank, sprinting back to the safety of their cars.

It was too late. Ciara had already slipped past them and was behind the line of police cars, punching large gashes in the gas tanks of several cruisers, including the large black van. Gasoline flushed out of them, flooding the dock as she slipped away, the police none the wiser. By the time they'd made it to their cars, Ciara was back at the warehouse, and Liora joined her, dragging Tabitha across the dock to the Rambler.

"Now it's your turn," Ciara said to Liora as she stuffed Tabitha into the trunk.

Liora stepped in front of the car, looking down the dock. The officers had noticed the smell of gasoline and were frantically fleeing the area. She waited for more of them to get clear before taking her sunglasses off, revealing her pale yellow eyes. A moment later, a gleaming pinpoint of pure white light pooled within them, now golden with power, and she carefully removed her gloves, revealing blackened fingertips charred by use. Her hands now free, she thrust them forward, and two searing beams of light pierced the darkness, streaking toward their target. As soon as they hit, the gasoline ignited. An enormous explosion hurled police cars into the air, creating a gap just large enough for the Rambler to cruise through.

"Brilliant!" Ciara cried, jumping into the driver's seat, her car growling to life.

"You seem to have a fetish for fire lately," Liora observed as she groped for the car door, momentarily blinded by her power. She'd noticed her sight taking longer to recover after each use, and she knew it was only a matter of time before her sight left her altogether. After some effort, she joined Ciara in the car, putting her sunglasses back on and carefully covering her hands with the cream gloves.

"What? That was all you, bright eyes; I just gave you the opportunity to join the show. So, you're welcome," Ciara said with a smirk.

On the other end of the dock, the fire raged and had already spread to several abandoned warehouses, threatening more. Ciara gunned the Rambler through the gap in the inferno as the officers dove out of her way, some even leaping off the dock.

23

THE STONE CHAPEL

IT WASN'T MUCH FARTHER until the Cadillac slowed, turning onto a forest access trail one could barely even call a road. The rains had rutted it out, and a smattering of fallen rocks littered the way.

"You're driving this thing on *that?*" Colm asked, leaning forward.

"It's the only way. It'll be slow going, but we'll get there," Liam said from the front seat. He pressed a button, and the car's shocks pumped, raising it a few inches higher. The car plodded down the track, Liam maneuvering carefully, cursing at the scraping sound of the undercarriage bottoming out in the ruts or catching an errant rock.

It was midmorning by the time they rolled to a stop at the end of the road. As they looked up the mountain, the ruins of the old abbey peeked out from the rocks and trees high above them. The sun crested the hill behind them, illuminating the old abbey in an ethereal glow, as if to announce its divine presence.

"There she is!" Liam stepped out of the car and pointed up the hill with his cane as the others scrambled out to join him. Colm stood looking up the mountainside as Rye strode past them, pulling her jacket on and tugging her stocking cap securely on her head.

"What are we waiting for, gents? Let's go find us a dead abbot," she called back from the entrance to the trail.

Before the others could move, Rye was already fifty yards ahead of them, picking her way up through the dense undergrowth that had mostly reclaimed the trail to the abbey. Clearly, no one had been this way in a long time, made even more obvious by the number of trees, some with trunks as thick as two grown men abreast, that had fallen across the trail. There was a fair amount of scrambling over the fallen trees and rockslides, and Liam often needed help, despite his vociferous objections.

Colm pushed forward, glancing at the gnarled and knotted old oak trees that lined the trail. From the right angle, he could have sworn they had eyes and were watching them like sentinels. A few days ago, it would've been silly to think that, but not now. Now, anything was possible. He tightened his backpack straps and hastened to keep pace with Rye, all the while keeping an eye on the trees.

With the sun bearing down on them, their tempers grew short, only aggravated by the rough condition of the trail. Still, they plodded along, and the abbey grew closer with each step. Soon they came upon a waist-high cobblestone wall covered in ivy that ran off into the forest on both sides. A rusted iron gate of intricate scrollwork stood open, falling off its hinges, and a pair of matching lanterns atop the fence flanked the trail. On the far side of the wall, the undergrowth hadn't yet fully reclaimed the grounds of the abbey, almost in homage to the hard work of the monks of the distant past. A number of crows fluttered about, loudly scolding the intruders.

Once they passed through the gate, the trail was distinctly

easier, and they took a break, resting on an oversized boulder that had been hewn into a bench. They'd come up several hundred feet, the Cadillac like a toy car far below. Rye sat gazing into the distance across the forested valley. Colm settled in beside her, wiping the sweat from his brow, looking out across the valley with her. It was sprawling, spreading out into the distance in both directions, all accented by the golden sun high above them without a cloud in the sky. They were in the middle of nowhere, with just the thin ribbon of road they'd driven in on cutting across the far side of the valley before disappearing over the top.

"Amazing! This is what it's all about," Colm said almost reverently.

Rye leaned back, resting her head on the boulder. "That it is. These are the moments—"

But a distant rumble of thunder interrupted her words, and her voice trailed off, confusion written on her face.

The thunder continued to echo through the valley without pause, and Colm could feel Rye's muscles tense until she stood, her hand to her brow to block the sun, peering across the valley. Her look of confusion was quickly replaced with disbelief. "Son of a bitch! How could they?"

Liam stood, following Rye's eyes across the valley. "Break's over. We need to get a move on."

Colm stood, joining them. "What is it?" he asked, but as the words spilled from his mouth, the noise finally resolved in his ears. It was the muffled rumble of the Rambler intruding on the silence of the wilderness.

"Are those the ladies from the museum?" Jake asked, dumbfounded, now looking across the valley with the others.

"None other," Liam said as he reached for his cane.

"Let's go," Rye commanded, and they all fell in line behind Liam, pressing farther up the hill into the abbey.

When they crested the hill, the modest grounds of the

abbey lay before them, engulfed by the same gnarled old oak trees from the trail. Liam stepped forward, pointing to the ruins of a large stone building just ahead of them. "That looks like the chapel."

Colm's eyes turned upward to the fallen spire that now lay in rubble littering the grounds. He followed the others as they crept forward, the sound of the Rambler pushing them forward, chasing them into the ruins. Unlike the cobblestone wall surrounding the abbey, this building had been made of dark, finely cut stacked stone, displaying the skill of the monks. It stood mostly intact, but the windows were shattered, and portions of the roof had fallen in. Ivy climbed the walls of the building, and the place where the door would have once stood was now just an arched opening.

"How do you know this is the chapel?" Jake asked as he glanced around at the other ruins on the grounds of the abbey.

"Well, I don't, but it's the biggest building, which is the way churchy folks usually do things," Liam pointed out.

"Umm, guys?" Rye called out from behind them.

Realizing that Rye wasn't with them, the three men stopped, turning back to see her off to the side, standing beside a large oak tree.

"I don't think that's the chapel. I think it's over here," she said, pointing to a smallish, nondescript stone ruin that the tree overlooked.

The three men joined Rye, taking in the simple beauty of it. Unlike the larger ruin with the spire, this one was not made of cut stones, but smooth, hand-chiseled stone. In fact, on closer inspection, Colm realized the monks had carved it out of a single enormous boulder. The windows were broken, but the roof was hewn from the same boulder, domed to shed the rain. At its apex, a small stone cross stood bathing in the morning sunshine. The large carved wooden door at the entrance stood slightly askew, revealing hints of the interior. Just above the door, carved into the stone, were two hands pressed together in prayer.

"I think you're right," Liam said, taking a step forward.

The others followed Liam toward the chapel, but Colm hung back, thinking over the last few days. He still couldn't believe he had a *magic* dice and had now met a genuine she-wolf and a leprechaun. Watching them, he half expected to wake up to the sound of his alarm clock blaring, but he knew that wasn't going to happen. This was all too real, and now was the time to see if Grigs had told him the truth about the bell.

Rye was the first to arrive at the door. She was running her hand along the carvings in the wood, deep in thought as Colm arrived at her side. Looking through the cracked opening, he could see a simple circular room, large enough for maybe fifteen people. The stone pews were arranged around a central lectern, and for the most part, everything appeared to be in good condition.

"Here, help me give this door a push," Rye said, and they both leaned in, but the door didn't budge.

Colm turned to Jake and Liam. "Give us a hand, guys?"

They both stepped forward, helping push it open. Inch by inch, the door submitted and scraped across the floor, triggering a few birds nesting in the chapel to fly out of the broken windows.

"That's good." Rye slipped through the opening, followed by the others.

The chapel had no other exits. The stone floor was littered with leaves and shards of stained glass from the narrow windows that circled the room. It was maybe twenty feet in diameter, with crosses and oak trees carved into the stone, but unlike the churches in town, there were no painted frescos or anything lavishly adorned with gold. This was a simpler, purer place of worship.

"Okay, so, now what?" Liam asked, posing the question that they were all thinking as they circled the room.

"What exactly did the Pict say?" Rye asked Colm, and all eyes turned to him.

Colm shrugged, sweat beading on his forehead. The memory of his discussion with the Pict was already getting fuzzy. "Well, he didn't tell me what to do once we found this place. He just told me we needed to come here to find the owner of the bell."

Colm diverted his eyes from the others, pacing around the chapel, the frustration clear on his face. He couldn't help but think that Grigs knew more, but Colm hadn't pressed him hard enough or asked the right questions. The same frustration spread to the faces of the others—all except for Rye. She was gazing around the room, studying the stone carvings on the wall as she spoke.

"There has to be something, a clue somewhere," she said.

"Well, if you've any ideas, lassie, I'm open." Liam leaned heavily on his cane before sitting on one of the pews encircling the central lectern.

Rye turned to him. "I've got nothing," she said, exhausted, crumpling onto the nearest pew.

Jake stepped toward the lectern, circling it, and finally leaned his body hard into it, trying to move it.

"That's pointless," Colm said, taking a seat next to Rye. "They carved this chapel out of a boulder, and that lectern is just a of part of it. It's not gonna move." He leaned forward, taking the handbell from his backpack, looking at the etchings even though he knew he couldn't read them.

With a gasp, Jake stopped pushing on the stone lectern and turned in their direction, breathing deeply from the exertion. "There has to be something we're missing."

"Maybe," Rye murmured. Then, "Wait—maybe that's it!" she said in an excited voice, springing forward with a bright look in her eyes as she turned to Colm.

"What?" Colm asked, sparked by her enthusiasm.

"Ring it!" she said, pointing to the handbell.

"It doesn't ring," Colm said, shrugging.

"I know, but just humor me. Just *act* like you're ringing it," she said with a smile.

All eyes again turned to Colm, and he slowly stood, holding the handbell, his doubt telegraphed in his slouched shoulders. "It's not gonna—"

"Just do it, please," Rye cut in, a bit more insistently.

Her look was intense. With the doubt still fogging his mind, Colm stepped toward the lectern, shaking the bell.

The chapel was silent. He turned back to the others, lowering his head. Even though he'd doubted her idea, deep inside, he'd hoped something would happen—anything. But it didn't. He dropped his hand to his side and stepped toward the pews, when a loud click came from somewhere in the rock deep below them. The sound of stones coarsely grating against one another followed, and the floor shook violently, causing Colm to lose his balance. Teetering forward, he fell toward Rye.

"Um, guys, you're going to want to see this!" Liam said from across the room.

As he turned, Colm saw the central lectern spinning, rising out of the floor until it ground to a stop just below the domed roof of the chapel. Cut into the newly exposed rock was a stone archway outlined with a series of runes. Beyond the archway, a stone staircase spiraled downwards, fading away into darkness. The staircase was covered in centuries' worth of spiderwebs, and an unlit torch sat in a sconce on the wall.

As the silence returned to the chapel, Rye stepped

forward, running her fingers over the runes carved around the archway. Liam joined her, looking over them as well.

"They're warnings," Rye said as she exchanged a concerned look with Liam. "They say not to venture down the stairs."

"I saw that look," Jake said as he joined them.

"What else is there?" Colm questioned, concern heavy in his voice.

Rye turned, her eyes fixed on Colm. "That one," she said, pointing to a particular rune carved into the stone of the archway, "means death."

"More precisely, it means, 'Death awaits,' or something like that," Liam clarified, rubbing his chin. "But any way you read it, it's not a good thing."

"Well, I'm mostly dead already," Jake quipped as he hoisted the shotgun from his belt, checking to confirm that it was loaded. "I didn't come this far to get scared away by some stone carvings made by someone who knows how long ago." He straightened his back with a stoic look. "I'm going down." He moved forward, but then Liam barred his way, pressing his hands against Jake's chest.

"Just wait. I didn't say I wasn't goin'," Liam said. "Let's just think for a moment, okay?" he suggested in a calm voice as they stood glaring at each other.

"He's right," Rye said, stepping to Liam's side as he gave her a grateful nod. "We just need a minute. These types of warnings aren't randomly thrown out. They're serious, so we need to be careful."

Jake shook his head, letting out a small breath of disgust. "Just a minute? I don't have many more minutes to give. It's obvious that the bell is leading us this way, and remember, those ladies can't be too far behind. So, come or stay—either way, I don't care. I just want to get rid of this cursed dice, and this is my only chance to do that," Jake said, his eyes fixed on Colm. "What about you, Gambler? You coming?"

Once the archway had revealed itself, Colm knew Grigs had been honest with him, and he also knew what he was going to do before this latest exchange got heated. Without hesitation, he stepped to Jake's side, drawing the Moonblade from his pack. "I'm going."

Liam released his hands from Jake's chest, taking a step back.

Rye pursed her lips, and with a resigned look, she placed her hand gently on Colm's shoulder, nodding. "Okay, let's go —but follow my lead," she said, turning to Liam. "You in?"

"So much for thinking about it for a minute," Liam said, shaking his head with a concerned look. He tapped his cane on the floor, gripping and re-gripping it nervously. "Lead the way." He motioned with his cane to the archway.

Rye turned, taking the torch from the sconce inside. It immediately combusted, illuminating the staircase in an eerie blue light that traced the edges of the walls, until several yards down, it was almost as if the stone itself disappeared into total darkness. The only sign of anything solid was errant points of light moving along the walls and ceiling, almost like shooting stars. She stepped through the archway, followed closely by Liam, Jake, and Colm.

Colm reached out, touching Jake's back for direction as they entered the darkness, with only the glimmer of the blue torch guiding them like the North Star. The darkness of the surrounding staircase was all-consuming, as if they were walking on the darkness itself. He could feel the floor as he stepped forward, but there was no floor to be seen. The sensation was a bit unsettling, but he eventually focused on the glow of the blue torch ahead. With his hand on Jake's back, they worked their way downward ever so slowly.

With his next step, Colm's hand suddenly lunged forward into the darkness. Jake was gone.

Lifting his eyes, he saw the vague silhouette of Rye against the faint blue light of the torch as he was overcome with a wave of nausea. His body quaked and convulsed as if it were being pulled inside out, his vision blinded by a sudden flash of white light. He jerked forward, tumbling to the floor, bitter bile churning up from his stomach, but he clamped down, holding it in. His head struck something solid, and then he rolled onto his back, opening his eyes.

Above him, impossibly, was the canopy of a forest lit by the noonday sun. It took a moment for his eyes to adjust as he loosened his grip on the Moonblade. He reached up, rubbing his head with his free hand and finding it smeared with blood.

His mind raced, trying to decipher what was going on, and he pushed himself up to his knees, surveying the surrounding woods to see those gnarled old oak trees watching him. Dashing forward, he stepped around the large oak he'd fallen by to see the crumbled ruins of the abbey a short distance away. "How is that possible?" he mumbled in disbelief as he ran his hands over his body to confirm that he was in fact here. He shook his head, confused as to why he was outside, until the image of Rye with the eerie blue torch-light flashed in his mind.

He'd left her alone, descending into the darkness. The words *"Death awaits"* echoed through his mind—and she was headed there without his help. He wasn't going to let that happen, but as he took a step forward, the ground swayed before him, and the pain once again flared in his head. Pausing, he bent over, taking a deep breath, pressing his fingers to his temples. With a renewed effort, Colm stood, taking another deep breath, steeling himself against the wave of nausea that was sure to come. And come it did, but this time he was ready for it. He pushed through it, determined to get back to the chapel, back to Rye.

Colm rushed into the chapel, but it was totally vacant—no Liam, no Jake, and no Rye. Stepping up to the archway, he glanced at the sconce, but there was no torch, which meant Rye was still down there. He took a deep breath and moved through the archway once again. It was even darker than before. The eerie blue light of the torch was nowhere in sight —and neither was Rye.

24

AN IMPROMPTU MEETING

LIORA LED the way as they followed the path slowly up the hill toward the abbey. Given her bum shoulder, Ciara was left with the unenviable task of lugging along their uncooperative baggage, which resulted in more frequent stops, slowing them down. Ciara did her best, but Tabitha also did her best to hinder their progress at every opportunity. However, they'd seen the Cadillac parked at the end of the road, so they knew they were getting close, and that kept them pressing onward. But the more Tabitha ignored them, the more Liora was seeing the logic in Ciara's viewpoint: their job would have been much easier without Tabitha's deadweight. But for some reason, their new employer required her alive and unharmed. It was clear that neither Liora nor Ciara enjoyed being told what to do, but that wouldn't last forever. At some point, the job would come to an end, and then all bets would be off. That was what drove them forward.

After an arduous climb, they finally arrived at the short stone wall surrounding the abbey, and Ciara unceremoniously threw their baggage to the ground. A muffled sound came from the bag as Tabitha's head struck the ground before she settled awkwardly against the stone wall. Ciara collapsed onto the large rock bench overlooking the valley, and Liora joined her, offering her a drink of water as they caught their breath.

"We can't keep going like this with her," Ciara said, wiping the dirt-caked sweat from her face. "She's slowing us down."

Liora nodded as she drank more water, still recovering from the climb. "Yes, she's definitely doing that. I'm not sure how we're expected to catch up with them as long as we have to drag her along."

"We could just say that she didn't make it—that she fell or something. It'd be easy to make it look like an accident," Ciara suggested. "My goal's the little golden child and her charm. She's never deserved that thing."

"Stop. There will be time for that later. Like it or not, we made a commitment to help find the Lady and fulfill the prophecy, and we won't truly be free until it's done. That's why we're doing all this, remember? Who cares about Rye? She doesn't matter anymore, so you need to bury the hatchet with her and let it go. We have a job to do," Liora said, gazing at Ciara, daring her to argue.

Instead, Ciara stood with a huff, stabbing her blade into a nearby tree. "Well, we can't keep on like this," she repeated. "We need to get her to cooperate with us."

"And how do we do that?" Liora asked in a sarcastically sweet voice.

Ciara turned back, glaring at her, but before she could answer, a strange popping noise sounded in the forest, just out of sight. Both whirled at the sound. Liora's senses were on high alert as she scanned their surroundings, looking for an explanation. However, the woods had wrapped their secret in silence once again, and she wondered if they'd somehow gotten ahead of their prey.

Reaching out with her good arm, she grabbed Tabitha's bag, struggling to drag it out of sight. Just as Ciara moved to help, the sound of snapping twigs echoed through the forest, freezing Liora in place. As she turned to Ciara, she smiled, seeing that she'd already disappeared. She reached down, gritting her teeth and pulling the bag the last couple of feet.

A deep voice from behind startled her. "Hello, Liora. Where's the dark one?"

Liora spun around, surprised to see it was one of the gents helping Rye. But beyond that, there was something oddly familiar about him, about his voice. She grinned, stepping closer to him. "Well, well, you seem to have found yourself in the wrong place."

He let out an eerie laugh, holding his ground firmly, showing no signs of concern. Instead, his hands dropped casually to his sides, and he took a step forward, looking into her eyes. "Or perhaps the fates wanted us to meet."

There was a sudden movement from above, and Ciara dropped from a tree, blades drawn. He did not even flinch, but stood solemnly smiling, Ciara's obsidian blades held firmly against his throat.

"Are you done?" he asked calmly, looking to Ciara with a chuckle.

Liora cocked her head to the side, wondering what he found so funny. This was not how people usually acted when confronted by them, so she mirrored him. "Are *you* done?" she asked sarcastically, matching his smile.

"Not quite," he said—and a swirling dark smoke enveloped his body. Ciara jumped back, her blades clattering to the ground, shaking her hands as if they'd been burned. Uncertain what she was seeing, Liora took a tenuous step back. A moment later, the smoke resolved, and the man who had been there a moment ago was gone, replaced with another.

"It's nice of you to finally join us," he said, looking upon Ciara with a scowl. "I was beginning to think I'd recruited the wrong two ladies to help me out with this … *situation.*"

Liora stood at attention, shock spreading across her face. "What are you doing here?" Even though she'd never seen him in person, the snarky intonation of his voice was unmistakable.

"I can be anyone I want, anywhere I want. You would be wise to remember that," he answered, taking a step to the side, unconcerned.

"But I don't understand. I thought you trusted us to do this job," Liora said in confusion. "That's why you hired us. We're following them, and we've dragged the girl along with us, unharmed. We're doing just as you ordered."

"Yes, that you are, my dear Liora—and a fine job of it too. But as a means of insurance, I've decided to join the fray. You see, I'll keep pulling them forward, and you two will keep pushing from behind. With that approach, finding the Lady is inevitable—and better yet, she'll be none the wiser." He bent over to pick up Ciara's blades, holding them out to her hilt-first. "And you, Ciara—always the tricky one."

Ciara stepped forward, snatching her obsidian blades with a menacing look, and he let out a chuckle as he turned back to Liora.

"Such a matched couple you are: the hopeful politician, and the fear-mongering murderer. Hope and fear, fear and hope, always working your devious ways. The Lady was wise to maintain your services for as long as she did, but I'm glad you've seen the light."

Liora knew his words dripped with deceit, and she couldn't have despised him more than she did at this moment. He never sought their services; he only manipulated them into doing his unsavory tasks—something they were currently powerless to avoid.

"Put the blades away, Ciara, and join us," he said, smiling. "We need to talk, and quickly, at that."

Ciara robotically returned her blades to their sheaths and joined Liora, her jaw clenched, frustration clear on her face. She resented this even more than Liora, but even her strong will was not enough to foil his dominance over them.

"That's a good girl, Ciara," he said condescendingly. "I assume that's Tabitha?" He gestured to the bag on the ground.

They both nodded. Ciara gritted her teeth, letting out a shallow, controlled breath.

"What is it, Ciara? You have something you want to say?"

Ciara nodded, but Liora spoke before she could say anything stupid. "We've got nothing to say to you. We're just trying to do as you ordered." Then she bit her tongue. She didn't like him or his tactics, but that didn't matter—not at this moment, at least. Waiting was her game. She knew that, and so she waited. For now, she surrendered to his control over them, feigning allegiance.

He looked at her sternly. "Don't get any foolish ideas. I'm not as stupid as you may think. In fact, I think just like the two of you do."

Ciara scoffed. Perhaps that was true in some regards, but not in so many other, more meaningful ways. Liora was nothing like him, and someday she would show him that— personally. Ciara leaned in, about to speak, but Liora placed a hand on her arm, giving her a knowing glance. Ciara relented.

"The girl," Liora said, "she's alive, as ordered, even though Ciara literally had to carry her ass up here because she refuses to help. Are you sure we need her? I mean, we're all here now, and we could just finish this and take Rye's necklace. The Lady would be sure to come."

Their employer cupped his chin, tapping his finger on his cheek. "You're right. I agree that the Lady would come, but she'd be ready for us, prepared. The new plan is so much better. She won't even see us coming. We'll be delivered right to her doorstep, and let in willingly, just as a cat brings a mouse to its master," he said, then remembered something. "Oh, and by the way, that was both risky and brilliant to have her call him, but it could've ended up not so great."

"Well, it went fine," Liora said, defending her decision. "Right now, Colm just thinks she's headed off to school."

"Yes, well, when he sees you two arrive with her, I'm sure that he'll have quite the surprise."

"That's assuming we can make it there with her," Liora said, frustrated. "She's been very uncooperative, refusing to walk or follow simple orders."

"Hmm, I think I can help with that," he said menacingly, stepping forward. "Get her out, quickly. You won't need the bag once I've ... *encouraged* her to see the benefits of her cooperation."

Ciara and Liora quickly unbundled Tabitha, untying her ankles, but leaving her hands bound behind her back with the gag in place. They struggled to get her to her feet, and she resisted every inch of the way.

"See the shit we're dealing with?" Ciara said, reaching for one of her blades, but she stopped as he nodded at her.

"That will not be needed," he said in a reassuring voice, and he reached out, removing Tabitha's gag. "Such a pretty young lady. It's Tabitha, right?"

She didn't say a word in response, and he stroked her cheek. "You seem like a smart young lady with your whole life ahead of you. Graduate school, even. Maybe a husband and kids down the road. But I'm here to make something abundantly clear to you: I don't care about you, or Colm. He's an orphaned child, lost to the world, and I could go back right now and kill him." He snapped his fingers. "Just like that. And the world wouldn't care, because he's a nobody—just like you."

Her eyes, laced with venom, now caught his. As she started to speak, he passed his fingers across her lips.

"Go ahead. Speak your mind if you've got something to say," he said with a smirk.

Her eyes widened as his hand dropped from her lips—only no lips remained. Where her mouth had been was now a smooth wall of flesh. She struggled to speak, but only faint and incoherent mumblings were audible. She panicked, her eyes growing wide as she fought to calm her breathing through her nose.

"No, nothing?" he asked mockingly. "That's a shame. It looked like you had something to say." Leaning in, he passed his hand over her nose, now sealing her nostrils, trapping her breath inside with her voice. "So fragile you humans are, but perhaps this gives you some motivation to play nice. No?"

Tabitha's eyes were pleading as tears rolled down her face, and her body convulsed, desperate for air. Her eyes met his, and she nodded hysterically, all her bravado gone.

He pressed his lips to her ear, whispering, "Do not test me, or I will kill you, just after you watch me kill Colm. And then, just for fun, I'll kill your parents too. Understood?"

She nodded fervently, her cheek brushing up against his as he passed his hand over her face to reveal her mouth and nostrils again. She gasped, falling to the ground in a lump.

He turned, looking at Liora. "I expect you'll find her very *helpful* from now on." Kneeling by Tabitha, he placed a finger under her chin, lifting her face. "Isn't that right?"

Her eyes met his, resigned. "Yes," she spit out, nodding

frantically in agreement, and with that, he slid the gag back into her mouth.

"But I want to be fair. So, if you do what these fine ladies ask of you, then I promise that you and Colm can live. What you do after that is up to fate. Fair enough?" he said, still looking at Tabitha, and again she nodded.

He rose, looking at Liora. "Now, back to you two. They're going to lead us right to the Lady if we let them, so stay on our tail, but don't confront us. I'll keep them pressing forward, and you stop them from turning back in case they get cold feet. Got it?"

"Got it," Liora said, nodding. She glanced to Tabitha to see the tears in her eyes. There were other ways to do things. She would remember this when the time came.

He turned to Ciara, stepping closer. "Do you understand me, Ciara? No confrontations."

She looked him in the eyes, nodding. "No confrontations. I understand," she said through gritted teeth.

He nodded back and turned, moving up the hill toward the chapel. The same swirling smoke enveloped him as he transformed back to his previous form.

Liora knelt by Tabitha, helping her sit up and taking off her gag. "I don't think we need this anymore. Are you okay?" she asked, and Tabitha nodded back, clearly flustered over what had just happened.

Ciara grimaced as she sat on a bench, watching. "Don't get all sappy on me now, Liora. We've a job to finish, and you know as well as I do that we have little say in the matter."

They held tight for a few minutes before they slowly crept their way toward the chapel, cautious to keep their distance, just as ordered. They paused, pulling Tabitha behind a large oak tree as Colm came striding out of the woods across the abbey grounds, heading back toward the chapel. Tabitha bolted upright, stepping toward Colm.

Ciara leaned in, her raspy voice whispering into Tabitha's ear. "Quiet now, Tabby, you'd best keep that deal you just made. Trust me, you don't want to cross him if you ever want to see Colm or that little college of yours again."

Liora leaned in, pulling Ciara back. "She gets it. We *all* get it. We may not like it, but we get it," she said, turning to Tabitha and continuing in a soft voice, "But you can see he's still alive, so just do as you're told, and it can stay that way. Okay?"

Tabitha let out a sigh as her body relaxed. She nodded, and they all crouched down behind the tree, keeping their distance.

INTO THE DARKNESS

COLM MOVED FORWARD into the darkness with no hesitation. Running his free hand along the gritty stone of the wall, he followed it downward, moving deeper below the chapel floor with each step. Without the eerie blue light of the torch, the staircase was cloaked in utter darkness. If not for the cold feel of the wall under his hand and the hard, smooth surface of the descending stairs beneath his feet, he would have felt adrift in the darkness. He gripped the Moonblade, slowing his descent as he approached where he'd descended to last time.

Just as he pulled in a quick breath to call out for Rye, a familiar wave of nausea overcame him. He again had the sensation that his body was being pulled inside out, followed quickly by the blinding light. He opened his eyes to find himself lying in a bed of leaves, looking up at the canopy trees, but by some stroke of grace, he hadn't hit his head this time.

"What the hell?" he mumbled as he rolled over, glancing at the noonday sun piercing through the leaves. Rising to his feet, he spun around until he sighted the ruined buildings of the abbey. He quickly collected himself, picked up his Moon-blade, and sprinted back to the chapel, where he found Liam and Jake waiting for him.

Liam had his foot up on the pew closest to the staircase, but stood at attention as he saw Colm come through the doorway. "Whoa, boy, slow down. This place is warded."

"Warded? What the hell is does that mean?!" Colm asked frantically, still thinking about Rye below them in the darkness, alone. He continued toward the stairs, looking at the ominous runes etched into the archway.

"It means it's somehow protected by magic," Jake said as he stepped in front of Colm, blocking the path to the archway.

Liam took the pipe from his mouth, stepping toward Colm. "I'm not exactly sure how it works, or why it let Rye through, but not the three of us."

"Well, we can't leave her down there by herself," Colm said, trying to step around Jake, but Jake held firm, not letting him pass.

"Colm?" a voice called up the staircase from somewhere deep below.

"Rye? Is that you?!" They all turned to the staircase now, moving closer so they could hear better.

"Yes, it's me," she said, her words floating eerily out of the darkness. "You need to put your weapons away."

"That's it? We just have to put them away, and then we can come down?" Colm yelled back in disbelief.

"Yeah, I think so," Rye answered.

"Well, let's get a move on," Liam said, handing his cane to Colm. "Here, hold this for me, would ya? Just a walking stick for you." He winked as Colm recalled the fight at the museum and Liam's deftness with the cane.

"Enough talk. Those ladies can't be far behind," Jake said, stowing his shotgun in Colm's backpack.

Colm fell in step behind Liam and Jake as they descended the stairs. Seeing as this was Colm's third time down, his body had learned the point where the wards kicked in. His muscles tightened as they approached it, but this time nothing happened, and they kept descending.

"Hmph, smart lassie," Colm heard Liam say as they moved farther down the stairs. Progress was slow in the dark, but they finally made it around the last bend of the spiral staircase to see a soft blue light emerging from a doorway at the end of a long stone passageway. As they moved closer, they realized the light was spilling out from an enormous cavern beyond. Torches were ensconced around the entire perimeter, all shining with the same eerie blue light as Rye's torch, which she no longer held.

Colm handed Liam his cane before he surged ahead, pushing his way into the cavern. "Rye?" he called out as he stepped through the arched doorway into the cavern beyond. The room was vast, perhaps ten times larger than the small chapel, though it too was cut out of the stone itself. Around the cavern at regular intervals, stone casements were carved into the rock, each with its own distinctive design. Some were nature scenes, some were forest creatures, and some were blank or not yet finished. Between the casements were hundreds of urns of various sizes, ranging from pitcher-sized to those as tall as a man.

"Over here," Rye's voice rang out, drawing his attention to the middle of the cavern.

Colm moved toward Rye, seeing a large, nondescript stone sarcophagus dominating the center of the cavern. The lid was off and broken into two pieces, and beside it stood a pale, solitary figure cloaked in a shabby brown hooded robe. Colm could see that they were in a bit of a debate, and the hooded figure had just said something to Rye that Colm couldn't quite make out. He quickened his pace toward Rye, but came to an abrupt stop when he saw that the hood was hiding a bony, skeletal face. It blankly fixed its empty eye sockets in Rye's direction, and she sat on the edge of the open sarcophagus, picking at her fingernails and rolling her eyes at something the hooded figure said.

"See, they haven't disintegrated," Rye said, motioning to Colm and the others.

Colm tentatively stepped to Rye's side, but was still in disbelief at what he was seeing, and even more so that she was talking to it. The hooded figure shrugged its shoulders, and Rye turned to Colm as the others arrived.

Motioning to the hooded figure, Rye laughed, rolling her eyes again. "He just keeps telling me he disintegrated you, but I kept hearing you coming down the stairs, and then, *poof!* Gone. Took me a minute to figure it out, but then it hit me," she said, motioning to them. "You guys had weapons. I didn't. The old fellow must have felt threatened by you."

"Well, not really threatened. I wasn't ever scared of them," the hooded figure said, reaching out his bony hand and indifferently waving them away as he too leaned against his sarcophagus.

"Right," Rye said, rolling her eyes again. "Anyway, guys, this is Gaetano. He was the abbot of this place—you know, before this happened to him," she said with a sweep of her arm. "Gaetano, this is Colm, Liam, and Jake."

Colm was uncertain of how to greet a skeleton, and was still shocked that he could talk, so he opted to remain silent in fear of somehow offending him.

Liam, however, stepped forward. "You mean *Saint* Gaetano," he corrected Rye as he looked reverently at the hooded figure.

"Saint? Oh, by no means, no," responded Gaetano dismissively. "No, not a saint. Just a regular old abbot—and a dead one, at that—so please don't go assigning me a station above my level." He laughed at the apparent misunderstanding, but his laughter sounded like a rock being thrown into a deep pool.

Now understanding what was going on, Colm reached into his pack, removing the handbell and holding it out so Gaetano could see it. "Is this your handbell?"

"What? Tomb raider! I've been looking for that! How dare you break into these sacred catacombs and steal my bell?! Your thievery will not go unpunished! I demand that you give it back to me now, or else!"

"Or else what?" Liam said as he stepped to Colm's side.

Surprising them both, Gaetano lunged forward with remarkable grace, reaching for his bell. Liam flicked his cane upward, rapping Gaetano's hand away from the bell, but in the process, he inadvertently knocked it from Colm's grip, sending it skidding across the stone floor without a sound.

Liam stepped between Gaetano and the bell, preventing the gaunt figure from retrieving it. "Let's keep this civil, Gaetano. No one needs to get hurt." He held Gaetano in place while Colm picked up the bell from the floor.

"You broke it!" accused Gaetano, pointing his bony finger at Liam as glowing blue flames sparked to life deep within his eyes.

"Gaetano! Liam!" Rye yelled, capturing everyone's attention. "Everyone, calm down. Gaetano, nobody broke anything. Just relax and hear us out."

Gaetano ignored her, the fire still raging in his eyes, fixed on Liam.

Rye stepped in between them, matching Gaetano's glare, and she slowly but firmly spoke. "Calm down, please."

"Don't make me snap your bony neck," Liam said from over Rye's shoulder as he held his ground.

"Enough! Both of you," she snapped, now glaring at them both. They all stood in a silent stalemate, and Rye seized the opportunity to move the conversation forward as she glanced at Colm. "Tell him what the Pict told you about his bell."

Colm stepped forward, joining Rye, and cleared his throat. "He said your bell's not broken; it's dumb."

The flames flared in Gaetano's eyes as he turned away from Liam, lunging at Colm, but this time Jake stepped in. Gaetano raised his hand, pointing at Colm. "*You're* dumb! Now hand it over, or suffer eternal damnation!"

Colm stepped to the side, where he could better see Gaetano. "No, you don't understand. It's not *dumb*, like stupid. It's just silent. It doesn't ring anymore. See?" He raised the handbell, shaking it in silence.

Gaetano's eyes subdued, replaced by what Colm could only interpret as understanding. The hooded figure paused, staggering back in shock as his bony hand rested on his forehead. "So, that means I've been sainted?"

"You're not just a saint; you're a patron saint," Liam said, a warm smile returning to his face.

Gaetano leaned back against his open sarcophagus, excitement in his voice as he laughed to himself. "After all these long years—a lifetime of commitment, really—to be acknowledged and my work respected... Finally! Yes!" He pumped his fist and stepped closer to them. "Tell me more, my friends, my bearers of good news. What or whom am I the patron saint of? Please, I must know!"

Rye started to speak, but before she could say anything, Liam stepped forward, blurting out the answer with genuine excitement. "You're the patron saint of Tyche."

"Tai chi? What is that? Do you mean that mindfulness-based martial arts thing from the East?" Gaetano asked, his voice revealing his confusion.

Liam continued, excited to share the news. "No, no, not tai chi. Tyche: T-Y-C-H-E," he spelled out. Gaetano just stared blankly at Liam, not saying a word as he continued. "You're the patron saint of Tyche, of Lady Luck. You're the saint of good fortune, luck, and, well, gamblers too."

"What?!" Gaetano cried, the disgust clear in his voice. He turned, throwing his hands in the air, pacing away until he turned back to them. "Don't I have any say in this?"

"No, not really. It's already done," Rye said sheepishly.

"It's already done… It's already *done!*" Gaetano mocked as he flailed his arms, continuing to pace around the cavern in a bit of a tantrum. "Oh, great, so that's it, then. A lifetime of hard work and devotion, all to be named the saint of scum, the saint of low lives, the saint of knuckle-dragging dice rollers and card sharks. I wish I would just die. Oh, wait—I'm dead already! Perfect! Worked my whole life, finally found my bell, and all for what?" He turned back to the group, his empty eye sockets looking directly at them. "Way to ruin a guy's life—or afterlife, or whatever! Thanks for nothing! You can all go now," he said, waving them away and returning to his sarcophagus, attempting to climb back in.

"Oh, boo-hoo, grow up, already," Rye said, taking a step toward him. "Are you done with your self-flagellation?"

"I most certainly do not flagellate myself, madam. I will thank you to leave my presence now," he said, finally scrambling back into his sarcophagus.

"You're thinking about it the wrong way," she said in a sweet voice.

He refused to look at her from of his stone bed, his bony hands now smoothing his cloak. He lay there, not saying a word, and Rye leaned against the side of the sarcophagus. Her voice softened, and she took his bony hand in hers. He finally turned, looking at her as she spoke. "As the patron saint of Tyche, you're the saint of good fortune. You're the giver of hope and fear, and most importantly, the giver of *love*. Hope, fear, and love are the essence of life. Without hope, there are no dreams. Without fear, there is no reflection, remorse, or moderation. Hope and fear held in a delicate balance—that's where life is lived to the fullest, and it allows for love to not only survive in the world, but thrive. That's where good fortune and luck live. That is what you're the patron saint of."

Gaetano sat up slowly, looking at her, stroking his chin with his bony hand. He started to say something, then stopped, turning away in reflection. "Hmm… Yes, there is much wisdom in those words. Saint Gaetano, the patron saint of hopes and dreams and fears," he said, pausing for emphasis, "and love."

Liam cleared his throat, correcting him. "Well, really, at the end of the day, you're the patron saint of good fortune, luck, and gamblers."

Gaetano turned to Liam, the fire igniting in his eyes as he snapped his fingers. With a pop and a flash of light, Liam disappeared. "I've had enough of his insolence," Gaetano said as he scrambled back out of his sarcophagus, standing before Rye. "Yes, I see it clearly now. You have wisdom beyond your years, young lady—much more so than that vile leprechaun."

"You are most welcome, Saint Gaetano," Rye said with a smile.

"Now, as for my handbell," he said, turning to Colm, reaching out with an open hand. "It's time for me to move on with my assignment, and to do so, I need my handbell."

"But where's Liam?" Colm asked fearfully, holding tightly to the bell.

Gaetano laughed. "Don't worry, young man, he hasn't been disintegrated. He's just been temporarily removed from my presence. I'm sure that pesky little man will find his way back."

Colm reached out to return the bell, but paused when he remembered the discussion with Grigs. "Wait—the Tin

Maiden. The inscriptions on the bell talk about the Tin Maiden. They say you'll unlock the secret way to the Forest of Blood and Bones, revealing the path that leads to her."

"The Tin Maiden? Why would you want to find that bossy git?"

"We seek your patron, the Lady, and to find her, we need to find the Tin Maiden," Colm answered, recalling the etchings on the handbell.

"Well, you're in luck. I can assure you that the secret way lies in this very room. It's just over there," Saint Gaetano said, nonchalantly pointing to an archway on the far side of the cavern, but where a passageway should have been was a stone wall.

"But it's solid rock. How the hell do we get through?" Jake asked, stepping to Colm's side.

"You possess everything you need to get from here to what you seek," Saint Gaetano said, smiling, reaching his hand out once again. "Now, my handbell, please."

Colm placed it into Saint Gaetano's bony hand, just as Liam came crashing back into the cavern. He was out of breath from the effort, gasping for air. He tried to say something, but it was indecipherable. As he finally caught his breath, actual words came out.

"Don't give it to him yet!" Liam blurted out, but it was too late. Saint Gaetano already held his bell, and he leaned into Colm.

"I respect your desire to brave that forest, even though it would have been much easier to just ask me to take you all to her. Hard work is underrated these days, but things that come with a bit of effort are always more appreciated, so bravo to you and your companions! I applaud you. But whatever you do, don't wander from the lights." As he finished speaking, he raised his bell, shaking it. For the first time, the bell let out a pleasant ring, and he disappeared in a flash of brilliant light.

Liam fell to the floor, still out of breath, rolling onto his back and looking straight up. "That's what I was trying to tell you. He could've taken us directly to the Lady with that bell."

"Shit," Colm said, running his fingers through his hair. "I'm sorry, guys. I thought I was doing the right thing."

Rye put her hand gently on his shoulder. "It's okay. We just lost out on a shortcut. So, nothing lost, nothing gained."

Liam pushed up on his cane, standing by Colm. "It's my fault. I didn't realize it right away, and by the time I did, he teleported me away. But Rye's right. We're still on track."

"What about the archway? How do we get through it?" Jake asked after they caught Liam up on what Saint Gaetano had told them while they walked to the archway.

Liam stepped up to it, pressing his hand against the rock wall, confirming that it was in fact solid stone. "Not an invisible doorway. So, I guess it's not that easy."

Rye stepped forward, running her hands along the stone of the archway, but it was devoid of any markings. "He said we have everything we need to open it, but what did he mean?"

"Maybe I have to wish it open?" Colm suggested, stepping forward.

"I don't think that's it," Jake said as he leaned against the wall, taking a sip from his flask and wiping his mouth on his sleeve.

Liam's eyes flashed to Jake's flask and turned away with a look of disdain. "I agree. That would be a last resort and probably wouldn't even work." He turned to Rye, motioning to the archway and speaking in hushed tones.

Colm stepped to Jake's side, leaning against the wall, fishing his pack of cigarettes from his pocket.

"Trade ya," Jake said, holding his flask out.

"I'll pass, but you can have a smoke." He handed Jake a cigarette, searching his pocket for a light. His fingers scrabbled against the funky matchbook the Whiskered Stranger had given him. Pulling it out, he chuckled. The pastel stars sparkled against the deep purple cover as he slipped it open, taking a match and striking it.

The match ignited and immediately flew out of his fingers, caught by an unexplained gust of wind. It swirled wildly, growing in intensity and picking up speed like a fiery dust devil. The inferno cast a reddish glow surrounded by a malevolent halo of purple where it mixed with the somber blue torchlight. Colm stood awestruck, the heat of the growing fire warming his skin as he glanced down at the matchbook with fresh eyes.

"What the hell?!" Liam said as he and Rye jumped aside to avoid the fiery tempest.

"I think I did it—or the Whiskered Stranger did!" Colm said, holding out the matchbook.

Before anyone could respond, the swirling fire slammed into the archway, flames licking the wall behind it until it fizzled, leaving sooty, blackened stone behind. As they gathered their thoughts, the stone archway blazed to life with the fiery amber of the tempest. The blackened stone inside the archway shimmered as waves rippled across the surface until it resolved, revealing the faded image of a darkened forest, with what looked to be a lamppost by a lone bench shrouded in a dense mist off in the distance.

"What do you mean, the Whiskered Stranger did?" Liam asked, coming to Colm's side.

"That night before he sent me to your shop, he gave me this," Colm said, handing him the matchbook.

Liam flipped it open, smiling in recognition. "These are not matches. They're Guiding Lights—magical flames that help those in need. Seems that he thought you might need some help. But you've only got two left, so no using them to smoke cigarettes," he scolded. "And that," he continued, tapping his finger on the cover of the matchbook, tossing it back to Colm. "That's the Lady's casino, The Lair. It's got to be where she's hiding."

"Do you think she moved it to Sidhe?" Rye asked.

"I'd bet my pot of gold on it," Liam said, but his mood turned dark as he peered through the archway. "Time is wasting. Follow me, and whatever you do, don't wander from the group. Those mists mark the borders between worlds, and within them, the passage of time, the tides, and every other reliable truth can shift unpredictably." He paused, concern heavy in his voice. "Moonfall will soon be upon us, so once we enter the forest, we must move with haste. The Unspeakables are forever listening in service of their master." As he finished, he exchanged an almost imperceptible nod with Rye and then stepped through the portal into the dark mist beyond.

THE ROAD OF REGRET

COLM STEPPED THROUGH THE ARCHWAY, his feet scuffing on the cobblestone path as he followed Liam into the shadowy mist. The moon hung veiled deep behind the clouds overhead, casting a subtle silvery sheen over everything. A brisk breeze tousled his hair, and he shivered as the cool mist saturated his skin. Glancing over his shoulder, he saw Rye and Jake emerging from the archway, the blue glow of the cavern illuminating the ground. He turned back, pulling his jacket tighter against the cool air, hastening his pace to catch Liam.

"Is this the Forest of Blood and Bones?" Colm asked.

"No. We're at the edge of it," Liam said. "The mists in this place have breached the fabric of magic that protects the fae underworld, a back door of sorts, allowing us to travel between these worlds. Now stay close," he said, reaching for Colm's arm, pulling him forward toward the lamppost as Rye and Jake hustled to catch up.

The lamp was wrought iron, similar to those Colm was familiar with in town, but it struck him as odd that the lamp itself was not lit. Instead, it stood with the bench, waiting in the darkness, the cobblestone path running by before disappearing into the mist. Stepping closer to the lamppost, he noticed a small iron signpost by it and bent over to read it.

"What does it say?" Liam asked.

Colm leaned closer. The markings were indecipherable to him, but as he looked at them, they jumbled and recast themselves into words he could read:

THE ROAD OF REGRET
Activate lamp for service

Liam turned away, looking down the cobblestone road and letting out a guttural sigh.

"Oh," Rye uttered at the same time, taking a seat on the bench.

"What is it?" Jake asked, looking from Liam to Rye. He stepped forward, retrieving his snubbed shotgun from Colm's backpack.

"This road is well known in Sidhe," Liam said, turning back, his voice distant as if he were puzzling something out. "The old stories say the road wanders the realms, never appearing in the same place twice, but it was also said to have been destroyed after the Fifth War, cutting off the last way for non-magical types to visit the city. It seems that's not entirely true, and instead, we've found her final resting place."

"You say that like it's alive," Colm said.

"Some say it is," Rye added ominously.

Liam shrugged it off. "It's just old magic, that's all. It does lead to the Lost City of Sidhe, but only after one successfully crosses the bridge."

"Successfully?" Colm echoed, not sure he wanted to know what Liam meant.

Liam stepped forward. "We'll have time to talk of that en

route, but now we must get going." He glanced back to the archway. The cavern beyond stood like a gouache painting against the veiling mists, its eerie blue glow reaching out. Stepping up to the lamp, he ran his fingers along the pole, searching. "Hmm..." He got on his tiptoes to look, but couldn't quite reach the top. "Some help here?" he asked.

Colm nodded, stepping up and opening the beveled glass window on the lamp. Inside sat a fat wick that disappeared into the pole below. As he leaned closer, the smell of kerosene wafted out from the lamp. Without a thought, Colm pulled the purple matchbook from his pocket, striking another match.

"What the hell are you doing?! I told you not to waste those!" Liam shook his head.

"I think we need to light it," Colm answered as he lit the wick, and the lamp flickered to life, casting a golden sheen on the bench below.

"Look!" Rye said, pointing.

Another lamppost flickered to life some distance down the cobblestone road, its light suspended in the mist, followed by another and another, until the darkness obscured everything beyond. Behind them, a loud clattering suddenly broke the silence, and Colm turned to see a gilded horse-drawn carriage, fine enough for a king, rolling out of the mist. But there were no horses pulling it. There was only a scarlet, horned fiend the size of a baby sitting on the driver's bench, its hoofed feet dangling over the edge. Colm stepped aside as the carriage rolled forward, coming to a stop.

The little fiend leaped off the bench, unfolding its wings. It fluttered in the air in front of Colm, its wispy forked tail whipping to help it keep its balance. "You called, Masster...?" it prompted, holding the three claws of its left hand out.

"Oh—Colm," he offered, blinking in amazement. Werewolves, talking skeletons, and now this… Could things get any crazier?

It smiled back. "What iss it that Masster Ohcolm asskss of Qariq?"

"No, it's just Colm," he said, correcting him.

"My apologiess, Masster Colm," it said, bowing its head. "Me'ss just here to sserve at your beckss and callss. And callss you have."

Liam stepped in, pulling its tail. "We've no time for this nonsense. We need a ride to the Lost City."

It hissed at Liam, struggling to get loose.

"Stop it!" Rye cried, smacking Liam's hand until he let it go.

"Yess," it hissed again at Liam. "Lissten to the ladyss. No needss to be meanss." It turned back to Colm. "You sseek passsage through the foresst to the Losst City, Masster Colm?" it asked, fluttering away from Liam.

"Yes, we're looking for the Tin Maiden," Colm answered.

"Oh, Dara. It'ss Dara you sseek. Sshe iss in Ssihde, sshe iss. Helpss you find her, I can. For the rightss fee, that iss." Its eyes narrowed as it rubbed its clawed hands together.

"You know the Tin Maiden?" Jake asked, stepping forward.

Qariq glanced at Jake, floating out of his reach. "Dara iss a friend of Qariq. Sshe protectss the wayss to the Lady'ss gaming housse. But ssshhh!" it whispered, putting a claw to its fanged mouth, its eyes darting to the side as it floated closer to Colm. "Not to tellss people aboutss the gaming housse. Dara ssayss to keepss it quiet, sso Qariq doess, but you carry her toyss in your pocket, sso you already knowss about her gamess."

Colm automatically felt for the dice in his pocket, wondering how Qariq knew, but he brushed it off, using it to his advantage. "Yes, that's right," Colm said. "We need to find Dara. Can you take us to the Lost City?"

It snickered, nodding enthusiastically. "It'ss been a long time ssince any vissitorss came thiss way. Youss don't wantss to walk through the foresst—very dangerouss, thatss iss, and me wantss Masster Colm to bess ssafe. Qariq givess you a good deal for a ridess." It paused, flapping its wings, tapping its claw to its chin in thought before its eyes settled on Liam with a wicked smirk. "Jusst ssome leprechaun'ss blood, and wess be ssafely on our way," Qariq said, smiling at Colm, his wispy tongue licking the air. "What ssayss you, Masster Colm?"

"It's not his to say," Liam objected. "You'll get no blood from me to use in your nefarious deeds. Name a different fee, and quickly."

"Payss the price or notss. There'ss nothing elsse Qariq wantss from Masster Colm."

Rye pulled Liam's arm. "Just give it the blood. We need to keep moving."

"Um, guys," Jake said, pointing back to the archway.

Through it, they could see Liora and Ciara entering the cavern, and Colm turned to Liam, echoing what Rye had just said, but more urgently.

"Shit. First Leilani, and now my blood," Liam muttered with a resigned look, holding out his finger to Qariq. "One drop. That's all you get."

Qariq smiled, clicking its claws. "That'ss allss I needss." In a flash, it collected the fee in a small, stoppered bottle, and the door to the carriage opened.

The interior was resplendent with silks and cushions, velvet drapes hung across the windows, and there was even a tiny chandelier hanging from the ceiling, casting a warm glow inside. One by one, they piled in, sitting on the plush upholstered benches that oozed the scent of jasmine. Colm glanced back to the archway to see Ciara standing in it, looking directly at him. The last time he'd seen those eyes, he'd planted his boot in her face. She smiled, pointing at him.

"Let's go, quickly," Liam said to Qariq, pulling the carriage door shut behind him.

The carriage lurched forward, the wooden wheels clacking along the cobblestones with a dull, rhythmic sound. Qariq's baseball-sized head popped through a window in the front of the carriage. "The ridess iss a long oness, Masster Colm. Qariq letss you knowss when we'ss closse."

As Qariq disappeared, the carriage picked up speed, hurtling down the road. Colm poked his head out the window to see Ciara, still looking at the carriage, but now she stood at the bench. Liora walked from the archway, her cream coat ruffling in the wind, joined by someone else hidden by the darkness. A moment later, they went out of sight as the carriage plunged deeper into the mist.

Turning his attention forward, Colm could see the magical mist dissipating over the cobblestone road ahead, only to be replaced by a somber fog that hung heavy from the sky. Above them, the moon fought to break through, but the layers of fog allowed only a faint specter of it to shine, casting unnatural shadows on everything below.

"Moonfall will be here soon," Liam said, leaning forward to look out the windows with Colm. "When the moon in the world above leaves the sky, it comes here to the fae underworld, blessing it with light and keeping the darkness at bay. 'Revere the rise, fear the fall.' That is the mantra of the fae underworld."

"Which means?" Colm asked.

"Which means Qariq is right: this is no place to be caught after moonfall. You want to be inside the city walls or protected by strong wards, and seeing as we have no wards, we must press on." He settled back into his seat by Jake as the carriage rattled over the cobblestones. "We're leaving the mists and entering the forest. It's best if you stay inside the carriage," Liam said to Colm, again surreptitiously glancing at Rye before looking back out the window, but it did not escape Colm's watchful eye. They were not telling him something, but he didn't know what.

The carriage rolled forward out of the mist, entering a marshy bog with a low-hanging fog obscuring the ground, rising up to kiss its counterpart hanging from the sky. The first trees that showed themselves through the mist were not trees at all, but paunchy stumps, hewn off close to the ground. But that soon changed, and dramatically so as the fog thickened and the trees grew larger with little space between them.

Liam rapped his knuckle on the carriage, calling out to Qariq, "Slow it down for a moment!"

The carriage slowed as Qariq called out, "I sslowss down, bosss."

The forest moved by at a more leisurely pace as Liam motioned outside. "This is the heart of the forest. I suggest we all take a look, because it's likely to be the only time we're ever here. But keep inside the carriage. No need to let them know we're in here."

Colm turned, looking out. At this slower pace, he could finally see through the dense fog to the trees closest to the road. The darkness tried to hide the secrets of the forest, but even the scant moonlight betrayed them, revealing something so strange that it was hard for him to comprehend. He recalled Liam saying the trees here grew from the remains of fallen heroes, but he'd had no idea he meant it literally. At the base of each tree, there appeared to be a person sitting down, leaning against it. Some were dressed plainly, but most were knights in full armor, some still holding their sword and shield, some holding a pike or lance, and some even bore banners lazily flapping in the wind, but all of them were dead. From their backs, stunted tree trunks sprouted, growing upward. The trees were a ghastly greyish color and held no branches or leaves. At the top, the trunks looked as if they'd just snapped off. Some trees were shorter, while others soared high into the sky.

Colm looked upward at a particularly tall tree that disappeared into the fog above as Liam spoke in a reverent tone. "The trees are called the Reborn. The taller the tree, the larger the hero in life. That one you're looking at––that's Éowyn, shield-maiden of Rohan and the niece of King Théoden of Rohan."

"What?!" Colm said incredulously. "She's not real! Tolkien made her up!"

"I told you that not all is as it seems in the fae underworld. What you know as truths or fictions can shift unpredictably, but in the realm of the fae, all heroes, even those only written about in books, are real," Liam said.

Colm turned to watch as a countless number of trees passed by, each with their own fallen hero, all of various sizes in monument to their stories. Suddenly, the carriage rocked violently, shuddering momentarily before clacking its way along the cobblestones again. Colm glanced outside as something in the fog caught his attention, and he leaned forward for a better look. The fog swirled from behind a tree, and two black eyes opened, staring at him.

Liam grabbed his shirt from behind, pulling him back. "Stay in the carriage," he warned, but then glimpsed what Colm had seen and rapped his knuckle on the wall. "Let's pick it up!" he called, glancing nervously at Rye.

"Sspeeding it up, bosss," Qariq answered as the carriage

resumed its speed from before, and the black eyes disappeared into the fog as its wispy tendrils snaked across the road behind them. The scene outside the carriage was dreary at best, but the little chandelier inside brightened the mood as Colm settled back next to Rye.

"You okay?" Colm asked, drawing her attention away from the forest. "You seem a little worried."

She glanced across the carriage at Liam. "I'm fine. I'll just be better when we're through the forest. I've heard too many secondhand stories to be relaxed."

A minute later, the carriage shuddered, and Liam and Jake flew forward, tumbling into Rye and Colm in a pile of arms and legs.

"Get off me!" Rye snapped, pushing Jake back to the other side of the carriage.

Colm leaned over, helping Liam back to his seat as he looked outside to see that they'd come to a stop. He reached for the door handle, but Liam thumped his hand with his cane.

"I said stay inside," Liam commanded, his mood turning dark as he scrambled to look out the window.

The cart stood still on the cobblestones, and on the side of the road, Colm could see several sets of black eyes revealing themselves in the mist. Wispy tendrils reached out toward them as Qariq swooped down from the bench, its wings carrying it around the carriage. It moved about effortlessly, spreading a glimmering dust from a patchwork bag slung around its neck.

Liam sat up, calling out to Qariq. "There's another drop of my blood in it for you if you get us out of here and to the bridge, ASAP."

Qariq glanced over its wing at Liam, nodding with a fanged grin. "Ssure thingss, bosss. I'll have uss out of heress in a jiffyss."

Colm watched as Qariq's tail and wings whipped feverishly around the carriage, its clawed hands spreading the glimmering dust everywhere. At first the dust just fell, but then it held, suspended in midair like distant stars in the night sky. A moment later, Qariq pulled a long metallic cylinder from its bag, blowing through it like a straw, sending out a golden arc that hit the suspended pinpoints of light. Tiny veins of light grew from each connection, repeating until the carriage was encased by what looked like a translucent mesh wall of tiny stars.

"Angel Dust," Liam said. "That explains how we can travel through the forest." He looked at Rye with relief.

"Is that why you two keep looking at each other?" Colm finally asked. "You didn't know if we'd make it through?"

Liam raised his hands in a settling motion. "There was no point in gettin' you and Jake all worried. I figured Qariq would manage the trip through the forest somehow, but you never know with imps. They're from Elsewhere."

"I don't even want to know," Colm said, looking to Rye. "But were okay now, right?"

She nodded. "I think so, but—"

"What are they?" Jake interrupted her as he looked out the window to the black eyes beyond the mesh barrier, taking a slow swig from his flask.

Liam leaned back, rubbing his shoulder. "They're the Unspeakables. They watch the ancient forest for the Black Nameless Thing and help guard it from thieves. Priceless things, from Stormbringer to Grayswandir to Excalibur, all lie forever at rest here. The Reborn, the forest, and all it contains are the province of the Black Nameless Thing, and I'm quite certain it wasn't thrilled when the Road of Regret was laid through the heart of this forest."

As he spoke, the carriage sprang to life again, surging forward and gaining speed until it flashed down the road, the glimmering mesh barrier sparkling in the wind, leaving a trail of glittering dust behind it like a comet through the night sky. The clatter of the cobblestones increased as Qariq pushed them onward at a quickened pace. It wasn't long before the mesh barrier dissipated, and they approached the far edge of the forest, where the sky cleared, revealing a starless expanse with only the moon starting its slow descent behind the mountains in the distance.

Liam adjusted his jacket, sitting up straight. "Now, there's the matter of the bridge that we should discuss. Do you know anything about it, Rye?"

"Not much, really," Rye said, shaking her head. "Just that it's the old way to Sidhe."

"Old, indeed. It was first constructed well before the wars began and was the primary way to traverse from other realms to Sidhe, but the people of Sidhe were always wary of those who came from the mists. To remedy that, the Bridge of Intentions was built, connecting this road to the city."

"What does it do?" Colm asked, sliding forward in his seat.

"It judges you—or at least, your intentions," Rye answered.

"Yes. It does that, but more," Liam added, glancing out the window and searching for the right words. "All who travel the road must walk into the darkness and cross the bridge to enter Sidhe, their intentions revealed. If one's intent is true and honest, then they pass through to Sidhe. If not, they disappear."

"What?!" Colm asked, shocked. "What do you mean, they disappear?"

"Well, I'm not exactly certain, but it's said that your soul is sacrificed to the mists. You have little to worry about though, but..." Liam glanced at Jake.

"What?" Jake asked, his voice rising. "Because of my dice,

or because of this?" He raised his flask, the electric green liquid peering out through the skull's crystal eyes.

"They're both concerning," Liam said. "You would be foolish not to be concerned about crossing the bridge. That's all I'm saying."

"Is there another way into Sidhe?" Colm asked.

"I'm afraid not," Liam said. "This is the only way for you."

"Well, foolish or not, I'm not turning back now," Jake said. "What would be the point of that?"

"Agreed," Liam said, turning to him and speaking gently. "I just wanted you to be aware of the risk you're taking. That's all."

"Fair enough," Jake answered, taking a swig from his flask. "But I made my bed long ago."

"Understood," Liam said, turning to Rye and Colm. "But you should be aware of the risks as well. Fae magic can be unpredictable at times."

Qariq's head popped in the window. "Youss sshould listenss to the meanss leprechaunss. The bridgess iss old, and magicss can tarnissh withss age." The carriage started to slow, then lurched forward, descending a steep hill. "We'ss approach the bridgess, Masster Colm," it said before slipping away.

Colm leaned forward, looking out the window. Below them, a dark valley spread out, lit by the fading whispers of moonfall. In the middle of the valley stood a shadowed city, its streets dotted with the glow of lamplight darting off and crisscrossing haphazardly in every direction. The streets were lined with oddly shaped cottages and buildings of various sizes, some lit with a welcoming amber light, while others remained hidden in the shadows. Just outside the city, an inky black chasm as wide as three city blocks surrounded it, and beyond the chasm, the valley swept out until meeting the mountains on the distant horizon, the moon slipping its way behind them rising once again into the world above. The cobblestone road drew a stark line through the landscape, the golden light of its lampposts following along like sentinels until it ended at a simple covered bridge that stretched across the inky black chasm into the city, with two lampposts standing guard on each end.

THE BRIDGE OF INTENTIONS

THE CARRIAGE PULLED TO A STOP, and Qariq opened the door, laying a red carpet on the ground outside, motioning for them to exit. "I expectss Masster Colm hadss a pleassant ridess? Not too sscared of thosse nasstiess?" it said, its tail lashing the air behind it.

"You did a fine job," Colm said, stepping out of the carriage, and uncertain of what to do, he bowed.

"Oh, youss flatterss Qariq tooss much, Masster Colm," Qariq said, fluttering to the ground, its hooves landing softly, its fleshy wings folding behind its back.

Colm stepped toward the bridge as the others climbed out and Liam settled his additional payment with Qariq. The base of the bridge was made of enormous rectangular stones impossibly laid against one another with no support below, spanning the entire chasm to the city. Covering the bridge was a quaint wooden structure painted a somber red ochre, with windows dispersed at regular intervals along its entire length, looking like something one might find on a quiet country road. A lamppost stood on each side of the bridge, casting its golden hue into the tunnel before the darkness was reclaimed by the same inky black as in the chasm below. Colm bent over, picking up a stone, and leaned forward, tossing it into the chasm. But there was not even so much as a distant clatter, which left him with an uneasy feeling. Perhaps people just fell into the chasm when their intentions were doubted. He shivered thinking about it, when a hand softly rested on his shoulder, startling him.

"Be careful," Rye warned. "You don't want to go falling in there after coming this far."

Colm laughed, stepping back. "Right, but it sounds like that's up to the bridge." She chuckled awkwardly, not saying anything more, and he could instantly tell something was off. "Are you okay?" he asked.

Her lips moved, but then she hesitated, turning to look into the tunnel. "It's complicated," she said finally.

"What?" Colm asked, stepping closer.

"I can't go back to her, to the Lady," she said, still looking away, but then she turned back to meet his eyes. "I'd thought I could go all the way with you. I really did."

"But..." Colm said, but he already knew what came next. He'd heard it before, but this time was different. This one would really hurt.

"But," she said, taking Colm's hands in hers, "I can't go any farther. You need to go on without me from here. I'm sorry, it's just that—"

Colm pressed his finger against her lips. "Shh. You don't owe me an explanation."

"No. I'm not breaking my promise to you without explaining myself," she said, holding his gaze, squeezing his hands softly. "I chose to leave the Lady's service, but you must understand that she views the Sorority as an immutable commitment. I tried to live within her rules, but when she refused to accept my relationship with Noah, that was the end for me. I left in the dark of night and never looked back." She pulled the necklace from beneath her shirt. "I always thought the Lady left this out for me that night to take as a gift, but now I'm not so certain. Nor am I certain she'd welcome me back with open arms, which could create … *issues* for you. I don't know, maybe I shouldn't have run away, and maybe she didn't give me the necklace—but one thing I know for sure is that I don't want to die finding out the answers by walking across that bridge." She lowered her eyes, tears glistening in the fading moonlight. "I meant it when I promised to help you. If not for what I just told you, I'd walk that bridge by your side. But because of who I am and what I've done, the risk is too high for me."

He reached out, lifting her chin and softly rubbing his thumb across the star tattoo, wiping her tears away. "I don't want you to die either—not for me, not ever. You've already given me a bigger gift than you can ever imagine," he said, and with his free hand, he reached into his pocket, taking out the plane ticket and handing it to her. "Take this and go. If I make it out of here alive, I'll find you in Dublin, and then we'll work on getting you home."

She clutched the ticket in her hand, resting her forehead softly against his, whispering, "Here I am, leaving you, and all you're worried about is me. I don't deserve your kindness. It's all because of me that you've been pulled into this, and now I'm leaving you when you've lost everything."

"I haven't lost everything," he whispered back. "Not yet, anyway. Plus, I have a feeling I'll be seeing you again."

"Ugh, you're not making this any easier," she said quietly.

"Sorry, but I really do understand." He wrapped his arms around her in a warm embrace. He didn't want to let go, but he knew they were already operating on borrowed time. "I'll have Qariq get you a ride out of here," he said as they turned, walking back to the others.

Qariq was stashing the carpet in the chest below the driver's seat as it turned to Colm. "Masster Colm, I sshowss you the wayss to Dara nowss."

"Okay, but first, can you get a carriage ride back for Rye? She's not coming with us."

"What?" Liam said, surprised, stepping forward. "If it's something I've done, just let me know, and I'll fix it."

"No, it's nothing about you, it's me," she said, glancing toward the bridge. "I think it's just best for me to stay on this side."

"You know her history," Colm said, looking at Liam, not wanting to share their private words. "She just can't go back to the Lady. You've both made it abundantly clear that the Lady's not the forgiving type, so perhaps it's even better for Jake and me." His words came out all wrong, not as he intended. He wanted Rye to come, but deep down, he knew it would be best if she didn't—not if she'd stolen from the Lady.

Jake agreed with Colm, and Liam nodded, tossing her the keys to his car. "Don't be too rough on her," he warned, pointing his finger at her. "And she only takes premium gas."

"Got it," Rye said, snatching the keys from the air.

Qariq leaped into the air, fluttering over to Colm. "Qariq can helpss you, Masster Colm, and your ladyss." It proceeded to clap its hands loudly twice, and an exact duplicate of the imp appeared next to it.

Colm's eyes widened, looking from one fiend to the other, and he took a step back.

"No needs to worryss, Masster Colm," Qariq said before turning to its duplicate. "Qiraq, pleasse takess the ladyss back to the archwayss in the misst."

Qiraq turned to Rye, motioning her into the carriage as

the door opened. "Pleasse, ladyss, Qiraq will takess you back nowss," it said and then turned, speaking to Qariq. "I will rejoinss you whenss I returnss."

Rye glanced at the two fiends, shrugging her shoulders before climbing into the carriage. Leaning out the window, she waved as the carriage made a wide turn before heading back. They stood silently, watching the carriage carry her off into the distance.

"Moonfall is upon us," Liam announced, turning away from the carriage and stepping toward the bridge. "We must go."

Colm watched as the carriage carried Rye farther and farther away. He knew it was the right thing for her, but it still hurt, the touch of her skin and the warmth of her embrace haunting him.

Qariq hovered in the air as they approached the bridge. "Walkss through. Qariq waitss here for youss to returnss."

Colm turned to the imp. "I thought you were taking us to Dara?"

"Qariq willss. You will sseess. Jusst walkss through," it said, landing and closing its wings, motioning them forward.

Slowly, they walked toward the bridge. Colm looked ahead, watching Jake follow closely behind Liam. Lowering his head, he walked past the two lampposts and was hit by a chill breeze whistling through the inky black tunnel, rippling his jacket. Liam glanced back over his shoulder, his face wrinkled with concern. Colm's feet followed, scuffing along the smooth stone, the darkness getting turned up with each step until he finally lost sight of Liam and Jake just yards ahead, now only hearing the steady tap of Liam's cane. The air was crisp, smelling of autumn leaves, and the breeze finally calmed as he walked into the darkness, its inky blackness swallowing him whole, leaving him blind. His pace slowed as he struggled to get his bearings, and his heart started to beat faster. He'd never liked the darkness—but then he felt her warm fingers interlace with his. He smelled the powdery floral scent of her perfume and knew it was not a dream. Her soft voice whispered to him, slightly out of breath.

"I couldn't leave you to the fates," Rye said. "I know her and her tricks better than any of you. So, if I'm to pay the ultimate price crossing this bridge to help you, then so be it."

"Rye, you can't. If you think you're not—"

She pulled him to a stop, pressing her finger to his lips. "Shh. I've made my decision. Now, let's find her and get rid of that dice," she said, turning and pulling his hand forward. From that point on, they walked through the darkness together.

The seconds dragged on into minutes as they slogged their way across the bridge, and he could feel the tension in her touch. At times, he thought he saw smoky images swirling around him, only to swipe at them with his free hand and find nothing. If not for the soft exhale of Rye's breath and the warmth of her hand, he wouldn't have even known she was next to him, but eventually the darkness faded. He felt that same woozy feeling he'd felt on the stairs down to the catacomb, and a sweaty sheen coated his forehead.

"You'll be okay," Rye said, squeezing his hand. "Coming out of the magic can be disorienting for some. Kind of like getting seasick," she said, ushering him forward. "Just keep your focus on the lampposts ahead."

As he followed Rye's suggestion, Colm's mind cleared, and he turned excitedly to Rye. "You made it!"

"*We* made it," she corrected him.

Looking ahead, Colm saw Qariq waiting on the ground just as they'd left it, but this time the city stood behind it.

Liam stood next to Qariq in a heated conversation. Colm glanced around, but Jake was nowhere to be seen.

Liam looked back at them with a look of relief as he dashed forward. "You came back?" he asked Rye with a smile.

"I made a promise," she answered, letting go of Colm's hand, "and I keep my promises."

"Where's Jake?" Colm asked, panicked.

Liam silently looked to his feet as Qariq fluttered over. "It wass alwayss a risskss, Masster Colm. Alwayss a risskss," it said, its eyes lowering now too.

"Well, we can't leave him in there," Colm said, turning back.

"He's not *in there*," Liam said, looking away. "He's gone."

"What do you mean, *gone*?!" Colm asked, his voice growing frantic.

"To the misstss," Qariq said. "They goess to the misstss when the bridge takess itss toll, but onss the bright sside, to only losse one iss a goodss deal. Ssometimess Qariq waitss and no one comess."

Colm glanced at the bridge and then at the city behind Qariq. "Why didn't you have to pass through?"

"Qariq iss sspecialss. Makess deliveriess, Qariq doess," it answered with a fanged smile.

Colm turned, looking to the city as he grappled with Jake's sacrifice. The moon was dipping below the horizon, hiding the secrets of the city that lay ahead, the fading light only revealing the darkened outlines of the cottages and buildings that were farcically stacked upon one another, each with a steep pitched roof. The streets wound away from their position and around the buildings, dimly lit by lanterns that dangled off black cordage strung between tall iron stanchions. The streets themselves were cobbled with a smooth, dark stone that absorbed the light, hiding all its imperfections. Directly ahead was a large archway in obvious disrepair, leaning precariously against the building behind it, and next to it stood a weathered bulletin board covered with papers, faded and flapping in the breeze.

"Thiss entrance iss not ussed much anymoress. Not ssince the war hass been overss. But Qariq sstill knowss the wayss," it said, waving them forward. "We goess to sseess Dara. Come, come with Qariq."

2 8

THE LOST CITY

Something about Sidhe was familiar to Colm, but also not. It was a strange feeling, only made stranger by Jake's absence. He pushed on, not willing to let Jake's sacrifice be in vain. Qariq flew ahead, turning back at the fallen archway leading to the city, waiting for them.

Slowly they gathered themselves and walked forward, joining Qariq as it spun away, pressing on. Colm quickly realized that having Qariq to guide them through the maze-like streets was a godsend. At each fork in the road, Qariq stayed on the streets that were lit by the dangling lamps. They passed by a variety of buildings. Some looked to be stores, and others stood dark and vacant. To the sides of the buildings, cutting away from the lit street were darkened alleyways. As they passed one, Colm paused, looking down it, only to quicken his pace to catch up as a set of pale, glassy eyes peered back at him. From that point on, he made it a point to keep his eyes on the street ahead. But one thing struck him as odd. Most cities he'd been in were bustling with people, but not Sidhe. They'd been walking for some time already, and they hadn't seen a single person.

"Where is everyone?" Colm asked, leaning closer to Liam.

"Anyone still out is at the Black Market, but moonfall is almost upon us, and even in the city, folks rarely venture out after dark," Liam answered, a fog of concern heavy in his tone.

"Pluss, theyss don't likess peopless who comess from the misstss. Ssusspiciouss of youss, they are," Qariq added. "We musst movess quickly nowss," it said, motioning for them to speed up. "Almosst theress."

Qariq led them through an increasingly complex maze of streets until it stopped by an alley, pointing to a darkened door at the end. "We iss heress. Dara iss theress," it said, moving into the alley, motioning again for them to follow.

Colm and Rye looked to Liam, who leaned forward, peering into the darkened alleyway. Seeing nothing concerning, he shrugged his shoulders, following Qariq. Rye and Colm followed, stopping at the door.

Qariq turned to them. "Waitss here," it said, "letss Qariq talkss to her firsst." With that, Qariq opened the door, slipping inside. A brief moment later, it emerged hastily, looking at them. "Sshess only hass a few minutess. Quickly," it said, holding the door open for them.

Colm looked through the doorway to see a dimly lit room with four chairs and another door at the far end as he stepped inside, following Liam and Rye.

Qariq fluttered by the door with a scornful sneer. "It'ss been a pleassuress to deliverss you dirtyss—"

But its words were interrupted by a deafening boom, followed by Qariq's body slamming into the doorframe, the black sheen of its blood streaking the wood as it slowly slid to the floor.

Colm stood in shock, uncertain of what to do as Jake reappeared, leaning through the doorway, holding the snubbed shotgun and speaking urgently. "They're slavers," he said. "We've got to go—now!"

There was a rustling noise behind the other door at the far end of the room as Liam quickly swung one of the chairs over, wedging it under the door handle before frantically turning back to the others. "That won't hold them forever. Let's go," he said, motioning to Rye and Colm as they stepped over Qariq's lifeless body, joining Jake in the alley.

Colm smiled, stepping forward to give Jake a hug.

Jake pushed him away. "There's no time for that now. We need to get out of here," he said sharply, his eyes darting back into the little room.

"But how did you find us?" Colm asked, his mind still adrift with questions, unaware of the danger they were in.

Jake motioned to the front of the alleyway, where the lifeless form of a second imp, Qiraq, lay, its blood pooling on the ground. Colm could see that there was blood splattered on Jake's shirt and fresh scratches on his face. "I saw that imp when I got loose from the slavers at the bridge, and I followed him here." Turning to Liam, he spluttered, "Do you know somewhere safe?"

Liam looked back, shrugging his shoulders as they heard the door on the far side of the room shudder. "I don't know where we are," he said in frustration. "It's been ages since I've been here, and they shift the roads and buildings to keep things unknowable to outsiders."

"That Dara thing was a load of shit," Jake huffed angrily, kicking Qariq's body into the vacant room and pushing the door shut. "It was delivering you to slavers. We're gonna have to find the Tin Maiden ourselves."

Rye stepped toward the end of the alleyway. "We need to go. We can sort it out—"

But before she could finish, there was a subtle smell of sulfur, followed by a burst of light, and they all turned, looking at Colm. He stood holding the purple matchbook in his hand, the last match flickering in the darkness. In a flash, it burst to life, jumping out of Colm's hand, streaking down the alley, leaving a sparkling trail of dust behind it. It stopped at the end of the alley, waiting for them.

Rye and Colm nodded to each other and charged off down the alley, following the sparkling trail of dust. Without even looking, Colm knew Jake and Liam were right behind them. The flickering match streamed forward around the corner and down the street, the harried group doing their best to keep up. The match would stop at corners, waiting, before streaking off again. Finally, they saw a few people in the streets rushing home, but they were quick to jump aside as the group barreled towards them. Coming around the next corner, they heard a loud din of voices ahead, and the street opened up into an enormous plaza full of drab tents and dimly lit booths with strange merchants and stranger goods. Above the marketplace, on the cordage, the lanterns mixed with small black flags bearing the faded white imprint of a troll cross, crisscrossing the plaza from stanchion to stanchion, lighting the entire marketplace as the remaining fae scurried about the plaza, buying and trading goods before moonfall.

The Guiding Light hesitated at the entrance to the marketplace, its head flicking from side to side, its flames licking the air. It drifted into the market, flitting from booth to booth, Colm and the others following. The tents and booths held bizarre things, and many of the merchants were closing up for the night as the match paused before moving on. On the far side of the market, they passed an open building with tables where some young fae were congregating over drinks and food. As the match passed by, there was a hushed silence, the conversation only picking back up once it was gone. As the match raced wildly around, it became abundantly clear that it was looking for something. It hesitated again, looking back toward where they had entered the market, when its flame sparked brighter, and they followed it to a small booth just inside the market, where it hovered at attention.

"Welcome," said a sultry female voice from somewhere in the darkness of the booth. "Got yourself a Guiding Light, huh?"

Colm approached the booth, stroking a silky black cat that sat preening on a wooden table. "We do," he answered, peering at the goods displayed. The items seemed random at best--a mummified raven's claw, a tiny spool of black thread, a petrified hand holding a candle, a small child's teacup, a lantern with a black candle, a necklace of baby teeth, a severed big toe, and much more. Behind the table stood two bookshelves. The first held mason jars of various sizes, containing liquids, locks of hair, and other mysterious items, while the other was full of jars that appeared empty, but bore small labels with markings Colm didn't understand.

"What can I help you with today?" said the voice, with a rhythmic thrumming to it. "We have everything. Curses, talismans, memories, potions, and more."

Colm looked deeper into the booth, searching for the merchant as the cat turned its head, allowing him to scratch its ear. Looking over the merchant's items, he had no clue why the Guiding Light had stopped here.

Rye leaned close to Colm, whispering in his ear. "You're petting the merchant," she said, her eyes directing him to the cat.

"What?!" Colm yelped, pulling his hand back.

"Oh, you had to go and ruin our fun," the cat said, looking at Rye as it strutted along the table, its tail high in the air.

"Yeah, well, sorry, but he's new to these parts," Rye said, glancing back at Liam for some help.

"Don't you think that's obvious to me?" the cat said, baring its teeth at her. "Now leave us to our trade, wench." It turned back to Colm, flicking its tail at Rye.

Growing impatient, Jake kneeled by the table, speaking in hushed tones. "We're looking for the Tin Maiden. Do you have something that can help us find her?"

"Hush!" the cat snapped, its eyes darting about. "Ears are everywhere in the Black Market, and questions like that will land you and me with the slavers, or worse."

"But she *is* in Sidhe?" he pressed, undeterred by her warnings.

The cat said nothing more as it leaped to a smaller side table, upon which sat a large bowl full of eyeballs. Quietly, it started pawing through them.

"What about this?" Liam asked, holding up the severed hand holding a candle. "I thought these are used to find things."

"Are you looking to rob someone?" the cat asked in a testy voice, not taking its eyes from the bowl.

"No," Liam answered quickly, offended.

"Then it's no good to you. Only good for thievery work," the cat hissed as it turned, leaping to the top of the cabinet behind the table. "Ah, yes, here they are," it said, gracefully leaping from the cabinet to the table by Colm, holding four blackened eyes, withered with age, tied together with lavender yarn.

"Oh my God!" Colm buried his nose in his sleeve. They had an oily pungency to them that he could taste in his mouth, reminding him of a skunk. "What are they?"

"Borrowed Eyes," the cat purred, setting them on the table. "But special ones. These have the gift of truesight."

"Truesight? What's that?" Colm asked, his eyes watering from the stench.

"It allows you to see places and things as they actually are, revealing them even if they're invisible or hidden by magic," Liam said, reaching for one as the cat batted his hand away.

"Not yours until the trade is done, leprechaun."

"But how do we use them?" Colm asked.

"You eat them, like a fine caviar. Just place it in your mouth, bite down, and *pop*!" The cat licked its mouth.

"*Eat* them?" Colm echoed, clearly distressed by the thought.

"Yes," the cat said flatly. "That which you seek hides in plain sight, so you're in luck that I had these. But I make no trades after moonfall, so time is wasting. Or you can come back at moonrise."

"We'll take them," Liam said. "What do you want for them?"

"I do not trade with your type," the cat answered and then jumped from the table, rubbing up against Colm's leg, purring. "What I want, only this one can give me. The naivety of a new Gambler is unmistakable."

Colm thought of shooing the cat from his leg, but the Guiding Light had led him to this booth for a reason. He kneeled next to the cat, tickling its ear, hoping for a fair trade. "What is it you want?"

The cat settled, sitting on its hind legs, licking its paw. "I want your next even roll."

Colm hesitated, thinking about the request, not sure what it meant or how it would even work. Still, he had no intention of ever using the dice again and would hopefully be rid of it soon. It seemed to him that he'd be getting these stinky magic trinkets for free. He chuckled, uncertain how to seal the deal with the cat, and reached his hand out to shake. "Agreed."

The cat slashed the back of his hand with its claw, leaving a jagged black scratch, but there was no blood. Colm rubbed it, but it held fast, like a tattoo. The cat leaped to the shelf behind the table, using the same claw to leave a mark on the label of an empty jar. "It is done," she said, turning back as Colm retrieved the Borrowed Eyes from the table.

The Guiding Light flared to life, dashing across the center of the market to a street on the far side, where it turned, waiting for them. They rushed across the market in pursuit, arriving where the match had been a moment ago, but now it had streamed down the street away from the market. Colm paused, looking back toward the black cat, then he caught sight of someone dressed in all black entering the market by the cat's booth.

"Impossible. It's them!" Colm said to the others, and they all turned back to see Ciara approaching the tent with the black cat. They quickly slipped around the corner and out of sight, chasing after the sparkling dust. It waited for them at the next intersection before speeding off and climbing a steep hill to the right. By this time, the moon had fallen behind the mountains, and the lanterns lining the streets were the only light other than the Guiding Light. It flared brighter, leading them up the hill until it crested, opening into an expansive, empty park, where it sputtered and went out, falling to the ground with a puff of smoke.

"Now what?" Jake asked, looking intently into the park before them.

"We eat them?" Rye suggested.

Colm pulled the eyes out, dry heaving at the smell. "I don't know if I can."

"We don't have a choice," Jake said, taking one and nonchalantly tossing it in his mouth.

Colm could hear the pop of the eyeball as Jake's teeth clamped down. It was almost too much, and a moist sheen again plastered Colm's forehead. Rye and Liam grabbed theirs, following Jake's lead, with viscous popping sounds bringing Colm's stomach dangerously close to objecting.

"I don't know if I can," Colm repeated, moving the blackened eyeball closer to his mouth and then jerking it away, the skunky smell overpowering him.

"Hmm, it's not that bad," Liam said, chewing fastidiously.

Rye wiped her mouth on her sleeve. "Liam's right. Just close your eyes, plug your nose, and eat it. We're wasting time."

Colm nodded, closing his eyes, but he was still struggling to put it to his mouth when someone shoved it in, forcing him to chew it. He gagged, almost vomiting as the eyeball popped, spilling its gelatinous stew in his mouth, the wrinkled flesh of the eye scraping his tongue. Struggling to get free, he opened his eyes to see Jake next to him.

"Sorry, brother. I promised to help you get rid of it, and I wasn't going to leave you behind." He reached down, offering his hand to Colm.

"It's okay. I just need a little help," Colm said as he gagged, chewing the rest of the eyeball before finally swallowing it.

Rye touched him on the shoulder. "Turn around. You're going to want to see this."

As he turned, Colm's eyes went wide, seeing a large manor house precariously perched atop an enormous outcropping of rock that now dominated the park. There were multiple steeply pitched peaks in the roof, all of various heights and sizes. Some were squared off and others were rounded, adding to the Gothic feel. The manor was awash with windows, all overflowing with an amber light that cast a glow on the park below, and the only apparent way in and out was an ornate wooden door atop a steep staircase that crept its way down the rocky outcropping. The staircase then spilled out into a small courtyard enclosed by a stone wall ten feet tall, which circled out until it ended in two fifteen-foot stone columns, each topped with an intricately carved gargoyle. Between the two columns stood a peaked stone archway with an ornate iron gate that stood open. Just inside the gate was a small stone building that looked like a mausoleum, except for the pleasant amber light spilling out of its windows and doorway.

"That's The Lair," Liam said, pointing to the manor house. He strode forward confidently, leading the group toward the arched gate.

"What business do you have here?" a gruff voice barked from above.

Colm stopped, looking up to see that the gargoyles' eyes were locked onto Liam with a pale yellow glint, and it struck him that these gargoyles weren't actually stone, but flesh and blood.

The second gargoyle sat down, its legs hanging off the column as it too glared at Liam, joining in. "She don't want you comin' around here no more, greenie," it said, chuckling as the first gargoyle piled on.

"Yeah, greenie. Turns away and go back to your rainbow."

"Hilarious, Clyde," Liam said in a dismissive tone. "I see your sense of humor hasn't changed, but I've some serious business with the Lady, so let us pass," he demanded, stepping forward.

"Sorry, not gonna happen. We've got our orders. No one comes in without an invite," Clyde said, yawning, his fangs glinting in the light from the manor.

"Do you have an invite?" the other gargoyle asked, already knowing the answer.

"I don't have an invite, Dwayne," Liam answered, fighting back his irritation. "But I assure you, she will want to speak with us."

"No invite, no entry," Clyde said. "Strict orders from the Lady."

"I've no time for this! I would like to speak to your manager. Now!" Liam demanded crossly.

Just then, a metallic scraping echoed from the small stone building inside the gate, and a shadow rolled past the window from inside. A moment later, a unicycle rolled out of the doorway, ridden by what looked to be a red-haired doll made from tin adorned with a turquoise jester's outfit and a matching hat. As the doll pedaled closer, Colm noticed the dull glint of her metallic grey skin, the bells on her dress jingling with the constant movement of her legs.

"Kidaran?" Rye said at Colm's side, running forward. Clyde swooped down, blocking her way.

"It's okay, Clyde. I know this one," the doll said in a well-oiled voice, spinning the pedals forward and back to keep herself upright.

"Got it, boss." Clyde flew back to his perch.

Rye stepped forward, looking at Kidaran. "Of course. *You're* the Tin Maiden," she said warmly.

"The one and only, but I go by Dara these days," she said, wheeling forward with a smile. "It's good to see you again. I thought you'd never come back after leaving with that hunk, Noah."

"Yes, well… Let's just say that was a big mistake," Rye said, rolling her eyes. "But tell me about you. When did you get become the Gatekeeper?"

"You know how it is with the Lady. You have to work your way into positions of trust with her. But sadly, there's not a lot of us left," she said mournfully.

"Well, I'm happy for you," Rye said, smiling before turning to the others. "This is Dara. She's an old friend of mine."

Liam stepped forward, sneering at Clyde and Dwayne. "That's great, but there'll be time for reminiscing later. Right now, we need to see the Lady."

"Oh, I'm afraid that's not possible," Dara said as she circled the group. "She's given very strict orders. No visitors."

"I don't think you're hearing me, dearie. We're not just

here to talk to the Lady; we're here to *save* her. We have a Haesel's prophecy that could save her life. We must see her now," he said, more forcefully this time.

"She doesn't need saving. She's under the protection of Sidhe," Dara said, not giving an inch.

Rye stepped forward. "She'll want to see me. You know that."

Dara pedaled in front of Rye, smoothly holding her place, weighing Rye's words.

"So, we're good, then?" Liam asked as he cautiously stepped forward, urging the others along until she rolled in front of him, blocking the way.

"I didn't say that. It's just that—"

"You don't understand." Colm stepped to Rye's side, pleading with Dara in a calm voice. "We are literally here to save the Lady's life."

Rye turned to Colm. "Show her the mandala."

"Mandala?" Dara wheeled closer, looking at Colm with renewed interest.

As he rummaged for it, Rye spoke of it to Dara. "The mandala holds a Haesel's prophecy foretelling her death. We have to give it to her, so she can see it for herself and take action."

Colm finally wrestled the mandala from his backpack, handing it to Dara. She took it, turning it slowly in her hands, reading the ancient script etched along its edge. A look of concern slowly spread across her face, and finally, her eyes raised to meet theirs.

Rye pleaded once again. "See? We speak the truth. We need to warn her, Dara. Time is short. The prophecy is already in motion."

Dara spun the mandala in her hands, rereading the etchings before speaking with a somber tone. "So, the prophecy —it's real. My apologies for the games, but I had my doubts, and I thought the Lady was being dramatic. I understand now why she went into hiding." Without another word, she handed the mandala back to Colm with a newfound look of resolve on her face.

"Lady boss," Clyde bellowed from his perch, directing her attention to the street beyond the park.

Dara's eyes lifted from Rye as they turned to see Ciara cresting the hill.

"You cannot let them in," Rye pleaded. "They're not who you think they are anymore. They're working with someone who wants to kill the Lady and take the Stone of Fates."

"I've heard similar things in the barrows," Dara said in a resigned voice. "I have to move the manor. Clyde, Dwayne, you need to hold them off for a minute while I start the shift." She turned to Rye as she pedaled back to the stone building, calling out, "Go! You must get the mandala to her."

Colm watched as Dara entered the stone building, pedaling to the edge of a glowing table that held an iridescent pyramid. Lifting it, Dara turned it one position to the right before rolling back to the arch, trying to pull the heavy iron gates shut. Out of nowhere, Ciara emerged from the shadows, kicking Dara's hand from the gate and knocking her to the ground, where she spun helplessly until Clyde swooped in, lifting her up. Dwayne dropped down, driving Ciara back from the gates, slashing with his wicked claws with a deep snarl.

Colm turned, racing to catch up with Rye and the others heading toward the stairs on the far side of the courtyard. Glancing back over his shoulder, he saw Liora's cream coat shimmering in the darkness outside the gate, but the air around the manor held an eerie translucent haze, and each step Colm took felt longer and longer, like he was being stretched out. Rye stood ahead of him on the stairs, grabbing his outstretched hand, and she pulled him up, pushing him ahead of her.

The stairs climbed quickly above the courtyard, and ahead, the large wooden double doors to the manor stood before them with a simple wooden sign above them: THE LAIR – WHERE FORTUNE LIVES.

Liam stepped forward, pushing the doors inward, and they were greeted by an entryway with a grand staircase reminiscent of the finest country manors in Europe. To the right of the entryway was an open room with endless tables of different games—blackjack, poker, craps, and roulette wheels. To the left was a room glaring with neon lights and the flickering bulbs of endless rows of slot machines, all garishly announcing their importance. The odd thing was, it stood empty. There were no people, no dealers, no servers passing out free drinks, no little old ladies plugging the slots, and no security guards with earpieces wearing sunglasses indoors, looking around nervously. The place was deserted.

They were walking toward the staircase when two figures emerged on an upper balcony, slowly descending the stairs to the entryway.

Colm looked up at the two figures, muttering in a confused voice, "The Whiskered Stranger...?"

HOPE & FEAR

"HELLO, Dara. Looks like the Lady has kept you well oiled," Liora said, standing at the gates, tugging on the rope to drag Tabitha along, her hands bound behind her.

Clyde and Dwayne hovered to each side of Dara as she righted herself, speaking bravely. "You're too late. The shift is almost complete."

"Why sacrifice yourself for her? She would not do the same for you," Ciara snarled, unsheathing her obsidian blades, baring her teeth at Clyde.

"Loyalty. It's something you could never understand. The Lady gave me a home when no one else would," she said stoically, facing the gates, holding her ground.

"Ha," Ciara mocked. "I'm not talking about the Lady; I'm talking about Rye. She tricked you—again. Just like when she convinced you to help her run with Noah—and look where that got you. Rye uses everyone to get what she wants, and now she's come to exact her revenge on the Lady."

"You're wrong. Rye's warning her about the prophecy," Dara said boldly.

"You stupid plaything. Rye *is* the prophecy, don't you get it? You didn't stop it. You've just fulfilled it by letting her in." Liora laughed, tugging on the rope to pull Tabitha forward.

Dara pedaled nervously, looking cautiously from Ciara to Liora.

"That's right. You just let the fox into the henhouse," Ciara added. "The Lady ordered us to stop them before they got through the gates, but you just let them waltz right in. You aren't serving the Lady; you're *killing* her," she snapped, spinning the blades in her hands.

"But," Liora added, "we're wasting time talking. There's still a chance that we can save her, if you let us through quickly."

"No. You're lying. She said you'd turned on us." But uncertainty had crept into Dara's voice.

"She's mistaken. It's Rye who has turned on *us*. Don't you see it? She's not one of us anymore. She abandoned the Sorority and the Lady. You helped her do it," Ciara scolded.

Liora leaned forward, speaking in a calm voice, pointing at the star tattoo under her eye. "You know what this is, right?"

Dara nodded, pedaling slower.

"We've sworn fealty to the Lady, unlike Rye. That's why we're here: to end all this before it festers any further," Liora added, her hand lowering to her side. "Now, please, let us pass."

"Before this gets nasty," Ciara added, glaring at the gargoyles.

Dara's hands fidgeted as she looked from Liora to Ciara.

"Please, Dara," Liora said again. "We used to be friends too, before Rye turned you on me. Do you remember that?"

"Oh, dear. What have I done?" Dara said, turning to Clyde and Dwayne. "Quickly, go find Breana, the healer, and bring her to the manor. The Lady is in grave danger and may need her services. Quickly!"

Clyde glanced at Ciara and back to Dara with a tentative look, not moving.

"Go!" Dara barked. "You are bound to follow my orders, and I need to stop the shift." She turned, wheeling back into the stone building, turning the iridescent pyramid back to its prior position as the gargoyles lumbered forward, heading down the street into Sidhe.

"Close the gates," Liora said to Ciara as she pulled Tabitha forward, waiting outside the stone building for Dara.

When Dara emerged, she carried with her a large silver needle as long as she was tall. "Let's go save the—"

Before Dara could react, Liora kicked her from the side, sending her unicycle off balance, and she fell spinning to the ground again, but this time Clyde wasn't there to help her back up.

"Are all you tinners this stupid?" Ciara asked, peering down at her, laughing as she walked by.

Liora said nothing, pulling Tabitha behind her, and they made their way across the courtyard as Dara yelled curses at them, pressing her silver needle into the ground, finally getting herself upright again. Just as Liora reached the stairs, she glanced over her shoulder to see Dara furiously pedaling across the courtyard, her silver needle held out like she was jousting.

"Quickly," Ciara urged, rushing them up the stairs, only to turn back and pause as Dara rolled up.

At the base of the stairs, each time Dara tried to climb up, her unicycle rolled back, unable to ascend as she wildly flailed her needle at them, repeatedly yelling, "I will not let you harm her!"

Liora stood watching as Dara backed up to make a run at the stairs and pedaled hard, making it up several steps before she lost her balance and tumbled back down onto her side, losing hold of her needle. She looked up, oil running from her eyes.

Ciara laughed softly. "Let's finish this," she said to Liora as they turned, climbing the stairs.

30

A ROLL OF THE DICE

DESCENDING the grand staircase was the same seemingly homeless man Colm had met just a few days ago. Next to him stood Saint Gaetano, now festooned in full saint's regalia in vibrant reds and blues, fringed with gold lace and adorned with solid gold buttons. Though he was a skeleton, he looked quite striking in his ceremonial robes compared to the drab brown robe he'd worn in the catacombs.

"That's them. They're the ones who desecrated my crypt!" Saint Gaetano screeched, pointing his bony finger at them as small blue embers lit in his eyes.

"Calm down. They're friends," the Whiskered Stranger said, placing a hand softly on Gaetano's shoulder, and the embers subsided.

Colm crossed the entryway with the others as the Whiskered Stranger descended the remaining stairs, stepping forward to address them, but Rye cut the old man short.

"I should've known," she said with disdain. "Enough of the games. I'm here, just like you arranged."

Colm stood shocked at Rye's tone, glancing at her and then back to the Whiskered Stranger. The old man said nothing, but a smile cracked his lips. Lifting his arms, he stepped forward, engulfed in a bright orb of light. Colm turned, covering his eyes until the light faded, revealing a beautiful lady not much older than Rye, her hair a mixture of black, blonde, and red streaks. She wore a splendid gown of azure silk trimmed with white fur and delicately embroidered with silver astrological signs. Dangling from her neck was a stunning pendant, an oval azure sapphire the size of a bird's egg mounted in an ebony pentagram that rested on her chest. Colm knew immediately that she was the Lady, the pentagram matching that from the book at Oliver's house, and the sapphire was the Stone of Fates.

"Welcome home, daughter," the Lady said in a melodic tone, lovingly gazing upon Rye.

Did she just say "daughter"? The Lady is Rye's mother? Colm felt played, and he turned to Rye, stunned. First she'd kept her membership in the Sorority from him, and now this. It seemed that Rye carried many secrets, but this was a big one. *Why didn't she tell me?* A wash of disappointment cascaded over him, his shoulders slumping as he quickly remembered everything she'd told him about her mother and the Lady— every last word. However, the more he thought about it, the more he became convinced that she hadn't lied to him—not exactly, anyway. She'd told him that her mother could be difficult and didn't like Noah, and that she had no desire to go home. But she'd also said the same things about the Lady and her Sorority. If he'd been paying more attention to her words rather than his own problems, perhaps he would have seen it sooner and connected the dots. She had told him, and her next words reiterated as much.

"Yes, Colm brought me *home*," Rye scoffed. "Just like you asked him to. I can't believe you'd stoop to this level with your own flesh and blood. We could've been killed, and for what?"

Listening to the exchange, Colm couldn't help but smile at the satirical nature of the whole thing. Unbeknownst to him, he'd actually done what he promised the Whiskered Stranger he would: he'd brought Rye home. He'd actually done it, even over her objections, but now he realized that he'd really made the promise to Rye's mother in disguise.

"Rye," the Lady said, stepping forward, her gown flowing behind her. "Please, just listen. I'm sorry for the games," she pleaded, "but I knew you wouldn't come without a good reason. You've always had a good heart. That's why I put all this in motion. I knew you'd help him—if for no other reason, then because he helped you." She looked at Colm briefly, then back to Rye, and at that moment, Colm realized he'd been played, manipulated—something that Rye had told him her mother reveled in doing.

Rye let out a deep sigh as she clenched and unclenched her fists, pacing back and forth. He could feel her anger building with each step. "With all you can see, you can be so blind sometimes!" she yelled. "And to think, I came to help *you*, but I'm so pissed that I fell for your crap again!"

"Rye—"

"Stop!" Rye cut in. "We can hash this out later, but for now, I need you to shut up and listen to me for once. You're in danger—the deadly type. The prophecy—"

"You must calm yourself," the Lady said, restraining her laughter. "I'm not as blind as you think."

Rye stopped pacing and faced her mother, her eyes full of venom.

"You must understand that I've chosen this," the Lady continued. "I cannot hide from my fate any longer, but I needed you here in my final moments with the Stone of Fates. It was the only way I could ensure your safety."

"You could've just asked," Rye snapped back.

The Lady rolled her eyes. "Please. You know as well as I

that you wouldn't have come. It saddens me to think of all that has transpired between us, but I'm here now to tell you I'm sorry. I've made many mistakes, but my biggest was not listening to you more, spending more time with you, and now…" She paused, collecting herself as a single tear ran down her face. "I'm just glad you're here. But I can no longer hide from my fate. That much is clear."

Liam stepped to Rye's side, wagging his finger at the Lady. "You're still not listening to her," he said. "We have a Haesel's prophecy about you." He took the mandala from Colm and held it out to the Lady. "See for yourself."

Her eyes narrowed, glaring at Liam as if noticing him for the first time. "I thought I told you to never insult me with your presence again," she spat, her demeanor changing instantly, her words sharp and cutting.

Liam stepped back, lowering the mandala. His lips moved, but no words came out. For once in his life, he had no snarky response. Colm wasn't certain what had transpired between the two of them, but whatever it was had clearly left a painful rift.

The Lady's eyes intensified. "You got your *freedom*. You got your *precious* little goblet. How dare you—"

Liam gathered himself and leaned forward, his tone now matching hers. "Myrna, stop it!"

Her eyes flashed, taken aback by his insolent tone. She glanced to Gaetano, but he just shrugged his shoulders with a blank stare.

"You know that's not how it went down," Liam objected. "I told you I didn't want my freedom, but you did it anyway. Maybe it was *you* who wanted your freedom from *me*?" Liam let out a deep breath, but his voice was still stern. "Now isn't the time to be reliving these old matters. Right now, you need to listen. I know you sent me away, but I only came here to help save you."

"That's funny!" she said, unfazed by his plea. "Since when do leprechauns think of anyone but themselves?"

Liam's body softened as a quiet solemness spread down his face. His eyes lowered as he responded in a soft voice, "Today, I guess." He glanced at Rye, then back to the Lady. "I had no idea that Rye is your daughter, or that you'd paraded yourself as the Whiskered Stranger. I'm here today because I'm genuinely concerned for you, Myrna. We came to share the prophecy and help figure out how to stop it or avoid it—or anything, really—but we're running out of time."

The Lady lowered her head, the anger draining from her face. "Oh, Liam," she said gently as his eyes raised to hers. "You don't understand. I'm already aware of the prophecy. Who do you think let it out into the world? Haesel was my sister. She gave me the mandala to keep the prophecy hidden from the world, but things have transpired that I can no longer ignore. To do so would have risked the lives of everyone I love, so I let Noah take the mandala. He thought he'd stolen it, but the reality was quite different."

In all the commotion, no one paid much attention to Jake. He stood by Colm's side, watching as the events strangely unfolded into a family feud of sorts. With the others engrossed in the exchange, he inched forward bit by bit, getting closer and closer to the Lady, no one paying any mind to him at all.

In the next instant, the hinges of the front door squealed in protest as the door swung open, drawing everyone's eyes that way.

Colm turned to see Ciara and Liora step through the doorway, a streak of venom pumping through his blood. However, on second look, they were not alone, and his heart sank when he saw Tabitha, an obsidian blade to her throat, her hands bound behind her back. She tried to call out, but the blade dug deeper, silencing her. The fear in Tabitha's eyes was palpable as she jerked away from the blade.

Colm took a tentative step forward, his hand pressing into his pocket, reaching for his only weapon. But he paused as he noticed the Lady motioning to Saint Gaetano. In the next instant, Gaetano's handbell rang out, echoing melodically throughout the casino, and the door slammed shut, a draw bar sliding into place. The melody continued cascading through the casino, accompanied by a strange feeling of electricity in the air, causing the hair on Colm's arms to stand on end. As the vibrations washed over Liora and Ciara, they dropped to their knees, holding their heads in agony. Tabitha fell from Ciara's grip, and with her hands bound, she hit the floor awkwardly, striking her head, and her body fell limp.

Looking at Jake, Colm noticed he'd taken two smooth black stones from his pocket, holding them out towards Liora and Ciara. It was odd to see them; they looked to be the same two black stones that Jake had used to stop Liora and Ciara at the museum. But how could that be? They were drained of their power, the remnants used by Grigs to make the Catholicon.

"Thank you," Colm said to Jake in a sincere voice, thinking he'd just stopped Liora and Ciara with the stones yet again, even though it made no sense. Things were happening so quickly that he was unable to keep his thoughts and memories in line.

"You shouldn't be thanking me. I should thank you." Jake smirked. "And I should thank Liora and Ciara for not killing you years ago, like I ordered them to. In fact, letting you live worked out better than I could've ever imagined. You found Rye, just as Haesel said you would, and then you led me right into The Lair, right to the Lady. Now the prophecy can finally play out."

Jake's words rattled around in Colm's head, but they

made no sense. He stood silently in shock, feeling like a marionette in some sort of bizarre theater production, but he snapped back as an azure light flared from behind him, casting ghastly shadows about the casino.

"Your magic will not work here, Jake—not in my home. Didn't Father teach you anything?" the Lady said, her voice echoing menacingly through the empty room.

Colm turned to see the Lady floating a few inches off the floor, her words sinking in slowly. She and Jake were *siblings*? This was clearly a family affair, and it seemed to be about as dysfunctional of a family as he could imagine—and he was caught up smack in the middle of it.

The azure sapphire around her neck flared brightly, as if it were the moon in the night sky. The Lady held her hands in front of her, pooling the light of the sapphire between them as it cast an eerie glow upon her face—but instead of one face, she now had three that flickered in and out of vision like a specter. One face was framed with thick black hair, another in smooth blonde, and the final was framed with red hair like Rye's. All the while, the sapphire pulsed brighter and brighter, until Colm turned, shielding his eyes.

"It has been a long time, brother," the Lady's three voices said in harmony. "But I knew you would come—just as our sister prophesied."

"Yes, this is quite the family reunion. It's been nice to get to know your daughters. I only wish we would've done it sooner," Jake said, holding the black stones in his hand, slowly separating himself from the others.

By the doorway, Liora and Ciara rose, a look of defiance knitted on their faces as they looked to Jake. With a fluid movement, they rapidly moved their arms up and down, their bodies once again absorbed into a faint mist, only to be replaced a moment later by the rhythmic beating of wings of a stark white dove and an inky-black raven.

Jake continued to move slowly, never taking his gaze from the Lady, raising the black stones up so that she could see them. No light reflected off them; it was as if they were made from darkness itself. "The magic of the stones may not work here," he said, "but they still hold their souls trapped for eternity, unless I choose to release them."

The Lady's voices boomed out, commanding the room. "Why have you come here, brother?"

"We're just here to share the prophecy with you, sister," he said, laughing, motioning to the mandala.

The Lady flexed her power, the sapphire blazing as she repeated the question. "No, why have *you* come here, Jake?"

"Isn't it obvious, sister? I come to claim what Father always intended to be mine. I come to claim the Stone of Fates. I come to claim control of the fates and fortunes of all in the Land Between and lay waste to all who aided you during your reign." He raised his empty hand in the air, making a fist, squeezing it tight. "Starting with Sidhe."

Suddenly, the whole manor house shook, followed by a series of thundering explosions from somewhere outside that shattered the windows, cascading broken glass across the smooth hardwood floor. Colm stumbled, glancing out the windows to see several large fires raging in the city below as alarms blared and water drakes took to the air.

"That is just the beginning of the pain to be inflicted, unless you bow to my demands," Jake vowed. "You and I both know the Stone of Fates was always to be mine, until Mother interfered." He regained his footing, holding the black stones out once again. "Once I learned that Haesel had made a prophecy about you and hid it from me, I really had no choice but to seek it out. I mean, it was a prophecy, after all, and Haesel was always so good at them. At first, she was reluctant to share, so let's just say she needed a little *push*."

The Lady let out a gasp, her faces flickering as her hands

raised up in surprise. "Mother was right: you are a monster! I knew Haesel wouldn't jump on her own just because Mother did!"

Jake chuckled. "Well, let's just say that they *both* needed a little push."

The light from the Lady's pendant flared, matching the intensity of her eyes.

Jake returned her stare, lifting the black stones up between them while speaking slowly and intentionally. "Let's not have it end this way, sister. You can choose to let them live, and I will honor that. The choice is yours: your life, for theirs. You won't get a better deal than that today."

Colm listened intently, suddenly realizing that Liora and Ciara were Rye's sisters, and the Sorority was her family. He glanced at Tabitha lying on the floor, and somehow, he knew she was okay. Turning back to Jake, he wasn't certain how the Siren Stones worked, but he was done waiting. Today was his someday. He took a deep breath as a warmth washed over him, and with little concern, he grasped the Moonblade.

Just as he was about to lunge forward, the raven crashed into Jake's face, raking it wildly with its razor-sharp talons. It opened sizable gashes in his cheeks, and blood flowed freely. In the next moment, the raven's beak jammed into Jake's left eye, pulling it out. In the mayhem, the white dove swooped in, picking the two black stones from Jake's open hand, one stone in each claw. Jake screamed in pain, blood oozing from his empty eye socket. With a wild swipe, he knocked the raven away—and in that moment, Colm saw his opening, his opportunity to end all this, his opportunity for revenge. The anger welled in him, and he lunged forward with his Moonblade in hand, his only thought to kill Jake and make him pay for what he'd done to his family.

But almost like a sad soliloquy on his life, things did not go well for Colm. Jake narrowly dodged the Moonblade, almost as if he could sense it, but the full force of Colm's body still slammed into him, and both fell to the floor. Jake rose above him in rage, landing a crushing blow to his face. With his other hand, he took the Moonblade and plunged it deep into Colm's chest, staring directly into his eyes.

"You again come to my aid," Jake whispered with a wild sneer. "This blade will allow me to end this once and for all."

Colm glanced down to his chest, seeing only the hilt of the blade before Jake's other hand pushed him off it, dropping him. He rolled as he hit the floor, the azure light from the Lady's pendant flooding his eyes. Rye called out his name as she came to his side, tears streaming from her eyes. The last thing he knew was pain—immense pain—and then Rye's face over his, her hands pressed against his chest, trying to stop the bleeding.

Then all went dark and cold.

RYE KNEELED over Colm's body, futilely trying to cover his gaping wounds with her hands. The blade had passed through his body, leaving open gashes on both sides, the blood flowing freely through her fingers. Unable to stop the flow, she raised her hands to his face, stroking it softly, her vision blurred through her tears. His eyes were vacant and his breathing raspy as blood spilled from his lips.

This was all because of her and the games her mother played. Death was his reward, even though he had always been honest and honorable. No one in her life had ever graced her with such gifts, and she felt compelled to help him, even if it cost her everything. She would not let him die this way. She owed him the chance to live.

Her hand reached beneath her shirt, taking hold of her necklace. The next moments were intentionally a blur; they had to be. Too much thought, and she might turn back. Blocking everything out, she lifted the charm from around her neck, placing it around his, the blood on her hands smearing the wood. His breathing was almost nonexistent, and he turned his head to her with a tear in his eye. She leaned in and gently squeezed his hand, softly whispering to him, "No more lies. I chose this for you."

With that, she spoke a simple incantation. There was a subtle flash from the charm, and a phosphorescent orb of white light moved from her body to his, engulfing him in an almost imperceptible but radiant light.

Rye glanced at her mother with tears in her eyes, her face streaked with Colm's blood. Amid all the chaos, the Lady's eyes, finally devoid of judgment, rested upon Rye, full of unspoken sorrow for her daughter's sacrifice. The Lady's faces flickered, the sorrow replaced with fury as she turned back to her brother. This was not over.

***

THE LIGHT from Rye's necklace permeated Colm's body as the charm itself melded with him, disappearing, leaving an impression of it on his chest. His body spasmed, and he gasped for air as the blood ceased flowing out of his body and the wounds started stitching themselves back together. His eyes shot open, and he turned his head to see Rye kneeling next to him, covered in blood, with tears in her eyes. Smiling, she squeezed his hand. "Welcome back," she said, her voice heavy with sorrow.

Colm's hands went to his chest, searching for the blade, but the only thing he found was the scar of her necklace on his skin and the cordage from which it hung. "I don't understand. How am I not—"

"Dead?" she asked. "I'm sorry for not telling you about my mother. You deserved—"

"Myrna, watch out!" Liam yelled, vanishing from sight.

Colm rose to his knees, watching as Jake lunged at the Lady with the Moonblade. But just as he was about to strike her, Liam appeared out of nowhere, smashing his cane down on the blade, shattering it, his momentum carrying them both careening into the Lady. The three of them rolled to the floor in an awkward pile of arms and legs, until Jake stood, an arm around the Lady's neck, dragging her with him.

"Enough!" Jake scowled, pressing a broken shard of the Moonblade to the Lady's side, the blood clotting on his face as he looked on with his one good eye. They all watched as he inched backwards towards the staircase, the Lady in tow.

To the side, a mist resolved, and once again Liora and Ciara stood side by side. But this time Liora held the black stones, handing one to Ciara. In unison, they crushed the stones, releasing a faint white smoke. Opening their mouths, they breathed in the smoke with a deep, wholesome breath. Almost immediately, a light of freedom flickered in their eyes as they turned their attention to Jake. Ciara drew her blades, spinning them menacingly in front of her, stretching her neck, and next to her, Liora removed her sunglasses, the light starting to pool in her eyes.

"Missing something?" Ciara sneered, spitting his eyeball to the floor. "You're going to wish you never came. Payback's a bitch, and there are four of us here."

"Stay where you are!" Jake barked, pressing the shard harder into the Lady's side, slicing through her azure gown.

Ciara paused, holding her position as Rye and Liora joined her. Liam was slow getting up and leaned heavily on his cane. No one paid any attention to Colm, but the magic of the charm continued working, weaving its unique power, restoring him.

"The Stone of Fates has grown weak under your reign, sister, and your control over it wanes," Jake said, tightening his arm around her throat. "Because of you, the Lost City is in flames, and that is only the beginning of my wrath upon the world. It's time for the fates to have their sting once again. I will make sure of that."

As if on cue, another string of explosions tore through Sidhe, the fires lighting the dark sky of moonfall. "This is your last chance, sister," Jake said, his voice competing with the sound of the city alarms now echoing through the empty gambling rooms. "Surrender the Stone of Fates to me now, or I will burn Sidhe to the ground and kill all who stand against me, including everyone in this room."

Colm had finally recovered, but could still feel the ghost of the blade in his chest and the cool chill of death upon him. Through that experience, he'd learned the solemn truth of death. There was no reason to fear it. It was a natural part of life, and it would call for him again whether he wanted it to or not. He'd felt his dice calling to him ever since he'd been brought back, and like death, he no longer feared it either. Instead, he'd made peace with its call, and he reached into his pocket, caressing it gently. There had to be some larger reason he'd been brought back from the other side. He looked at the others and glanced out at the burning city. He could pray for them, but that was not his power. His was the power of the wish, something the Lady had gifted him. It was meant to be used, and he'd finally embraced that, not wanting this second chance to slip by. He simply needed the courage to do what had to be done. Trading one for many seemed like the only real choice to be made. It was the only way to save them all—to save Rye.

Leaning over, Colm voiced a myriad of wishes to kill Jake, each wish darker than the last as visions of his parents and Andrew flashed in his thoughts. He rolled furiously, unable to quell its call any longer, but it seemed his luck had completely escaped him as he rolled odd after odd after odd —at least ten times, perhaps more. He'd lost track of the rolls, but with each one, the dark veins spread on the dice, turning it a smoky black, and his bones creaked and his muscles ached beyond his years.

Jake heard the clattering of the dice and started laughing. "You can't use that trinket against me! All you're doing is killing yourself—*again*," he taunted.

"What he says is true," the Lady confirmed through gritted teeth, her faces looking at Colm. She spoke softly, now addressing Jake. "If I surrender the Stone of Fates to you, you must swear to let my daughters go free."

"I swear it," Jake said without hesitation.

"Swear it on our father's grave," the Lady demanded.

He hesitated, his eyes coming to rest on her daughters.

"Swear it," she repeated. "You can only take the Stone of Fates if it is freely given. You know that."

"Fine. I swear it," he answered.

"You can't give it to him!" Rye yelled, stepping forward, the anger growing in her face, fur sprouting on her arms and her jaw cracking. Ciara and Liora joined her, advancing on Jake.

"Stay put!" Jake yelled, pressing the blade harder into the Lady's side, inching backwards.

"This is my fate," the Lady said, looking upon her daughters. "I've known it ever since Haesel shared it with me many years ago. It is time for my brother to take the mantle and fulfill the prophecy. But please know I am at peace—"

"Enough," Jake interrupted, growing impatient. "Do you give me the Stone of Fates of your own free will?"

"I do," the Lady said.

The sapphire pulsed brightly as Jake took the pendant from her neck.

Colm looked on in horror, wondering what would become of the world, the people of Sidhe, and Rye. He simply didn't believe Jake's promise to the Lady. His dice again called to him, and he again answered, now wholly incapable of ignoring it. "The fates do not control me!" he yelled out. The only thing coursing through his mind was that Jake could never be allowed to have the Stone of Fates—not after Colm had seen what he was capable of doing even without it. He whispered to his dice as he held it close, "I wish the Stone of Fates would be destroyed." As he let the dice drop from his hand, it skittered to a stop, landing on three X's. His shoulders slumped as he worked to muster the strength for another roll, but before he could, the pulsing of the stone increased. Just as Jake was about to place it around his neck, the stone shattered, sending streaks of light outward with a gust of wind, staggering everyone in the room as the light from its implosion passed through them all and then faded away.

"You insolent little—!" Jake yelled, turning his attention to Colm, still holding the Lady by the neck. "What did you do?!"

The Lady, no longer of three faces, but back to the one he'd first met, smiled at Colm. "He tried to use his dice against the Stone of Fates. It seems Haesel did not tell you everything, as she did me."

"What does that mean?!" Jake asked her frantically, trying to make sense of what had just happened.

She closed her eyes, speaking softly. "It means you don't get what you seek."

As Colm looked on, the dice called to him again as Jake pulled the shard of blade back, his face full of vitriol, ready to plunge it into the Lady's side. Colm reached for his dice, making the only wish he could think of to save her from the blade. "I wish the Moonblade had never been made." He let the dice drop, and it spun, settling on two X's, and he looked up to see his wish fulfilled. But as he turned, he instead saw the shard plunge deep into the Lady's side. He didn't understand; he had rolled an even! It should've worked, but when he turned his eyes back to the dice, it was awash in an aura of light that whisked away out the window toward the Black Market. He glanced at the back of his hand, and the black cat's scratch was gone.

Colm watched helplessly as Jake threw the Lady to the floor, the broken blade lodged in her side, its magic wasting no time webbing outward from the wound, turning her to stone. Above her, Jake stood gathering a swirling pool of darkness between his palms, growing and crackling, spinning off tiny bolts of lightning. The glint of Ciara's blades caught the light as she descended on Jake. Liora's eyes radiated with a bright glow. Her hands were still gloved, but this was no time to be vain. She raised her hands toward Jake, and out of the corner of his eye, Colm saw Rye transforming, following Ciara's lead.

At the foot of the staircase, Jake slammed his pooled magic into the floor, and lightning arced through the room. A sooty wall cascaded outward from him, blasting everyone off their feet and sending them flailing backwards.

Looking to his side, Colm spied Gaetano cowering, backpedaling up the staircase away from Jake. Remembering his trick from the catacomb, Colm yelled his name, and Gaetano finally turned to him, as if waking from a deep slumber.

"Get us out of here!" Colm yelled.

Gaetano nodded, and amidst the chaos, a single bony hand rose into the air, snapping its fingers.

31

ST. AUGUSTINE, FLORIDA

THE EARLY MORNING sun peeked through the windows as Colm rose to his feet, seeing the others gathering themselves, shaking off the effects of Gaetano's magic. Glancing around, Colm saw that they'd been transported to what looked to be some sort of shop, the walls lined with shelves full of trinkets, with a single rack of brightly colored T-shirts and flannel pajama pants. In the middle of the shop, a strangely carved boulder was embedded in the floor, surrounded by a circle of moss-colored terra-cotta tiles upon which Myrna lay motionless, the blade protruding from her side. Gaetano was the first to reach her and lifted her up, resting her against the boulder as the carvings on it immediately pulsed with light. He smoothly pulled the Moonblade shard from her side, and the spread of the stone across her skin stopped.

"Where are we?" Liam asked, wearily pushing himself up with his cane until he stood by Colm.

"Make sure the door is locked," Gaetano ordered, ignoring the question.

Colm turned, confirming that the door was locked, sneaking a look outside. Sunlight dappled the street lined with palm trees, and immediately across the way, he saw a sign touting the waters of the Fountain of Youth. A moment later, Liam's hand rested on his shoulder, and he too looked outside and let out a chuckle.

"Well, that's right smart, bringing us here," he said, turning to Gaetano.

"Where's here?" Rye asked, already wearing one of the brightly colored shirts from the rack, now bent over to slide on a pair of the pajama pants. Her old clothes were torn and tattered, lying on the floor, but at least she was able to calm herself. Her fur was mostly gone already, her bones back to their previous petite size.

"Florida. St. Augustine, to be exact," Liam answered. "The alleged home of the Fountain of Youth and its legendary healing powers." He turned back to Gaetano in a mixture of excitement and wonder. "Do you know Saint Augustine?" he asked.

"Not all is as it seems here," Gaetano said, looking to Liam. "Saint Augustine wasn't a real person. He was created by the Lady to hide the power she's been collecting in this place for centuries, knowing that this day would come. It was her retirement plan of sorts. This boulder," he said, patting it with his bony hand, "it's a powerful and ancient artifact that she found in this very spot long ago and immediately understood its innate magic. It holds the power to heal, and she fashioned that to her favor," Gaetano said, his hands dropping to his sides.

"So, the boulder—it will heal her?" Rye asked.

"Not exactly heal her," Gaetano said. "The magic of the Moonblade is potent. But as long as she remains within the boulder's aura, it will keep her alive, counteracting the Moonblade's effects. As for now, she's dangerously wounded and needs its direct touch."

"When will she be healed?" Liam asked.

"She will never be healed, not completely," Gaetano answered gravely. "She can never leave St. Augustine. This will be her home for as long as the power resides in this boulder and her life force resides within her."

"So, she's trapped here?" Rye asked, stepping out from behind the clothing rack.

"Not trapped; hidden. There is more to the magic of this artifact, which is why she chose this place. Imbued with her stored power, the boulder also acts as a shield of sorts. St. Augustine is protected by an invisible barrier—one that hides all magic within it, even from Jake. For that reason, St. Augustine is itself a safe haven, not only for Myrna, but for countless fae who prefer not to live in the darkened barrows deep underground. This is actually where Myrna has been in hiding, but she couldn't reveal it to you all until Jake tried to fulfill the prophecy. Now that is done, and here we are."

Myrna roused, leaning against the boulder as the light continued pulsing through it. The stone that had been ravaging her body was now mostly gone. Her eyelids heavy, she glanced around, seeing them all.

"Good," she said, turning to Gaetano. "It worked."

Gaetano kneeled by her side. "Yes, just as you planned."

"It was the only way," she said to him, not happy, just satisfied. "But I'm not certain what happened to the Stone of Fates. That was unexpected, and I can only feel whispers of it left in my blood. I guess we shall now see what Haesel meant when she said 'reborn,' but as for the prophecy, it is done."

"What about Jake? Where is he?" Ciara asked, pacing the room as Liora looked on.

"He is not our concern right now. Now we must heal and prepare," Myrna answered.

"We could've beaten him if you'd just told us what was going on," Rye said, kneeling next to her mother.

Myrna, still weary, reached out, taking Rye's hand. "You

like to think I'm blind," she said with a faint smile. "But you forget the powers I held. I saw Haesel's prophecy to be true. Sacrificing the Stone of Fates was the only way to save you all. I only did what any mother would do."

Liam limped to Myrna's side, slowly dragging his leg behind him before settling next to her with a thud, his cane clattering to the floor.

"Your leg!" Colm said in alarm, noticing a shard of the shattered Moonblade protruding from Liam's calf. It was surrounded by a ring of stony skin, but for some reason, the stone wasn't spreading as it had on Myrna.

"Don't suppose this rock will work for me?" Liam asked, leaning closer to Myrna.

"I'm afraid it won't," she said, pushing herself up to face him.

"Thought not," Liam said, smiling at her as he clutched Jake's tarnished silver flask adorned with the skull-and-rose motif, its electric-green liquid peering out through the skull's crystal eyes. Twisting the stopper, he took a small swig, wincing as it went down.

"The Green Fairy?" Myrna said, concerned.

"It'll keep it from spreading," he said, twisting the stopper back in place.

"She always takes more than she gives," Mynra warned, reaching out for Liam's hand, a tear falling from her eye.

"Ah, it's nothing," Liam said. "And as I've always told you, if there's one thing a leprechaun can do, it's hold his liquor." But no smile came from him this time, only a resigned breath. "What about this Fountain of Youth?" he asked, glancing out the window.

"I'm afraid not," Myrna said. "The water here is sweetened by the power of this boulder, so it can help heal some simple ailments, but not the wounds caused by the Moonblade shard."

"Hmm. Well, so here we are," Liam said, taking her hands in his. "You're stuck here forever, and I'm stuck with the Green Fairy."

"And with me," Myrna said, squeezing his hands. "I'm sorry, you were right. I was scared of commitment, and it seems I've badly misjudged you." Her eyes glistened as Liam softly stroked her cheek.

Colm looked to Liam's wound, Myrna's words echoing in his mind—*"but not the wounds caused by the Moonblade shard."* The word "shard" reverberated in his mind, until finally, he couldn't ignore it, recalling Grigs using the same word. Without any thought for himself, Colm's hand disappeared into his pocket, pulling it out.

"The Catholicon, from Grigs," Colm said excitedly.

All of them, except Rye, looked at him strangely. Rye reached out, placing her hand over the Catholicon. "You don't need to sacrifice any more," she said, her eyes pleading with him. "You've already given enough."

Colm knew she was right. But at the same time, his dice had taken hold of him, and if he used the Catholicon on himself, he knew he'd just waste the years away again with more failed wishes. To use Grigs's magic that way felt wrong. He saw the pain in her eyes, matching the resigned sadness in his. "I have to try," he said. "Grigs told me I'd know what to do when the time came. This is what I need to—"

Rye's finger came to his lips, hushing him. His sorrowful look spread to her, and she nodded. "I understand, Colm. Trust me, I do." She glanced at the bare leather cordage that hung loosely around his neck. She reached out, gently placing her hand on his cheek. "Today, we all make sacrifices."

"What in the blazes are you two talking about?" Liam asked, turning to Colm.

"It's something Grigs made for me in exchange for your

Hawaiian girl," Colm explained. Without warning, he reached down, pulling the shard from Liam's leg and replacing it with the Catholicon.

Grigs's craftsmanship was immediately apparent as a slight greenish-yellow glow emanated from the Catholicon, and tendrils slowly crept out into the stony skin around the wound. The Catholicon pulsated wildly, and the tendrils created a web over the stone. A moment later, Liam's wound turned pasty white, matching the surrounding skin.

"Well, I guess that Pict isn't such a git after all," Liam said, misty-eyed. "But I hate owing people things, especially him. He'll never let me live this one down."

Myrna's eyes lifted from Liam to Liora and Ciara, and she rose, sitting atop the boulder, her strength returning slowly. "Hello, Liora, Ciara. It has been too long since you fell prey to Jake's designs. What do you have to say for yourselves?"

Ciara looked to Liora, suddenly at a loss for words, but Liora stepped forward, filling the silence.

"We have no excuse, Mother," Liora started. "Yes, it's true that we were intoxicated by his promises to us, but once we submitted to him, his manipulations became clear to us. Too late did we see the truth, and he held us by the stones. Every time we tried to resist, he reminded us of his power over us," she said, tears in her eyes.

"Oh, Liora," Myrna said softly, "you always were the optimist, and I did go into hiding, but where was your faith in me?"

"I'm sorry, Mother," Liora said, breaking down. "I really am, and—"

"It's not her who is to blame," Ciara cut in. "It was me who pushed her to entertain Jake's offers. She reminded me of our commitment to the Sorority, to you, but I pressed her and convinced her that we needed to venture out on our own in your absence. So, it's me who lost faith, not Liora."

"That is big of you to admit, Ciara," Myrna said, turning her attention from Liora. "I am not without blame in this matter, that is certain, and looking back, perhaps I could have done things differently. But what's done is done, and I'm relieved that we all stand here alive, able to talk to one another like family once again."

"So, you're not—"

"No, I'm not cross with you. Disappointed, yes, but I'll get over it, like I always do," she said with a subtle smile. "For now, let's celebrate that your bondage to my brother is over." Myrna wiped a tear from her eye as she looked to her three daughters. "I'm sorry you were all pulled into this by my brother, and your necklace," she said, turning her attention to Rye. "I did not foresee your sacrifice."

Rye stood by her mother, taking her hand. "It's okay, really. It's a choice I made, and I'm at peace with it," she said calmly, stroking her mother's hand softly. "And you were right about one thing: if it weren't for Colm, I probably wouldn't have come home."

Her mother nodded, taking her daughter's hand and squeezing it tightly.

Liora and Ciara stepped toward Rye. There was still a hint of jealously in their demeanor, Ciara openly glaring at Rye as Liora stepped between them. "As for us girls," Liora said, "I hope we can bury the hatchet and move forward as a family. But much has passed between us, and that may take a bit more time."

"Maybe we can start with an apology for what you did to me, and to Noah," Rye said, glaring back at Ciara.

"I'm not going to apologize to you," Ciara said, leaning forward. "You need to apologize to *me* for what you did. This all started long before, with you always thinking you were better than us."

"Girls!" Myrna shouted. "Now is not the time for this. It's

time to consolidate our powers so that we can fight Jake. This was not the end, it was only the beginning, and it's uncertain what has become of the power of the Stone of Fates in the aftermath of Sidhe. We must stay hidden in St. Augustine and prepare, together."

"Fine, but I'll apologize when she does," Ciara huffed, turning away.

Colm wasn't certain what the issue was between Rye and her sisters, but his anger was boiling over, and it took everything he had to remain quiet. Apologies would never be enough for him to forgive what Liora and Ciara had done—especially to his parents and his uncle. As far as he was concerned, they were as much to blame as Jake himself. They had taken his only family from him. The wound was deep, and somewhere in that pain and anger, he felt his dice calling to him. But it was interrupted by a female voice mumbling out, hidden behind the boulder.

"Shit—Tabitha!" Colm muttered. In all the commotion, he'd forgotten about her. Rushing across the room, he found her starting to regain consciousness, and he kneeled by her side. Unbeknownst to him, Liora had followed him, offering to help him with Tabitha, but he pushed her away, sending her bouncing off the boulder and onto the floor.

"Haven't you done enough?" he spat, his anger boiling over.

Myrna rose, moving closer to Colm as Liam walked with her, steadying her, as she was still weak from her near-fatal wound. She kneeled by Colm, taking his face in her hands. "And to you, I owe the biggest debt of gratitude, and the sincerest of apologies. But you should not blame my daughters. They were simply pawns, just like you, ensnared in a wicked plot by a petty man. However, that in no way diminishes the loss of your parents and uncle, and for that, you should blame me. All this has happened because of me, due to my actions, and the Haesel's prophecy concerning me."

Colm looked at her coldly. None of what she said changed anything, and the reminder that he'd lost his parents and uncle because of this prophecy did not sit well with him. She was right: this was all because of her. He slammed his fists on the floor in anger. "Why me? Why ruin my life?!" he demanded, his rage building as he stood.

"Your fate was tied to Rye's and the Stone of Fates, and thereby to the prophecy. Haesel foresaw that and told me as much. That's why Jake sought to eliminate you, and that's how I knew only you could do what needed to be done," Myrna said standing up, her eyes locked on his.

At that moment, Colm hated her more than he'd ever hated anyone in his life. She'd just admitted that his whole family had been killed because of *her*, and on top of that, she'd cursed him with the dice, taking his life too, piece by piece.

Beneath his anger, the dice called to him, reminding him of its power. He was free from her control, free to use his power as he wished. And then it hit him. He didn't owe these people anything—not even Rye.

"I brought her home," Colm said menacingly, motioning toward Rye. "You owe me payment in return, and I want it now."

"Rye has already repaid my debt to you," Myrna said, clasping her hands together. "She rescued you from certain death by surrendering her necklace to you."

"What?" Colm's eyes softened. He had known that somehow she'd saved him, but he was unaware of how she'd managed it.

"Her necklace, it graced her with the power of life from death, but she could also choose to relinquish it to another. She chose to give it to you, to save your life," she said, pausing. "So, we've both lost something in all of this, and I suggest we consider your debt paid."

Colm hesitated, looking to Rye for an instant. The prophecy had not only taken everything from him, but from Rye too. Myrna was only making it worse with her explanations. His anger rekindled, and he turned back to Myrna. "That was hers to give, not yours," Colm said. "So, *you* still owe me a debt, and I want to be paid."

Myrna reeled back at Colm's words, and Liam spoke up, taking a step forward. "Colm, I suggest you calm down. Take a moment to think about who you're talking to."

"Why?!" Colm yelled. "Why should I care who she is? Screw her, and screw you!" he cried, pointing his finger at Liam. "I didn't ask for this—for my parents to be killed, for my uncle to be killed, for Tabitha to be kidnapped, or for your stupid dice! She said it herself," he said, his finger now wagging at Myrna as spittle rained from his mouth. "*She's* the one to blame for all of this, and she owes me! No, I'm owed a debt by her, and I want it paid!"

Liam stood speechless as Colm took the dice from his pocket, its dull black surface absorbing the morning light as he tumbled it in his wrinkled hands. "Are we on the same page now, Daserii?"

"Calm down," Liam said slowly, raising his hands. "You just saved my life; you don't want to go and kill me now. It'd be a shame to waste the Pict's magic like that," he pleaded, trying desperately to settle Colm down before he did something he'd regret.

Colm rolled the dice around in his fingers, pausing as he felt warm fingers interlacing with his, followed by the gentle press of her body. The powdery floral scent of Rye's perfume filled his senses as she leaned forward, her lips caressing his. He submitted fully, closing his eyes as all the venom drained from him. She held her body against his, her heart racing with his, and the dice fell from his hand to the floor, his mind clearing. If he'd wished for anything, this would have been it —and now it was happening in real life, no dice needed.

"I'm still here," she whispered to him, slightly out of breath as she leaned her forehead against his, "and I'm not going anywhere."

Colm trembled, a tear coming to his eye as he reached up, gently stroking her cheek. "You broke your promise," he said quietly.

"I thought this was a better solution," Rye said, "but I hope you're okay that I did."

"Yeah, I'm good with it," he said, smiling, not wanting to let go.

"Remember why you came here," she whispered, leaning back, her eyes locked with his. "Don't let it corrupt you."

That's when it hit him. He'd grown accustomed to the dice and its power, both welcoming it and pushing it away at the same time. Part of him didn't want to give up the dice, but the part of him that was in control right now did, and he knew Rye had been right all along. The dice was too much for him, and nothing he could do would bring Andrew or his parents back. But perhaps he could get his own life back—at least, what still remained of it.

He nodded, and Rye turned to Myrna, holding his hand in hers. "And my mother still owes you something," she said in a stern voice.

Myrna nodded and stepped forward, looking from Rye to Colm. "It seems that I do owe you something. By bringing you into this, I can see that I've caused you much grief. You not only brought Rye home to me, but you saved her in ways that perhaps even you do not yet understand. For that, I again thank you," she said with a slight nod of her head. "Now, what is it you ask of me?"

Colm hesitated, glancing at his dice on the floor. "I would

like you to take the dice back," he said, forcing himself to say it. As he heard the words come out, he was struck with a profound sadness, and he immediately felt he'd made the wrong decision. Rye squeezed his hand in reassurance, but he could only muster a weak smile.

"So be it," Myrna said, summoning a black iron brazier that appeared at her side, flickering in and out of reality. It was there one moment, and then gone. She tried again, but nothing came this time, and she turned to Gaetano with a puzzled look.

"It seems your powers have faded," said Gaetano, stepping to her side. "I thought I sensed a shift when the Stone of Fates was destroyed."

"So, you can't take it back?" Colm asked as a spark relit somewhere deep within him, but he quickly pushed it down, knowing what it meant for his life.

"It seems not," Myrna said, somewhat distraught. "But you must know you cannot use it here in St. Augustine, ever. It would compromise our location, revealing us to the world."

Liam leaned down, picking up the dice, handing it to Colm with a fatherly eye. "You will need to learn to live with it," he said, placing his hand softly on Colm's shoulder. "You're the last Gambler."

The last Gambler. The gravity of that was not lost on Colm, and he hadn't really thought of it until Liam said the words. He nodded his understanding, and Liam stepped aside. Across the room, Colm spied a mirror on the wall that reflected an older man with silver-tipped hair standing next to a hauntingly beautiful redhead as Rye leaned in, kissing his cheek.

"We'll fit in perfectly in Florida," Rye said. "There're lots of gold diggers down here."

"Are you the gold digger?" Colm asked with a chuckle.

"I guess I am, assuming you want to stay," she said.

Tabitha mumbled again as Colm looked down toward her, catching a glimpse of the red stone of his mother's Claddagh ring on his finger—something that Tabitha had worn just days ago. He recalled her giving it back to him at dinner, but any remaining anger he had at her flushed away, and in its place was only sorrow that she'd been dragged into this, just like he had. She was so innocent, smart, and beautiful.

Then he thought of Rye, her wild eyes glaring at him from the darkness of a clearing at midnight. She was dangerous, and part of a world full of magic that he'd known nothing about just days ago. He didn't belong in Rye's world; he knew that. He looked at the ring, and then from Tabitha to Rye, and he knew where he belonged. There was no turning back.

"I do. I want to stay with you." He turned to Rye, sealing it with a kiss. There was no doubt in Colm's mind: he belonged with Rye and her world now.

Unbeknownst to them, Myrna listened to their exchange as tears moistened her eyes. "I wish I could give you back the years the dice took from you, but..." She paused, wiping away her tears. "But I no longer have the power to weave that kind of magic."

A bony hand tapped Myrna on the shoulder. "I think I can help you with that."

"What?" Myrna said, turning to Gaetano.

"You can use the magic of my soul to weave one last miracle. I can't think of a better way to solidify myself as the greatest saint ever," he said softly, as if from far away.

"No," Colm said, "too many people have died. It's enough."

"But I'm dead already," Gaetano objected, holding his arms out. "And there should be enough in my soul to restore your years and perhaps a touch more. I don't ask for this; I *demand* it," he insisted, getting irritated.

Tabitha stirred, drawing Colm's eyes from Gaetano. Colm didn't have any ill will towards Tabitha, and he turned to Gaetano. "Can I ask one more thing of the great Saint Gaetano, as the last Gambler of his domain?" Colm asked, purposefully speaking in grandiose terms, having learned that Gaetano responded well to them.

"I would like nothing more than to hear your request. You may proceed," he said, sweeping his bony hands before him.

Colm glanced at Tabitha, smiling. "Can you make her forget all of this—forget about me—and send her home?"

Gaetano's hand went to his forehead. "Can I make her *forget* all of this?" he said in a mildly offended tone. "A baby could do that! I thought you'd have some grander idea for Saint Gaetano's last act."

"If you could do that for me, I'd be forever grateful," Colm said with a deep bow.

"Oh, stop it," Gaetano said. "Now you're just pushing my buttons. But yes, I can do that for you." He raised his hand, swirling it in the air, then snapped his fingers. With a pop, Tabitha disappeared from the shop into a pinpoint of light as Gaetano bowed back to Colm. "It is done. And now, to imbue your life with mine..." He turned to Myrna, nodding as they clasped hands, and Gaetano's robes fell to the floor, resting on a pile of bone dust.

Myrna turned to Colm, holding her hands in front of her as a ball of white light tinged with azure formed between them. She pushed it toward Colm, and as it hit him, the years he'd gambled away returned, leaving the young man whom the Whiskered Stranger had met just days ago.

PICKING UP THE PIECES

THERE WAS a flash of light as the sooty wall of Jake's power crashed into the walls of the casino. Jake looked around wide-eyed, seeking Myrna and the others, but he found himself standing alone, only the sound of the fire alarms in Sidhe breaking the silence. He turned, slamming his fists down hard onto the railing of the staircase, the wood splintering beneath his fury. He'd missed his chance to end this with his sister once and for all. Now, it would be *more difficult* for everyone.

He stepped to the window, looking at Sidhe in flames below him, the water drakes making steady progress on the fires, quelling the damage. A single black bat whooshed past Jake through a shattered window, its wings fluttering rapidly, only to be replaced by a puff of smoke. In the bat's place now stood a gaunt figure with a light complexion and dark, wavy hair, his black cloak reaching to the floor.

"Did you succeed, my liege? Did you get the Stone of Fates from her?" he asked, taking a small step forward, slightly out of breath.

Jake turned to look at him, dried blood marking the edges of his missing eye. "You're late, Veldor," he snapped, his mood sour.

Veldor gasped, taking a step backwards. "What happened to you, sir? Your eye—it's gone!"

"Where are the others?" Jake asked, ignoring the question as he stepped forward, tearing a strip of cloth from his shirt and wrapping it around his head to cover the missing eye.

"I-I'm sorry sir," Veldor stuttered, taking a step back. "We were waylaid by the Sidhe guard. They still battle in the city below, but I escaped to come to your aid. Did you get it?" he asked again.

"I did not," Jake answered, turning away, the frustration clear in his voice. "I don't know exactly what happened, but one thing is certain: my sister no longer holds the Stone of Fates either." He paused, pacing back and forth in front of the stairs before turning back to Veldor, speaking softly. "It's strange. I can feel whispers of the stone's power within me, but each time I try to grasp it, to use its magic, it's not there."

"Perhaps there is some secret to it that she hides from you," Veldor suggested.

"Hmm…" Jake reflected. "Perhaps, but I fear it's something beyond even her designs. It feels as if the power of the stone itself has been torn apart."

"They can't have gotten far," Veldor said. "We can scour the city for them—"

"No, they're gone," Jake cut in, gazing out the window. "You will not find them in Sidhe. They've gone back into hiding."

"What are your orders, then, sir?"

Jake stood quietly at the window for a moment longer before he turned, speaking calmly. "Gather everyone from Sidhe who knows them, or has ever seen them, smelled them, or heard of them, and bring them to me. Someone must know where they hide."

"Consider it done," Veldor affirmed, and he left the room the same way he arrived.

33

SHARING FATE

THE ELECTRIC-GREEN EYES of the skull stared back at Colm as he sat alone in the dark by the fireplace. The warmth of the fire chased away the chill evening air, its flickering light glinting off the tarnished silver flask. He gazed into the fire, watching the flames dance as he swirled the flask, thinking of home, knowing he couldn't go back. Too much had changed. *He* had changed.

Taking the stopper from the flask, he pressed it to his lips, tilting his head back, smelling its bitter licorice notes as it burned his throat. He'd bet everything on the chance to get rid of his dice, but instead he was forced to make his peace with it, convincing himself it might come in handy someday. However, staying in St. Augustine with Rye meant he needed to find a way to control its call, and the Green Fairy was the only way he knew to do that and keep her safe. That's when he'd asked Liam for the flask, which Liam reluctantly gave him after a litany of dire warnings and protestations. He didn't understand why Liam disliked the Green Fairy so. Colm's experience with it so far had been uneventful, but Liam's warnings left him wary of it. However, even Liam had partaken of the Green Fairy when his life was at risk, so that provided him with some solace.

Still, even under its influence, he could feel the call of the dice. But it was distant now, muted to a point where he could ignore it. He thought back to the battle with Jake and how easily the dice had overwhelmed him. Ever since then, Colm had fought to stay vigilant against it for the sake of everyone in St. Augustine, but it was exhausting.

As for St. Augustine, it was a quaint coastal town that reminded him of home. Both towns had been settled by the Spanish, so adobe buildings were prolific, but the warmer climate here was a welcome change. However, it seemed that Myrna had not only stored her power in this sleepy town, she'd also made several wise real estate investments and had purchased a block of buildings in old town St. Augustine, each with a storefront below and a nicely appointed condo above. The shop that held the strangely carved healing boulder was called *The Lucky Lady*, and Colm later learned that it sold lucky charms. There were rabbit's feet, four-leaf clovers, horseshoes, lucky pennies, acorns, and many more oddities that lined the shelves and display cases. The tourists swarmed her shop, swearing by her wares. She'd always just smile, but Colm couldn't help but think that there was more to her wares than mere superstition. Around town, the Sidhe refugees blended well with the normies, who had no clue that their city was a sanctuary of sorts, now more than ever.

Shortly after they'd arrived in town, Ciara and Liora had left. They'd said they were going on the hunt, and their prey was Jake, but Colm knew the real reason was to give them all some space and time to allow for healing. They'd wreaked more than their fair share of havoc, and even Rye was not sad to see them go.

Colm bent forward, taking the poker and adjusting the logs as he heard a familiar clicking behind him.

"Mind if I join you?" Liam asked.

"Not at all." Colm patted the chair next to him.

Liam's cane clicked around it, moving slower than before, the wound of the Moonblade still not fully healed. He sat in the chair with a sigh, resting his goblet on the small table between them as Colm took another sip from the flask.

"You need to slow down with that stuff," he warned. "It's not for sipping, like bourbon. It's maintenance, a medication. A few times a day—that's it."

"I know, but I kind of like the taste of it." Colm stoppered the flask, putting it away.

"Trust me on this one," Liam said, lifting his goblet and taking a stout drink. "I've been around a long time, and I've never seen a happy ending with the Green Fairy on board."

Colm nodded, his attention back to the fire.

"Mind if I smoke?" Liam asked.

"He doesn't, but I do," Rye said out of the darkness behind them as she walked over, joining them by the fire, sitting on Colm's lap. Her fingers wrapped around his, and he felt the smooth curve of his mother's Claddagh ring on her finger. "Did you ask him about it?" Rye asked, looking at Colm.

"Ask me about what?" Liam said, looking from Rye to Colm.

Colm reached over to the side table, picking up a small card. "I found this in my pocket, and I was just wondering, do you think Grigs could help me with this dice?"

"Maybe. He's pretty crafty." Liam reached out, taking the card from Colm. "Do you know what this is?" He chuckled, holding it out.

Colm shook his head. "It was just something he gave me with the Catholicon."

Liam leaned forward, tossing it into the fire. "It's a calling card. We can just ask him."

A moment later, the flames flickered, and a familiar face

formed in the fire, its eyes searching the dark room before settling on Liam. The next thing Colm knew, the room was full of a dozen or more Picts, with Grigs at the forefront, but they looked much different than when he'd seen them last. Their clothes were disheveled, and many of them were bleeding and wounded, each holding a straw broom in their hands. Grigs stepped forward, a blackened cut scarring his face, and he wore a white hammer on his back.

"We seek sanctuary," Grigs said, looking at Liam. "Will you grant it?"

Liam stumbled on his words, but then a voice came from behind.

"He cannot, but I can." Colm turned to see Myrna enter the room, which was now overflowing with visitors. "You are always welcome, Grigs. I'm happy to give you and yours sanctuary here."

"Thank you, Lady," he answered. "I'd heard you might have a hidden sanctuary, but not even my magic could find it."

"I am no longer the Lady," she corrected him. "The Stone of Fates has been destroyed and the fates reborn."

Grigs stepped forward, rubbing his chin. "So, that's what I felt."

"It is. But we don't know what it means yet."

Grigs glanced around the room, looking at Liam, Rye, and Colm, and then back to Myrna. "Do you not see it?" he asked her.

"See what?"

"You all carry the whispers of the magic from the stone, a remnant shadow of sorts. I can see it in your auras," he answered.

"Curious." She walked toward the fire, resting her hand on the mantel. "What do you think it means?"

"I don't know, but there's something there. I can feel it as you get closer," he answered. "But for now, we need to send word to the others of your sanctuary. Jake is seeking all who ever aided or befriended you, he's torturing them, even killing them, hell-bent on finding you. He came to our Dun in the late hours of the night. Those of us here were lucky to have our brooms handy, but many did not. This is all that remains of the Picts," he said grimly, motioning to his fellow Picts in the room.

Myrna leaned heavily against the wall to the side of the fireplace, her gaze empty. "I am sorry for your loss and that of your people, Grigs. But as for opening St. Augustine to all in need—I cannot do that."

"Are we to just leave them out there to die?" Grigs asked in disbelief.

Myrna stood silent. Her answer was obvious without a word spoken.

Grigs lowered his head, slamming his hand on the small side table, crushing it, unable to restrain his anger any longer. "He's burning Sidhe to the ground, Myrna! To the ground!"

"I understand what you're saying," she said, consoling him. "But we are not strong enough yet. If we reveal our location, then we all die. At least if we stay hidden, we can bring the fight to him when and where we want. Ciara and Liora are already on the hunt."

At the mention of Ciara and Liora, Grigs raised his eyes to her. "They fight for you, for the Sorority again?" he asked.

"They do," she answered. "Jake had them under the command of the Siren Stones, but their souls were released and the stones destroyed."

Grigs stood, taking a deep breath. "What of Jake? Was he with you when the Stone of Fates was destroyed?"

She nodded. "He was, but my patron whisked us away, leaving Jake in Sidhe."

"Then he likely wears the same aura as you, and we can only assume he either knows what it means, or will be seeking the same answers as us," Grigs added.

Liam joined in, stepping to Myrna's side. "He cannot be allowed to hold even a whisper of its magic, whatever shape it takes in its rebirth."

"Much is unknown about that at the moment, but yes, it's agreed. Jake cannot be allowed any part of it," Grigs said.

"So, it is settled," Myrna announced. "We must see that it's magic doesn't fall under my brother's control, no matter what the cost."

END OF BOOK ONE

ENJOYED THE LAST GAMBLER?

Thanks for joining Colm, Rye and Liam on their supernatural adventure in *The Last Gambler*. If you enjoyed the book, a review would be much appreciated as it helps other readers discover the story.

Looking for more writing from me? Please visit my substack, *detect magic*—there you can subscribe, keep tabs on what I'm writing, and read other stories I've published. Let me know what you think and join the community in the comments.

Visit, read and subscribe at:
https://danblakely.substack.com/

And there's more good news! Colm and the gang will be back in *Pieces of Eight*. Subscribe to my substack to keep tabs on it and get sneak peeks along the way.

Still hungry for more magic? Check out my other novel, *no extra lives* — a fantasy adventure for anyone who's ever wished real life came with a respawn button.

ABOUT THE AUTHOR

My journey started in a sleepy Midwestern town in the summer of 1971, pretty much at the dawn of all that was to be awesome in the world. I still remember watching Star Wars erupt on the world and the late nights playing D&D. Like a gaggle of other kids, that's where my love for fantasy stories took root. I grew up on Tolkien and Donaldson and Moorcock and Herbert and more. Sure, I played soccer and hung out with friends, but I was always looking for fantasy stories to devour. It didn't matter if it was a book, comic, movie, magazine or video game (even Zork!). The endless worlds and stories the human mind can imagine remain irresistible. There's nothing quite like strolling through a freshly created world—simply magical.

Before landing in California, I bounced around from coast to coast. Along the way, my love for fantasy never left. I've always kept journals and notes of ideas. Over the past few years, I've been weaving stories using those ideas to create worlds and the people living in them. I want to introduce you to people and worlds that inspire you, perhaps even surprise you. Hopefully, after meeting them and living in their worlds, you'll long for more, always wondering what happens next. Maybe their stories will even change you along the way. Oh, and of course, a little magic in a story is always a good thing.

Since this is my first book, I don't have a list of other books to direct you to. But if you're interested in reading more from me, please visit me at:

www.DanBlakely.com
https://danblakely.substack.com/

And again, if you loved this book and have a moment to spare, I would really appreciate a short review on the page where you bought the book. Your help in spreading the word is gratefully appreciated and reviews make a huge difference to help new readers find their way here.

The last thing that I would ask is whether you could find one person in your life to recommend this book to—referrals are the lifeblood of stories and I be honored if I've earned that from you with this story.

Thank You!

—

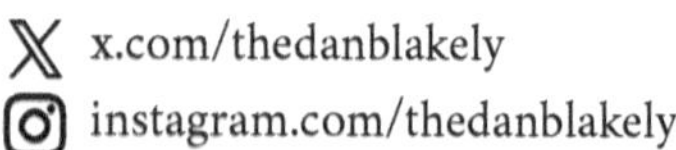

X x.com/thedanblakely
instagram.com/thedanblakely

ACKNOWLEDGMENTS

Thanks to my family, friends, beta readers, editors, proofreaders, and cover design team. It truly does take a village publish a book after that initial draft. It's been a long process for my first book, but with help of my village we finally made it to the finish line.

I also want to thank you for taking a chance on a new writer and picking up this book. Without you, I'd just be writing into the void. You're the reason why I scratch those words onto paper.

www.ingramcontent.com/pod-product-compliance
Lightning Source LLC
Chambersburg PA
CBHW020227010826
48973CB00006B/1411

9 798991 581004